Sign up for our newsletter to hear
about new and upcoming releases.

www.ylva-publishing.com

OTHER BOOKS BY LEE WINTER

VENGEANCE PLANNING
FOR
AMATEURS

LEE
WINTER

ACKNOWLEDGEMENTS

My beta readers and experts for this book were so wonderful.

From author Jess Lea, who shares my love of angular, icy, fictional women named Margaret, I acquired an in-depth knowledge of the inner working of book clubs. And academia. It's hard to say which was more alarming! Thank you, Jess, for your excellent comments, gentle humour, and insights into Prahran.

From author Roslyn Sinclair I learned about French philosopher Paul-Michel Foucault and even more alarming insights into academia. I'm eternally grateful for both the suggestions and verbal arsenal to carve up one annoying character. Smart women are the best! (Yes, I mean Roslyn.)

From Martin Borchert, my best mate at high school and now a high-flying top librarian, I learned all about how Aussie university libraries are structured and run. Much love and appreciation, my friend! Stay fabulous.

Thanks to my publisher, Astrid Ohletz, who somehow squeezes beta reading my books into her packed schedule. Invaluable feedback as always.

Sam, my fiancée and long-suffering occasional beta reader, ponied up for five chapters of this book and profoundly altered the course of it through her usual blistering critique. She is responsible for squishing my "absurd subplots that strained credibility beyond belief" and explaining to me that I can do better. I'm so grateful.

An extra big *mwah* goes to my alpha reader Carolyn Jaye, who gave me such a lovely reminder that I was writing a *romantic comedy* and helped me stay true to that path with her excellent suggestions.

I also give a standing ovation to my editors, including my new editor Genni Gunn for all her hard work in polishing up my book.
Finally, to my awesome readers: I appreciate you coming on this eccentric little journey. I know I leap about sub-genres as the mood takes me. I'm grateful you bounce from book to book right along with me. Love you all!

DEDICATION

Sometimes all you need is a penguin and to be wanted. Or is it to be needed and want a penguin? Either way, the answer is clearly penguins.

For Sam, who always makes me laugh and, for some reason, wants me even after twenty-five years. (The jury is out on the penguins.)

CHAPTER 1

THE MOST BEAUTIFUL PLACE ON EARTH

Olivia Roberts parked behind heaven's own bookstore and turned to her penguin. "What brings you joy?" she asked Trip. If anyone would know, it'd be her feathered companion of a decade who'd seen more sights than most, despite being, well, taxidermied. But his stuffed and not-actually-alive status was neither here nor there. Trip was an *excellent* listener.

However, her penguin chose to stare into the car park, which housed a couple of customers' cars, the rusty old Mazda owned by Kelly, Olivia's sister, and one beautiful black Jaguar.

Three guesses who owned that one.

"Well then, I guess it's up to me to decide." Olivia popped the glove box on her Love Muffins Kombi van and rummaged through a pile of round button pins which all bore sayings that, in theory, spread joy to her clients. She pulled out two for closer consideration.

"It's Tuesday, so we have *Hooked on a Filling* or *Muffin Compares to You.*" She held them out for Trip's perusal.

He stared even more intently at the bookstore owner's shiny Jaguar.

Right? It was a bloody showy car. Trip wasn't wrong. How did she afford it on a bookstore boss's salary, anyway?

Olivia made an executive decision and pinned *Muffin Compares to You* to her flannel shirt. It seemed fitting since it was book club day. After baking, reading was a close second to perfection in her mind. "Yes?"

Trip's gaze was definitely approving this time.

"Thank you. I'll be back soon. You watch the van."

Heaven was not overrated. Mary Bugg's Bookstore and Coffee House was the most beautiful place on earth, in Olivia's humble opinion.

The shop had large, gleaming glass windows framed in bronze, beyond which lay an enticing array of Australian crime novels in the front display. An engraved plaque sat next to the door.

> MARY ANN BUGG (1834-1905) WAS AUSTRALIA'S MOST PROMINENT FEMALE BUSHRANGER, ALTHOUGH SHE IS LARGELY OVERLOOKED BY HISTORY. THE ABORIGINAL WOMAN USED HER SHARP MIND AND BUSH SKILLS TO OUTSMART POLICE AND KEEP HERSELF FROM CAPTURE, ALONG WITH CAPTAIN THUNDERBOLT, HER INFAMOUS OUTLAW LOVER.

A peacock's tail feather intricately wound its way around and through the lettering of the bookstore's name, the shiny blues and greens beautifully contrasting with the bronze framework.

Once you stepped inside Mary Bugg's double doors, polished boards creaked underfoot, leading past a row of wooden stools lining a long bench in front of a side window.

The smell of roasted coffee beans, pastries, and Olivia's own homemade artisan muffins swirled around this small cafe area, a divinely scented invitation that reached those passing the bookstore.

Beyond lay shelves on bandits, murderers, detectives, and tales of crime, mystery, and derring-do. Most of all, Mary Bugg's focused on Australia's bushrangers—roaming outlaws who rustled livestock and horses, fought, stole, and sometimes killed, lived off the land, and battled furious police.

Thanks to her sister being the full-time barista and occasional book sales assistant, Olivia knew the cafe was the source of most of the bookstore's profits, not the rollicking tales of crime and punishment.

Kelly had worked out a deal with the owner on Olivia's behalf, which meant Olivia had a reason to come to this beautiful shop every day at the crack of dawn to drop off her Love Muffins baked goods.

Tuesdays, like today, were extra special because she had an excuse to return at three in the afternoon to run the Women in Crime Book Club meeting.

Her favourite part of the store was at the very back, past the rows and rows of books, just before you reached a short hallway, from which split off the manager's office, staff bathroom, and storerooms.

A ring of deep armchairs in soft, pale-green leather surrounded a small glass coffee table, inviting readers to sample their books before purchase. Olivia loved this peaceful place more than anything in life except baking. It was her escape. And, in fifteen minutes' time, this warm, inviting space also would play host to Olivia's book club.

She slid onto a cafe stool and admired the funky, coloured paved laneway outside, grateful for a breather. Catching sight of herself in the window, Olivia combed her fingers through her wild collar-length chestnut hair. In the slightest breeze, her fine strands would blow around like a dandelion gone to seed.

"Hey, Liv," came Kelly's voice. A steaming cappuccino slid into view. "Everything okay? Not like you to be perched over here when your book club's about to start."

Olivia took the coffee gratefully and turned, thanking her big sister. They were close, given they shared a house together and were in general agreement on the big issues: their parents sucked, cereal was a soup, and pineapple belonged on pizza.

Kelly wore her usual uniform of black pants and a black, long-sleeved T-shirt, covered by a white apron with the words *Mary Bugg's* embroidered in navy in one corner. With her slim figure, wavy, dark-red hair, and elfin features, Kelly had definitely scored the looks in their family. Whenever Olivia pointed this out, Kelly would always huff and reply she'd rather have Olivia's "mad baking skills".

Sure. Because whipping up a mean muffin was so much better than having beautiful people falling all over themselves to date you.

Kelly leaned in. "Liv? You okay? Why does your face remind me of a sad little puppy?"

"Aren't you supposed to be working?" Olivia glanced around hopefully for customers, not ready to confess her latest episode of Olivia Roberts' Hapless Misadventures in Dating. But there was only a businessman at the end of the counter, reading a newspaper and sipping a midafternoon coffee. She inhaled in disappointment.

"You're out of luck; stop dodging." Kelly eyed her gently. "Spill."

"Tina's been blowing up my phone." Olivia's confusion leaked. "Like, a dozen messages in an hour."

"Ah." Kelly offered a sympathetic cluck. "What's that thieving mole want now?"

"To get back together." Olivia traced the handle of her mug. "She says she's really sorry and she'll do better. And she misses me. A lot."

Kelly's face scrunched up in disbelief.

"She's in therapy now," Olivia rushed on. "Apparently, her stealing was just a cry for help. She sounds genuine."

"As a two-bob watch." Kelly folded her arms. "Liv, I know you like to see the best in everyone, but she was selling your stuff for party drugs. You were her bank."

"But what if that *is* all behind her now?" Olivia asked.

Kelly shook her head. "Do not allow that woman back into your life. Trust me. Tina's like all the others."

"But…" Olivia hesitated. "I think she really misses me."

"What's not to miss? You have a good and gentle heart. I really hate how many people take advantage of it."

"I'm no different to anyone else," Olivia protested. "I'm not attracting *extra*-awful partners, am I?"

Kelly's eyes narrowed. "Okay, do *not* make me cite Annalise."

Annalise. Bile rose at the reminder of the worst of her exes. "I know Annalise was bad," Olivia said. "Of course I do. But that's also why I was thinking of giving Tina another chance. She's actually making an effort to change. She even asked after Trip."

"She asked after your manky old penguin? But not you?" Kelly scowled. "That woman comes with more red flags than a Chinese military parade. Remember, you dumped her ass for good reason."

Actually, Tina had dumped *her*. Pre-emptively. Right before Olivia could throw her out after catching her in mid theft. And also, *manky*?! She glared. Trip couldn't help that he wasn't a spring penguin anymore.

Kelly studied her silence with suspicion. "Okay, we'll table this topic for at home tonight. But speaking of exes, mine's lurking around here somewhere. Sasha's still trying to get into my boss's pants."

Olivia rolled her eyes. "Still trying to get into yours, you mean. You get he's trying to make you jealous, right?"

Sasha Volkov was an ex-Russian ballet dancer turned wannabe actor and occasional model. He was square jawed, moved with swoonworthy grace, and had beautiful dark hair and darker eyes. He was an unrepentant flirt who could charm the stripes off a zebra.

"He's welcome to try to make me jealous," Kelly said. "But I'm not interested in anyone who tries to flirt with the waitress between courses when he's on a date with me. He said it was a reflex, that it meant nothing." She snorted. "So I told him *his* charm meant nothing. I wish my boss the best of luck in dealing with him."

Olivia tried to imagine the bookstore's owner, Margaret Blackwood, being propositioned by Sasha, but it was difficult to picture given Olivia had never even met the woman. There had been a few rare glimpses from behind, when Kelly had pointed her out, but the woman was *fast*. She would stride about as if channelling "Anne Lister engaged in Very Important Business", but Olivia would never be able to identify her in a line-up: "Tall and blurred, officer? Uh, female? Drives a fancy Jaguar?"

By all accounts from Kelly, Dr Blackwood was imposing, intellectual, and highly introverted, preferring to hide out in her office doing paperwork than engage with customers. She left all the Mary Bugg's "people duties" to Kelly and Stephanie, the part-time assistant who sold the store's books between college literature classes.

Olivia used to be offended by how much Dr Blackwood actively avoided her, despite how many new customers Olivia's award-winning muffins had brought in. That was until Kelly pointed out that her boss avoided absolutely everyone. All of which made Sasha putting the moves on her extra hilarious.

"How *did* Dr Blackwood take Sasha's seduction attempt?" Olivia asked curiously.

"That's private and confidential," a deep voice from behind said.

5

Olivia turned to find Sasha grinning at her. He kissed her on each cheek. "Olivia, *dorogusha*! It's been too long! You look as fabulous as ever."

"Crash and burn, huh?" Olivia said dryly, noting the swift topic change.

"Alas, this was not my most excellent triumph." He clutched his heart dramatically. "I would have more success talking to door. Which was what I ended up doing. The fierce Dr Blackwood slammed her office door in my face. So much force! I am greatly deaf now." He pouted.

Kelly cocked an eyebrow. "I did wonder what that unholy bang was."

"This is of no matter." Sasha ran his fingers through his fabulous hair, which caused his sculpted bicep to flex. He held the pose for effect and added with a winning smile: "It frees me up for other opportunities." He offered Kelly a hopeful look under his long lashes.

"No." Kelly shook her head adamantly. "Thanks."

Sasha's lips curled up. "At least you are polite. Your Dr Blackwood…I'm not sure I've ever been told no with so much…what is the word? *Venom*. She's most blunt—like Russian woman." He sounded almost impressed now.

"I wouldn't take it personally. People as a whole top her shit list."

"It is puzzling."

"What, someone turning your pretty ass down?" Kelly asked sweetly.

"I would," Olivia said cheerfully. "Sorry, Sasha. I've seen the light: It's the ladies for me."

He waved their words away. "Yes, yes, you are both very funny. I meant, why does Dr Blackwood have this business involving people if her nature is to be…" He mimed slamming a door. "Begone, irritating humans!"

Kelly tilted her head, considering that. "Yeah, not a clue. I've often wondered that myself."

A shudder sounded on the window in front of them.

An angelic child's face had appeared, with splayed, sweaty hands on either side of it. The boy gave Olivia a cheeky grin. "Wiviaaaa!" came a dramatic wail. "I'm staaarving!"

"Wivia" laughed at his little smooshed-up face—because since when was Toby Garrity, aged four and three-quarters, ever *not* hungry? Olivia hid her smile when his exhausted mother slipped into view, pulling a threadbare green cardigan closer to her gaunt frame. Samantha Garrity hauled her son from the window, mouthing *sorry* at Olivia.

Bringing up the rear was a ten-year-old girl sporting a tangled, reddish-brown ponytail and a worried expression. Her eyes brightened briefly at the sight of Olivia, whom she waved to enthusiastically before turning to trudge after her mother and brother.

Oh boy. Olivia slurped the last of her cappuccino and slid off her stool to render assistance.

Kelly chuckled. "I'll tell book club you'll be a little late."

"Thanks." Olivia grinned.

Taking Olivia's empty cup, Kelly said good-naturedly: "Hey, can you try to remember we *also* need food?"

Olivia affected an innocent look. "I have no idea what you're talking about."

"Sure you don't. Right, I better get back to it. Gotta start clean-up before my area closes."

Sasha took that as his cue to escort Kelly the whole twelve feet back to her coffee station, flirting up a storm as he went, Dr Blackwood's appeal apparently forgotten.

So fickle.

One look at Samantha Garrity told Olivia the exhausted woman was at the end of her tether. She worked two jobs and had been forced to live in a clapped-out old station wagon with her kids while they were on a waiting list to get into public housing. For all that, Samantha had somehow produced two of the most charming children Olivia had ever met.

Toby was an active little scamp. He'd try to climb any tree, no matter how tall, his strong little arms strangling the trunk, legs propelling him up like a caterpillar. Toby also hoovered up food like an industrial vacuum cleaner.

His reserved, watchful sister Emma, with freckles sprinkled across her pale cheeks, was a voracious reader who loved nothing more than a book discussion with Olivia. Unlike her brother's bright blue eyes, hers were the palest cornflower blue.

If life had handed the Garritys lemons, they were still a whole lot of sugar away from making lemonade.

Olivia had met her first Garrity many months ago when she'd spotted Toby's brown legs and bare feet sticking out of one of Mary Bugg's big skip bins. Two wooden crates had been stacked up wonkily to get him in there. Pulling him out had produced a wild-haired boy with each hand firmly wrapped around a stale muffin and his jaw chewing madly on a third. She'd had to bribe him with fresh muffins to get him drop the binned ones.

While escorting him back to the day care centre three streets away, she heard his entire life story, matter-of-factly told—from his dad dying to losing their home to living in a car that "smelled bad, specially since it died-ed" up to and including how he'd scaled the day care's side gate when no one was looking.

"Olivia," Samantha said tiredly. "It's good to see you." The cautiousness that was always in her eyes lifted slightly before her walls shot back up.

"What's wrong?" Olivia asked quietly, leading the trio around to the back of Mary Bugg's into the open-air parking area.

Along the edge of the gravelled area sat a low wooden bench and two green industrial bins filled with stacks of flattened book boxes in one and food scraps and leftovers in the other.

"A lot's wrong." Samantha answered Olivia's question softly enough that her children couldn't hear, then gave a wan smile. "But that's life, isn't it?"

Olivia handed her the van keys. "Go sit for a moment. Just move Trip. I'll sort out the kids, and then we can talk properly."

It was a sign of how tired Samantha was that she didn't even argue.

Pulling a notepad and pen out of her backpack, Olivia summoned Toby and Emma over to the bench. She crouched down and gave them instructions for a game: Emma had to describe a rhinoceros to Toby—an animal her brother had never heard of. And Toby had to draw it just from Emma's description. If their mum correctly guessed the animal, they won.

With the kids diverted and Toby giggling about any animal having only one big horn, Olivia headed back to her van, slid into the driver's seat, and faced Samantha. "Right-o, what's going on?"

Samantha sighed. "I'm losing two of my cafe shifts, so things are tighter than normal. I still have the supermarket weekend job, though. I'm making do." She attempted a smile. "But Toby's been asked not to return to his day care because he's disruptive and too 'high energy'."

"Too nimble, you mean."

"Right. They've never forgiven him for how much the new fence extensions cost them to go above that child-proof gate he managed to scale."

"Ah."

"An elderly woman in a nearby building has offered to look after him while I'm at work. It's a tiny place, but it's secure. Emma already goes there after school every day. While Toby loves Mrs Clarke and her endless supply of sweets and attention, Emma doesn't. She'd much prefer to be in a park reading till I finish work, but that's not safe. I've seen drug deals there. I can't risk it."

"No," Olivia agreed.

"And I just found out that Emma's been eating only half her lunch and bringing the rest back to Toby because her baby brother is always saying he's hungry. I feel terrible. What kind of a mother can't feed her own kids enough?" Guilt and shame etched her face. Samantha rubbed her temples. "Even with the Centrelink payments, I'm still short, repaying all the debts Pete racked up on our joint credit card."

"I think Toby's a bottomless pit when it comes to food," Olivia said with an encouraging smile. "Any family would have trouble keeping up with his appetite. But, on that note, I can help. I overordered last week, and now Kelly's giving me hell for crowding out our kitchen. So the non-perishables are in my van." She gestured over her shoulder to the back. "Maybe you can take some of them off my hands?"

"Olivia," Samantha said with a half protest, half sigh, "how many times can one woman overorder? This is the fourth time now. You're either hopeless at inventory or being very kind."

"Look, it's just...I've been there." Olivia closed her eyes for a moment. "Not as bad as you, but I spent a little while living in my van in my early twenties when I got into a bad situation. And unlike you, I had family to get me out of my mess. This isn't charity, Sam. It's just...I remember how it feels—like you're invisible and worthless. But you're not. I just want to help."

Samantha exhaled. "I *will* pay you back, you know. When I get back on my feet."

Olivia waved her comment away, but Samantha shook her head and repeated: "I will."

Children's cries of "finished!" came from the bench.

"That reminds me," Olivia said with a grin as she reached for her door handle, "whatever they show you, you see a rhinoceros."

"Of course," Samantha deadpanned. "What else?" Her gaze locked with Olivia's. "Thank you," she said sincerely.

"It's nothing. I mean it." Olivia climbed outside.

Emma and Toby ran past, holding a drawing of what looked like a cockroach with booted feet, a horse's nose, and a unicorn horn. The siblings talked all over each other, and then silence fell as they awaited their mother's verdict.

After much earnest consideration, Samantha suggested: "Erm…a rhinoceros?"

"YES!" came a pair of joyful cries. "You guessed it!"

Olivia laughed to herself as she rummaged around the back of her van for a copy of *Matilda* she'd snagged last week to give to Emma, along with a cheesy muffin for Toby and a small bag of non-perishable essentials. After a moment's thought, she also pulled forward the bags of fresh fruit she'd just bought and sorted through them.

Well. Maybe Kelly wouldn't notice if some of them never made it home…

CHAPTER 2

THE BOOK CLUB

OLIVIA SETTLED DEEP INTO HER favourite armchair at Mary Bugg's. It was hard to focus since her thoughts were still on the Garritys. She couldn't help but worry about them. Olivia glanced around the four pairs of eyes watching her.

Breanna was the oldest, a retired public servant with curly, wild, brown hair streaked with grey. She folded her arms over a *Fuck the Patriarchy* T-shirt. Evidently, the patriarchy was resisting because the shirt was faded and decades old.

Next to Breanna sat Tess, a young Aboriginal drama student who was writing a "deadly outback Indigenous sci-fi" novel in her spare time. *Deadly* meant *cool*, apparently. Tess was curious and sweet and had been tucked firmly under Breanna's protective wing.

The most easygoing of the group was a dead heat between volcano-shaped security guard Derek, and Bo, a short and solid butch stagehand. She was working on a *Les Misérables* production for Prahran's community theatre which kept her too busy to actually read most book club selections.

Derek was the opposite: an avid reader ploughing through books on his night shift security desk job at an inner-city apartment building. His forbidding size made for an intimidating first impression, but he was gentle and laconic, and nothing ever seemed to bother him. Except sad endings. And cheese.

"What did you all think of the book?" Olivia asked the group.

"Why *this* book?" Breanna jumped in first, sounding exasperated. "I thought you'd lost the plot!"

Right on cue, the door to the manager's office snicked behind Olivia's left shoulder. She twisted to look. The normally closed door was now ajar, as it always was once book club was in session.

Margaret Blackwood was in attendance.

Olivia didn't remember when it first started. Maybe even two years ago—which was how old the group was. But at some far-back point in time, the reclusive bookstore owner had started "joining" their weekly meetings. That was weird, wasn't it? Or, maybe not, when you considered a bookseller probably loved reading too.

When Olivia had first realised what was going on, she'd done the polite thing and knocked on the office door before book club one week to invite her to attend in person. Her raps had been ignored. She'd called out her offer through the wood and had been ignored even harder.

"*The Mystery of a Hansom Cab* is a hundred years old!" Breanna raced on and waved her Kindle, which showed the cover of Fergus Hume's novel.

"Try a hundred and thirty-eight years," came a faint, feminine murmur from the office.

The voice was barely audible—and, as Olivia's chair was closest to the corridor and the office door a little way down it, she could *just* make out the words.

She almost fell off her seat in shock. Dr Blackwood, woman of mystery, was speaking? To her? Or, hell, at all?

Olivia scanned the group to see if anyone else had noticed. No one gave any indication. Okay, had she just imagined it? She waited. No other murmurings fell into the silence.

Finally, Olivia replied to Breanna: "Well, I thought it might be interesting, given we're a crime and mystery group, for us to read Australia's original international bestselling mystery. To broaden our horizons."

"My horizons are already broader than the author's," Breanna retorted. "Did you notice how every woman in the book except for the heiress is an old, ugly crone? One's even called Mother Guttersnipe! Then there's the bitter landlady who screams constantly that *all men are brutes*!"

Well, that was no exaggeration.

"Heh! That's *so* funny." Bo shifted in her chair, banging her Doc Martens together. "I'd have thought that'd be right up your alley, Bree."

Breanna snorted and pressed on. "And the only decent woman, the heiress, is praised because she's pretty and a great *support* for her fiancé when he's accused of murder. She has no agency of her own. Oh, and the insipid creature keeps fainting!"

"Well, to be fair," Damien said, "one of the blokes fainted too."

Olivia suppressed a laugh. She liked Damien a lot. "True. The author was equal opportunity regarding fainting."

Breanna narrowed her eyes for a moment—her way of reluctantly conceding a point—and then started round two. "It was also terribly written. The POV kept shifting midscene; one scene had *no* point of view at all; the protagonist for the first half of the book, the detective, was just *gone* in the last half, no explanation. There were no scene breaks, no paragraph spacing. It was one long screed of text broken up by full-page ads for Bovril."

"What on earth *is* Bovril?" Tess asked with interest. "That wasn't in my copy."

"It's grotesque," Breanna replied with a grimace. "A brown, meaty yeast extract that looks and tastes like shoe polish. I had to eat it as a kid."

"So it's basically just meat-flavoured Vegemite from the 1800s," Damien mused.

"The 1800s? Just how old do you think I am?" Breanna demanded, swinging about to look at him.

He grinned and tapped his chin. "Well—"

"Okay!" Olivia jumped in far too brightly. "I think we're getting off track here!"

"You don't say," came that low, goading voice behind her.

Olivia blinked. Trust Dr Blackwood to have heard all that. "Please, can we get back to the plot?" she begged the group.

"The *plot*?" Breanna repeated. "The one *without* a woman protagonist or a woman author, despite us being the Women in Crime book club? Or the plot we know is happening because every character says their thoughts out loud? That plot?"

"Look!" Olivia said, at her wit's end, "this book isn't perfect, I know, but it's a piece of Australian history. It was self-published by an author living in

Melbourne and became a massive hit. But why I chose it is that it inspired Arthur Conan Doyle to write Sherlock Holmes! See? It's Australian literary history! Give it some respect!"

"Literary. *Right.*" Dr Blackwood's words were much louder than before. Loud enough that Olivia knew she couldn't have been the only one to hear her.

Everyone froze.

Anger flared in Olivia. She was being heckled! It was as rude as hell. She spun around to glare at the ajar door. "Do you *mind*?!"

"Liv?" Tess asked, brow wrinkling. "Who're you talking to? I mean, who's talking to us?"

"No one," Olivia said and turned back in her seat. "An incredibly annoying flea in my ear."

"Sounded like someone to me," Damien said curiously.

"Arthur Conan Doyle," murmured said annoying flea, "was only inspired to write Sherlock Holmes because your *literary* book was so bad, he thought he could do better."

Olivia gritted her jaw.

Bo wrote on her notepad, then held it up, tapping her scribbled words dramatically with a pen: *Are we just going to ignore The Voice?*

"Please disregard our heckler," Olivia said with a long-suffering sigh. "The bookstore owner—who is supplying commentary—clearly has too much time on her hands. Any other thoughts? About the plot? The murderer?"

That set them off arguing about how the detective hadn't wondered why a supposed impulse killer just happened to have chloroform in his pocket. Still, at least they were finally discussing the right topic.

Olivia exhaled in relief.

"You're far too easily pleased," purred that low voice as the others argued amongst themselves. "You have all of Australia's crime and mystery books at your disposal and the best you could come up with was a sub-par read from 1886 by an English hack; a book that Conan Doyle called 'a slight tale, mostly sold by puffing'. He was being kind."

It was the most Dr Blackwood had ever spoken to date, so it stilled the room to silence.

Bo, eyes wide, waved about a new note: *Garbo talks!*

It would be funny, except their heckler was derailing book club. The group was chaotic enough as it was. Olivia scowled and flapped a hand for Bo to put the note down.

Bo dropped her notepad and said, "Hey, next week, can we all read *The Marmalade Files*? That's a cool story. Love it."

"You love Anna Torv, you mean," Breanna suggested slyly and glanced around at the blank faces. "Star of *Secret City*, the TV series based on *The Marmalade Files*."

"I cannot deny it," Bo said. "She's my celebrity wife; just doesn't know it."

"You just want to get out of reading the book," Breanna challenged. "Did you even read this one?"

Bo looked sheepish. "I meant to, but Prahran Community Theatre needed me to fix their *Les Mis* barricades because the chairs rammed on the top keep tumbling into the audience. How could I say no to that? I don't want the French Revolution to claim any more victims."

Everyone laughed. Bo being a stagehand made for some entertaining tales. Breanna, looking exasperated, turned to Olivia. "I don't think the hotness of actresses on a TV show is any reason to select a book title," she said with an arched eyebrow, "do you?"

"Dunno about that," Damien said thoughtfully. "Seems valid."

"You would say that," Breanna said with a heavy sigh. "You're such a *man* at times."

Tess inserted helpfully: "I loved Anna Torv in *Fringe*. Do you think we could read a sci-fi novel next?"

And just like that, Olivia's meeting careened into another black hole of Topics Not Even Remotely Related to the Selected Book. Good Lord, she was bad at running a group. Or was her book club just bad at focusing?

"And once again we have chaos," came the soft murmur. "Regular as clockwork."

"All right, that's it!" Olivia shot to her feet.

Everyone stopped in mid discussion to stare.

"Liv?" Bo asked, concern flickering across her broad, tanned face. "You okay, mate?"

"Fine," she muttered, sinking back into her chair, feeling ridiculous.

Why was no one else as annoyed by the maddening intruder as she was? Maybe because they hadn't tried to invite Dr Blackwood to join the group once and been totally snubbed. That still stung. "Look...next week's book should please everyone: It's modern, Australian, has a female lead and author. And," Olivia turned to Bo, "*Crimson Lake* by Candice Fox has also been made into a TV series for any of us not able to read it in time, so that checks everyone's boxes."

"Does a woman die in it?" Tess asked worriedly. "Lately, I'm starting to hate that to enjoy crime books we have to accept so many brutal murders of women."

Olivia felt a headache coming on. "I...have no clue. I haven't read it yet. There are...crocodiles," she added feebly. "That's all I know."

Tess leaned forward. "I'm concerned we're not addressing how many awful murders there are in our chosen books."

"You're in a *crime* group," goaded Dr Blackwood.

No shit, Olivia wanted to snap back. She cleared her throat and repeated the bookstore owner's words to the group. "We are in a crime group."

"Oh, very original," came a reply, louder and mocking.

Grr.

Damien hooted with laughter.

"Well, about that," Tess said, "it seems sexist that all the worst murders always happen to women characters. Maybe we should make a new rule about the books we read."

"Or *don't* read," Breanna said, eyeballing Bo pointedly.

"Shouldn't we be eliminating the books that kill off women for kicks?" Tess argued. "I mean aren't we pro-women?"

"There goes Shakespeare." Dr Blackwood's amusement was clear in her drawl. "As noble as the sentiment is, the reality would leave you with few books to read."

Olivia slumped back into her chair. Dr Blackwood had a point. Then again, so did Tess. There *were* a lot of gratuitous women's deaths in crime fiction.

"Isn't that censorship?" Breanna asked, her brows drawing together. "I don't favour it when governments do it, so I'm definitely not a fan of it in my downtime. Like here." She waved at the group. "All crime titles should be free for discussion."

"Killing's just the side stuff anyway," Damien argued amiably. "I mean, guessing who and how it happened is the point. Using the clues. The spray of blood on the wall; the placement of bullet holes—*that's* what crime fic is all about."

"So bloodthirsty!" Bo laughed and slapped Damien's arm lightly.

He shrugged. "I'm not wrong though."

From there, the discussion tumbled into how many classic books they'd miss out on versus not giving money to misogynistic authors. Olivia's headache began to pound.

"Um, can I also put in another request?" Tess interrupted.

Olivia sighed inwardly. "What is it?"

"We really need more Indigenous crime books included. I never see myself reflected in the books I read."

"Hang on," Breanna said gently, "do you want to read Indigenous authors or Indigenous characters? They're not the same."

"Both!" Tess said with enthusiasm. "And make it a mystery! Why can't we do that?"

"Because in Australia, at least, that's a tiny pool of books," Olivia said with regret.

"I could research it for you," Breanna offered, "but off the top of my head I can't think of many titles. Unless we turn to non-fiction. I mean, need I remind us of who this bookstore's named after?"

They fell silent. Yes, this was still a bit of a sore point for the group when they'd read a biography about Mary Ann Bugg, an amazing woman who rode and dressed like a man and kept her outlaw lover alive with her knowledge of living off the land. Unlike most in her circle, she could read and had brilliantly defended herself in written form over the theft of twelve bolts of fabric, swinging public sentiment to her side and getting the charges dropped.

Outlandish myths also swirled around her, such as the time she allegedly rescued Captain Thunderbolt from jail on Cockatoo Island, swimming there with a metal file between her teeth.

All in all, she was a worthy subject for a bookstore name. A worthy subject for a book in her own right. But historians loved to focus squarely on her famous male companion. Indeed, the one biography dealing with her life was called *Captain Thunderbolt and His Lady*.

"That did suck," Bo said. "I mean, I didn't get a chance to actually read the book, but she deserved better than being an afterthought on a book title."

"No truer words," came a low murmur.

An actual endorsement from Dr Blackwood? Olivia would die of shock later—once she'd recovered from dying of shock at her engaging in the first place.

"Good book otherwise, though," Damien conceded. "Top research. Excellent action scenes. Exciting stuff. I mean, right?"

"You *would* focus on the wrong thing," Breanna huffed. "You *do* get that the only reason Captain Thunderbolt outwitted everyone was because his woman was the brains of the outfit?"

Damien gave a good-natured wave. "He was smart. Like how he had Mary Ann teach him to read and write. That's top leadership when you think about it—knowing his weaknesses and using the experts around him to overcome them." He glanced at everyone. "Don't you think that's good life advice for everyone?"

"He should have stuck to his own advice, then," Breanna said dryly. "He broke up with Mary Ann—his smartest resource—and only *then* did the police finally catch up with him. Coincidence? Hardly." She snorted. "There's a reason she lived to old bones and he didn't. Hell, she even had time to pop out fifteen kids before she finally curled up her toes."

"We're getting way off track," Olivia tried.

"I agree," Tess said earnestly. "The most important point is, can we please stop picking books with so many women getting murdered in them?"

"We'll discuss your suggestion next week."

"And not do it," Tess said sadly.

"We'll see what Breanna's research reveals," Olivia said diplomatically. "Our time's up. Thanks for coming, everyone. Remember, *Crimson Lake*."

The group gathered up their notes. Breanna took off first, still arguing with Damien, who didn't seem to mind in the least. Tess, on her way to her college classes, was asking Bo about what else went into making a proper French Revolution barricade.

Olivia, however, was more interested in who hadn't left. She climbed to her feet and rounded on the office behind her. Dr Blackwood's intrusion into book club had to be addressed.

Just as Olivia reached the door, it suddenly closed with a click. "Excuse me, what *is* your problem?" Olivia asked. She tried knocking.

A lock made a *clunk.*

"Oh, very mature," Olivia muttered softly, her natural politeness warring with her mounting agitation. She knocked harder and lifted her volume. "If you want to talk about our books so badly, why not join the club? Like when I asked you last time!"

Silence greeted her.

She sighed. She supposed she could stick around and wait to have it out with the woman once and for all. Except Mary Bugg's was an excellent daily customer of Love Muffins' baked goods. Did Olivia really want to jeopardise that by picking a fight? Or even worse, run the risk of being banned from the most beautiful place on earth just because its owner loved to do a weird, murmured critique of Olivia's book club in real time?

Fine.

Dr Blackwood could do whatever she wanted because it was her store. She might be the most annoying woman Olivia had ever met.

Or, rather, not met.

Diary of Dr Blackwood

Tuesday, March 3
Day 1123 post H

Sunset: *7.57pm*

Temp: *14.7C-19.5C*

Rain: *0mm*

Noise: *Neighbour 1B's air conditioner @ 65dB @ 10pm! To monitor further.*

Drink: *Trentham Estate Shiraz 2020. Two glasses. Acceptable.*

Reading: Non-fiction—*Just arrived, my* Journal of the Australian Library and Information Association, *Vol 69, issue 1. Article on digital curation bears further examination.*

Fiction—The Mystery of a Hansom Cab *(Fergus Hume). Poorly formed drivel by a hack with delusions of literary talent. Worst book club read in three months.*

General Observations: *The sunset from my apartment balcony tonight is particularly beautiful. Streaks of reds and orange look like an artist's brush daubed across the sky. Its serenity as I sip my wine and scribble my daily thoughts is a counterpoint to the day.*

That persistent Russian danseur attempted to be overfamiliar again, no doubt in a bid to entice his ex-girlfriend back. If my barista wasn't so inexplicably fond of Sasha, I'd ban him from the store. His batted eyelashes and absurd muscle flexing reminded me of a baboon presenting for mating. The only thing more pleasant than slamming the door in his face was the surprise he registered as I did so.

Book club. Chaos as always. Olivia made occasional arguments on book themes that bordered perilously close to substantive; won't hold my breath for the anomaly to repeat itself. Her attempts at herding cats back onto topic with that idiotic group yielded the usual predictable results. Apparently, I should now offer <u>sci-fi</u> *books in my* <u>crime</u> *bookstore! What's* next? Fifty Shades of Grey?! (H, of course, would call me a snob for that line. Under the circumstances, I wear the title proudly.)

It was too difficult to hold my tongue this week. All this time, all these months, I've muttered my sarcastic rejoinders under my breath. Not today. I've gone from passive observer to vocal critic. The only person more shocked than Olivia— based on her repeated little explosions—was me.

Speaking of Olivia: I was in the storeroom today when the Garritys entered the car park right outside. Olivia's experience at herding cats clearly came in useful. She wrangled those children like a pro. I also observed her hand off what looked like a good proportion of her weekly shop to Samantha Garrity. Does Olivia have no plans to eat too? With a heart that soft, I'm not sure how she survives in this world.

CHAPTER 3

TAKING A TRIP

OLIVIA SETTLED BACK IN HER Kombi, the final drop-off for Wednesday morning complete. She was exhausted and running on fumes since yesterday. Kelly had had some very firm thoughts on the subject of Tina, and they'd talked late into the night.

First thing in the morning, Olivia had politely texted her ex-girlfriend a firm no.

She'd told Tina she wasn't giving her a second chance. Kelly was right. Tina might say she was reformed, but it'd only been a few months. *Why don't I ever see the red flags the way Kelly does?*

Trip was in a contemplative mood, staring out the window. He'd been willed to her by Olivia's late nana. When she was seventy-one, Betty Roberts had acquired him after romancing a taxidermist while on her many travels— which had inspired Trip's name. Betty and her faithful penguin took a lot of trips together.

Trip had a short, orange beak and was slim even by penguin standards. He boasted black-and-white feathers and was roughly the height of a shoe-box on its end. Given he'd gone everywhere with Betty, it wasn't surprising he looked a little worse for wear around the tips of his once sleek feathers.

Olivia didn't care that he was past his prime or that he didn't say much. He was a first-rate companion and never minded her early starts.

"I mean, I could reassess in six months' time," Olivia told Trip, suddenly having second thoughts. Was she being a cold, unforgiving person? If

Tina was still interested and still putting in the work on herself, of course. Tina really could change. She'd feel terrible if Tina was better and Olivia had never even stopped to find out.

She pursed her lips, gripping the worn steering wheel tighter, glancing at Trip. "Don't look at me like that," she protested, although Trip was still resolutely contemplating life. "You never know. The universe has the capacity to surprise us all."

The traffic lights turned green and Olivia accelerated—although that wasn't exactly the word for it given the state of her ancient yellow Kombi she'd repurposed as a food van. It was the other thing Nana Betty had given her—wheels. It allowed her to ply her artisan muffins all over Melbourne's best coffee hubs.

She puttered slowly through downtown Prahran, a busy, cafe-studded suburb five clicks from Melbourne's city centre, which lured coffee snobs, market lovers, and would-be hipsters. Prahran was a contradictory mix of shabby-chic shops, the fashion mecca of Chapel Street—hanging on to its groovy title by a thread these days—and trendy apartments. The latter were populated by old money, now way out of Olivia's price range. It was the reason she and her sister rented a little house half an hour away, much deeper in suburbia.

Olivia pulled up at a small park that drew office workers on their breaks like seagulls to hot chips. It was later than usual, almost noon. She had finished all her other daily muffin drop-offs to coffee houses, lunch bars, cafes, and, of course, heaven's own bookstore.

Rolling open the heavy door on the side of the van—which had the embarrassing effect of contracting her painted company name to "Love Muff"—Olivia pulled forward a set of shelves containing two trays of muffins.

Her reputation meant she never had to wait more than an hour to be sold out as passers-by snapped up the remainder of her baked goods. It was always a nice end to her day, which started at four-thirty in the morning. And it meant, if she was lucky, she might also see her favourite sight: Book Woman.

She turned in anticipation. There she was. Seated at the bench in the middle of the same park where Olivia plied her unsold muffins, her patrician nose buried in a novel. She often did this: devoured novels on her lunch break. Actual books too—she was old school, which Olivia found interesting—paperbacks that she flicked through at some pace.

Judging by the rate at which the colours on the covers changed, she read one a day. And given most of the covers were in blacks or reds, her genre was probably crime.

The woman looked like a sinister, short-haired Morticia Addams—all elegant, broody, and aloof, as if she knew how to commit half the murders in her books.

Book Woman's most notable feature was her sharply pronounced cheekbones that set off her pale skin, black hair, and dark-framed glasses. The entire effect, unsoftened by make-up or any hint of colour or expression other than indifference, radiated complete disdain. Indeed, at this moment, she was impersonating a lean, haughty human vulture hunched over its paper prey.

While she might scare away everyone else with her harbinger-of-doom aura, Olivia was utterly mesmerised. She often wondered what Book Woman did for a living. Her clothing was always impeccable but interesting—masculine-cut ebony pantsuits hugging her long, narrow body, paired with polished black ankle boots. One day Olivia might even approach her and ask.

Yeah, right.

"Hey, Love Muff! Been waiting ages!"

Olivia's attention snapped back to her customers. Well, customer. Andy, one of her regulars, gave a dramatic sigh to punctuate his agony. The engineering student always looked half starved. He smiled his big, dopey, boyish grin, and Olivia could almost forgive him for using that appalling nickname.

"Yeah, the Kombi's been acting up again," she explained. "But I've got your favourite today, if that helps." Olivia slid her biggest three-cheese-and-herb-crust muffin onto a paper plate. She'd set this one aside just for him.

Practically drooling, Andy slapped down his money...all in spare change. He was already munching happily as he got out: "Mmph. Mnnnks, Livvy. Best. Muffins. Ever!"

Not Livvy. Not Love Muff. Olivia—or Liv in a pinch.

Still, she didn't correct him. He was a good customer, as well as harmless and sweet in a rumpled kind of way. She forgave him again and smiled as he retreated to sit on a low wall, where he slouched over his phone and devoured his lunch.

An hour flew by relatively smoothly until Olivia had only one muffin left: a sweet-potato-and-heirloom-tomato creation with a crusty Parmesan topping. Maybe the name needed work: Parma Sutra. Damien from book club had come up with it. She didn't want to say no in the face of his delight at his own "genius", so she'd used it.

No one wanted the last Parma Sutra today, though. It seemed a shame to throw it away, and she'd learned years ago not to eat her own leftovers or her bum wouldn't thank her. She was always a little self-conscious about its slightly roundish proportions, thanks to the ex who used to mock it mercilessly.

She'd often wondered why you'd date someone in the first place if you thought them so unattractive? She never did find an answer to that.

As Olivia began packing up, she spotted the muffin she'd failed to sell and glanced around hopefully for one last customer. She noticed Book Woman again.

Olivia paused. She loved to watch the way she'd snap the pages over on her book—crisply, as if to do it slowly was inefficient. But then she'd smooth the new page flat like an act of benediction for a lover. As if apologising for any abruptness.

As Olivia's eyes darted back to the Parma Sutra, an idea occurred. Did she dare?

Okay. Yep. *Okay.* She was doing it. She straightened her button pin: *Done and crusted.*

Scooping the lone muffin onto a small paper plate, Olivia drew in a deep breath and straightened. She would offer the woman her baked goods and not be a total chickenshit.

She was halfway to the other woman when it occurred to Olivia it was time to panic. She, a complete stranger, was about to accost someone and shove home-made muffins at them, even if said home-made muffins had been named "Best Food Truck Baked Goods (Savoury) in Prahran" in last year's esteemed *Good Food Guide*.

What if the woman thought it was some ploy to poison her?

Olivia slowed, fear drying her throat.

The woman glanced up, and their eyes met. A shiver ran through Olivia at the power of that gaze.

An eyebrow sharp enough to draw blood rose in question as she peered at Olivia. Her dark eyes scraped across Olivia's battered sneakers and up her jeans, wide hips and belly before sliding past her flannel shirt and white tee to settle on her face, with its doubtlessly frozen-deer-in-headlights expression.

The woman slowly lifted her chin, as if she had graciously allowed *one precious minute* to Olivia.

"Um, hi." Olivia fidgeted as she came to a stop in front of her. She tried to figure out her opening line. *Idiot.* She should have worked this out before she got here!

Would you like some Parma Sutra? No, that sounded weird as hell.

Would you like to taste my delicious muffin? Jesus! No!

Hi, I'm Love Muffins and… shit!

Had her hands always been this clammy?

Olivia blushed, hating that her fair, freckled complexion would almost certainly accentuate every beetroot-red capillary. She wished she had some witty introduction because this was now awkward as hell.

The woman's lips twitched as if considering expressing amusement, but she faltered as her gaze drifted past Olivia's shoulder.

At the same time, there came a shout from Andy, near the road. "Hey, Livvy! Someone's stealing your…"

What? Olivia spun around.

He squinted at the road and pointed. "Penguin?"

Trip?! Horror flooded her. *No!* A shadowy form was running from her van with Olivia's feathered companion under one arm.

"Oh my God!" She flung the muffin, still on its little paper plate, onto the bench and bolted.

Olivia puffed after the thief, every muscle protesting the unexpected physical activity. She'd curse how out of shape she was later. Right now, the most she could pray for was that she had no witnesses to this indignity.

"You go, Livvy!" Andy called out encouragingly from somewhere in her periphery.

Then there followed a female's soft snort of laughter from behind her. Most definitely not Andy's.

Olivia winced, knowing only too well who that'd be. Just great: witnesses confirmed.

Perhaps the thief hadn't actually expected to be noticed in mid thievery because Olivia rounded a corner to find the scoundrel leaning against a wall, catching their breath, holding Trip under one arm like bagpipes.

It was a thief Olivia recognized only too well. "*Tina?*"

"Oh, hey, Livvy. Great seeing you again." Her ex-girlfriend took a gulp of air and flapped her hand in an absent wave.

"What the actual hell?"

Tina supplied a relaxed, genial grin. "Okay, so it's not what it looks like. You *so* need to chill, girl."

"What, you didn't just steal my penguin?" Olivia lunged to snatch Trip.

Tina danced away with ease.

Olivia glared at her annoyingly agile form. With her wiry, gym-honed body and bleached blonde hair, she always gave off a wasted, rich socialite vibe. It wasn't far from the truth. Tina's massive sense of entitlement came from being an only child to wealthy parents who had given her everything she'd ever wanted.

They'd cut off her allowance after she got into party drugs. That apparently had meant that Olivia's possessions became Tina's to pawn. She hadn't even known about Tina's habit until Olivia's worldly goods started vanishing.

"Okay, hear me out." Tina drew in a breath and struck the *you-know-you-want-me* pose that always got her likes on social media. "I got your text this morning, and I was just *so* sad. You know?" She pouted. "I didn't want to end it over a stupid text. I didn't want us to be…" she reached out to stroke Olivia's button pin, "Done and crusted."

If Tina was weaponising her joyful motivational puns, Olivia was going to be very cross in a minute.

"Don't we deserve more?" Tina finished, and now her wide blue eyes pleaded with her. She was so earnest.

"Oh." Olivia blinked in confusion. "But…I mean…" She then pointed at Trip. "Why?"

"I needed to get your attention, that's all. I missed you so much. Weren't we good together? Didn't we click when things were good?" Her smile was soft and cheeky, like it had been in the early days. "So I've been spending all my time at home reflecting on how I've screwed everything up. That's it." She swayed in. "I truly just wanted to see you again."

She offered Trip to Olivia who snatched him back warily.

"I know how much you loved this little guy," Tina went on, "and I figured, well, you may hate the sight of me right now, but you'd definitely want to look at Trip again. I just wanted to talk to you. Properly. Face to face. Trip was never in any danger. Sorry if I scared you."

Doubt streaked through Olivia. Tina sounded so sincere. And now that she'd handed back Trip, this wasn't exactly a hostage negotiation anymore. Tina's eyes were beseeching as she waited for a reply.

"I don't...hate you," Olivia said, squeezing Trip tighter. "I was really disappointed in you. You stole my things. You broke my trust. That was gutting."

"I know, babe, I know. I'm so, so sorry." She swayed even closer. "Can you ever forgive me? I'm so much better now. My therapist says she's never seen anyone more committed to getting off drugs than me. It's because I'm motivated. I thought about how much I wanted to win you back. Didn't we have a blast together when we weren't hung up on the little stuff?" Her eyes were wide and hopeful.

"It wasn't *little stuff* stealing my mum's bracelet, though," Olivia protested. "That wasn't little stuff at all. That was a family heirloom she'd given me."

"No, you're right." She hung her head. "My therapist was shocked when I told her what I'd done. Stealing the love of my life's precious family heirlooms is the worst. Never again, though." She reached out and grasped Olivia's hand. "Never again."

Tina's hand felt dry and cool against Olivia's own sweat-slicked skin.

"I'm...the love of your life?" she squeaked, deciding not to point out that Tina had in fact already nicked another of her precious heirlooms not five minutes ago. But that had been to get her attention, so it wasn't the same thing, was it?

"Yeah, you are." Tina smiled. "Didn't you know that? You're my girl. You're why I want to get better. You're just so...good. So sweet. You're probably the only person on earth who'd ever give someone like me a second chance." Tina drew in a breath, looking nervous, then kissed Olivia's cheek.

"So I'm taking a risk and putting myself out there. Asking: one more chance?"

Olivia's skin lit under the warmth of the sweet kiss. She'd missed that sensation. The simple closeness and affection between two people who shared intimacy.

She'd never realised Tina loved her. She'd always seemed so dismissive of "mushy feelings" before, as if they were an intrusion on good sex. Or... average sex. Because Tina didn't always *entirely* remember to take care of Olivia's needs too. But then, she'd had a lot on her mind, hadn't she? Trying to keep all her secrets? Addiction was difficult. And here Tina was, trying so hard to be better.

Olivia inhaled. Maybe she was crazy, but she couldn't help wanting Tina to be the woman she claimed she was. She couldn't help wanting her to keep trying. Wanting her to...want *her*. Because in all the time they'd ever dated, Olivia had never felt truly wanted until this moment.

Come to think of it, in all the time and across all the people Olivia had dated, she'd never felt really wanted. More...convenient. It was a dream to be wanted. "Yes. But, so help me, you'd better not hurt me again," Olivia said. "Anything but that."

"Anything but that," Tina agreed, and this time she captured Olivia's lips in a kiss that hinted at passion. "It's Wednesday, right? So Kelly'll be out bartending tonight? How about I come over and make up for lost time? I'll even cook." She laughed.

Cook?! Tina had never cooked even once for Olivia before. And it was nice she remembered her sister's schedule so as to not inconvenience Kelly. Although that probably had more to do with the fact that the two got on like cats and dogs. "You'll cook?"

"Yeah, babe. I will. Like I said, I'm making amends. See you tonight. At six? I know you like to have dinner and bed early because you work bakers' hours."

Olivia's heart melted a little more at her consideration. It was true she was usually asleep by nine-thirty. "Six," she agreed.

With a smile from ear to ear, Tina said: "Can't wait." With that, she sauntered off, giving her ass a sexy little sway.

As Olivia watched her go, she reminded herself not to be too hopeful. Maybe Kelly was right. But still…Tina sounded a hundred times better than she had before. Wasn't she worth a second chance?

Olivia looked down at Trip. Well, now. She'd always said the universe was full of surprises.

Trip made no comment.

Sunset: *7.55pm*

Temp: *13.6C-23.5C*

Rain: *0mm*

Noise: *Neighbour in 1B did not run a/c despite warmer day. Odd behaviour. To monitor further.*

Drink: *Trentham Estate Shiraz 2020. Two glasses. Still acceptable.*

Reading: Non-fiction—*JALIA, Vol 69, issue 1. Article on financial management for libraries. Nothing I didn't already know.*

Fiction—*Land's Edge by Tim Winton. Overly descriptive nostalgia for Australian beach lovers. Well-written wallowing.*

General Observations: *I witnessed a penguin theft today. Olivia—because of course it was her; she is at the heart of every single one of life's absurdities—was embroiled in the saga. A blonde waif sprinted off after wresting said penguin from the Love Muffins van.*

(Note I'm no longer sneering at the name—it's only taken a year, and I've exhausted all my insults. Still, the van name is about what I'd expect from someone who wears buttons each day with another baking pun that's more awful than the last. Some of the puns are so bad, they make me appreciate my former life in academia, where the wit was sharp enough to cause internal bleeding.)

I'd have pointed this penguin heist out to Olivia as she was standing just three feet from me at the time, clutching baked goods to her chest. But a customer called out to her first.

I strongly suspect I was about to be offered a muffin. I wonder how she might have phrased her offer? "Please accept this stale, sad baked good I was unable to sell?" After all, Olivia does come out with the most surreal...blurtings... at times.

I'm most sorry we were interrupted and I did not get to hear her awkward pitch.

CHAPTER 4

SECOND CHANCES

Tina arrived for dinner with mounds of takeaway food from a nearby curry place. Olivia couldn't help but stare at the bulging bags as Tina shunted them onto the kitchen counter.

Her ex-girlfriend then waved at the aromatic fare as if she'd accomplished something amazing. "As promised, food of the gods." She glanced around and paused. "Why's all this out?" Tina peered at the frying pan and utensils stacked neatly beside the cooktop, where Olivia had placed them in anticipation of Tina actually cooking.

This did not look like cooking.

Maybe she'd simply forgotten she'd promised to cook? That could be it. In which case, Olivia shouldn't make a fuss because Tina had still brought food, and that was a miracle in itself.

But no, she had to know. "Weren't you going to cook?" Olivia asked as diplomatically as she could.

Tina's brows furrowed. "No, I said I'd bring food. And here it is. Your favourite. Three types of naan bread, too: cheese, garlic, and butter."

Olivia bit her lip. Naan bread was Tina's favourite. They'd had it together, it was true, but usually Olivia would nibble one corner, and Tina would devour the rest while announcing how long she'd have to spend on the spin bike in her apartment's gym to work it off.

"You said you'd cook," Olivia said, at least wanting the record straight if nothing else.

"What? Are you sure?" Tina asked, confusion spilling across her features. "Yes."

"Oh. Well. I mean, if it's that important to you, let's put all this stuff away and I'll do my best. It's a shame, though, because Tandoori Palace's dishes are best when just prepared, not as leftovers the next day." She made a small huff as she started gathering it all together. "Will you have room in the fridge? I know you keep all your baking supplies in there too."

"Stop." Olivia felt ridiculous. Tina was right; the food was here, and it was fresh and hot. Why was Olivia making a fuss? "Since it's here, we may as well eat it."

"Great idea," Tina said, brightening. "That's smart."

For the weirdest moment, Olivia felt…managed…but then the feeling slipped away as Tina started chattering about her day and shooting Olivia sunny smiles. She reminded her often of the good times they'd shared, and for a while, it was easy to pretend they'd never been apart.

Tina was diving into the food and making obscene moans that made Olivia forget many of her grievances against her ex. Former ex? Wait, where were they in the scheme of things?

"Livvy, you have *got* to try the cheese naan," Tina sighed happily. "It's the best ever." The dreamy look caught Olivia at her weakest moment. She was captivated completely by that heated gaze, loaded with desire and lusty satisfaction.

So, before long, she'd tried the naan bread. And then Tina's curving lips. Her neck. Her breasts. And then Tina was in Olivia's bed again as if she'd never left it. She was rocking and moaning and clutching and releasing Olivia's hair. Then she was pinning Olivia down, her body pressing her possessively into the bed, and rutting against her, gasping and panting, until…

Well. Sometimes the universe was incredibly repetitive after all.

Tina had rolled off her after her orgasm, stroked Olivia's hair twice, and gone straight to sleep.

Olivia blew out a breath in frustration. She studied Tina's naked beauty—the smooth, soft planes of her body and the childlike innocence that her face relaxed into whenever she was asleep.

Tina was trying to be better, she reminded herself. Rome wasn't built in a day. And maybe, in the morning, she'd take one lust-filled look at Olivia, remember what she'd forgotten to do the previous night, and give her make up sex for the ages.

Feeling a little more hopeful, Olivia closed her eyes.

The next morning, Olivia was up at four as usual, disappointed to find the bed empty beside her. She should have remembered that Tina rarely slept over. Olivia did, however, find something new—a note on her dresser, in Tina's uneven scrawl.

Thanks Livvy, that was exactly what I needed.

She ground her jaw for a moment at the self-centred choice of words, but again reminded herself about Rome and its speed-challenged builders. She made her way to the kitchen and began robotically starting her muffin bake for the day.

On her sack of flour, she found a new note; this one in her sister's handwriting.

I won't ask who you brought home who left that Indian food mess for me to find, but if it was Tina, I swear, woman, we have GOT to have another talk. She's like a bag of self-hitting hammers.

Maybe Kelly was right—Tina would hurt her again. Or maybe Olivia was right. But there was no evidence either way. You never knew until you put yourself out there and tried. People were worth giving a second chance, right?

Right.

She'd pretty much convinced herself of that as she loaded her fresh muffins into the Kombi.

Dawn had well and truly broken across Melbourne when she finally rolled the side door closed on her deliveries. Olivia decided she should focus on the positives of last night. She'd had a good meal and shared intimacy with a beautiful woman after a dry spell. That part had felt nice if you didn't focus on the lack of reciprocation. Or the fact she'd had to fix that particular oversight in the shower this morning or remain pent-up all day.

She shook her head. Back to the positives: Tina was trying to get her life in order. Nothing was missing from Olivia's bedroom or wallet this morning, although she still felt a little guilty for checking.

And, after her muffins run, she had exciting plans to kick back and relax and stream a few shows she'd been missing. That was something to look forward to. It was a toss-up between some zombie series with a feisty teenage girl in it and a Mexican drama about a baby swap and lesbians. *Decisions, decisions.*

Olivia climbed into the driver's seat. "What do you think, Trip? Mexican lesbians or zombie apocalypse?" she asked, turning to him.

Trip's seat was empty.

She choked. Olivia frantically looked all around and under his seat. She considered running inside and waking her sister to see if Kelly had borrowed her penguin for some reason. *What reason? How absurd!*

Instantly, she knew what had happened. It hadn't been enough for Tina to try to steal Trip earlier. When she'd been caught red-handed, she'd simply pivoted. She'd schmoozed her way into Olivia's bed for one last fuck-you shag and then taken him anyway.

How could she?

How could anyone do this to another person? Pretend to like them and then betray them in the worst way? It wasn't just Tina who'd done that to her. Her three other exes had been self-centred users, all taking advantage of her kindness. But now Tina had surpassed even their shitty deeds. Tina had taken Trip. Worse, she'd done it knowing he meant everything to Olivia.

Her world tilted for a moment, as if about to collapse. And then, for the first time in Olivia's entire life, all she could see was red.

CHAPTER 5

IT'S ALL OR MUFFIN

WANTED: ONE HENCHPERSON

Duties: *Assisting in vengeance planning and execution of a revenge bucket list.*

Skills required: *Sabotage, reconnaissance (not in a stalkery way), wet work, brainstorming, and implementing various schemes as required. Experience not necessary, but extreme annoyance at one's exes a bonus.*

Payment: *Six months' supply of assorted baked goods from Love Muffins.*

Apply in person to: *Olivia Roberts, c/o Women in Crime Book Club, Mary Bugg's Bookstore and Coffee House. Next Tuesday, March 10, from 4pm.*

OLIVIA PINNED HER AD ON the community noticeboard that sat just inside the doors of Mary Bugg's. It was the first thing customers would see as they entered. She attached a dozen application forms underneath the ad.

The noticeboard was supposed to be for customers offering piano classes or selling a bookcase, not soliciting henchpeople. Henchpersons? But desperate times etc., etc.

Her gaze fixed on her typed words. Funny how bold and challenging the ad looked now that it was up for all the world to see. But Olivia had tossed and turned all night last night over what had happened, her fury rising. Apparently, once she'd uncorked that bottle, there was no returning.

For most of the night, she'd relived, over and over, her visit to the spectacularly uninterested Victoria Police. They'd signed and dated her stolen penguin report before shooing her out, explaining that they had to focus on "important" matters.

Important. As though Trip wasn't one of the most important people in her life. Well, companion. Whatever. They didn't understand and weren't interested in listening when she'd tried to explain his family heirloom status.

Pawn store staff had laughed outright when she'd called to see if anyone had tried to offload a penguin.

Olivia's calls to Tina had gone unanswered, and she'd pretty much been stewing ever since. Yes, *stewing* was the word. All day yesterday and last night, she'd marinated in rage and a sense of injustice. She'd picked over every single former relationship in unflattering, excruciating detail.

By two this morning, she'd confirmed what she already knew: that everyone she'd ever seriously dated had either carelessly and callously hurt her or taken advantage of her—or both.

When Olivia stopped and fully took stock of those four disastrous exes, her anger grew to white-hot. Why did she attract such people? Why did none of them care about her enough to treat her better? Why had none of them cared that they had lost her?

Am I not worth wanting?

By four-thirty in the morning, when she rose to bake, utterly exhausted after twenty-four hours of fuming, she'd concluded their excuses were irrelevant. All that mattered was what she did about it. It was long past time to take action. Payback was *on*.

Of course, to actually have payback, one needed a plan. Olivia was self-aware enough to acknowledge she didn't have a conniving bone in her body. She didn't have even the first clue how to come up with clever schemes that "sure showed them".

Okay, small setback. She slid the trays into the oven and set the timer just as the answer arrived. She needed a partner in crime as clever and cunning as Mary Ann Bugg to outwit her enemies and enact a little vengeance.

How hard could it be to find someone like that?

"Oh, you have *got* to be kidding me!" Kelly's incredulous voice sounded from behind. Her sister came to stand next to her and glared at the ad Olivia was regarding on the noticeboard. "Seriously?"

"Not kidding." Olivia folded her arms. "Deadly serious."

"Are you trying to get me fired?" Kelly dusted down her crisp barista apron. "Dr Blackwood might have a few things to say about you soliciting help in committing crimes!"

"If your boss is unhappy, she can tell me to take it down. And what crimes are you talking about? It's an expression of interest at this point, nothing else."

"You're asking for *henchpeople*! And what about wet work?" Kelly tapped the words. "That's assassinations and blood and bodies!" Her eyes widened. "You will *not* turn to murder on my watch, even if your exes all deserve it."

Wait, was *that* what wet work meant? Olivia's mouth fell open.

Her sister's eyes grew even wider. "How can that not have come up once in your book club?"

Olivia squirmed with embarrassment. "It does come up rather a lot but I"—her cheeks warmed—"I just thought it was about, you know, wiping down wet areas in the house, tidying up a little before the cops arrived, not…the rest." Okay, now that she said it, it sounded ridiculous.

"Dr Blackwood will definitely know what wet work means," Kelly warned. "She runs a freaking *crime* bookstore. If she claps eyes on that, I'm fired and your precious club's dead."

"Fine!" Olivia reached into her pocket, dragged out a pen, and put an arrow beside *wet work*, then scribbled a note next to it: *NB: not in the murder sense.* "Happy now? Even Her Majesty can't complain—although God knows she loves to."

At the thought, she glanced towards the end of the bookshop to where the manager's office was. She couldn't see it from the front of the store, but she imagined Dr Blackwood in her office, seated in some huge power chair, peering out through the slatted wooden blinds, watching for any infraction so she could pounce.

To be fair, Olivia didn't actually *know* whether Margaret Blackwood stared out at the people in her store all day or not. But she assumed that was the case. Because what else did she have to do in that little office for hours on end?

Kelly shook her head. "If you get my ass fired, you'll have to pay both our rents."

"Why would your boss fire you? You're her best barista."

"I'm her *only* barista. And around Melbourne, baristas are a dime a dozen." Kelly sighed. "Do I want to know why you're doing this? Is this about Annalise's text last week? I know that was a bit of an entitled move—"

"A *bit*?" Olivia scowled at the reminder. Years ago, when they'd been dating, Annalise had scammed and wheedled all Olivia's savings out of her before sleeping with Olivia's then boss. When she'd caught them, Olivia had been fired and her former girlfriend had moved in with him. The cherry on the top had come last week: Annalise had texted to ask Olivia to make them a wedding cake. For free! "No, it's not because of Annalise's text. It's because of Tina."

"Oh my God, please tell me it wasn't her you were with on curry night?" Kelly asked incredulously. She looked closer at her sister's face. "Oh, hell... what'd she steal this time?"

Olivia's lips quivered before she forced the word out. "Trip."

God. Voicing it hurt even more.

Silence fell. "Trip?" Bafflement laced Kelly's voice. "She stole your *penguin*?"

Nodding, Olivia blinked back tears.

"I knew that witch was up to something! Making contact out of the blue? Was this why she asked about Trip? What'd she want with him, anyway?"

"I don't know. She won't return my calls, and the police are no help."

"Oh, hon. I'm sorry."

"So, you see?" Olivia waved at the ad. "I was up all night thinking about all the exes who've hurt me and how I said nothing. Well, I'm not going to take it anymore."

Kelly eyed her in surprise.

"God, why's it always me? I've had the worst luck with relationships."

"Olivia," Kelly said with a long sigh. "It was never about you or luck. It was just assholes being assholes. That's on them. You somehow always stumbled across the most manipulative bastards, who took advantage of your kindness and sweet nature. It's been almost physically painful to watch you putting up with their gaslighting bullshit and thinking it's something you've done wrong. Although any time I did warn you, you just couldn't believe that anyone could be so terrible and calculating, so you went ahead anyway. As for Tina, she's the worst gaslighter of them all. I can't believe you gave her a second chance."

Olivia's cheeks flamed. *Me either.* "Well, now I'm not putting up with it," she said defensively. She tapped the button pin on her shirt she'd chosen with deliberate care this morning: *It's All or Muffin.* Then she added with iron in her voice: "No one steals Nan's lucky penguin and gets away with it!"

"I'm glad you're finally fighting back," Kelly said gently, "but you know only a bunch of creeps will answer that ad, right? Or worse, professional criminals."

"Actual professionals will not be working for muffins."

"Good point. So you'll attract the amateur criminals, then."

"Maybe a couple," Olivia conceded. "But, see, that's why interviews are being held here. Public place; lots of witnesses. I'll weed out the creeps. You can even watch me while you work if it'll make you feel better."

"If you're absolutely hellbent on doing this, why not do it alone, without any witnesses to get in the way?"

"Come on, Kel, you know me better than anyone else," Olivia said in frustration. "Do you seriously believe I have the mind of someone brilliant at subterfuge and plotting and all those twisty schemes that make you go *ooooh* at the end of a crime novel?"

"Eh." Kelly rubbed her cheek. "Yeah. Good point. No. No scheming bones in your body."

"Right. I need smart, slick vengeance, not whatever lame plans I'd dream up. And a henchperson will keep me focused too."

"Why not brainstorm with your book club for ideas?"

"I said smart and slick," Olivia said, dryly, "not something outlandish from a murder mystery. Besides, they are impossible to keep on topic."

"Excuse me?" An older woman's tone cut through the room. "If you two are done gossiping, I'd like to buy this book now. And one of those muffins. The one with the chocolate bits on top."

Kelly snapped to attention. "Gotta go. I'll see you at home tonight." She pointed at the noticeboard. "We are *not* done with this."

"Yeah we are. And unless your boss rips my ad down, I'm officially recruiting a henchperson."

Sunset: *7.52pm*

Temp: *15.9C-19C*

Rain: *7mm*

Noise: *Neighbour 1B is apparently away. No a/c.*

Drink: *Lemon, lime, and bitters. Two.*

Reading: Non-fiction—JALIA, *Vol 69, issue 1. Article on the history and future of reading. Shock findings: we <u>were</u> reading and we still <u>are</u>.*

Fiction—The Fatal Shore *(Robert Hughes). Hard to work out what was more brutal—the treatment of the convicts or the tiny type size. Atrocious.*

Note: Get reading glasses prescription updated.

General Observations: *Further to my comment a few days back that Olivia is at the heart of every single one of life's absurdities: Today she posted an advertisement seeking a henchperson. Because of course she did. This is officially the most ludicrous event to ever transpire in the history of Mary Bugg's.*

As an aside, I truly didn't think the woman had it in her. I've seen no evidence of a ruthless or cunning streak in Olivia Roberts. She exudes an abundance of kindness and empathy. Puppies, kittens, and orphans everywhere are unsafe from her attentions. I detect not the slightest drop of darkness in her. But it's a ruinous state to exist in: those who run too much on heart suffer grievously when bad things happen to them.

So now she's doing this? What happened, I wonder, to elicit this response? No matter the reason, I'm awaiting Olivia's henchperson interviews with more than passing interest. It may well be the highlight of the month. What a depressing thought.

CHAPTER 6

INTERVIEW WITH A HENCHPERSON

Applicant One: Damien

"Okay," Olivia said, shuffling her papers on the coffee table. "Thank you for coming."

She was in the little area at the back of Mary Bugg's, where she had just finished her book club. Unexpectedly, her fellow book club members had wanted to discuss her henchperson recruitment plans in detail instead of *Crimson Lake*. Which was a shame because Olivia had really liked the book.

After the book club broke up, Damien had been the first to stand, move one seat over, and drop into the chair directly opposite her. He slid his application across the table.

She blinked up at him. "Thank you for your interest, Damien." She glanced at her clipboard and the first question. "What could you bring to the table as a henchperson?"

"Um, okay, right, I'm big. Ah, strong." He held up his arms, bent at the elbows with hands curled into fists, and beamed. A large mass of flesh moved, not necessarily into muscles. But it was indeed impressively broad.

She nodded.

He paused. "That's kinda it."

"Any previous experience?"

"Not at henchpersonning. I mean it's a bit out of the ordinary, isn't it? But security? Sure. Eight years doing that. Before that, I taught high school geography."

"You did?" She stared.

He shrugged. "Got bored and needed more money."

"Well, if it's more money you're after, there's only muffins in this gig."

"Yup," he said. "I know."

"So why do you want to do this?"

"Um, well you're kinda little, and I don't want to see you beaten up." He grinned. "But mainly I'm really down for those muffins. The, ah, non-cheese ones," he clarified.

"I see. Well, thanks for your time, Damien, I'll let you know."

"That's it?"

"Yes."

She sighed inwardly as he left, unimpressed his motives were purely muffin related. Olivia filed his paperwork and looked around for the next applicant.

Applicant Two: Tess

"My turn." Tess slid into the chair Damien had vacated.

"What?" Surely, she'd misheard.

"I'm applying too." Tess plopped an application form onto the table. "I know I'm young, but I'm good at taking direction—I mean, I'd have to be, being a drama student. Also, I can squeeze into small spaces. And I don't mind getting my hands dirty. So please consider me?"

"Are you sure? I mean, why?" Her gaze took in the woman. She was such a sweet kid—innocent, tiny, with romantic views of the world. Her enormous brown eyes were just so sincere. Olivia worried she'd be spending all her time acting as a bodyguard if she chose Tess. And there wasn't that much body mass to Olivia to start with, despite that one ex's views on the size of her bum.

"It sounds so exciting," Tess enthused. "Daring! Like a real adventure from the books we read. I could be a modern-day Mary Ann Bugg!"

"Except it'd be a lot more boring. Stake-outs, hiding in bushes, waiting for hours, that sort of thing."

"Really?"

"It wouldn't leave you any time to write your Aboriginal outback sci-fi story."

Tess sagged. "Oh. What exactly *are* you planning to do to your exes, then?"

Good question. Olivia had no clue. "Need-to-know basis, Tess. And until I have my chosen henchperson, you don't need to know."

"Well, okay. Hey, can I blog about this? If I'm picked, I really want to capture our adventures and share them with the world."

"No! This is a top-secret mission! There will be no glory beyond the muffins."

"Oh." Tessie sagged all over again. "Never mind, then. I don't really eat muffins anyway. No offence." She rose. "Good luck, Liv."

Non-Applicant Three: Breanna

"Just stopped by to say wish I could help," Breanna said, leaning over the vacant chair. "But I'm not applying."

"No?" Olivia said curiously. Revenge planning would be something she was sure would be in the activist's wheelhouse.

"I know half your exes are women. I can't in good conscience make it my life's work to tackle the patriarchy while going after women at the same time—even if they deserve it. Sorry. I know that sucks."

"I understand." Olivia sighed.

"Good luck, though." Breanna raised a fist in solidarity and marched off.

Applicant Four: Sasha

Kelly's ex was as beautiful as ever as he crossed his leg over one knee and settled back in the armchair. He could be a painting, arranged like that. And he knew it.

Sasha smiled. "Now you will consider me," he announced, giving his floppy hair a shake to settle back where it was: perfection.

"Don't you have somewhere else to be?" she asked suspiciously. If he wasn't chasing Kelly, or trying it on with Dr Blackwood to, once again, chase Kelly, he had no reason to be in the bookstore at all.

"Why would I be anywhere else when I heard about this most exciting job offer?" He leaned in. "A henchperson?" He chuckled, low and deep. "This is something I very much wish to have on my CV."

"You've never shown any interest in dark deeds before," Olivia noted. "Why now?"

"You do not know me at all," Sasha said, pouting. "I have many interests. As for my skills, I am athletic. You need me to jump into high place? This I can do. Or maybe you wish me to play the role of handsome jilted lover to make your exes worry they should not have let you go?" He grinned. "Also, I can do this."

Olivia snorted. "I don't think any of my exes would believe you were ever with me."

"Did I not mention I am an actor now? I can be most convincing." He shot her a look of pure lust that made her confused more than aroused.

"Um…"

He dropped the look. "You see?" Sasha said earnestly. "My acting coach says that I am 'coming along with bounds and leaps'." He smiled, and his even, white teeth gleamed. "I could also be a great Mata Hari, if you need one—or whatever is the male version." He turned just the slightest amount in his chair, and his pecs bulged, causing his shirt to strain at the fourth button. "Maybe I can be useful as a distraction on a mission?"

Too much of one, most likely. Sasha's arresting looks would never blend in anywhere, ever. Besides, that wasn't her main concern. "Why are you *really* here?" Olivia asked. "I know this job doesn't interest you." Suspicion flared anew. "Wait, did Kelly put you up to this?"

"Who?" Sasha asked innocently.

"She did!" Her sneaky sister! "You're here to spy for her!"

"Okay, she is most worried." Sasha lifted his hands. "And I am trying to get into her forgiveness books after the…misunderstandings…on our last date."

"Where you flirted with the waitress and Kelly broke up with you."

"You make it sound so final. But, yes, I am here to be her eyes and ears."

"I don't need a minder." Olivia shot him a peeved look. "You're fired!"

Sasha appeared unruffled by this news. "I was not hired, so you cannot actually fire me."

"I don't care. Take your sneaky ass outta here."

Sasha rose, giving his sneaky ass a suggestive jiggle. "This is your great loss."

How did he make everything sound like a line? Unbelievable.

Applicant Five: Emma

"Emma?" Olivia eyed the ten-year-old Garrity girl in confusion.

"Hey, Olivia." Pale blue eyes met hers.

"Why are you here?"

"For the job interview." She made a *duh* face.

"Shit! I should have put an age limit on this."

"Olivia! You swore!"

Oops. "Sorry."

"So, about the job. I'll work really, really hard. I'll do research on any-thing. I'm well-read, so I know a *tonne* of fictional schemes, but I'm sure I can think up some of my own, whatever you need—"

"I need you to stay in school, sweetheart. In fact, shouldn't you be there now?"

"Um, Olivia, it's, like, four-thirty? School's been out *forever*. What does *wet work* mean? And why's it crossed out?"

"It's about cleaning up."

"Like bathrooms and kitchens?"

Right? It wasn't just Olivia who'd thought that. "Sort of."

"And the spying? Who are we spying on?"

"There's no spying for you. As a full-time student, you'd have no time for henchpersonning."

Emma peered at her. "That's not a word, you know."

"Are you sure?"

"Yeah."

"Well, it should be. And I think your mum mightn't be too thrilled about you learning about vengeance schemes."

"I've *already* learned about vengeance schemes. It's all through children's books. Hansel and Gretel? They threw the witch in the oven! Matilda? She terrorised Miss Trunchbull for being abusive to the kids and Miss Honey."

"*Miss Honey*," Olivia repeated, a dreamy sensation overtaking her. "I love her."

"Me too." Emma then gave a tiny smirk. "Although I don't think I love her the way you do."

A soft, amused snort sounded from the office behind them.

Great. Olivia sighed and felt her cheeks burn. Meanwhile, Emma Garrity was far too sharp for her own good.

She cast around for a good reason to say no to a smart, well-read, would-be henchperson, who'd tick most of the boxes except for the not-insignificant fact that she was only ten. And it was highly doubtful she'd had any exes to be enraged at.

"Look," Olivia tried, "the bottom line is, if I gave you your fill of muffins—and we both know you'd really be giving them to your brother—it'd be a disaster. Toby would eat me out of business!"

Emma giggled. "You say that as if you haven't been giving us a tonne of muffins and other groceries for months."

"What other groceries?" Olivia asked, trying to sound clueless.

"You think I don't notice how many of Mum's groceries smell like your van? Come on, Olivia."

"My van smells?" Olivia was aghast.

"Good smells." This time, Emma fully smiled. "And we're really grateful. You've been awesome to us. So now I want to help *you*. Please, let me?"

"I can't, Emma. Education is your top priority, no matter how worthy the vengeance cause."

"Let me come to the strategy meetings, at least? If you have them here at the same time, I can walk over, straight after school."

And it all became clear.

"You want to be away from where you're supposed to stay after school?" she asked gently.

A guilty look crept onto Emma's face. "I'm sorry," she whispered. "I really do want to help too, but yeah. Basically, Mrs Clarke's place is tiny, really stuffy, and filled with old-lady smells. Like roses and perfume and soaps, and it's so sweet and icky. It's also too dark to read there, and it hurts my eyes to try."

"That sounds hard, sweetheart. I understand why you'd want somewhere else to hang out after school. But I'm usually only here Tuesday afternoons for book club. And even if I did have late afternoon henchperson meetings here every day, this isn't my bookstore. It's not my place to give you permission to hide out here doing your homework."

"Oh." Her voice was small.

"Isn't there a public library you can go to?"

"The local one's been closed for ages since it was flooded."

A low voice from behind Olivia said: "She may attend Mary Bugg's after school if her mother approves it."

Olivia blinked in surprise.

"But only as long as the child doesn't adopt your appalling taste in books. I'm not in favour of infecting the innocent."

With an eyeroll at that, Olivia looked at Emma, whose eyes had widened. "That was the bookstore owner, Dr Blackwood. You have tentative approval."

"Why does she say I'm not allowed to agree with you on book stuff?"

"Because she's eccentric and *loves* to be mean. Just roll with it."

"Eccentric!" came an outraged mutter.

Glancing at the ajar door, Olivia called: "I notice you didn't argue with the *loves to be mean* part." Turning back to Emma, she said, "Just get your mum to call me, and I'll run it past her."

"Thanks, Olivia." Emma bounced to her feet. She turned to face the office and called out politely: "And thanks, awesome bookstore boss."

There was a pause and then the low, approving voice: "At least *someone* has discernment."

Emma's normally serious face creased into laughter.

Applicant Six: Harmony

"Hi, I'm Harmony," a strange woman said, bustling in to sit down, pushing her wide-rimmed sunglasses onto her head. She was thin, wrapped in a likely home-made knitted cardigan and sunny yellow frock. It had different types of mushrooms all over it. Catching Olivia studying it, Harmony smiled brightly and said, "They're fun-gi, get it?"

Fun fungi? Olivia nodded politely.

"I don't have to tell you that I'm the perfect person for this job." Harmony pulled out a day planner, snapping the elastic holder off the pages and flicking forward at a rapid pace. "You might say I've been working up to this my whole life."

"You have?" Olivia stared at her in surprise.

"Oh yes. As soon as I saw your ad, I thought: 'Wow, this is me. It's everything about who I am', you know?"

"Really? What do you do for a living?"

"I run the Harmony Whole Foods stall at the Queen Victoria Market." She waved her hand, and an armful of plastic purple and pink bangles clinked and clanged.

Olivia frowned. "Um, so what credentials do you have that will help me?"

"Okay, years of experience. I started out doing this when I was only young, just trying it a little bit, you know? Seeing if it was for me. Then, when I was a teenager, I thought maybe I could go all-in? Fully commit? And I did. There was no looking back."

"No looking back," Olivia repeated.

"No. I went from vegetarian, and I've been a vegan now seventeen years."

"A…vegan? So how does that help me?" Confusion filled her.

The woman paused flicking through her diary and looked up in surprise. "Aren't you looking for someone to help you with vegan planning? It's on your bucket list, I believe? I'm available next week. I'm always happy to take someone through the journey."

Olivia sighed. "The ad says vengeance planner. *Vengeance*. As in hurting one's exes."

"Ohhh." Harmony closed her planner book with a slap. "I did think that part was a bit odd. Now it makes more sense. I just assumed you were going to learn the vegan lifestyle while simultaneously annoying your exes. And I have to say, as a woman, I could totally appreciate your multi-tasking there. That really seemed on point."

"No, no multi-tasking, just straight-up vengeancing. Sorry."

"Well, I see we have a vision mismatch." Harmony rose. "I could leave you my card, though, if you do want to try some of my vegan recipes on my website? VivaLasVegan.com."

"No, that's okay." Olivia forced a smile. "Thanks for stopping by."

The woman bustled out.

Applicant Seven: Davo

"Davo" as he called himself on his application form (no other name listed), was a short, squat man in his forties with unkempt, dirty hair and nails.

His eyes darted all around as if assessing the joint for exits. Or just casing the joint. "Where's yer boss?" he asked, having another look around. "No point starting till he gets here."

"I… What boss?"

"The bloke who put the ad up?" He tilted his head, and there was a small scar along his jaw.

"The, uh…"

"You his secretary, then?" Davo nodded. "Guess it makes sense not to expose yourself at this early stage in proceedings. Well…"—he waved at his paperwork—"it's all there. Experience and so on. I've seen the inside of Boggo Road too, if that helps." He smiled a cold smile.

Boggo Road? Where the hell was…and then it clicked. That was a notorious jail in Queensland, wasn't it? They'd shut it down a few decades back for being too awful. So she actually had a career criminal on her hands. Kelly would give her hell after this.

"I…um…am not sure this position is suitable for you," Olivia tried.

"Why not?" His brown eyes narrowed. "I'm not good enough for you? That's rich, given what the job is!"

"Look, there's no boss, just me. And the pay is in muffins!" Did he not realise that?

He blinked then, absorbing this info. "Oh." He scratched his chin. "I didn't read the whole ad, gotta admit. It was so fucking long."

It wasn't even a hundred words!

"'Sides, I'm not real interested in working for some *fee-male*," he sneered. "For muffins or otherwise. No offence, woman. I thought I'd be fuckin' up some troublesome bitches, not helping one roast the poor bugger who pissed her off. *Shit*." He looked appalled.

Olivia wasn't about to tell him that half her exes *were* women. For some reason, he didn't seem the sort to embrace the queer community.

"Right, then. I'm outta here." Davo rose, then paused. "Uhm, can you not tell anyone I was here?" His eyes darted around as though his mates might be lurking. "Don't want word to get out I'd consider working for… *you know*." He shot her a loaded look.

"A woman?" she asked sweetly.

"Muffins."

"Of course. Perish the thought."

"I mean it's not like you offered beer." He leaned right into her space and lowered his voice conspiratorially. "But a bit of advice? A freebie, from one asshole to another."

She swallowed back a protest at his over-ripe body odour and being called an asshole.

"Hire the cleverest bastard you can find, got me? Not the biggest or the meanest-looking shithead. They're a dime a dozen and good in a brawl but aren't what ya need here." He tapped his temple. "Revenge is a science not a blood sport. Remember that."

Then Davo offered her a grin so creepy that Olivia wanted to leap from her chair and hide behind it. Fortunately, and thank every deity in the universe, he turned tail and was gone.

Applicant Eight: Kelly

Kelly sat down next. "Kelly Roberts," she said, sliding an application form Olivia's way. "Age thirty-four. Full-time barista, part-time bartender."

"Here to see if I was sucked in by Sasha?" Olivia asked a little more tartly than she'd intended. In truth, Davo had rattled her rather badly.

"Here to apply."

"Apply? You're not serious." Olivia knew that for a fact.

"If I'm going to see my little sister get up to all sorts of dangerous things, I'd rather I was there too."

"Bull. You're really here to talk me out of it."

"It's a *terrible* idea!" Kelly flung up her hands. "What could you possibly accomplish? What's done is done. You'll end up arrested!"

"Not if I'm careful."

"Careful? Careful! You're *already* not being careful! Don't think I didn't clock that reprobate in here five minutes ago!"

"Davo? He was fine. Gave me some good advice and left. We're cool."

"So cool you rushed off to the bathroom after he leaned right in and whispered in your ear?"

Well, that was true. She'd just needed to splash some water on her face and…

"Don't do this."

"It's happening. With or without your support. May as well be with, don't you think?"

"You're impossible." Kelly sighed and rose when she saw a customer waiting at the coffee counter. "Just be careful."

"Of course."

Olivia reviewed her list of applicants. Big, strong Damien, who was only there for the muffins. Tess, there for the adventure and glory. She'd get neither. Besides, she made dandelions looks tough.

Sasha, just a spy for Kelly. He was too noticeable to be of much use on any undercover mission. Emma wasn't a serious contender (although she'd been better than most), and the vegan, Harmony, hadn't meant to be there at all.

Much as she hated to admit it, Davo was right. She needed someone sharp and clever, with schemes and brilliant ideas. Not anyone tough or big. It wasn't enough.

No one who'd applied was even close.

Had this been a pointless exercise? Did no one understand how this felt, being so hurt you just had to strike back or feel like a victim forever?

Applicant Nine: Book Woman

"Hello?" A low murmur sounded. "I'm here to interview for the hench-person position."

Olivia's head snapped up. She gasped as she stared into the face of the woman from the park. "I...I..." She waved excitedly at the chair opposite. "Yes! Please sit!"

The woman eased into the leather armchair and looked around. She was in an ebony suit, tailored beautifully for her angular body. Her gaze raked Olivia from behind black-framed glasses. Instead of introducing herself, she asked: "Why this place?"

"It's where I'm most comfortable. I'd live here if I could."

"I wonder how the owner feels about that," the woman murmured.

Olivia craned her neck to check her office door before answering. *Huh. Closed.* "She'd hate it. Pretty sure she hates me."

"Is that right?"

"I think so." Olivia smiled. "Hi, I'm Olivia Roberts."

"And I'm interested in the job." The woman's expression was inscrutable.

Suddenly, Olivia had the oddest sensation of familiarity. How did she know this woman's voice?

"My expertise is in crime, so I feel I'd be suited to carrying out your *dastardly deeds*," the woman continued, her tone the faintest bit mocking. "I have a double degree in criminology and information technology at Monash University, a masters by research from the Royal Melbourne Institute of Technology, a PhD from RMIT, and was the director of Scholarly Services at the RMIT's university library for some years, where I ran an internationally-renowned special Australian historical collection. It focused on bushrangers, especially Aboriginal bushrangers, who are greatly overlooked by history."

Olivia blinked as her brain lurched into overdrive, her subconscious screaming for attention, even as she registered in wonder that there'd surely never been a better suited candidate for a job. Not to mention she was so damned clever, as per Davo's advice. "That's impressive."

"It is." She crossed her legs at the ankles as she agreed with utmost confidence. Her beautiful pantsuit rode up a little, revealing polished black boots.

Oh, Olivia *so* knew that smug voice. She did, but where…how…

"Aboriginal bushrangers," Olivia repeated dumbly as her subconscious finally kicked through the wall and supplied her the blindingly obvious answer. "Like…Mary Bugg?"

"Exactly like Mary Bugg." Her mocking smile was pure victory. "We haven't formally met. I'm Dr Margaret Blackwood."

CHAPTER 7

DR BLACKWOOD, I PRESUME?

OLIVIA'S MOUTH FELL OPEN. "Y-you..." The book woman she'd been drooling over was also the smug manager from Mary Bugg's who'd been taunting her at book club? "Is this some game to you? Because it's not to me." She stopped as a new realisation hit. "You knew who I was, didn't you, that day I offered you my muffin?"

"Don't forget *and* saw someone steal your penguin." She sounded vastly amused now. "Yes, of course I knew who you were. I know all my suppliers, and your van isn't remotely subtle. Not to mention, I've observed the masterclass in chaos that is your Women in Crime group. Honestly, it's like watching someone juggling rattlesnakes seeing you run that absurd little book club. You've reinvented farce."

Olivia glared. "You're so rude!"

"I'm accurate. Do you deny it?"

Well, she couldn't *exactly*. But so what if her group tended to enjoy their absurd tangents? "So, now here you are pretending to be interested in my henchperson job just to mock me some more? Is that what this is?"

"Oh no, I'm genuinely interested in the position."

She was? "Why?"

"I have such little amusement in my life." Dr Blackwood gave an innocent look. "This will be an acceptable distraction."

"So you're just applying for kicks."

"Yes. But I *do* promise to give it my all." Her lips quirked up at the corners.

"Then no thanks. I'm after serious contenders only." Olivia folded her arms.

"Why does it matter why I'm offering my services, so long as I am? Especially given the choices: the Cro-Magnon security guard with no discernible skills beyond giving your muffins salacious names."

She'd heard Damien name Parma Sutra? Olivia winced internally.

"The naive young woman who thinks romances are real-life," Dr Blackwood barrelled on, defaming Tess next.

"The former danseur who assumes his good looks will get him anything or anyone. The primary school student or the inattentive vegan—the less said about either, the better. And by the way, fungi are never fun. Your sister, who'll sabotage your henchperson job to keep you out of trouble. Or the misogynistic, barely literate professional felon who couldn't even read to the bottom of the ad to ascertain that your job pays in muffins."

Dr Blackwood gave a dramatic pause and continued: "Or there's me: one of Australia's leading experts on the criminal mind, author of multiple peer-reviewed papers on historical convicts and criminal figures, and an internationally respected authority on Australia's various outlaws and bushrangers."

"You left off *modest*."

"You wish me to feign a mediocrity I don't possess?" Dr Blackwood's eyebrow lifted. "No."

"If you were all these wonderful things in academia, why are you running a bookstore?" Olivia asked reasonably.

A shadow passed across her eyes, and Dr Blackwood's mouth tightened. "Irrelevant."

"Were you fired?" Olivia couldn't resist asking. Fair was fair, given the goading Dr Blackwood had inflicted on her.

"Absolutely not." Dr Blackwood's voice contained enough chill to frost over the glass coffee table in front of them.

"You expect me to believe you're just…needing a distraction?" Olivia eyed her. "So much so, you'd team up with someone you hate?"

Dr Blackwood snorted. "If you think our butting heads briefly on matters of fictional crime literature constitutes *hate* on my part, you've clearly never worked at a university. Academics can peel the skin off a rival in two bloodless sentences, then offer the poor corpse a coffee."

If that's how the woman treated her former colleagues, Olivia would hate to see what she'd done to her enemies. Wait, did that mean her mocking book-club interactions with Olivia counted as friendly banter in Margaret Blackwood's twisted world?

"So you really *are* just…bored?"

"As I keep saying." She certainly looked bored right now.

Olivia eyed her suspiciously.

"Or maybe I just really enjoy your muffins," Dr Blackwood drawled. Her expression gave nothing away.

Great. Now Olivia didn't know whether to believe her or not. "Then how come you ignored the one I offered you in the park?"

"Except you didn't offer it to me. You clutched it to your chest while you gaped at me and stuttered for a bit. Then you flung it down and puffed off after your stolen penguin." She cocked her head. "Did you get the bird back, by the way?"

At the reminder, Olivia's heart clenched in agony. "Yes and no," she squeezed out. "Well, it's no now. Trip's gone."

"I see." The other woman's expression lost any hint of mirth.

That was odd. Olivia would have laid bets on Dr Blackwood milking that humiliating scene for all it was worth.

"All right, then," Dr Blackwood continued, "we'll just have to include penguin retrieval in my services."

Olivia bit her lip as she mulled over the possibility. Could she really work with this annoying, conceited, condescending woman? A woman with a skill set that was, unfortunately, also far beyond Olivia's wildest dreams?

"You need me." Dr Blackwood seemed to read her mind. She flicked lint off her sleeve.

Olivia did need her. Not just because she was someone clever and cunning for dastardly scheming purposes but also because, truthfully, if she didn't have a partner in this operation, she was afraid she'd lose her nerve and give up. "I…suppose."

"There, now. That wasn't so hard. So, who are the exes we'll be attending to?"

Olivia stared, astonished by how easily she'd taken control of the conversation and had just given herself the job. "I didn't say I'd hire you," she protested.

"You will."

The cockiness rankled. "Will you just tell me why you're applying, *really*? I can't believe the foremost expert in all those criminal mastermind-y things you listed is interested in hanging around with me out of boredom."

"Fine." Dr Blackwood leaned back in her chair. "Perhaps I have a vested interest in ensuring free muffins for my cafe."

And now it all became clear. What a sneaky move! It would be impressive if Olivia wasn't so outraged. "Hey, that's cheating! My muffins offer was only ever supposed to be for an individual, not an entire cafe. You're taking advantage!" Anger rose in Olivia. Wasn't this how she'd gotten into this mess in the first place? People just took and took, with no consideration for her feelings?

"Then perhaps you should have said that in your ad. It's the minor details like these that I can help you with. Another reason to hire me."

"I'd go bankrupt if I supplied all your bookstore's muffins for free."

Dr Blackwood looked unconcerned and waved a hand. "I'm well aware. Despite you neglecting to include that in your terms, you can just pay me what you would have paid any other individual."

"Really?"

"I just said so, didn't I?" Dr Blackwood gave an impatient huff. "Now, do we have a deal?"

Olivia sighed. She supposed she could do far worse. "Fine," she said. "You're hired. But no more mocking book club meetings."

"I make no promises. Now, tell me: how many of your exes are we planning to make rue their existence?"

"Four. Two men, two women." She held her breath, wondering if Dr Blackwood would have any issues with Olivia having dated both sexes.

Dr Blackwood took her in and didn't speak for a moment. "I...see."

"What do you see?" Olivia asked, an edge in her tone.

"I didn't realise you were bisexual."

"Do you have a problem with bisexuals?" she asked with even more edge. This deal would be over in two seconds if she did. Some of Olivia's favourite people were bi.

"Not at all." Dr Blackwood looked faintly startled by the notion. "I just assumed you were a lesbian."

Olivia choked. It had taken her years to reach the same conclusion. Dr Blackwood had just figured it out on sight!

"I am a lesbian, but I only worked it out after the boyfriends," Olivia muttered, eyes tightening. "Can we *please* move on?"

"I'm not the one dragging this out. Did you have a mission to plan or not?" Dr Blackwood paused. "Or four of them? Plus the penguin, of course."

"The penguin is tied to one of my exes, actually."

"Wait! That skinny blonde thief was your ex?" Dr Blackwood looked askance. "The one racing off with your penguin who looked like a strung-out Paris Hilton? The woman, not the bird, to be clear."

"Yes." Olivia gritted her teeth.

"What endeavours have you made so far to retrieve your penguin?"

"I went to the police, but aside from filing a report, they weren't interested because it's a 'low priority' crime. Tina's ducking me. She doesn't have a job and spends almost all her time in her apartment. But I can't just bang on her door because there's a lot of security on her building. I can't get to her floor. Her parents bought her this luxury penthouse."

"And yet she resorts to theft?"

"Well, they cut off her allowance since then."

Dr Blackwood mulled that over. "All right, we'll stick a pin in that case for now. What of your other exes?"

With a scowl, Olivia recalled her first boyfriend. "There was Timothy. We dated throughout high school. He was this man-child, car-loving rev-head. He and his brother both treated me like an annoying third wheel. We broke up when I was eighteen."

Dr Blackwood peered at her. "Teenage love? I'm sure most young people make mistakes, so whatever he did…"

"You have no idea what he did!" Olivia's cheeks bloomed with shame at the reminder. "It was awful. And trust me, he's very worth making my list."

Dr Blackwood waited.

Swallowing hard, Olivia said, voice hoarse, "You know, I think we'll skip him for now." It was too soon to tell this story to a complete stranger. "We'll come back to him another day."

Dr Blackwood's gaze was filled with questions. To Olivia's relief, instead of asking them, she said quietly, "Understood. Who's next?"

"Martin. He was this older marketing guy. He adored the fact I was only eighteen. He wanted to be my svengali." She shuddered. "Martin loved to be a pseudo intellectual and show how smart he was. He really hated when I had an opinion of my own."

"Did he do something particularly awful?"

"Yeah." Olivia nibbled on her lower lip. "He abandoned me in a seedy, dark street after we had a fight. No phone, no money. Just me and a bunch of drug dealers, prostitutes, and cruising customers."

Idly, she wondered if Dr Blackwood would ask what the fight had been about because everyone else had, as though it were her fault. Olivia stared down at her fingers, which she was anxiously knotting and unknotting.

"What a pitiful human." Dr Blackwood's words were low and cold.

Olivia snapped her head back up. Warmth filled her chest. "Thank you for not asking why he did it. What *his* side was."

Dr Blackwood's nostrils flared. "For heaven's sake," she said, sounding almost irritated. "There's no excuse conceivable for abandoning and terrifying a young woman like that. None. His reasons are irrelevant."

"Thanks," Olivia mumbled. "Really. Thanks."

Waving her hand as if to swat away a fly, Dr Blackwood said: "So, who came next, after your thin-skinned narcissistic svengali?"

Olivia couldn't hold back a giggle at that. Martin would *hate* being described in that way. "Ah, okay. So, as bad as Martin was, there's no outdoing Annalise. I wound up giving up my university dreams to fund her law degree."

Dr Blackwood blinked in surprise. "You weren't always a baker?"

"No. I'd always enjoyed cooking, sure, but I had other plans. I was doing a bachelor of arts, majoring in literary studies at Monash when I met Annalise. I thought I might become an academic one day—to spread my love of literature to others."

Respect edged into Dr Blackwood's eyes.

Olivia had seen that look before on others, many times. People who'd dismissed her as *just a baker* before learning about her other career path. She glared. "Ah, so I'm worthwhile now because I wanted to pursue academia the way you did?"

"No one could have pursued academia the way I did," Dr Blackwood murmured. She didn't sound smug for once, just resigned. "Continue. How did you go from an earnest literary major to Prahran's award-winning muffin purveyor?"

"Wait, how do you know I'm award winning?" Surprise shot through Olivia.

"You think I'd sell just anything in my store?" Dr Blackwood asked with a tut. "I researched you when your sister first approached me about stocking Love Muffins goods. Why did your academic ambitions fall by the wayside?"

"I fell in love." Olivia winced. "I thought Annalise loved me back. She was so charming and sincere. She convinced me to help her out with a few small debts here and there—just while she was getting through law school, she said. Once she became a lawyer, she'd pay it all back and I could return to uni."

"Return? You'd dropped out?"

"She needed more and more money until it was more than I had. She talked me into pausing my degree while I took up a baking job to pay for my debts—well, her debts. That job turned into an apprenticeship when it became obvious to Joe, the boss who owned that bakery, that I had a knack for baking. But before I could finish my apprenticeship, I caught Annalise in bed with Joe." She sagged. "I lost everything. And Annalise moved straight on to him like I hadn't even been there. She found her way to the next cashed-up, fully funded life."

"That's terrible." Dr Blackwood's eyes narrowed.

"And that's not the worst of it. Last week, she texted to ask me to bake their wedding cake for them. Hers and Joe's. For free! For old time's sake, she said. As if she hadn't ruined my life by running off with him. And even though she still owes me tens of thousands!" Indignation filled her.

"That's... *Dear God.*" Dr Blackwood hissed in a tight breath. "No wonder you were pushed over the edge to this vengeance plan."

"Oh, no, that's not why."

"No?" Dr Blackwood looked truly shocked now.

"It was Tina. When she stole my penguin."

Dr Blackwood peered at her. "The penguin theft did it? Not the free wedding cake request? Or the tens of thousands of dollars of debt? Or being abandoned in a crime street?"

"Yes!" Olivia growled.

The other woman's expression clouded in puzzlement. "So, what on earth is that thief planning to do with some tatty old penguin?"

"Hey! Trip is *not* tatty. Okay, he's a little worn around the edges. Who isn't?"

Dr Blackwood's eyes crinkled. "I meant no offence," she drawled. "I didn't get a good look at your…bird. But I'll have you know *I* am most certainly not worn around the edges." A half smile tugged at the edge of her lips. "Still, I promise not to impugn the honour of your penguin in future."

"Good," Olivia said crossly. "And I know no one else understands, but Trip's special. I love him. He's a family heirloom—he was my grandmother's on all her trips, and she willed him to me as a good-luck charm." She swallowed back a choke. "And I was supposed to continue the tradition and take him on adventures too. She'd be so upset I've lost him. Tina knew how much I loved him, and she still…lured me into bed and stole him."

"But I saw her take him on the street," Dr Blackwood said in confusion.

"I got him back that time. Um…" She gritted her teeth before making the admission. "Tina talked me into giving us another chance."

"After she'd stolen your penguin just prior?" The scepticism was clear in Dr Blackwood's voice.

"Yes." Olivia's voice was small. "And so now you can see she screwed me over twice." Fury rippled through her. "Just like everyone else I've seriously dated. That was the last straw!"

Dr Blackwood gave a slow nod. "Semi-related note, did you know the literal Chinese-to-English translation of penguin is business goose?"

Olivia blinked. "It is?"

"Indeed." She cocked an eyebrow. "And a kangaroo is a pouched rat. And jeans translate to cowboy pants."

Olivia peered at her, then chuckled in spite of herself. Her tension eased.

At Dr Blackwood's pleased twitch of her lips in response, Olivia wondered if that had been the intention.

"How do you know all that?" Olivia asked.

"I thought we'd established I'm well-read?" Dr Blackwood's lips threatened a proper smile. "Never forget that."

"As if you'd let me," Olivia grumbled.

Dr Blackwood ignored that. "Let's get down to business. Who's first? Svengali Martin or Entitled Annalise?"

"Martin." Olivia had already thought about this. They needed something simple to ease their way into vengeancing. Martin wasn't clever; he just thought he was. He'd also be the easiest to get access to. Besides, Annalise was far too tricky, Tina was out of reach for now, and Timothy just didn't bear thinking about.

Dr Blackwood nodded. "All right. Tell me everything you know about Martin. Then we'll work out how to crush him."

And damn if she didn't actually look enthusiastic for once.

CHAPTER 8

SVENGALI MARTIN

Dr Blackwood clicked her pen and picked up a notepad. "Let's get the basics. Who Martin is, where he works, and how long were you dating him for."

Olivia paused then and had the rather startling realisation that she'd have to tell a complete stranger some pretty embarrassing personal information. Not just any complete stranger. Her client, furtive book-club eavesdropper, and occasional heckler. Was this even a safe space to share any of this? Although, did that even matter? This was important background intel her henchperson needed.

But as Olivia looked at Dr Blackwood's steady gaze, she saw it contained no sharpness, no judgement. She simply waited patiently to be briefed.

Here goes nothing.

"Martin's now a marketing *guru*, or that's what he tells everyone," Olivia began slowly. "He loves showing off: how clever he is, how successful, how lucky I was to have him. He picked up on the fact I was feeling low after Timothy, and he was so charming at first, so smooth. He's always been great at schmoozing people. And he loved that I was young enough to be moulded." She paused. "His actual words."

Dr Blackwood scowled. "He sounds lovely. Let's talk about the night he abandoned you. What happened?"

"We were driving to a restaurant for dinner. He was going on and on about this autobiography he'd just bought about the founder of Sony, Akio Morita. Martin was so full of himself, and I was just too tired that night to puff up his ego. I said nothing. He demanded to know, in not so many words, why I wasn't impressed by his highbrow book selection. So I said, truthfully, that I'd read the book months ago."

"Oh dear," Dr Blackwood said with dry amusement. "What did he say?"

"Nothing at first. He went very, very quiet. Then he pulled over and politely asked me to get out. I was confused but did so, figuring we'd arrived, and looked around for the restaurant. But then he just roared off into the night before I could even get my bag from the back seat. Then I noticed how dangerous the area was. The further I walked, the scarier it got." She shuddered. "We broke up not long after that."

Dr Blackwood's lips pressed into a thin line. "How long were you there? And where was 'there' exactly?"

"Greeves Street."

"As in Melbourne's red-light district?" Dr Blackwood's gaze bored into her.

"Yes. After dark, it's wall-to-wall dealers and the meanest streetwalkers, not to mention men driving by really slowly looking for drugs and sex. The prostitutes kept swearing at me as if I were the new competition. I pleaded with them to let me use their phone, and then their pimp turned up and told me to fuck off, with threats of smashing in my face." She shivered. "It was the longest twenty minutes of my life. Martin decided to come back for me then, after I'd learned my lesson not to prick his ego or outdo him. I learned a different lesson, though: for all his charm, Martin was a bastard."

Silence greeted the end of Olivia's story. Perhaps Dr Blackwood thought being left on the road in a bad neighbourhood for only twenty minutes was a silly thing to get worked up about. Maybe it *was* silly if you were as imposing as Margaret Blackwood. But Olivia had had nightmares for months. She'd wake up chilled, remembering how it felt, trembling in that thin dress. The wild-eyed pimp screaming obscenities at her. Men calling out disgusting things as they cruised past—one just idling his car and ogling her with a creepy expression.

"Your boyfriend left you in Greeves Street for…twenty minutes." Dr Blackwood repeated quietly. "You were there the whole time?"

"Yes." Suddenly Olivia wondered if Dr Blackwood thought she should have moved to a safer location and had been foolish not to. "I thought Martin would come back looking for me when he'd calmed down and that if

I wasn't there, he wouldn't be able to find me. I was afraid it'd be worse if I wandered off and got lost. So I-I hid behind an industrial bin for a little bit, making myself as small as possible. My clothing reeked of spoiled food and other gross things." She bit her lip at the reminder. She'd ended up burning her favourite dress. "Martin even demanded I pay for car cleaning after the smell from my clothes got into the upholstery." She twisted her fingers again. "And I did. I paid."

Dr Blackwood's jaw worked.

"I know it all sounds lame." Olivia looked down, ashamed. "The worst part is any time I'm in a sketchy area, it makes me so anxious. He lives in my head rent-free. I hate he did that to me."

Now Dr Blackwood's lips pursed. Was she going to say something scathing? Make Olivia feel small and stupid? She wasn't sure how she'd keep it together if she did. After all, hadn't Dr Blackwood said academics enjoyed verbally eviscerating people? She braced herself for the worst.

"How shall we destroy him?" Dr Blackwood asked in a soft, dangerous voice. The cold look in her eyes did not bode well for Martin's future wellbeing.

Olivia's head snapped up. "You don't think I was an idiot?"

"Oh, you are definitely an idiot. Some of your views on what makes for a good book are laughable. Inflicting that *Hansom Cab* nonsense on others was a crime against humanity. However, fearing for your safety when ditched in Melbourne's worst street isn't foolish. It's wise. Had I been there, however, I would have billed him for the cost of my clothing and shoved his car-cleaning receipt up his left nostril."

The visual picture made Olivia burst into laughter.

Dr Blackwood let a smile slip out, just for half a second.

"I wish you'd been there," she murmured.

"I'm sure that's a first," Dr Blackwood said, amusement leaking into her tone. "But thank you." She straightened. "Well, we can sort this out. Let's review: Martin saw himself as the leader, the guru of your relationship. He was the literate, intellectual patriarch, and you, his student. Your having read the book he'd selected to boast about ruined the image he had of himself in his head. How can he share his vast wisdom if you know more than he does on a topic? How frustrating. How…embarrassing. He decided to punish you for that."

Olivia nodded. "Ego's really important to him."

"How long did you date him?"

"Two years. From age eighteen."

"A long time to endure his idea of affection."

"Unfortunately. But he was so confident and charming, and I was too young to realise what he did wasn't normal. So many girls wanted to date him. I couldn't believe he chose me—the shyest, quietest girl you could find."

"That's no accident, as I'm sure you now know."

Olivia gave a snort. "It's embarrassing now that I look back. What I wouldn't do to be able to rewind history."

Dr Blackwood shook her head. "History makes us who we are. It's important no matter how desirable it is to erase bad memories. Trust me, I lived with a historian once."

She *had*? Olivia blinked. Oh, she had so many questions. Why was the historian in the past tense? How long was "once"? Who was it? Some smooth, media-savvy university lecturer always in the newspaper? A nerdy academic who hid away in their department and published one impenetrable paper after another every other year?

"But we can fix history a different way," Dr Blackwood declared. "Did you have any vengeance plan in mind for him already?"

"I was hoping to brainstorm with my henchperson for that step." She looked pointedly at said henchperson.

"Such an excellent addition to my CV, that title," Dr Blackwood said and leaned back in satisfaction.

"It'll slot nicely in after Director of Scholarly Services at RMIT," Olivia countered with a grin.

"Given how cutthroat the politics were there, yes, I believe you're right." Her eyes lit up. "I should send my new credentials to my former colleagues. Also, I believe my mother would be so proud. She's vice chancellor at Monash University, after all."

This time, Olivia choked. *Vice chancellor!* "She's...she's Professor Neubold?"

"She is." Dr Blackwood nodded. "Did I mention *so* proud?"

"It'd be no trouble to send her a formal, congratulatory email about having hired you as my henchperson," Olivia suggested with a laugh.

"Oh, *would* you?" Dr Blackwood's smirk turned positively gleeful. She appeared to consider it. "I'll get back to you on that."

They stared at each other for a moment.

Whoa. Had they shared an actual joke about a personal matter? It was kind of shocking how much fun that had felt.

Then Dr Blackwood seemed to remember whom she was talking to. Or maybe it was that she didn't particularly like Olivia. It was hard to say, but she looked to be in acute discomfort as redness rose up her cheeks and she turned away, clearing her throat. "Never mind," she muttered. "I was not being serious. Obviously. So…Martin. Thoughts?" she asked crisply.

And just like that, Dr Blackwood's thousand-foot walls had shot back up. Olivia instantly missed that other side to her. She wondered what it would take to entice it out of her again. But not right now, not when Dr Blackwood looked so disconcerted.

"Off the top of my head," Olivia said flippantly, "what about I mess with Martin's car so he gets abandoned somewhere bad? I'd love him to get a taste of what I went through. And he needs to be without his phone or money."

"And by mess with his car, you mean…?"

"I don't know? Cut the brakes or something?" Olivia threw her hands up. "I haven't really thought about it at length."

"What could possibly go wrong? A manslaughter charge will be fun when the brakes die at a pivotal moment."

"Well, okay, no brake cutting." Olivia huffed out a breath, trying to think of something else. "Okay, we snatch him off the street, blindfold him, drive him somewhere creepy, and leave him there. Wait an hour and call for help for him."

Dr Blackwood's look was blistering. "Seriously?"

"What?" Olivia's voice rose to defensive.

"Kidnapping charges instead of manslaughter? And you realise he'd recognise that eyesore of a bakery van the moment you pull up, even if you blindfold him later."

"So we use your car."

"Absolutely not. My Jaguar is not to be directly used in criminal enterprises."

"Hire a car?"

"Well, that wouldn't be traced back to you in two minutes. How do you call yourself a dedicated mystery and crime reader when this is the best you come up with?"

"I know! We steal a car!" Olivia brightened.

"You're ridiculous." At least her expression looked amused this time, as opposed to cutting.

"Well, if you're so smart, what's your best idea?" Olivia demanded.

"Get him to drive *himself* to where you want him to be. Obviously."

"Get him to…" Olivia stared at her. "What, we just call him up and tell him to go to some deserted place if he pretty please wouldn't mind?"

"No, we use his ego against him." She paused and thought for a moment. "We call and explain how he's been selected for a top 100 list of Melbourne's Rising Stars of Marketing."

"Oooh." Olivia was actually pretty impressed.

"Inform him the photo shoot will be at some grungy industrial estate of our choosing miles out of town. It will add atmosphere for the photo shoot, we'll say. Explain that the photographer will meet him there. And a reporter will interview him later after the photos."

"And then we destroy his car and abandon him there?" Olivia asked hopefully.

"You really are *so* violent." Dr Blackwood rolled her eyes. "Destroy the car and it's an insurance and police matter."

"Not really. It's my car. I bought it."

"It's…your car?" Dr Blackwood asked in surprise.

"Yes. I bought it as an old clunker, but he loves it because it's a good collectible brand and he thinks retro's cool. I never asked for it back. When we had our last fight, I just walked away."

"Well," Dr Blackwood's eyes seemed to light with possibilities. "I don't suppose you have a spare key to your former car?"

Olivia puckered her brow as she thought. "Yes."

"That makes things much easier. We tell him to leave his phone in the car as a security measure—because we don't want leaked pics all over social media ruining the impact of the photo shoot. And then we tell him to meet our photographer at some distant spot inaccessible by vehicle. While he's walking there to locate our fictitious photographer, you sneak to his car, let the air out of his tyres. Then, get inside the car, find his phone, take the SIM card out of it so he can't call for help."

"Why take his SIM card not his phone?"

"The cost of a SIM card is only a few dollars. It's a minor matter if you're caught. Phones can run to a thousand dollars and thus invoke heavier penalties."

"Oh." That made sense. "Then what? We leave him there?"

"You'll call the RACV breakdown assistance number for him after an hour."

"That's sneaky." Olivia nodded. "I like it. So, you'll play the journalist on the phone?"

"Don't be ridiculous. Do you think I sound like a member of the gutter press?"

"No, but maybe someone serious from the arts page of *The Age.*"

"Who would have zero interest in marketing hot shots and top 100 lists. I'm fairly sure you know someone involved in drama who'd be better suited."

"Who, Sasha?" Olivia blinked. "Wouldn't his accent be a little memorable? Besides, I'm a bit worried he'd go off script and start improvising. You know what he's like."

"Regrettably." Dr Blackwood rubbed her temple. "And I didn't mean that lascivious Lothario. What about Tess from your little book club? Isn't she a drama student?"

"Huh. Actually, yeah. I'm sure she'd love the real-world experience."

"Mmm."

"You really do listen to everything that happens in book club, don't you?" Olivia shot her an amused look.

"It's either that or do my paperwork."

"Sasha will be so disappointed he's missed his big chance to impress you with his acting." Olivia grinned.

"He'll live. Besides, I'm sure he's used to rejection. I tell him *no* often enough." The glint was back in her eye, the one Olivia couldn't decipher but that seemed to spell danger to someone.

"Not interested in stud-muffin Sasha?" Olivia asked, suddenly feeling bold.

"Not interested in an off-topic subject." Dr Blackwood's tone was chilly now.

Olivia realised the dangerous glint had been a warning directed at her. "Fine," she said.

"Now, then, shall we run through possible deserted locations on Google Maps?"

"Um, sure. You mean...now?" Olivia asked.

"Why not now?"

Olivia stopped. This was suddenly feeling a whole lot real. Wasn't this what she wanted?

Visions of Trip being stolen by her unrepentant ex flooded her mind, and she straightened. "Yes. Now."

Sunset: *7.47pm*

Temp: *10.3C-22.3C*

Rain: *0mm*

Noise: *Neighbour 1B remains away. I fed his cat today. I'm not sure who was supposed to be doing this task. I trust the absurdly fluffy black animal returns to its cat-sitter soon.*

Drink: *Yarra Yering Dry Red, two glasses. Don't hate it.*

Reading: Non-fiction—*JALIA, Vol 69, issue 1. "Coding with XML for Efficiencies in Cataloguing and Metadata". In my day, everything was efficient in my department because I made it so. Reports to improve efficiency were not required.*

Fiction—*Crimson Lake (Candice Fox). Deranged woman + crocodiles. The latter were the superior characters. Doubtlessly, Olivia will love it. She'll say things like "It was so absorbing" and "couldn't you feel the man's pain?" Oh, I felt pain all right.*

Unfortunately, due to the book club's excitement about a certain advertisement, no one discussed the book, and so my incisive interjections remain unspent. It would be frustrating, except...

General Observations: *I am a henchperson. Yes, I did just write that.*

No, I didn't expect to be so anointed when I got up this morning. It just...happened. I'm still not entirely sure what possessed me. One minute I was listening to a series of inferior applicants, appalled that they thought they could offer anything useful to Olivia's endeavours. I could see them getting her arrested or killed, so useless were their skills. So, call me magnanimous, but when I could take it no longer, I offered my services to ensure Olivia's continued freedom and my regular supply of highly sought-after muffins. Not that she thanked me. A stunned mullet comes to mind.

Further, she confirmed my long-standing view that she's a lesbian. All that unironic flannel-wear did not render her pronouncement much of a shock. It was funny how surprised she was by my educated guess. But nothing surpassed her expression of astonishment when she put the pieces together at last: Why, yes, I am the woman who reads books in the park and spots penguin thefts. Thank you for noticing.

She also declared me mean and eccentric. I'll file that away under life goals.

I digress. I am a henchperson!

I trust it will be diverting.

Unrelated note: What possessed me to tell Olivia who my mother is? I've not had an egregious lapse into revealing personal information since...well, not in decades. Still, Olivia's offer of alerting Monash University's esteemed vice chancellor as to my henchperson status is so tempting. I'll see how my maternal unit acquits herself over family dinner this Easter. If she reminds me of all the many, many ways I've disappointed her and disgraced the family by leaving academia to run a common crime bookstore, I might just nudge Olivia into action.

I admit it felt nice for her to offer, even in jest. It was... unexpected...feeling like I have a friend in my corner against my mother.

Well, maybe not a friend. Obviously, Olivia doesn't class me as such, or even particularly like me. I don't blame her. I'm...challenging, or so I'm told by one and all. Either way, I appreciated her gesture more than I'd ever admit.

Postscript: I've allowed the Garrity girl to spend time in my bookstore after school each day, given that her family sleeps in a car and has few opportunities. Emma seems a bright child. Education should be nurtured not endured.

I trust H is laughing at my uncommon lapse into generosity. Although H is likely still in guffawing fits over "mean and eccentric".

CHAPTER 9

BREADY TO RUMBLE

Courtesy of their extensive mapping research, Margaret and Olivia had found the perfect spot: an abandoned, unfinished industrial estate in outer Melbourne that had fallen prey to graffiti artists and vandals when developers had gone out of business. It had twice been written up in newspapers as the worst area in Melbourne. Olivia, who still had Greeves Street burned into her brain, begged to differ.

Tess seemed genuinely delighted by the assignment to play the part of a reporter in a call to convince Martin to take part in the fictitious photo shoot.

"He's so keen," she reported back excitedly on the phone when she'd finished. "He didn't question how weird the location was or how he had to leave his phone in the car. Or any of it. He was all, 'Is this because I was nominated for an Effie award?'" She paused. "I have no clue what that is, but I said, 'Why, yes, yes, it is.'"

"Great." Olivia beamed. "That's great."

"Thanks." Tess sounded earnest now. "I'm trying to get better at improv. It's harder to get into character when you don't have a text to go off, but I just tried to channel my best inner 'puff-piece *Herald Sun* reporter' voice."

"Well, I'm impressed."

"Oh, I'm so glad." Tess's smile was evident even down the phone. "What about your partner in crime, Dr Blackwood?"

Wait, how did Tess know whom Olivia had selected as her henchperson? The book club gossip network, most likely. Or Kelly.

Olivia slid a glance to Dr Blackwood, who'd been listening in on the call with an expression fixed somewhere between "mentally making a shopping list" and outright bored.

"Oh yes, she looks very impressed."

Tess gave a happy squeak. "That's excellent. I'm two for two! I think if you win over even your toughest critic, you've won the whole audience. And I know from book club that she's such a fierce critic…"

Dr Blackwood's eyebrow slid up at that.

"…so, I'll take her approval as a standing ovation!" Tess said her good-byes and hung up.

"You think this is my impressed look?" Dr Blackwood asked. "You'll only encourage her to think I have one."

"She did this for free," Olivia fired back lightly. "Stop your bitching."

Margaret Blackwood finally, fully, smiled.

Olivia jumped from her van and jogged to the idling Jaguar behind Mary Bugg's.

"What on earth are you dressed as? Beat-poet ninja?" Dr Blackwood called from her car's window.

At least the woman was punctual and ready, although Olivia had expected nothing less on mission day from Margaret Blackwood. But did she have to be quite so acerbic?

Olivia glanced down at herself. Black turtleneck, black jeans, black Doc Martens. She didn't own a beanie, so she'd borrowed Kelly's black beret to hide her distinctive chestnut hair. "What? I'm trying to become a *shadow*. So I don't attract attention."

"It's the middle of the day. There are no shadows. You look like a French cat burglar about to eat a baguette and recite *On the Road*."

Olivia put her hands on her hips. "Okay, first, Jack Kerouac is overrated. His writing's just a series of well-described scenery. He's the reason we have to endure pretentious words like *zeitgeist*. Secondly, how the hell am I supposed to know what to wear for a mission? It's my first one!"

Dr Blackwood bristled. "Excuse me? Kerouac's writing conveys complex images and ideas with such originality that he deserves to be lauded. He wrote a *genuine* classic. Further, *zeitgeist* is a perfectly excellent word to bludgeon one's academic rivals with. Now, as for mission garb..." She eyeballed Olivia's outfit. "Are you cosplaying *To Catch a Thief*? Did you seriously just copy your look from the movies?"

Glaring, Olivia pointed out the obvious. "Where else am I going to copy it from? My team of expert criminal advisors? And, by the way, as my official henchperson, I'd have thought that advising on correct mission attire would fall under *your* duties."

"Oh *really*." Dr Blackwood's gaze raked her again. "I missed the part in your advertisement that said *must think for me too*." She paused and peered at Olivia's button pin, her shapely brows meeting. "*Bready to rumble*? Oh my. So...punny. I'd have made it *Bready to Crumble*, though, to maximise the sheer awfulness of it."

That did sound better...not that she'd ever give annoying bloody Margaret Blackwood a win. "For God's sake, can we just get a move on? Martin'll be arriving at the site soon, and we can't miss him because we're too busy bickering."

"Fine." Dr Blackwood sniffed. "So, Beatnik Ninja, are you ready?" The question was delivered without bite for once and sounded like a genuine query.

Am I ready? No. But Olivia was committed now. "Yes."

"And you know the plan?"

"Once we arrive at the co-ordinates and you drop me around a corner, I surveil and wait for Martin to exit his car—well, *my* car—and head to the building he's been given directions to. I nick his SIM card, let down the tyres, and run back to you."

"Yes."

"Are *you* good?" Olivia asked. "I mean henchpersonning is a big responsibility."

"Is it?" Dr Blackwood's eyebrow lifted. "Somehow I *can* cope with dropping you off and picking you up without cracking under the stress."

Ignoring that dig, Olivia opened the passenger's door to Dr Blackwood's Jaguar and slid in. "Well, good." Luxury assailed her senses from the wooden trim and leather-stitched steering wheel. "Oh my God. This car is amazing."

"Of course it is. Now, then: time to take you for a ride." Her smile was not in the least bit safe.

Olivia cracked the car door a foot the moment they reached their destination. It was an abandoned access road that vehicles had likely used when the site was being constructed. Rusty scaffolding was still visible in a few places, but mostly they were surrounded by a cluster of one- and two-storey concrete buildings covered in graffiti.

No one was around. Nonetheless, Olivia tumbled to the ground, rolling to one knee, keeping her centre of gravity low.

"What on earth are you doing!" Dr Blackwood called to her. "Role-playing Captain Kirk planetside?"

"You watch *Star Trek?*" Olivia's head shot up so fast in surprise, she wrenched her neck. "Ow." She rubbed it. This never happened to Kirk, she was quite sure.

"Just get into position." Dr Blackwood pointed at a wall they'd decided from their mapping research would make a good hiding spot to peer around. "I'll be out of sight, not far. Text me if you need assistance."

"Roger wilco that," Olivia said promptly, tightening her backpack around her shoulders and stomach.

Dr Blackwood shot her an incredulous look, then accelerated smoothly away.

Olivia properly looked around for the first time. Yep, *creepy* was the word. She could smell waste. It was likely from stray animals. Or dead ones. Some of the partially built industrial buildings were being reclaimed by nature and were now overgrown with weeds.

In the distance, a car pulled up, startling Olivia, who'd been daydreaming. She pressed herself against the building and clocked it. Yep. That was her old Holden Torana, all right. Still orange.

Martin, unmistakeable in his slick suit and slicker combed-back hair, slammed the Torana's door and glanced at a paper in his hands. He was a little portlier than Olivia remembered, his cheeks ruddier and fuller—probably too much booze from all those long client lunches had taken their toll. But he was still good-looking and—given the way he stood, chest out, chin up, in his Master of the Universe pose—he seemed to know it.

Martin looked around, then strode off in the direction of one of the buildings.

Go time.

After Martin disappeared behind a wall, Olivia crept up to the car and tried the door handle. It didn't budge. She fumbled for her key. The door snicked open. Thank God he'd never changed the locks. He probably thought she was too much of a sap to try and reclaim it. In truth, she'd been so glad to be rid of Martin that she'd never dwelled on the fact he still had her old car.

She glanced wildly around, half expecting Martin to come striding back and catch her, but he was out of sight. She could hear him in the distance, though, calling plaintively for the fictitious photographer. "Hello? Anyone here?"

Right, tyres first.

She let down the first with her keys, muttering *come on, come on*, as it slowly hissed down. It was taking too long. Her heart was thudding in her chest. Were tyres normally so slow to deflate? They should have tested this first! Why didn't they? Or ask someone?!

Finally, it was pancake flat. Olivia fretted for a moment over her choices. Maybe she should get the SIM card next and do the other tyres later.

She crawled into the car, making sure her head was below the dash at all times, and hunted for Martin's phone.

Nothing. Had he taken it with him? Had Tess not impressed upon him the need to be phone-free?

Wait. Was it in the back? The boot? He'd always thrown all sorts of crap in there.

Slithering out of the car, she sneaked to the rear and popped the lid. Gym bag. Briefcase. *Jackpot.* Spare tyre. *Oooh.* She began deflating that with a key pressing into the valve while her other hand reached for the briefcase. Olivia popped it open. *Phone*! Great.

After a few more minutes, the spare had been flattened enough to abandon it and she reached for the phone to open its innards. Except…it wouldn't open. She'd brought a paper clip in case it was one of those models where the case and phone backing lock together too well. And…no luck.

Fuck, fuck, fuck.

Martin's calls of "hello?" were getting closer. He was on his way back!

She flung the phone back, closed the briefcase, and paused, staring at the haphazard interior of the car boot. Did she dare?

Olivia hadn't discussed this with Dr Blackwood, and, hell, she'd been of two minds about bringing it. But she wanted him to remember back to a night when he'd left his girlfriend alone in a creepy place. Maybe he'd even have regrets?

Reaching into her backpack, she withdrew her old copy of Akio Morita's *Made in Japan* and carefully placed it in the boot next to Martin's briefcase—the book that had started the fight that ended in terror.

If nothing else, it'd give him something to read while he waited for a rescue.

With a grim nod, she lowered the lid on the boot and quietly clicked it shut. A flash of suit in the distance between pillars caught her eye so she relocked the car, dropped to her hands and knees, and scuttled away.

Dirt and dust coated her black jeans and boots. Her knees and hands hurt as jagged pebbles dug into them. Some ninja she was.

Back to the safety of the wall, she texted her accomplice: *He's heading back*

Dr Blackwood: *On my way.*
Olivia: *Roger that*
Dr Blackwood: *Do. Not.*

Olivia snickered. Also, who put full stops in text messages?

Within moments, the Jaguar purred up. Olivia leaped inside. "Go, go, go!" she cried.

"Excuse me?" Dr Blackwood said, turning to her. "No need to get excited." She pulled away and cruised off. As they reached a higher road, they could see down, far below, to where Martin was. He didn't look up; he was too busy staring at a flat tyre.

"Why is there only one flat tyre?" Dr Blackwood asked. "That wasn't the plan!"

"I ran out of time! I did flatten the spare, though."

"That's something, but..." Dr Blackwood's voice began petering out at seeing what Martin was now doing. "*How* is he making a call?"

"I couldn't get his phone open! I really tried. It was stuck." Olivia gave her an indignant look. "But I left him a souvenir. Maybe it'll give him something to think about while he's waiting for the RACV to arrive."

Dr Blackwood inhaled sharply. "You what?"

"I…put a copy of *Made in Japan* in his car. To remind him of our fight and what happened next. Maybe he'll think about how it'd have felt to be me that night."

"You…just told him *you* did this." Dr Blackwood stared at her incredulously.

"I…" *Oh shit.* She supposed she had. Accidentally, but still. "Um."

"You are *useless* at criminal enterprise!"

"I guess." Olivia swallowed. "Sorry. I assumed I'd be better at wreaking revenge."

"Well…" Dr Blackwood frowned. "It's our first time avenging. Mistakes will be made. But as your henchperson, I expect certain standards. I will not be a party to incompetence."

"Maybe Martin won't figure any of this out? Like, maybe he'll think the one flat was bad luck. And spares are often flat due to neglect."

"And the book?"

"Oh. Right." *That.*

"And the call to be there in the first place to meet no one? He's not that stupid. He'll put it all together soon thanks to your obvious clue. Expect an enraged ex to be visiting you shortly."

"Oh no." Olivia's head sunk into the neck rest. "No, no, no."

"On the plus side…"

There was a plus side? Olivia looked up hopefully.

"I did get a good laugh out of you ninja-crawling on all fours away from his car."

She'd seen that? Of course she had. She never missed anything. Olivia scowled. "You are the *suckiest* henchperson going. You know that, right?"

Dr Blackwood's lips twitched.

Sunset: *7.38pm*

Temp: *9.3C-26.5C*

Rain: *0mm*

Noise: *Neighbour 1B remains away. His cat returned again. I fed it, allowed it two minutes on my lap while I searched its collar for a tag with a phone number. I found neither. I'll make inquiries with other residents to see who's supposed to be minding it. Spent five minutes trying to get black cat hair off my pants. Will buy a clothes roller.*

Drink: *Yarra Yering Dry Red, one glass. Found cat hair in it. Liking it less.*

Reading: Non-fiction—JALIA, *Vol 69, issue 1. "A Model for Librarians to Assess the Digital Capability of Research Teams". My own approach was vastly superior: Step one, inform the team if they're not up to date on digital research skills, they will be fired. Step two, fire the failures. Step three, replace, rinse, and repeat. Problem solved. Hardly worth a whole paper.*

Fiction—*Re-read of* The Marmalade Files *(Steve Lewis and Chris Uhlmann). I hate to concede that the TV series,* Secret City, *was an improvement on the book, and that it was in large part due to the casting of Anna Torv. Bo would doubtlessly smirk at that. Although, why she persists on attending the book club but not reading any of the books remains a greater mystery than any in my store.*

General Observations: *Day One of active-mission henchpersonning had mixed results. While I acquitted myself to the best of capacity, Olivia's effectiveness was lacking. Which is to say, she made a mess of it. I'd be peeved at the loss of professional standards if she had not given me the greatest laugh in three years. I still wheeze when I remember her ninja-crawling away from the car, breath puffing out her red cheeks like a paper-mâché carnival clown. Not that she's a* *clown. Absolutely not. Her absurdity is in her personality not her keen mind (despite her dire taste in books).*

I'm anticipating greatly our next mission. And when was the last time I anticipated anything at all?

Postscript: Emma Garrity has settled into a nook I've set aside for her at the back of the store, near where the book club usually gathers. She attends after school from 3.20pm to 5pm daily. She even allows me to offer an occasional opinion on her English assignments. Her passion for books is con-siderable—and commendable. It turns out she acquired the passion from her mother, who used to read voraciously until their circumstances changed. A pity. I suspect Emma greatly misses discussing books with her mother.

CHAPTER 10

STITCHING UP A SVENGALI

FOR SEVERAL DAYS, OLIVIA LIVED in fear of Martin banging on her door, demanding to know what the hell she was thinking by luring him out to the middle of nowhere, letting down his tyres, and leaving him a book as a parting gift. On the fourth day, she relaxed, settling in a little early for book club at Mary Bugg's, when she heard a familiar voice.

"Hey, Livvy!"

Oh shit. She looked up to see Martin sauntering over to her, expression smarmy. With his hair slicked back and the shiny navy suit paired with a striped shirt and maroon tie, he looked like an extra from *American Psycho*. Some things never changed.

Lowering her voice, Olivia hissed: "You know I hate being called that."

He shrugged. "Why? It's a pet name."

"I'm not a pet."

He laughed.

Well, that seemed a little encouraging, she supposed. Maybe he wasn't about to make a scene?

"I'm on a mission of peace. Relax." He dropped into the chair opposite her. "Saw your van when I was driving by, and it reminded me I had to talk to you." Martin glanced around curiously. "Huh. Never actually been inside this place. It's a bit..." he scrunched up his face, "*olde worlde*, isn't it? And what's with the peacock tails twirling around all the genre signs? Why peacocks in an Australian crime bookstore?"

Olivia had never really thought about it before. She glanced at the nearest sign. It said *Thrillers* and, sure enough, a delicate purple and green inked peacock tail wound around the word. He did have a point about it being out of place—a bit like he was. "You said something about being on a mission?"

"Oh, right. Yeah, Livvy. Here." He slid a paper bag across the desk.

Nervously, she opened it and pulled out her copy of *Made in Japan*.

Shit. He'd definitely put all the pieces together. Oh no. "Look, Martin—" she began with a placating tone.

"Not sure if you remember," he cut her off, like always, "but years ago, we talked about this book. I know it's not my copy, so it must be yours. I found it in the boot the other day when I was looking for a spare tyre. I guess you must have stowed your copy there, back when the Torana was yours?"

It's still mine! The gall of him. But his other words suddenly bounced around her head. *Wait...*

"I think it's been stuck there ever since until it finally bounced loose when I had to go on a seriously dodgy bit of road the other day. I'm a man of character, and I'd never keep what's not mine."

"He kept your car," came a goading murmur from the office behind her, too quiet for Martin to hear.

"—thought you might want your book back," he finished. "I recall you liked it or something?" He eyed her uncertainly.

Olivia stared at him. Then at the book. And back at him. "You don't remember that we had a fight about this book?" she whispered.

"We did?"

"And then you ditched me in Melbourne's creepiest street over it?"

"Huh?" Martin looked truly puzzled now. "What are you talking about?"

"I was left cowering from druggies and pimps behind a skip bin while you drove off."

He snorted. "Oh, come on, Livvy. Even if that happened as you say— which I highly doubt cos you know how emotional you get—that was *years* ago. You know I'm a good guy. See? I found your book and I'm returning it. Do you want it back or not?"

She clawed the book towards herself and wondered what to do now. "You said you needed a spare tyre. What happened?"

"Oh, I had to go to some industrial estate. So many sharp rocks. I probably should check my spare every once in a while. That was flat too. But it was fine. I have a mate who didn't live too far from where I was. Got it sorted out in twenty-five minutes." He smiled, that charming, oily smile she used to think was handsome. "I'm all good. Better than good, actually. I probably shouldn't say this, but who are you going to tell?"

He leaned in and whispered, excitement edging his voice: "I'm going to be in a spread for 100 top marketers." His eyes were bright. "Waiting for a reschedule. Was supposed to do it the other day, but the photog didn't show." He shrugged. "Shit happens. But, yeah, I'm going amazing. Engaged now too. To a model." His eyes slunk all over her and took on a pitying expression.

Bastard.

"And you? You're still..." he waved around. "Driving around in your nana's weed van?"

"It's not a weed van!"

"Sure smelt like it." He laughed. "Damn, that old bat loved to party."

Before she could protest that okay, sure, Nana Betty liked a joint—or three—for her arthritis, but that didn't mean her Kombi was a 'weed van', he added: "At least tell me you don't still have her stupid penguin. Cos that'd really be a loser move." He laughed harder.

The door behind them suddenly banged open.

Dr Blackwood appeared, framed like some sort of avenging angel in her trademark gothic black. At six feet tall, arms and legs spread as if about to leap into flight, she was an impressive sight. Olivia's breath caught in spite of herself. She did not, of course, find Margaret Blackwood in any way impressive. Well, okay, she did, but that was the residue from back when she'd admired her as Book Woman.

Margaret spoke, her voice dripping with condescension. "Oh, hello." She raked sharp eyes over Martin. "Are you a friend of Ms Roberts?"

Martin chuckled as if the mere idea of being friends with Olivia was hilarious. "Nah. I just brought her back something she lost."

Dr Blackwood's eyes narrowed as she took him in from the top of his gelled hair to the bottom of his polished shoes. "Law or marketing?" she asked.

Prickles skittered up Olivia's spine at the faintly mocking tone.

"Marketing," he said, surprised. "Wow. You guessed that?"

"You *reek* of it."

"I…thank you."

"That was not a compliment."

Olivia swallowed back a laugh as his eyes widened in surprise.

"Yeah? Well, I'm not some hack marketer." He stood, as if no longer able to take being so much lower than this towering woman. "As a matter of fact, I'm one of the top 100 marketing stars on the rise. They're doing a story about me."

"Is that so?" Dr Blackwood drawled. "Well, I'd be sure to put that all over social media if I were you. Self-promotion is important. Make sure to alert your bosses too. As an employer myself, I like to be aware of which of my staff is doing well and worthy of a promotion."

"Oh." Martin thought about that and suddenly nodded. "Yeah. I mean, of course I should, but I don't want to jump the gun. I have to wait for it to be written up in the newspaper. I mean…it's an outside chance—um, a way, way, outside chance—but what if they change their mind and I'm cut from the list?"

"Nonsense," Dr Blackwood said with a careless wave. She spoke with utter authority. "Get in first, be loud, be bold. Make sure everyone knows to look for the story. That is how to get noticed in life. Be a shark. And as for being cut? They'd never dare after you've promoted their story for them. They might even bump you a few numbers up the list."

He grinned, and it had a wolfish quality Olivia knew only too well. Oh, he'd so be doing this. "Yeah. A shark," Martin agreed.

"Indeed," Dr Blackwood said. "Now, if you'll excuse us, I need to consult with Ms Roberts." She waved at Olivia. "Profits are up significantly since we began selling her award-winning baked goods."

"No way." Martin looked amazed and glanced at Olivia and back. "I've seen her van. She only makes muffins, right?" He waved at her button pin of the day and snorted at *Life is What You Bake It.*

Olivia gritted her teeth. *Thanks, Martin, for undermining my entire career.*

"Award. Winning. Muffins." Dr Blackwood eyed him. "It seems you've been out of the loop. Ms Roberts's goods are much sought-after all over the city. I tell her she should also engage in social media to get the word out, but she's too modest."

Wait, what?

"A pity," Dr Blackwood continued. "The modest don't prosper nearly so well as the bold, do they?"

"No." Martin looked back on firmer ground, given he was apparently more impressive than Olivia. He shot her a smug look. "They don't."

"Mm." Dr Blackwood folded her arms. She all but tapped her foot, waiting for him to leave.

"Okay…" His gaze was back to dismissive as he addressed Olivia. "Well done, I guess."

He *guessed*? God, she was so tired of being treated like this. How did she put up with him for two years?

"I want the Torana back," she suddenly blurted, surprising herself.

"What?" Martin's voice was shocked and high. Worry flitted into his eyes.

By contrast, Dr Blackwood's expression suddenly took on an approving, interested gleam.

"You heard me." Olivia's gaze drilled into him.

"You don't even like it! You got the Torana cheap as an A-to-B car, you said. You said its colour clashes with your hair!"

"And it's still mine, and I want it back."

"So this is the thanks I get for bringing back your book?" he asked with exaggerated outrage. "You take away my car?"

"Except it's not your car. It's mine. It's always been mine. You didn't even know me when I bought it."

"I pay the registration on it every year, though," he protested. "And the insurance!"

"And now you won't have to." She studied him evenly. This slippery, smarmy man had cowed her so much when she was younger. "I'm serious."

"No!" He took a step closer, then lowered his voice. "*No.* That is…that's not happening. I won't allow it."

Allow it? And did he actually think he looked threatening, invading her personal space like he was? With so many witnesses around? She glanced about to confirm that and spotted Damien watching from the Mystery section with a dark glower. Emma, fittingly, was staring daggers from the Young Adult section. Breanna, peering at them from Bushrangers and Convicts, looked ready to bury a body if need be.

Martin seemed oblivious; his entire focus was on Olivia. "Enough with this bullshit," he spat out. "You only want it because I have it. You don't need it. You have your nana's van. It's obvious you don't appreciate the Torana the way I do."

He meant, of course, its value. How much it had gone up. She wasn't oblivious that her classic car was worth ten times now what she'd paid for it. That's what Martin appreciated the most, she had no doubt, that he was driving a valuable collectible.

"Don't be immature," he pressed on. "Let's just keep the arrangement as it is. Like adults." And *there* was the patronising tone she knew and loathed. Oh, that had worked on her once, when he'd seemed so much older and more knowledgeable. And what arrangement did he think they had? He got to drive her car for free? Without even asking? *That* arrangement?

"I want my car back because it's mine." Olivia stared at him evenly. "I don't need to give you a reason. I'm not backing down. Not this time."

"Sure you are. It's you," he mocked. "What are you gonna do about it if I say I'm keeping it? Nothing. You always do nothing." He gave her a slimy smile and turned to go. "Catch you around, *Livvy.*"

"Don't call me that." This time when she said the words, there was no pleading. Her tone was angry and low. She shocked herself she even had it in her.

Not that it mattered. He laughed, flipped her the bird over his shoulder, and strode off.

Olivia ground her jaw. Then she turned to Dr Blackwood. "Okay, what was all that about? Telling him I'm lousy at social media? You know, Love Muffins has its own Facebook page. It has 3,700 followers."

"I'm just being an exceptional henchperson. Apparently, you had doubts."

"How? By telling him he's a legend and should boast about it? Ugh, he's got a bigger head now than he had before!"

"You told me ego matters to him. I've egged him on to plaster his social media with news of this accolade. For some reason, he was too stupid to realise, despite all the clues, that he'd been set up. And after he's announced he's going to be named in the paper, I'll contact an acquaintance at the *Herald Sun.* I will alert her that a con artist is using their paper's name to big-note himself in a non-existent story. At the very least, she would be per-suaded to publicly say no such top 100 list exists."

"Okay," Olivia said, collapsing back into the chair. "That's actually clever."

"Don't sound so surprised." Dr Blackwood smiled faintly. It fell away at Olivia's expression. "What's wrong?"

"He didn't even remember what happened," Olivia muttered. "One of the most traumatic moments of my life, and he didn't remember it."

"From his point of view, he taught someone a lesson and thought noth-ing more of it. Maybe he teaches women so many lessons, this is just back-ground noise to him."

"Yeah." Olivia swallowed. "I can't believe that for all our planning, he never got to feel what I felt that night. He didn't have a moment's unease after the flat tyres. He called his friend and was gone in no time."

"He'll be professionally humiliated soon enough. It wasn't a total waste of time. And, from what I've seen of him, that will be more scarring to him than what we'd planned."

"I guess so." Maybe Dr Blackwood was right. She stared down at her hands and realised they were shaking. "Thanks."

"Don't thank me. This is a professional transaction: my assistance, your muffins." Her tone was brisk, but Olivia wondered if she really meant it.

"You were kind, making sure he got some payback."

"Unlikely." Dr Blackwood straightened. "I'm not a kind person. Ask my former colleagues. Our fights were legendary. Besides, if I recall, you said I love to be mean."

"I didn't mean that in an evil way. More like a nitpicky way, like how you sliced and diced everyone at book club."

"Nitpicky?" Her nostrils flared as if smelling something rancid. "I'm quite sure you mean *accurate*."

"Whatever helps you sleep at night. Look, you let Emma come here every day after school," Olivia pointed out. "That sounds like something kind to me."

"What sort of a monster would I be if I prevented a vulnerable child from doing her homework in a safe environment?" Dr Blackwood folded her arms, eyebrow arching. "That's proof of nothing. Now, I'll leave you to it. You have that rabble you call a book club to oversee." She waved at the milling members talking animatedly near the shelves. "By the looks of things, it'll be even more off topic than usual."

"Wait!" Olivia said hastily. "Stay for the club? I'd love you to meet everyone. I mean properly. And I know you'll already have read *The Last Woman in the World* by Inga Simpson. That's this week's read."

"Oh? Is it?"

"You know it is." Olivia smiled at her feigning innocence.

Dr Blackwood sniffed. "Of course I've read it. But as scintillating as it sounds to experience that undisciplined mob up close, I'm busy."

"But it'd be more fun if you were there. That way, we can all, um, benefit from hearing your nitpicky...and accurate...comments."

"I'm not interested in interacting with anyone," Dr Blackwood said. "My comments were only intended for you. Unfortunately, your little group turned out to have exceptional hearing."

"What..." Olivia trailed off. That sounded...intimate. Did Dr Blackwood not realise that?

Maybe she did. Her cheeks pinkened, and Dr Blackwood opened her mouth like a fish gulping at air. Suddenly, she backed away into her office, closing the door with a little more force than was usual. Or necessary.

What. The. Hell.

The chairs filled up, and before long, the club members were talking over each other as Tess and Bo were brought up to speed about Martin's dramatic appearance at the bookstore and the failed mission. Emma slunk into a chair by the window, now her unofficial after-school homework spot. Given the angle of her body, she was definitely listening in.

Maybe Olivia should relocate her to Kelly's cafe area at the front of the store. Post-apocalyptic thrillers were not suitable for ten-year-old ears. Except Dr Blackwood was also likely right. They wouldn't be doing much talking about Inga Simpson's book today.

While the book club discussed Martin's showdown, Olivia stewed over her ex-boyfriend's parting remark that she'd do nothing about getting her Torana back. Because that's what she always did, wasn't it? He wasn't wrong to think that. And, hell, it burned.

The door snicked open behind her just as Damien turned to her.

"You know," he said, "your original plan was flawed, even if it had gone off without a hitch."

That caught Olivia's attention. "How so?"

"Even if you'd nicked his SIM card, he could have still phoned for help. Many phone companies allow emergency calls without a SIM card. And those that don't? You just call 112—that's the emergency number for mobile phones worldwide."

"Oh." Olivia sagged. How amateur did they look now? "Do you think he knew that?"

"Guess we'll never know. But don't sweat it," Damien said kindly. "Wasn't that, like, your first mission? You guys are still ironing out the kinks, yeah? I'm sure it'll go better next time. But I'm thinking, if you need to run any plans over the pits, we've got a pretty good cross-section of people at book club."

"You think we need help?" Olivia asked slowly, unsure whether to laugh or cry at how obvious it was she'd screwed up everything.

"Everyone needs help," Damien said easily. "It's just a matter of how much. Should we talk about your vengeance plans for Tina, for instance?"

Olivia blinked. "How do you know about Tina? Or that I'm planning anything against her?"

Damien lifted one shoulder in a lazy shrug. "Wasn't she your last girl-friend? Since the ad went up after you two broke up, doesn't that mean she did something super shitty to start all this?"

"I...suppose." Logic for the win.

"And given where she lives—Lonsdale Heartland Tower, right?—and that you used to say she never liked leaving home much, then I'm imagining you've got yourself an access issue? Now, see, that's something right up my alley."

Suddenly, Olivia remembered what Damien did for a living. He worked the front desk security at a fancy apartment two streets down from where Tina lived. Olivia had bumped into him so many times at the bookstore nearest Tina's place that she'd invited him to the crime group.

"I don't suppose you know a way up to the penthouse suite in Tina's building?" Olivia asked hopefully. It really sucked, right at this moment, that Tina's parents had never reclaimed her luxury apartment when they'd cut off her allowance.

"No." He rubbed his jaw. "And those top-price, la-de-da places don't allow anyone to access any of the floors without permission from a person who lives there. Front desk security has a list of approved guests. Wouldn't Tina have revoked your permission?"

"Yeah. She had my name taken off her list when we broke up."

"Right." He nodded. "But I know the day security guy at Lonsdale Tower. I see him at the local every few weeks. I'd be happy to buy him a beer and find out all the building's vulnerabilities. Subtly like."

Olivia tried to imagine what vulnerabilities he'd come up with. They wouldn't be able to sneak past the front desk with all those cameras.

"Lemme get back to you on options," Damien said. "Okay? Like I said the other week: Mary Bugg's Thunderbolt feller had the right idea—you've gotta make use of the resources you have."

Why not? "Okay. Yes. Thanks, Damien."

Emma was writing furiously, which made her far too suspicious to just be doing homework. Olivia suddenly stood and walked up behind her, getting a look at her page. Scribbled in big scrawl were the words: *Lonsdale Heartland Tower.*

"That is not homework, young lady."

Emma jumped, looking guilty, and offered her a hopeful smile. "If you don't want me as a henchperson, at least I can be the notetaker, right? That's useful, yeah?"

"Sweetheart, you are *not* taking notes on my vengeance schemes. That's not going to help you pass maths, now, is it?"

"No." Emma said, then grinned. "But it might help me pass English. We're reading *Rebecca* by Daphne du Maurier next semester. I want to get a head start on studying women plotting tricky schemes."

"Isn't *Rebecca* a little advanced for kids your age?" Bo broke in curiously.

Breanna looked askance. "Nonsense! Children should have their minds open to all sorts of books and not be pigeon-holed by age. I hate gatekeeping or censoring books at any age. Every child is different. It is such a slippery slope having arbitrary limits."

Annnd off they went again. New debate topic. They'd be there a while because censorship was Breanna's chief bugbear.

Olivia leaned in and told Emma quietly: "My official answer is still no unless your mum tells me to my face that she's fine with her daughter playing stenographer to vengeance-planning meetings."

Emma slumped.

"But I also know, notes or no notes, that you're going to listen in regardless of what I ask you to do, so can you please at least not make it so obvious?" Olivia gave her a small grin.

Emma raised her little finger and said, "Pinkie-swear. I promise to turn the pages of my maths book every two minutes."

"Thank you." Olivia smiled and returned to address the rabble. "Okay," she said in a *let's wind-this-up* tone, "censorship is bad, kids are all different, books should match their maturity level, and can someone *please* tell me they've got a single thought on Inga Simpson's book?"

Friday, March 20
Day 1140 post H

Sunset: *7.31pm*

Temp: *16.1C-22.7C*

Rain: *0mm*

Noise: *Neighbour 1B remains away. Black cat now meows for food in front of my door. I have explained I am not its caretaker. It explains that, apparently, I am. A standoff ensued for ten minutes before I decided the decibels it was emitting exceeded noise regulations, and I'm nothing if not about quiet environs. Food was administered. Peace resumed. I really must find the animal's acting guardian, however. I did not sign up for this. I'm quite sure H would laugh at me now being a cat lady, albeit involuntarily.*

Drink: *Water. Three glasses. Vanquishing enemies while henchpersonning demands rehydration not alcohol.*

Reading: Non-fiction—JALIA, *Vol 69, issue 1. "Checking the Pulse of LGBTIQ+ Inclusion and Representation in the Academic Library". Not before time, I suppose. Maybe there's hope for some of Australia's dinosaur institutions yet.*

Fiction—That Deadman Dance *(Kim Scott). It might have won the Miles Franklin award, but it didn't win me over. I think you'd have liked this one, H. The mythology mixed with real storytelling needs a certain creative soul to enjoy it. My soul insists on being entirely grounded.*

General Observations: *If ever there was a man's face worthy of being slapped it is Olivia's loathsome ex, Martin the marketer. How he ever persuaded her to date him is a mystery. He's clearly unworthy. The sliminess of him reminds me of eels.*

It took everything in my power when I overheard him deriding Olivia's hard work not to tear strips off him, pointing out in detail his impressive mediocrity. I wanted to ram one of her larger muffins down his throat so that he might experience their excellence personally.

Instead, a superior plan occurred to me that will destroy him far more effectively.

As to Olivia's ridiculous comment that I am being kind— what rot. The truth is I'm protective of those in my immediate orbit whom I deem worthy of my time or attention. Thus, I will ensure no harm comes to the neighbour's hungry cat, the homeless girl, or the absurd muffin maker. That's not being kind. I don't know what it is, but it's not kind. Territorial at best.

Postscript: Emma's mother came to speak with me. I was pleased to be able to reassure Ms Garrity that her child is safe and in no way a burden to Mary Bugg's. As if anyone who loves books as much as Emma does could ever be an encumbrance. How absurd. I told the woman as much. She looked entirely too surprised for a statement of fact.

We also had a brief discussion on books. It turns out Emma wasn't exaggerating. Her mother is remarkably well-read, especially in the crime and mystery genre. She even supplied a clever, little joke about the Dewey decimal system that startled me. Civilians never usually crack librarian jokes. This is a woman who has spent a lot of time in libraries.

The wistful way Ms Garrity gazed at Mary Bugg's shelves was not lost on me. I offered to give her a book or two of her choosing, but she politely refused and said I was already doing enough by keeping an eye on Emma. A shame. The soul of a reader should never be starved.

CHAPTER 11

THE WATCH PEACOCK

THREE DAYS LATER, OLIVIA RUSHED into Mary Bugg's, her phone opened to a screen that had made her shout so loud, she'd probably stopped traffic. On Martin's Instagram page was a post about how he was going to be named in the *Herald Sun*'s Top 100 Rising Star Marketers list—along with a boastful screed about how he'd worked so hard and was excited to be recognized as one of the best.

And, under his post, just ten minutes ago, was a reply from @ RealJMMorrison, deputy editor of the *Herald Sun*, saying, "No such award exists. Can't imagine our readers would care about ten marketers, let alone a hundred! You have a good imagination, though."

Under the deputy editor's comment were dozens and dozens of laughing emoticons and comments from strangers as well as Martin's friends and colleagues, mostly suggesting that the time to delete the post was two seconds after he'd posted it. But the pièce de résistance was a comment from his boss: "Sorry, Martin. Seems despite what you've been telling us all, you're not the greatest!"

That would have burned. She'd already taken screenshots of all the comments to keep forever.

Olivia hurried through the bookstore, weaving around shelves, waving off Kelly's called out, "Liv? What's up?", and running straight up to Dr Blackwood's office door.

She knocked enthusiastically. Getting no response, Olivia decided this was too much of an emergency not to involve her henchperson and threw the door open. "We did it!"

Dr Blackwood visibly jumped, her pen went flying, and then she scowled from behind a stark, minimalist, wooden desk. "By all means, burst into my office uninvited. Were you raised in a barn?"

Olivia rushed over, too excited to quail in the face of her irritation. "Sorry, it was an emergency! High-order henchperson business. Look!" She thrust her phone under Dr Blackwood's nose.

Sighing, the other woman tilted her head forward to examine it.

"Martin did *exactly* what you told him to!" Olivia said. "And now he's being roasted on social media. And see that guy?" She pointed at a comment. "That's his boss telling him he's not great. This will *crush* Martin!"

For a moment, Dr Blackwood didn't react at all, then a faint smile curled her lips. "I see Janice didn't disappoint."

"Janice? Is that @RealJMMorrison?"

"It is."

"You know the actual deputy editor of the *Herald Sun*? It's only the largest newspaper in the whole of Victoria! If not Australia! You sure buried the lead!"

"I know the editor too. But Janice especially. She was at my wedding. Gifted us a punch bowl, of all things." She frowned as if trying to remember where it was.

"You're…*married*?" Olivia sank into a chair opposite as shock washed over her. "You never said."

"You never asked." Dr Blackwood's expression was such a perfectly bland variety of neutral that she had surely practiced it in a mirror. "But in the interest of accuracy, I'm no longer married."

"Oh." Olivia felt terrible. "Sorry. I'm… Shit. Divorce sucks."

Dr Blackwood's face flashed with a pinched, raw pain. The kind of pain that said Olivia had made the wrong assumption. Which meant…

Oh fuck. Fuckity fuck. Trust Olivia to put her foot in it. What if this loss was recent and Dr Blackwood was still in mourning? Her cheeks flamed in humiliation. "Oh God. Hell, I'm really, really sorry."

Dr Blackwood's jaw worked. Her eyes turned to flint. She suddenly shifted forward, shoulders hunching over like a threatening gargoyle…if gargoyles were also disconcertingly attractive when enraged. "This topic is *not* up for discussion. What *is* to be discussed is that you are to never again burst in on me in my office. Are we clear on this? You might have disrupted some extremely important work. *No one* comes in here!"

Olivia blinked in surprise. Now that she'd said it, Olivia realised she never *had* seen anyone else step foot inside this office. She wondered what that was about.

Curious, she sneaked a peek around the room, half expecting to find contraband items which might explain her ferocity. But the decor was tasteful, refined, with a few Australiana nick-nacks and some framed old maps next to degrees on the wall.

The longest wall, which faced the bookstore, held a wide window hidden by horizontal slatted timber blinds. Due to the blinds' angle, you could see everything going on outside Dr Blackwood's office while being invisible from her side. Quite the tactical advantage.

"Are we clear?" Dr Blackwood repeated through gritted teeth.

"Clear," Olivia said lightly. "Sorry. I was excited. But you're right. It was rude. I won't do it again…" She faded out as a flash of blue and green drew her attention. A large bird was on a shelf near the window. An actual, full-size, formerly alive *peacock*. It was a gorgeous, well-preserved specimen.

"Wow," she whispered, walking over to it and inspecting it closely. "Beautiful." No wonder Dr Blackwood had never given Olivia any grief about driving around with a penguin. Dr Blackwood was now only the second person that Olivia had ever met who had a taxidermied creature in their possession—after her nana, of course.

And a peacock? Did that explain all the imagery around the store? Was Dr Blackwood a bit of a peacock fancier?

"Um…" Olivia whispered respectfully into the feathers. "This is unexpected."

Dr Blackwood didn't speak for a moment. "That is a historical artefact. Allegedly."

"An artefact?" Olivia asked in fascination. "And why allegedly?"

"This is all unproven, but…" Dr Blackwood hesitated for a moment, then said, "An academic at Monash University's history department was bequeathed this peacock by a deceased estate, along with a letter that told an incredible tale. In it, Helen was informed that this was the infamous 'watch peacock' belonging to Ned Kelly's grandfather, James Quinn."

Mentioning Ned Kelly, the most iconic Australian bushranger of them all, would absolutely get any historian's attention. And to suggest his grandfather owned this—what had she called it? "A watch peacock?" Olivia asked tentatively. "What's that?"

"Think of a watchdog but with feathers." Amusement darted into Dr Blackwood's eyes.

"Oh, I've gotta hear this story." Olivia grinned and ran back to sit opposite her.

Dr Blackwood steepled her fingers. "James Quinn had a hideout at the back of his homestead that frequently housed bushranger friends or family on the run. His watch peacock..." she waved at the stuffed bird, "would alert them if police were near."

"How could a peacock do that?" Olivia asked, entranced.

"According to stories at the time, the bird would 'perch and parade on the roof and announce the approach of a visitor by continuous and penetrating calls'. It was an unbeatable system until the night of June 5, 1870." Dr Blackwood's tone warmed to telling her tale.

"What happened that night?"

"Harry Power, known across the land as the Gentleman Bushranger, was using Quinn's hideout. A huge rainstorm blew in, and the peacock took cover. With no peacock patrolling that night, the police were able to sneak in and capture the entire bushranger gang. It all came down to bypassing one bird."

"So is this why you have a peacock motif throughout your store? It's in homage to your bushranger's peacock?"

"Yes. Although I have to reiterate that it's all speculation. I have some natural scepticism about whether it's the same bird. But Helen loved the idea of it possibly being true, so I didn't have the heart to get it verified, in case it was just a tall tale. In families with intergenerational collectibles, myth becomes fact more often than not as the years go by. It also didn't feel right to display it in my bookstore as a historical artefact as it hadn't been officially verified. I won't endorse poor science. So my solution was to just..."

"Hide it in your office?" Olivia lifted her eyebrows. "Well, that works too."

Dr Blackwood gave the faintest of shrugs. "It does."

"Well, I love it." The bird was old, but there was a grandness to it. And it had a snooty condescension to its expression which matched Dr Blackwood very well. Not that Olivia was about to tell her that.

Silence fell.

The words "I didn't have the heart to get it verified" did a rapid loop around Olivia's brain. Dr Blackwood hadn't wanted to hurt this Helen woman who clearly adored the peacock and its exciting backstory. "Why do you have it?" Olivia asked. "I mean, if it was given to Helen?"

That flash of pain returned, the one etched with so much raw misery that Olivia had to look away. *Ah.* So. Helen was the dead spouse? What else made sense? Hadn't Dr Blackwood once said she'd lived with a historian?

Desperate to remove the vulnerable look from the other woman's eyes, Olivia quickly said, "Does your peacock have a name?"

"Why would it?" Dr Blackwood snapped, her voice thick with emotion.

Olivia gentled her expression. "Why wouldn't it? Watchdogs have names. Why not watch birds?"

"It's known only in the history books as James Quinn's Watch Peacock."

"That's a bit of a mouthful." Olivia gave her a tiny grin. "We can do better than that, can't we? How about Quincy?"

Dr Blackwood stared at her.

"Or not."

"Or not," Dr Blackwood ground out. She folded her arms and glowered at Olivia. "Now, was there some reason for you bursting into my personal space besides gloating about your ex's downfall?"

"Isn't that enough?" Olivia asked amiably. "We got lucky with Martin not being the brightest spark. We have a much bigger challenge ahead of us for Annalise. She's a lawyer, after all. She has so much charm, it should be a crime. And, worst of all, she's a master manipulator." Olivia added glumly, "As I can attest."

For a moment, Dr Blackwood said nothing and just regarded Olivia as if deciding something.

"All right," she finally said, sounding resigned now. "You have my attention. We can sit here and discuss the next assignment. How shall we destroy Entitled Annalise?"

They worked on their destruction plans for Annalise until Olivia yawned, apologised, and called it a day. After all, everyone else's four in the afternoon was Olivia's midevening. Bakers' hours were a hell of a thing.

She headed home, mind still awhirl with what she'd learned.

One: Martin had finally had his oversized ego crushed. Sure, it hadn't been crushed the way they'd originally planned, but they'd gotten there in the end—thanks to Dr Blackwood using his ego against him.

Olivia was still stewing over the fact he couldn't remember dumping her in a crime street or even the book fight. Nor did he have any plans to surrender the Torana. She'd think about that later.

Two: Dr Blackwood had been married. To a woman. *A woman!!!* Olivia hadn't expected that. Maybe she should have, given how often the bookstore boss delighted in shooting down gorgeous Sasha's advances. Except that her hands-off aura was directed at everyone, so Olivia didn't feel bad for not guessing.

There had been other clues, though: Like the mannish black suits, lack of make-up, short nails, powerful stride, and the way she blew into a room with such force, as though one cape swirl away from being a Tim Burton villain. A shiver ran down Olivia's spine. She greatly appreciated watching Margaret Blackwood enter a room. In fact, it was her favourite thing ever since the woman had swept up to Martin and destroyed him without the idiot even realising it.

It had felt…God! Wonderful. Like having a vicious, commanding wolf as your best friend. Well, not friend. Dr Blackwood didn't think much of Olivia, she was quite sure. But…it was just…comforting. Olivia felt protected.

Three: Dr Blackwood's spouse was most likely named Helen. The same Helen who had been a historian and academic at Monash University until, most likely, she'd passed away.

Well, what good was Google for if not a little benign cyberstalking?

As Olivia waited for her tomato soup to heat, stirring occasionally, she went through page after page of Google on her phone, looking for the elusive academic.

It turned out she wasn't that elusive. As an author of two dozen papers on early Australian history, someone called Professor Helen Spencer popped up in the news fairly often. Several newspaper obits had been written, talking mainly about her academic success and fame. One university article had a small piece on her that mentioned Dr Blackwood in detail.

VALE PROF HELEN SPENCER

Monash University's Indigenous Studies Centre pays tribute to its highly regarded director, Professor Helen Spencer, who has passed away after a short illness, aged 45.

Prof Spencer authored twenty-six papers, led the way in the world's understanding of Oceanic Indigenous cultures, and helped spearhead the research project, Global Encounters & First Nations Peoples: 1000 Years of Australian History. She was the author of the critically acclaimed memoir Through My Grandmother's Eyes: Beyond the Stolen Generation.

She will be sadly missed by staff and students who loved her vast knowledge and enthusiasm for history.

Prof Spencer is survived by her wife, RMIT Director of Scholarly Services Dr Margaret Blackwood, who also built the world's foremost library collection on Australian bushrangers. The couple married four months ago.

In lieu of flowers, Dr Blackwood requests donations be made to the Global Encounters & First Nations Peoples project.

A service will be held at Monash University's Aboriginal Garden on Thursday at 10am.

Attached was a photo of an arresting-looking woman with light brown skin, blonde, wavy hair, and mischievous eyes. She wore an elegant white blouse.

Olivia closed her eyes for a moment. To die at only forty-five... Her heart clenched. And worse, to die only months after marrying. She flicked a look at the date on the article. Dr Blackwood had lost her wife of four months some three years ago. And they couldn't have married much before they did because Australian law prohibited same-sex marriage before then. How long had they been together for?

Putting down her phone, Olivia decided to face dinner. She slurped her soup mournfully as she processed what she'd turned up. She knew from Kelly that Mary Bugg's Bookstore was only two and a half years old. Had Dr Blackwood walked away from academia because she'd lost her wife?

Had working in academia, surrounded by so much history and historians, reminded her too much of what she'd lost? If so, then why had she then started a bookstore focusing on Australia's past? Especially given she wasn't even remotely a people person. Why get into customer service at all?

She had no answers by the time Kelly came home and murmured, "Hey", then sniffed at the pot. "Tomato soup? Are you depressed or premenstrual?"

"Can't a girl just like tomato soup?"

"Not you." Kelly studied her. "Spill? Was it Martin? Still brooding over him not coughing up your Torana? Do you have any plans to get it back? I'm all for that, by the way. That's an expensive car you walked away from."

"No… That's not it. I'm… I dug up some stuff on your boss today. Um, from Google."

Kelly paused. "Really? Like what?"

"Did you know Dr Blackwood married a woman?"

Kelly looked at her for a beat, as if waiting for a punchline that hadn't come. "Really?"

"Yes."

"Huh. No, I didn't. I'm surprised she's never come by. The wife, I mean. It'd be interesting to meet her."

"Well, she can't. She died. Three years ago, before the bookstore even opened."

Sympathy washed Kelly's face. "Shit. Poor Dr B. And poor wife, of course. God, that sucks."

"Yeah." Olivia slowly stirred the dregs in her bowl, then attempted another mouthful.

Kelly began helping herself to the leftovers in the pot. "Okay, for your own health and safety, I'm going to strongly suggest you never tell my boss that you know all this stuff because you snooped on her. Okay? Actually, for your sake and mine."

"I know." She sighed. "I wouldn't. I just feel bad for her. Losing her wife who was only forty-five. That's way too soon."

"It's tough," Kelly agreed. "God, that is really shitty. I plan to neatly avoid this agony myself, of course, by never getting married."

"I'll let you break the devastating news to Sasha."

Kelly snorted. "Please, he only wants me because I don't want him. It's the challenge for him."

"Are you sure about that? He's perilously close to besotted."

"I'm sure. He flirts with far too many women to only have eyes for me. Which is a pity because he was *phenomenal* in bed."

"Ew. TMI." Olivia scrunched up her nose.

"So prudish. On this topic, any new prospects for you? Or has Tina ruined you for life?"

"I'm not sure I'd be a great dating choice right now. Imagine going out with me and asking what I do. And I'll say, 'Well, by morning, I'm a baker; by afternoon, I work out various ways to screw over my exes. I have this whole vengeance bucket list, plus a henchperson'. Cos that sounds normal and sane."

Kelly laughed. "When you put it like that, yeah, I'd run. So, who's next on your vengeance list? Annalise?"

"Yep. I brainstormed with Dr Blackwood this afternoon. So far, it's looking like I'm baking Annalise a cake—"

"No!"

"Wait, not a wedding cake, just something generic, but I'll be writing in icing the amount of money she owes me. I'll deliver it to Reception at her office. Wouldn't take long for the whole building to hear about it. Lawyers are the worst gossips. About the only thing Annalise holds sacred is her professional reputation. I'll leave a message for her that I'll repeat this every two weeks until she pays up. And I'll add the cost of the cakes to the money owed, so the amount written in icing will keep going up, cake after cake."

"That's a really smart-alec way to make a point. I like it."

"Me too. It was Dr Blackwood's idea." She sipped some more soup, then put her spoon down. "I suppose she understands all about the value of reputations from surviving in academia. It's a big thing in that field, your reputation."

"I guess so." Kelly side-eyed her for a moment. "I can't help but notice you're not enraged by my boss as much anymore. You used to hiss that she was avoiding you. Then you'd announce she was spying on your book club every time I mentioned her."

"Don't read too much into it." Olivia's heart gave a sad little twang as she added, "We're business partners not friends. I'm in it for the brainstorming and backup. She's in it for the free muffins."

Kelly looked thoughtful at that. "Huh," was all she said. "Interesting."

Monday, March 23
Too long since H

Sunset: *irrelevant*

Temp: *irrelevant*

Rain: *irrelevant*

Drink: *irrelevant*

Reading: *irrelevant*

General Observations: *My neighbour in 1B has passed away. They found him this evening, but he'd been dead three weeks. THREE WEEKS! No one missed him. He had no friends, no family. Only a cat.*

I tried to picture him in my mind, and I can only remember his unruly, white hair and a brown and green jacket he often wore when collecting his mail. I knew his voice from him calling to his cat. But I don't remember anything else. Not even the cat's name.

It hits home, the thought of having no one to mourn you. Really mourn you. As I watched them wheel the gurney away, I wondered who'd think to look for me if I lay dead in my apartment.

Who would even bother to come to my funeral? Aside from my family, of course. My mother would make it all about herself in the eulogy. I wonder if she'd surreptitiously slide in a few regrets over my unfortunate failings. My fall from grace into—dear God—crime literature.

Would she remember to mention you, H? How you were once my everything?

I miss you beyond the imprecision of words. I know it's been three years, but I can't fight it. I feel the loss of you in my skin. In the roots of my hair, in my nails, under my breast, in my throat, inside my ribcage. Missing you is like a groove worn in a rock by dripping rain. It's more a habit now. But even habits of so long find a way to ache.

I hate that even hearing your name or thinking of you directly throws me all the way back to the start of the grief. I get angry at anyone for making me remember you. How dare they!

I'm not sure I'm strong enough to face it all again. Yet here we are.

Helen...I miss you.

—Margaret Blackwood
Bookstore owner, henchperson
Cat lady (now official)

Tuesday, March 24
Too long since H

Sunset: --

Temp: --

Rain: --

Drink: --

Reading: --

General Observations: *I'm embarrassed about my breakdown yesterday. Helen has been gone a long time—over a thousand days—and I should be stronger. It hit hard, though, the neighbour dying alone and unnoticed. Apparently, only my asking around to find out who was supposed to be feeding his cat while he was away spurred the building manager to investigate.*

Why didn't I wonder how odd it was that he'd stopped feeding his cat? Or remember that in the past six years, the man has never once gone on holiday? The building manager figured it out immediately; why didn't I?

Instead, without any curiosity or deeper thought, I fed a starving animal that had escaped an open window and sought food from a neighbour.

I'm slipping. This is a level of surface thinking I used to deride in students. Is this lapse a concern? A pattern? It's something to keep an eye on.

Issue one: Evaluate my mental reaction times, looking for deficits.

Issue two: Analyse my unsettled feeling following Olivia storming my barricades—well, my office—sitting in that visitor's chair as if she belonged there. As if she had a right to my space. No, that wasn't what rattled me. It's that she seemed to really want to be there.

It felt strange under my skin that day, letting someone inside the four walls from which I keep the world at bay.

I'm out of practice at being human, I think.

Unrelated note: Book club took place today. I did not so much as open my door, let alone interact, as I have been doing recently. I ignored Olivia's knocks afterwards. I was not in the mood.

CHAPTER 12

ENTITLED ANNALISE

"I'm not sure I'm up for this." Olivia drew in a tight breath and turned to Dr Blackwood in her passenger seat. It was actually weird to see her there. Not just because she'd lowered herself to be inside a van called Love Muffins, but because Dr Blackwood was sitting where Trip should have been.

"We've been over this. You'll be fine." Dr Blackwood's gaze was intense yet reassuring. "You know this. Go to the receptionist, tell her you have a cake for Annalise. Offer to show it to her, and of course she'll say yes. Receptionists all have a nosy gene. She'll gossip all over the building about what she's seen. You've left your number in the cake box. When Annalise calls you, tell her you'll repeat your cake deliveries regularly until she pays up."

Olivia swallowed. "Okay. What if I see Annalise? She can make me forget my own name. I get all lost and tongue-tied. She's got this weird villain superpower. She's impossible to say no to, and it's hard to remember to be mad at her, no matter how badly she treats people. She makes complete strangers want to give her the shirt off their backs because her smile makes them feel special." Olivia scowled. "I was no exception, obviously. No one's immune. Annalise Marbeck could start a cult if she wanted to."

Dr Blackwood snorted. "Well, she won't win me over. I eat cocky upstarts for breakfast. Just ask Sasha Volkov."

That was surprisingly comforting.

"Just remember, I'll be there as backup," she continued. "I'll be sitting in the foyer while you're at the reception desk. Just look over at me if you need to remember why we're here. Or to…break her spell." Dr Blackwood's lips quirked. "I promise she's nowhere near as powerful as you've built her up to be in your mind. You *can* do this. Never forget why you're here."

"I'm here because she used me." Olivia bit her lip.

"Used, abused, manipulated, and cheated on you." Dr Blackwood's eyes were cold as she added: "She needs payback. Focus on that. She *deserves* this."

"Right."

Dr Blackwood waited a beat, then smiled coolly. "Shall we unmask a villain?"

Olivia stood at the reception desk of Singh, Slater & Howard Legal Services, clutching a white cake box. "Hi," she began, trying to project confidence.

The receptionist held up a finger and said, "Mmm. I see."

Olivia blinked.

The woman was blonde and model-thin with raspberry-red lips pursed into a pout. Her eyes met Olivia's but seemed to stare right through her.

Olivia glanced helplessly over to the foyer, thirty feet away. Dr Blackwood was seated elegantly on a leather two-piece sofa, apparently studying a *GQ Australia* magazine, except Olivia could feel her dark gaze over the top of the Liam Hemsworth cover.

"I'll be sure to tell Mr Singh you called. Thank you." The receptionist tapped her ear.

Oh. Right. Wireless phone thingies.

Swallowing nervously, Olivia patted the cake box. "I have a delivery from Love Muffins for Annalise Marbeck."

"Just leave it here," the receptionist said, flicking her eyes to the box and away again.

Okay, that was the first time someone had had absolutely no reaction to Olivia's company name. Like, not even a flicker of a smirk at Love Muffins?

"Would you like to see it?" Olivia asked a little too forcefully as nervousness kicked in.

"Why would I?" Her tone was as bored as it could be before crossing over into rude.

What? She's supposed to want to see it!

The receptionist lifted her finger and tapped a keyboard, then her desk phone, then her ear again. "Ms Marbeck, I have a cake delivery in Reception for you from a…Love Muffin?"

"Love Muffins," Olivia corrected by rote before suddenly realising her ex was being summoned to Reception. Annalise would be here. *Right here!*

Sweat slicked her palms. She shot a panicked glance to Dr Blackwood, who had lowered Liam Hemsworth a little, observing intently.

"Love Muffins," the receptionist corrected. She tapped her ear again and looked at Olivia. "Ms Marbeck will be right down."

"I have to show you my cake!" Olivia blurted just as the lift dinged.

A trio of men in smart suits and big lawyer energy disgorged from the steel box, headed for the exit.

"You really don't have—" the receptionist began as Olivia flipped the box open anyway, "—to."

The lettering was plainly visible: *You owe me $32,000. Pay up.*

The receptionist glanced at it for a moment, murmured, "uh-huh", then turned back to her computer and resumed typing.

What the hell? Who wouldn't react to that? Olivia's gaze flicked helplessly between the cake and the receptionist, wondering what to do now.

"Whoa!" boomed a masculine voice suddenly beside her. "Nice cake!"

She turned, startled. It was one of the lawyer bros from the lift, who'd stopped in his tracks to read the words on the cake. Then he laughed. "Who's that for?"

Just then the lift dinged again. The doors slid open. And there she was… Annalise.

A cold shiver ran through Olivia. So poised. She wore her light brown hair in a swirled, newsreader bob that made her look older. Her conservative navy skirt suit was paired with glinting gold jewellery at her throat and de-signer six-inch heels. She looked a million bucks, especially when she walked with that sultry hip sway. Did she do that for Olivia? Showing her what she was missing out on? Or was this for the whole world to enjoy?

"It's for Annalise Marbeck," Olivia croaked out to the man, not taking her eyes off her approaching ex. Christ, even now the woman's smooth, confident, head-bitch-in-charge aura made Olivia's breath catch. Annalise had looked like that when she was a student too, as if she owned the place.

Annalise neared them, all smiles and oozing her trademark, *you* wish *you were me* persona, obviously anticipating a free wedding cake or a sample of one at the very least.

The smile dropped the moment she saw the iced words. Darkness edged her narrowing grey eyes, and her crimson mouth pressed into a thin line of displeasure. Annalise slid the lawyer bro a wary look.

"It's fucking genius," he proclaimed, eyeing them all, pointing at the cake. "Genius!"

It was? Olivia stared at him in confusion.

He whipped out a phone and took a photo. "Shit, I know who'll love this."

"Genius?" Annalise prodded.

"Yeah. Great way to think outside the box, Annalise. I presume you've got a client with a problem getting money out of someone? It's really creative ordering this!" He shook his head in awe. "Debt collecting in cake form. Just brilliant."

He glanced at Olivia's tomato-red button pin. "I guess that's why you're wearing that? *Bake it Happen*? Great niche marketing! Serious kudos. You're working it."

The man left, still shaking his head, and called over his shoulder: "Hope you get 'em to cough up the dough! You deserve it with that stunt."

Olivia's jaw clenched. Why hadn't she put Annalise's name on the cake!

"Oh dear," Annalise said softly into her ear. "So sorry to disappoint." Her knowing eyes remained sharp on the receptionist, who was typing away and ignoring everything. "It seems your clever little bid to embarrass me has failed spectacularly."

Olivia slumped before she remembered this was only round one. "Next time, I'll be sure to write 'Annalise Marbeck owes me $32,040. That extra forty will be the cost of this cake and the next added in."

"There will *be* no next time." Annalise smiled her most engaging smile, the one that people would sign away their life savings for. The one that had done in Olivia so often. Then she leaned in, close enough for Olivia to smell her Armani perfume and see the smoothness of the delicate, movie-star skin at her throat. It was so confusing.

The alluring scent swamped Olivia with memories of kissing that swan-like neck and finding Annalise's pulse points. She used to love that she could make aloof Annalise scream. Of course, it was the same soft neck her boss, Joe, had been taking advantage of too. And Olivia was quite sure Annalise found his neck extra alluring these days, given he now owned a whole string of bakeries across Melbourne and was richer than sin.

"You can't stop me doing this," Olivia said quickly, but it was weird how her voice did an unconvincing wobble.

"Oh, Olivia, I most certainly can." Her voice was that same low, throaty, assured tone that always sounded like she'd stepped out of a cosmetic commercial after assuring women she knew them better than they knew themselves. "I'll just explain to our receptionist how I have a stalker problem and that any deliveries of cakes to me are to go straight in the bin. I mean, what if they were...*poisoned*." She gave her sculpted eyebrows a comical arch and her crimson lips curled into an intoxicating smile.

Even though she'd just been mentioned, the receptionist typed on, seemingly oblivious, occasionally tapping the piece in her ear. Amazing. And, yes, Olivia could see how this particular receptionist would obey without question any order given.

Annalise shot Olivia a triumphant look.

"How do you live with yourself?" Olivia muttered in defeat.

"Very well," Annalise replied, eyes lit with victory. "So very, *very* well. Joe is an excellent provider, and, oh my, the things he can do in the bedroom. I've upgraded on every level. You do understand you were my piece of rough trade, don't you? A little walk on the wrong side of the tracks while I was bored and needing a diversion? You were never a serious contender for my affections. I mean," she leaned right into Olivia's space and murmured in her ear, "look at you...my sweet, gullible, baby dyke, always wearing those style-challenged flannels and smelling of muffins. And now look at me." Her smile was mocking. "You had to know you were never in my league."

Olivia stumbled back, away from that taunting mouth and confusingly alluring scent, feeling as if she'd been gut punched. Humiliation and anger threatened to drown her. Of all the nasty...*mean*...things to say. The cruelty. How unnecessary. Yes, of course she'd understood later Annalise had been after her money. But she'd had the conceit to believe the woman had also enjoyed being with Olivia. Apparently, she'd just been *bored*? Olivia had been what—someone to toy with between draining Olivia's bank account dry?

Olivia grasped her stomach and tried to think of a powerful retort, even as tears of embarrassment filled her eyes. She blinked them away with fury. "Well, I *won't* be making your wedding cake!"

"Yes, I *did* get that," Annalise purred. "Thanks for the heads-up." A speculative gleam appeared. "You know, you could have really screwed me over by agreeing to do it and never delivering it, right? Or baking up something laced with a laxative? Everyone would have assumed it was the chicken. It's *always* the chicken. But aren't you lovely?" She chuckled. "You just spared my caterers a lawsuit over their 'dodgy' chicken."

Olivia couldn't believe her ears. Who would be so cruel or unethical as to mess with a bride on their wedding day? What monster would do that?

Annalise would.

"I love that the thought never even occurred to you," Annalise said. "But, then, you always were so unbelievably naive. My best advice, dear harmless, hopeless Olivia, is to stay out of the payback business. You're *terrible* at it." She patted Olivia's cheek dismissively. "Now, I have work to do. You can run along." She flicked a glance at the cake. "And thanks for the laugh."

With that, Annalise slapped the lid closed on the box and dropped it into the bin next to the desk.

The furiously typing receptionist didn't so much as twitch at the sudden *thunk*.

Incredible.

Annalise swirled away, back to the elevators, the picture of cool elegance. Even after they whooshed her away, Olivia couldn't move. Her cheeks were an inferno and probably matched her hair.

A reassuring warmth was suddenly beside her, but Olivia was too afraid to look at Dr Blackwood. What must she think? She'd probably heard most of that. The insults. The mockery. She'd have seen Olivia stand there and take it too. Impotent and useless. She hung her head.

Dr Blackwood tugged her arm. "Come on," she said softly, and it was the gentlest Olivia had ever heard her. "Not here."

Olivia found herself a few minutes later sitting in her van, staring out at the road in front of her, unmoving.

"I'm sorry," Dr Blackwood said quietly, regret lacing her tone.

"For what? Witnessing that car crash? For her telling me there was never an *us*? Apparently, I was just a naive, trusting bit of *rough trade* providing her with a diversion while she systematically ripped me off?"

"I'm sorry for not stepping in before she said those things." Dr Blackwood inhaled. "And I'm sorry I sat there, unable to think of a single biting thing to wipe the smirk off her smug face. That is an experience I'm greatly unaccustomed to. Clever insults come naturally to me—you may have noticed. But with her…" Dr Blackwood shook her head. "I understand what you mean now by the power of her personality." She sounded so annoyed with herself. "Olivia, I fear I've failed as a henchperson. I provided no backup."

Olivia turned to properly look at her, surprised by the frustration in Dr Blackwood's voice. "This isn't your fault."

"I came up with our plan. I was so sure the receptionist would be a source of gossip. She wasn't. I was so sure we could manipulate a woman you'd already warned me repeatedly was clever and cunning. She was exactly as you said. Perhaps you didn't quite convey just how charismatic she is. How strong a force she is."

"Yeah, well, I wouldn't have given all my savings to someone dull and unaffecting, now, would I?"

"No. I suppose not. I do understand how she enamoured you so well. A fly in a spider's web comes to mind."

Olivia winced. "I'm a fly, am I?"

"Yes. And I'd rather be you than her any day of the week."

"Yeah, right." Olivia snorted at the lie.

"I'm serious. At the end of the day, she will always be cruel and manipulative. And you will always be…you."

"And what's that?"

"Decent. Good. Unaccountably kind."

Olivia inhaled in surprise. Dr Blackwood almost sounded…fond of her. But that couldn't be right, could it?

"I did hear what she said about her upgrading from you to Joe." Dr Blackwood's gaze bored into her. "Olivia, no one deserves that. Besides, she was lying. If you really were beneath her notice, she wouldn't have bothered engaging you at all beyond tossing out the cake and leaving. I think you do affect her in some personal way, so much so that she had to go out of her way to hurt you for it."

"Or she's just a nasty piece of work and hurt me because she could." Olivia's cheeks bloomed. "But thank you," she murmured.

Dr Blackwood nodded tightly, breaking their gazes, and glancing away.

"I think she was right about one thing," Olivia said after a few moments. "I'm terrible at payback."

"We're still new at this." Dr Blackwood blew out a long breath. "However, it occurred to me after this morning that I'm not the whiz at vengeance planning I thought I would be. I assumed that two competent, intelligent women could take care of problematic exes with ease. Just a bit of clever planning and...*done*." She scowled. "Apparently not."

"You think I'm competent and intelligent?" Olivia asked in surprise.

Dr Blackwood snorted and looked about to say something dismissive—as was her way. But she hesitated and instead said: "Well, obviously. Look at how you turned your life around after that schemer took all your money. Now you have a delicious range of award-winning goods that you supply all over Melbourne. That takes competence and intelligence, wouldn't you say?"

"Delicious?" Olivia perked up. "Wait, you've tried my muffins?"

Dr Blackwood rolled her eyes. "Who stocks a product in their store untested?"

"I assumed you relied on the reviews." A thought suddenly occurred. "Did you actually eat the Parma Sutra I gave you that day at the park?"

Dr Blackwood looked away again as a pink tinge slowly climbed up her neck.

"Oh my God, you did!"

"There was so much going on," Dr Blackwood suggested airily. "Penguin pursuits and the like. Who can remember the small things?"

"You SO did!"

Dr Blackwood huffed. "Fine! I was hungry; it was there. Happy now?"

"Yeah." Olivia leaned back and smiled. "I really am. Thank you."

"Mmmph." Dr Blackwood couldn't entirely keep a trace of amusement from her voice. "You know, I might have just said that to improve your mood."

"Uh-huh." Olivia knew she was now beaming.

"Just don't let it go to your head. I can barely remember eating the thing."

Olivia gave Dr Blackwood a soft look. "Thank you," she repeated. Without thinking, she leaned across and grabbed Dr Blackwood's hand, giving it a squeeze.

"Nothing to thank me for," Dr Blackwood said gruffly. She inhaled and looked down at their commingled fingers. Surprise flickered across her face.

Tingles of awareness shot up Olivia's fingers, and she retracted them quickly, shocked at the intensity of how it felt to touch her. God, what must the other woman think of her for randomly grabbing her hand in the first place, then jerking back?

Dr Blackwood stared at her own now-empty hand for a beat. "Are we ever getting out of here? I can feel the smarminess of Singh, Slater & Howard infecting me even being near it." She sniffed pointedly and glanced around the Love Muffins van. "Although apparently, my standards have been slipping lately." The edges of her lips threatened a smile.

Olivia grinned. "Don't worry, your reputation is safe. I'll tell no one you ever set foot inside my van."

"See that you don't." Dr Blackwood's dark brown eyes crinkled—had they always been so beautiful?—and right then, Olivia felt okay. Despite their mission being an absolute screw up from start to finish. Despite Annalise treating her like a boot scraping. Despite everything.

How…unexpected.

Thursday, March 26
Day 1146 post H

Sunset: *7.22pm*

Temp: *13.7C-19.8C*

Rain: *0mm*

Drink: *Raidis Estate "Cheeky Goat" Pinot Gris 2019. Two glasses. Ridiculous name, light taste. Acceptable.*

Reading: Non-fiction—*JALIA, Vol 69, issue 1. "Systematic Searching: Practical Ideas for Improving Results." Paper suggests using social media as a "source of evidence for both information gathering and information retrieval". Over my dead body will social media ever be a source of anything but a sneer and a headache.*

Fiction—*Mullumbimby (Melissa Lucashenko). Unusual and authentic Indigenous woman's story. Curiously, the author used third-person POV almost like a first-person unreliable narrator. Not sure if I approve or not. Will revisit later.*

General Observations: *The late neighbour's cat persists in yowling if not promptly fed, but otherwise, peace has descended at last. I have purchased assorted toys, trays, and beds that internet animal experts inform me are essential for a mature cat's wellbeing.*

I keep finding cat hair in the unlikeliest places. How did that creature deposit hair inside my kettle?

Note to self: get a vet check. This much moulting cannot possibly be normal.

One positive: my newest acquisition appreciates my evening ritual of sitting on the balcony while I update my diary and enjoy a wine. The animal seems to have pronounced my lap acceptable and purrs like a jackhammer.

I've found the feline's evening presence not too terrible. The creature was a balm after the day I had.

I'm left to wonder yet again about the state of my mental acuity. Today, Olivia faced her demons in the shape of the scheming, slippery Annalise Marbeck and what did I do? Nothing. I remained a silent witness to a verbal mugging.

During the entire encounter, I was struck by two things: one, how much I loathed someone I didn't even know. I had this urge to throttle Annalise for the way she hurt Olivia so casually. And two, how overwhelming that woman was. Oh, I've met plenty of powerful, attractive people in my time; hell, I grew up with the apex predator of academics. But Annalise Marbeck exudes a charisma the likes of which I've never seen before. Even I felt drawn to her...or more like, frozen by her, caught up in her sticky web. How can one so horrific be also so alluring?

I was appalled at myself for even noticing her surface attractiveness despite not wishing to. It was unnerving.

So transfixed was I by the energy and confidence Annalise exudes, I did absolutely nothing. I simply sat there and waited for Olivia to deal with her potent demon.

But she didn't do that, did she? She was crushed by a vastly superior opponent.

And I did nothing.

It reminded me that the sad truth about humans, upon learning someone has been scammed, is to immediately think of all the reasons why it would never happen to them. I'm no different. I admit I judged Olivia somewhat for her "failing". I knew with such certainty that I'd be incapable of being hoodwinked into paying off a romantic partner's debts just because they batted their eyelashes at me.

But with a personality as strong as Annalise's, with that overwhelming charisma and confident awareness of her power—combined with promises convincingly made—it would take a hardcore cynic to be unmoved.

Olivia is no cynic.

Now I'm left to wonder if, in her place, how I'd fare if charming Annalise Marbeck had turned her "superpowers" on me when I was in my early twenties. The answer is troubling. I'm disturbed at the feeling it provokes. Then again, no one likes facing the suspicion they're not as strong as they assumed.

I considered resigning my henchperson position over my inexcusable inaction. But who would be there to look out for Olivia? She needs someone in her corner. I know only too well how it feels to stand alone against enemies. I suspect it's why I volunteered for this ridiculous job in the first place.

Unrelated note: I can't believe I confessed to eating that Parma Sutra muffin. At this rate, Olivia will worm all my secrets out of me, and then where will I be? I'm jesting, of course, but part of me wonders: how did she do that?

Somehow, she just looked at me, so filled with gratitude and happiness at my simple admission that I'd enjoyed her muffin. I was helpless to refuse her the truth. Then she seized hold of my hand—a move that shocked me because no one touches me. She dropped it as soon as she came to her senses, but it had felt nice—genuinely—to the point of confusion.

I digress. The solution for dealing with Olivia's own apparent superpower over me seems rather simple: don't do any favours that would result in her feeling grateful.

(I'm not entirely sure if I'm joking. Further analysis required.)

PS: Olivia loves H's peacock. Is it proof she has no taste? On that, I really am joking now.

Oh, how Helen would love Olivia. She'd probably sit back, sipping a vodka and lime and laughing her head off while I try to cope with the cyclone of absurdity that is one Olivia Roberts.

CHAPTER 13

REVENGE IS A DISH BEST SERVED BOLD

DAYS AFTER THE AWFUL FAILURE to bring Annalise to account, Olivia had been granted access to Dr Blackwood's office—actual, proper, not-a-mistake access to her inner sanctum. When it had first happened—a little tilt of the head indicating Olivia should follow—Olivia had glanced over her shoulder to check Dr Blackwood hadn't meant someone else.

The other woman caught Olivia's furtive glance. "Who else would I be inviting in to strategise on how to get access to Tina?" she asked dryly. "My sales assistant or my barista?"

Good point. Olivia's cheeks flamed. Still, she felt like the anointed one and smiled in pleasure.

"Let's get to work," Dr Blackwood said briskly, settling into her chair and flipping open a notepad.

Olivia was more focused on the room, with its tasteful, austere décor, its big, slatted-timber blind, and Quincy* the peacock. (*Not its actual name.)

This whole space felt lived in, fully inhabited by its secretive owner. Every nook had something in it, as if it had been carefully assessed to be the exact spot for that book or this folder or some box.

The smell was divine—bringing to mind venerable old libraries, vanilla, and fragile paper. That faint aroma probably came from the large pile of ancient tomes in one corner, their spines faded and peeling and looking over a century old. Olivia couldn't make out their titles. Yet, for all the ancient, timeworn, and historic feel radiating from the room, there wasn't a speck of dust anywhere.

"What is a day in Tina's life like?"

Olivia blinked and returned her focus to Dr Blackwood.

"Sad." Huh. Olivia had said that without thinking. "But that's how she likes it, I guess." She wondered if that were true. Whether Tina did like her life as it was.

Dr Blackwood arched a curious eyebrow.

Olivia explained how Tina was unemployed aside from her popular YouTube make-up tutorials, had few friends since she'd stolen from all of them, and now rarely left her luxury apartment.

Food was delivered to her regularly, and the security guard on the ground floor would drop it off in person rather than allow a stranger up to the restricted-access penthouse floor.

While Tina occasionally used to go out at night to "hang out with her cousin"—which Olivia now knew was her code for scoring drugs—she wasn't sure if she still did. Olivia wasn't sure if she really even had a cousin. Either way, it meant Tina had no set schedule. Even her workouts were done in her apartment building's basement gym. If not for Tina's rear balcony, she'd be severely vitamin D deprived. As it was, she was plenty pale already.

"Just our luck," Dr Blackwood noted, dropping her pen back to her notepad with a frustrated plop when Olivia finished her rundown. "You dated a shut-in."

"Don't call her that," Olivia said. "Some people just don't like socialising. Take you, for instance."

Dr Blackwood's genial expression instantly darkened. "Excuse me?"

Uh-oh. "Sorry. Nothing."

"It was clearly something if you felt the need to say it." She folded her arms and let loose a death glare.

Double uh-oh. "Um," Olivia said hastily, "it's just an impression I get. Aside from the bookstore, you don't talk about any other interests. Like, ever."

"And so, based on nothing at all, you've decided I have no life," Dr Blackwood said dangerously. "Tell me, other than baking, book club, and destroying your exes—the latter being only a recent development—do *you* ever go out socially? Have friends over? Entertain?"

Olivia lifted her hands in a sign of surrender. "Look, I didn't mean it that way, as a negative. Hell, if you want to stay home every night slugging back craft beers while you finish the latest Tom Clancy, I'm hardly one to judge. I just really hate the word *shut-in*. It's such a mean term. And I happened to have really enjoyed that Tina was a homebody. She never demanded we try a new club every night or, I don't know, go camping." She wrinkled her nose. "I'm not built for that. Most of the time we just hung out at my place."

Dr Blackwood lost her defensive air. "Well." She retrieved her pen. "The last time I went camping, I was five. The outdoorsy gene bypassed me entirely as well. I'll swap the craft beer for a good red and watching the sunset from my balcony every night. But I wouldn't be caught dead with the latest Tom Clancy. What will it take for you to develop better taste in books?"

She sounded so aggrieved and yet *not,* judging by those dancing eyes, as if making fun of Olivia's book taste constituted actual entertainment.

"Oh my God," Olivia said in wonder. "I finally get it."

"You get what?" Dr Blackwood asked suspiciously.

"You weren't lying, were you? When you applied for the henchperson job. You really *are* bored at work."

Dr Blackwood's eyes narrowed as if deciding whether to start another round of bickering. "I think," she said instead, "we need to work out how to get access to your *homebody* ex." There was no denial.

"Wouldn't an expert in criminals, convicts, and bushrangers like you find all their dreams had come true running a bookstore on that exact theme?" Olivia asked, puzzled.

"You'd think that, wouldn't you," Dr Blackwood said with a tired sigh. "I certainly did."

Olivia detected her ruefulness. "Did the reality not match the dream?" she ventured.

Dr Blackwood's expression turned sour. "Something like that."

"I'm...sorry."

"I wouldn't mind how it worked out except for..." She faltered and flicked a glance at Olivia. "Well, I didn't fully appreciate that there would be *customers* to take into account," she said, her lip curling in derision.

"*Nooo!*" Olivia teased.

"Who all kept wanting to talk to *me*," she added for clarity. "And they're just so dim-witted half the time with their requests and inane comments.

I had to hire a sales assistant to deal with them because my refusal to sell books to the unworthy was making my losses mount."

Oh hell. Olivia could see it now. Margaret Blackwood throwing out some poor customer who'd made some ignorant, unscientific comment she could not abide.

Dr Blackwood shook her head. "I once had some know-it-all try to tell me that Ned Kelly wore armour made of *tin*. He actually argued with me when I explained it was made from the iron mouldboards of ploughs donated by farmers sympathetic to his cause. As if tin could stop a bullet."

She sniffed. "I politely offered to prove he was wrong by firing a bullet at him while he was wearing a tin chest plate. That resulted in him scuttling off like a diseased cockroach while calling me a psycho. Honestly, some people are so difficult."

Olivia snickered.

"I also hadn't fully realised how much Australians are obsessed with Ned Kelly, as if he's the only bushranger in our history. Do you know how many times I've been asked if I sell Ned Kelly posters? Or asked why I'd name my bookstore after some 'unknown rando' when I could have called it Ned Kelly's Bookstore?" She ground her jaw. "Honestly, I've half a mind to write a biography." Her eyes gleamed. "I'd call it *Why Bushranger Mary Ann Bugg Is Better Than Buckethead.* Subtitle: *Ned Kelly's An Overrated Son of A Bitch.*"

Olivia burst into laughter. "You should do it. You have all the right credentials."

"I do, don't I?" Dr Blackwood's voice was filled with amusement. "Then, anytime someone comes into the store asking about Ned Kelly merchandise, I'll just point them to my display of books and tap the title subheading."

"A sound plan," Olivia said. "But speaking of plans, we really do need to sort out Tina."

"Yes." Dr Blackwood sighed. "Sorry to be diverted."

"I'm not. That was too much fun. I love it when you go off on your rants."

The other woman lifted an astonished eyebrow. "I'm fairly sure you're the only one."

Their eyes met and held for a few moments. And that was when Olivia felt it again. It was the same as that time Dr Blackwood had mentioned her mother: a sense of connection, of being in on a joke that no one else shared.

Then it was gone.

Dr Blackwood said: "Let's do a stake-out. Didn't you say that sometimes Tina would go to her local coffee house on a Saturday to get some special blend of coffee beans?"

Olivia shrugged. "Yeah. It's about the only thing she can't get delivered. But it was only every now and then. Always on a Saturday, but there was no pattern as to which one."

"All right." Dr Margaret opened her calendar. "Is this coming Saturday suitable for trying our luck?"

Flicking through her plans mentally, Olivia realised she had none. As usual. Maybe Dr Blackwood's point about her having a limited social life was closer to the mark than Olivia appreciated. "Yes."

"And if we're successful and see her come out of her building, what then?"

"I need answers on Trip first. Vengeance can come second." Olivia's shoulders slumped. "I miss him. I've been calling the police station every other day to see if they'll follow up on the theft. They said they sent a constable to visit her and make inquiries but that Tina was out. Which, given her homebody lifestyle, made me think they're lying. I suggested that the constable might not have actually gone up to her door, and they got really snotty. They told me to stop calling and that they were *looking into it*. Then they hung up."

"I'm sorry." Dr Blackwood seemed sincere.

"Thanks. You know how it feels." Olivia's eyes darted to the peacock. "I'm sure you'd miss Quincy if someone took him."

"That's not its name," Dr Blackwood said evenly.

"Right." Olivia grinned unrepentantly, just as her phone rang. She answered: "Olivia Roberts."

"Hi, it's Geoffrey Hart from the *Sunday Herald Sun*," came a man's deep voice. "Is this the owner of Love Muffins?"

"Uh, yeah?" Olivia pressed the speaker button and lay her phone down on the desk. "Why does the *Sunday Herald Sun* want to talk to me?"

"Well, I write the *Weird About Town* column—you know, quirky or funny stuff around Melbourne—and I got a tip-off from a friend that you baked a cake for a debt collection? He sent me a photo of the cake. That's a hell of a thing!" He laughed. "I'm wondering if you can tell me more? Who it was for, how it came about? Is this a sideline for you? Baked demands for payments?"

Silence fell. Olivia stared at the phone in astonishment, then glanced up at Dr Blackwood. Her expression was mischievous. Dr Blackwood scribbled a note and held it up.

Get his info, say you're busy & will get back to him.

Olivia nodded and did so. She put her phone away. "So that lawyer guy in Annalise's foyer must know this reporter."

"So it seems." Dr Blackwood's expression was cool and deadly. Then her eyes crinkled. "I have an idea. And it will kill two atrocious birds with one stone."

She outlined her plan, and Olivia's eyes went wide. "That's—I mean it's—um…audacious?"

"Revenge is a dish best served bold." Dr Blackwood smirked. "You know, that saying would look good on a button." She pointedly looked at Olivia's *Ryes and Shine* pin.

"Um, my buttons are supposed to be joyful and uplifting," Olivia protested. "Motivational?"

"You don't find wreaking revenge boldly on someone who deserves it to be *highly* motivational?" Dr Blackwood purred, her tone laced with anticipation. And then she smiled, wide and full.

And damn if that didn't do funny things to Olivia's insides.

Two hours and much diligent work later, Olivia's anxious gaze met Dr Blackwood's where she sat behind her desk. The call, on speaker, connected.

To Olivia's surprise, Annalise picked up on the second ring.

"Are you a glutton for punishment?" came her ex's mocking tones. "Back for round two? Let me guess, you finally thought of a killer comeback you wish you'd said?"

"Actually, I thought I'd give you the heads-up on something," Olivia said. "I just had a call from Geoffrey Hart from the *Sunday Herald Sun*. He writes the *Weird—*"

"—*About Town* column," Annalise cut in. "Yes, I know it."

"The lawyer guy in your foyer who thought my cake was 'genius'? He called the reporter and sent a photo. Now I'm being asked about a story on debt collection via baked goods. With a full explanation of exactly why I made the cake. Naming names, outlining the background behind the cake, all of that."

There was a sharp inhalation. "What did you tell him?" Annalise's voice was tight now.

"I said I'd call him back. I thought we should talk first."

A beat passed, and then came the strangled question: "What do you want?"

"A bank deposit of $32,020."

"I can't just…"

"And one free lawyer letter."

"A free… To whom? Why?"

"I want you to demand my ex-boyfriend return my Torana. I bought it. It's mine. I have the paperwork. I want it back." Irritation at all the ways her various exes had taken advantage of her flooded her, making her voice sharp.

"Well, I can do that. But I don't have thirty-two grand lying around! I have a wedding to plan!"

"Maybe cut a few stops off the honeymoon, then," Olivia said, a rush of daring filling her. Because of course Annalise's honeymoon would be lavish—she had never grasped the concept of understated.

"Olivia…" And this time, her tone was pure honey. Oh, Annalise could turn on the charm when she wanted. "I know I said some things earlier, and I'm sorry if I was a little rude. You must understand my point of view: I was just so excited at the thought I might be getting a wedding cake from you, and instead it was…that *thing*."

Olivia said nothing. Dr Blackwood's gaze narrowed.

"And I'm aware, in the past, you did give me a lot of money…"

"Loan. It was a loan. You said you'd pay it back. I have Kelly who witnessed that at least once."

"Fine. *Loan*." She massaged the word as if it were nothing. "But no one has thirty-two grand just lying around."

"Thirty-two thousand and twenty," Olivia corrected. "The cake you threw out wasn't free. And I'll be happy to draw up a payment plan, but if you miss even one payment, I will be calling Geoffrey Hart back to explain that photo in detail."

Silence fell.

"Come on, Olivia, be fair," Annalise protested. "I'll get your car back for you, and I can pay you fifteen. Thirty is beyond me right now."

"Thirty-*two* thousand *and* twenty, *and* you get my Torana back." Olivia's heart was racing at her own audacity. Was this really her? She felt so bold. "I'll drop the twenty bucks if you get my car back in a week."

"That's not a compromise! It's close to extortion!"

"I never said I'd compromise. And I'm only asking for exactly what you owe me. What you promised me. You've had years to do right by me, and you've just ignored me like it didn't happen."

"Olivia, that's unfair!" A note of panic had crept into Annalise's voice now.

"No. I'm done waiting for you to develop a conscience. If you fight me on this, I'll also ask for interest. And if you ignore me like last time, I'll take you to court. That'll be fun, won't it? Having everyone at work know what you've done? And for the cherry on top, I'll make sure to brief that journalist too, just so he can cover his debt collection via cake story from every angle."

Dr Blackwood's dark eyes were burning into Olivia, radiating with approval. Having her respect filled Olivia with warmth and pride; she could move mountains right now. Was this how everyone else felt every day? Demanding what they deserved and getting it? It was addictive.

"Fine," came a strangled voice down the phone.

Olivia didn't speak she was so shocked.

"FINE." Annalise ground out the word louder. "I'll pay you."

"Good." Olivia tapped on her phone. "I've just emailed you an agreement to sign, outlining what we've discussed and the late-fee penalties if you don't meet all the terms. You'll also find the information about the car I want back, proof I own it, and my ex-boyfriend's contact details."

Now a silence dragged out for half a minute. "Well, well, haven't you changed?" Annalise drawled the words, half annoyed, half impressed. There was a ping noise. Another silence. Then: "I've received your email. I'll send the contract back, signed, shortly."

"Good," Olivia said. "Don't forget to CC me a copy of any of your emails with Martin."

"You want them CC'd?" Annalise queried. "Not blind copied?"

"Yes. I'd like him to know I'm happy to be screwing him over. He seemed to doubt my sincerity at follow-through last time we spoke."

This time, the silence drew out even longer. "You are *not* the woman I remember," she muttered. "I'll email the little prick today. All right?"

"Perfect."

"Well, then," Annalise said, "that's settled. Now kindly fuck off." She spoke so sweetly, as if she'd just thanked a host for a lovely dinner. Then she hung up.

Olivia stared at her phone in surprise. "That…went better than expected. In fact, I thought she'd put up a bigger fight."

"Never underestimate fear as a motivator," Dr Blackwood said. Her eyes were warm and bright as she added: "That was delicious. You were utterly perfect." Her voice was so approving.

Oh my God. Olivia's stomach did a flip and a half pike. In the face of all that unexpected appreciation, her body had apparently briefly forgotten that she found Dr Blackwood entirely too smug and condescending.

Did she, though? Or did she find it kind of sexy now? Especially getting those peeks behind stern Dr Blackwood's mask?

An hour later, Olivia was copied into a sharp, threatening email to Martin from Singh, Slater & Howard demanding her car back or police would be called.

While Olivia hadn't seen too many lawyer's letters in her time, she could tell this one was especially nasty. It seemed Annalise was taking her bad mood out on Martin.

Within two hours, Olivia's Torana was parked outside Mary Bugg's, and Martin threw the keys at her head.

She side-stepped and caught them easily. Olivia was tempted to ask how he knew she'd be here. Had he seen her van around the back? Or had he taken a punt, given how often she hung out here? It's funny how she'd never really thought about how much Mary Bugg's had become her second home lately.

"Fuck you, you vindictive little cunt!" Martin screamed to her—and half the street—before he took off on foot. He paused only to kick the side of the orange car he'd claimed to love so much.

Apparently, it really had been all about the cachet for him, having a collectible in his possession.

Dr Blackwood appeared by her side, wearing a pensive expression. "Are you okay? That idiot has quite the mouth on him."

"Yeah, fine." She pocketed her keys and then peered inside the windows of her old car. It all looked in order. "I half expected him to dump a bucket of snakes in here or something."

"Just to be on the safe side, why don't you get it detailed and mechanically inspected before you drive it," Dr Blackwood suggested. "In case his imagination is as good as yours was when we were brainstorming his vengeance."

"He has the imagination of a goldfish." Olivia grinned. "And I didn't really mean it when I said we should cut his brakes."

Dr Blackwood cocked an eyebrow. "You know, if you want him charged for damaging your property, my security camera would have caught that kick." She pointed up to the discreet security device above the door.

"No. I'll keep that in reserve for now. But it's nice that, for once, I'm the one who gets to choose how this all plays out. I like that it's in my control now."

"Mmm," Dr Blackwood said. "Well, on the subject of cars, can we opt for my Jag for Saturday's stake-out? I refuse to while away the hours in anything orange or something smelling of stale baked goods."

Olivia elbowed her lightly in the ribs. "This again? I'll have you know my baked goods aren't stale."

Dr Blackwood merely smirked. "My car it is, then."

"You're impossible."

"So I've been told. By the way, if you had to name a black cat, what would you call it?"

Olivia stared at her, utterly mystified.

That evening, Olivia emailed Dr Blackwood a shortlist of her very best black cat names. It had taken a while to come up with them. Her favourite was the perfect name for a cat associated with a woman who looked like a goth-librarian Morticia Addams.

Finally, assured she'd passed the woman's mysterious test, she went to bed feeling oddly satisfied.

Thursday, March 31

Sunset: *7.15pm*

Temp: *12.2C-21.4C*

Rain: *0mm*

Drink: *Old Vine Barossa Valley shiraz—one glass. It turns out I'm not in the mood for this one. Another night.*

Reading: Non-fiction—JALIA, *Vol 69, issue 1. "Building Political Support for Library Funding." Some things never change. I don't miss the politics or "working the room" for benefactors.*

Fiction—The Other Side of Beautiful *(Kim Lock). An agoraphobic Australian doctor with PTSD takes an unplanned road trip and faces her fears. The protag's journey back to "normal" sticks with me. I related a little too well to burying oneself after a tragedy and putting distance between you and the world. Not engaging, not connecting, is comforting.*

The timing of having read this just when Olivia accused me of having no life is not lost on me. My defensive hackles went straight up. But...truth hurts. I admit that, like the fictitious Dr Mercy Blain, I'm also crawling—just as involuntarily—slowly back into the light.

That thought fills me with trepidation. Perhaps it's not before time, though. Maybe I should stop avoiding people to the extent I do. Maybe I should stop marking every day of Helen's passing.

General Observations: *Did we just have a win? Another one?*

Maybe we are better at vengeance planning than I thought. No, that's not honest. It was entirely luck. We fluked a win because a passing stranger who got the wrong end of the stick shared a photo with a journalist. Without that random individual, we'd have failed comprehensively.

Next time, I must pay closer attention to Olivia's analyses of her exes. She tried to tell me Annalise was clever, sharp, and tricky. I assumed I would be able to challenge her if needed because I'm, quite frankly, masterful at beating people. My mother did not raise someone without a ruthless edge or a brutal tongue.

But occasionally, one meets a rival with skills in other areas. Annalise's devious and charismatic nature can distract, manipulate, and make an adversary lose focus. The result was she was especially dangerous as it wasn't anticipated. It was certainly a lesson.

Incidentally, Olivia is woeful at naming black cats. I did not ask for the best pun names. I wanted a regular name. She acted as if she were trying to pass a test. How mystifying.

First, she gave me Cilla. No, one must not sully a legend by giving their name to a cat.

Eightball is just insulting. Cats have dignity too.

I'm also not about to call "Satan" to her food bowl each night.

I'm rather partial to Wednesday, though. As in Addams. The character's attitude and unorthodox fashion choices were always exemplary. I'm just not sure why Olivia included a smiley face after that option. What is she suggesting?

Meanwhile, the veterinarian says my newest family member is an eight-year-old spayed, healthy female cat. She set up an account for me for regular check-ups. So I'm a mother at last. Maybe I should inform Monash University's venerated vice chancellor that she's a cat grandmother. I'm sure she'd appreciate that.

Postscript: I've acquired for young Emma Garrity a copy of Anne of Green Gables—*because how can any little redheaded girl never have read this? I'm fairly sure that's a crime of some sort. I've informed her she may discuss the characters or themes with me afterwards if she wishes. Naturally, I have no concern in this matter either way.*

CHAPTER 14

OF SNACKS, SPIES, AND STAKE-OUTS

IF YOU'RE GOING TO HAVE a stake-out in a car, Olivia decided nothing beat doing it in a Jaguar with tinted windows and heated reclining leather seats. Especially when the heavens had opened up in a miserable, constant downpour.

Olivia privately thought the weather would drive even the most sociable indoors, so it was unlikely Tina would brave it. But she found herself surprisingly reluctant to put off spending half a day with Margaret Blackwood.

What was that about?

She pushed the troublesome thought away and reviewed their surroundings.

They were parked outside Lonsdale Heartland Tower, Tina's apartment building, within easy view of the front doors. Olivia had brought two bags of snacks, mainly a cross-section of muffins and water bottles. Dr Blackwood had brought attitude and questions as to why they needed the food.

"Because we're going to be here awhile," Olivia had answered. "And I'm not going to miss my chance to confront Tina because I got low blood sugar and had to rush off to find food. Nor do I want to brave that rain just for a snack."

Dr Blackwood had sighed at that and reclined her seat, replacing her usual serious-looking nerd glasses with dark sunglasses. Honestly, she looked like a fictional super spy.

Olivia stared so long and so hard, with so much appreciation, she forgot Dr Blackwood could actually see her from behind the black lenses.

"What?" Dr Blackwood murmured.

"Nothing. I mean, you look cool."

"Don't I always?" She sounded amused now.

Well, Olivia had to concede that. "Yeah," she said grumpily. "I guess."

"You guess." Dr Blackwood's lips did that twitch around the edges that emerged when she was amusing the hell out of herself. "Get back to me when you're more decisive."

"You're hilarious."

"Thank you."

Olivia leaned forward and put the radio on, then changed the station three times as news, ads, or sporting results blared out. Finally, Dr Blackwood slapped her hand away and chose a USB setting. Soft music began to play. Not classical…it was more… What was it, exactly?

"World music," Dr Blackwood explained without being asked. "This track's from the Middle East."

Was that a horse whinnying?

Dr Blackwood skipped tracks. Pipes and monk chants started up.

"I really thought you'd be into classical," Olivia said. "Aren't all librarians into sweet-old-lady music?"

"Just for that, I'll find my Otken album. That's a Siberian Indigenous folk band with a really unusual sound. It'll broaden your horizons." She leaned forward, fingers outstretched over a button.

"You know what? Silence works too." Olivia pressed the off button. "It's too early in the morning to have my horizons broadened."

"Suit yourself." Dr Blackwood didn't seem put out. She returned to her reclined position, still looking super-spy cool. Maybe it wasn't the sunnies so much as the black turtleneck and black slacks. Very Agent 99.

Silence fell. It was the awkward kind.

Then it fell some more.

"Want a muffin?" Olivia asked.

"No."

Five minutes passed.

"How about now?"

"Still no."

"I thought you liked my muffins."

"Not at eight-thirty in the morning." Dr Blackwood lowered her sunglasses a little to convey her incredulity over the top of them.

"Oh. Right."

"Maybe focus on the building, not my stomach." She glanced at Olivia's button pin. "Or do you always keep your *eyes on the pies?*"

Olivia didn't dignify that with a response. Her phone beeped with a message alert, and she opened it up to find an email from Annalise saying her money had been repaid. *Really?* She switched over to her bank account. Sure enough, thirty-two thousand dollars had been added to her balance. The depositor was not Annalise, though. It was Joe Hillsop, the old boss Annalise had cheated on Olivia with—now Annalise's fiancé.

She didn't know why she was surprised. *Of course* the scheming woman would get someone else to pay her debts. Did she ever pay for anything herself? But, still, making Joe cough up thirty-plus grand had to hurt her standing with him.

Olivia suspected she'd been right the first time: they'd be having a cut-price honeymoon…and probably a few fights about this. Maybe it was petty, but at that thought, Olivia couldn't help but smile.

She sent the journalist an email apologising for the delay in getting back to him and explaining she couldn't help him with his story due to customer confidentiality. She blind copied the email to Annalise.

Next, she debated sending Annalise some heartfelt email about how it wasn't naive to expect the best from those we love and that Olivia's only mistake was wasting her love on someone incapable of it.

"You're making a face."

Olivia turned. "Annalise just paid up."

"All of it?"

"Yes. Now I'm considering some biting, final farewell pointing out how I'm not a fool for loving someone. My only mistake was choosing her."

"No."

"No, that wasn't my mistake?"

"Yes, that was your mistake. No, don't send it. Someone like her? Not even acknowledging what she did will eat her far worse than anything else. If you send her anything at all, it should be two words: funds received. She'll hate that more than any impassioned appeal that she underestimated you."

Huh. "You're right." Olivia grinned, sent *funds received* and closed her phone. "Thank you."

"No need. I just know more than most what pisses off narcissists."

"Oh?" Olivia turned to look at her with interest. "Why?"

Dr Blackwood hesitated.

"Your mother?"

"Mmm." It was an acknowledgment, barely.

"That sucks." Olivia reclined her own seat a little so she was more in line with Dr Blackwood. "It's hard to know what's worse: a narcissistic mother or one who forgets you exist." She gave a rueful laugh. "My parents have been grey-nomadding all over Australia in a campervan for at least fifteen years. You'd think they'd be sick of it by now—and maybe they are—but I think they're too stubborn to quit."

"Really?" Dr Blackwood asked. "That's different. Do you all keep in touch?"

"Not really. Occasionally they remember Kelly and me, but they're in their own little world. Always have been. They were spectacularly uninterested in parenting. Kelly and I learned early we really only had each other for emotional support. We raised ourselves. Our parents only went through the motions. They turned up at parent-teacher conferences and listened and said nothing. They made sure we were clean and fed and so on but never offered an opinion on careers or grades—low or high—or friends or dating. And as soon as Kelly and I were out of the house, they sold up everything and off they went."

"How could they afford to roam the country for fifteen years?"

"Dad injured his leg at work and got a big payout, so he retired early. Mum was a personal assistant and couldn't wait to retire either. So she threw in the job, and they fulfilled their dreams. I'm happy for them, don't get me wrong, but it was a lonely way to grow up. The irony is that I was really close to my grandmother on my dad's side, Betty, who gave me Trip and my Love Muffins van."

"Why's that ironic?"

"Because she roamed even farther and wider than my parents. She was the original nomad in the van, driving all over Europe and, later, North and South America—I think that's what inspired my parents, all the fun she was having. Nana Betty was far less physically present in my life than my parents, but we were so much closer. She was actually interested in me. Kelly and I got postcards from all over, calls on our birthdays, although it was me she connected with most. And we shared such wonderful emails. But when she was out of contact, I just had Kelly."

"It's good you had your sister."

"It was. Is. Although she does get over-protective about me as a result of our childhood. Do you have any siblings?"

"I have a brother—a mathematics professor at La Trobe uni. He has a wife, two kids, a goldfish, and excellent parental-approval ratings."

"Ah." Olivia could hear the faintest tinge of bitterness. "The golden child?"

"Definitely. What's not to love?"

"Are you two close?"

"Not especially. He thinks on a different wavelength to everyone else. He's brilliant but…distant."

Wait, yet another distant Blackwood?

Her companion must have caught Olivia's expression because Dr Blackwood said dryly, "Yes, even more than me." Her brief smile fell away quickly. "Roger means well, but he's just all about maths. I think he forgets I exist half the time. Hell, he even forgot to…" She faded out and then looked away.

"He forgot to what?"

"I… It doesn't matter."

"I think it probably does," Olivia said kindly. "Tell me?"

Dr Blackwood regarded her for a moment. "He was so caught up in solving something for a maths challenge that he forgot to attend Helen's funeral." She paused and said haltingly: "Helen…was my wife."

Yes, Olivia knew that, of course, but they'd never had that discussion. "I'm really sorry," she said sincerely. "That must have been gutting."

Dr Blackwood turned and stared out the window as her jaw worked.

Olivia's heart went out to her.

"It wasn't ideal." Dr Blackwood's voice sounded thick. "You find out how much family means to each other during funerals. Not weddings. Oh, everyone's expected to attend those. But funerals? Those are interesting. They're the most optional of all maybe-should-attend obligations."

"I suppose they are." Olivia hadn't really thought about it like that. But no one really batted an eyelid about someone being unable to attend a funeral. Everyone noticed when someone was missing from a wedding.

"Helen and my mother got on like oil and water," Dr Blackwood said. "Due to a rather awkward first meeting."

"Oh?"

"The first time I met her, Security were in the process of tossing her out of a university fundraiser. They thought she was a gate crasher until someone recognised her as being from the History Department. She'd just come in from reclassifying boxes of dusty old artefacts and hadn't changed her clothes. Helen had been distracted by some huge find and wanted to tell her department head about it immediately. The most fun was the murderous look on my mother's face when she realised she'd *have* to allow her in. Helen even flipped my mother the bird—not realising who she was at the time. She thought she was just some meddling, overly officious bystander. In Helen's defence, my mother had only just been appointed vice chancellor and no one had really gotten a good look at her yet." Dr Blackwood exhaled, glee clear in her voice. "*That* was a night."

"I'm guessing it's hard to come back from that—you falling for a woman your mother didn't like very much."

"Well, my mother and I eventually reached an uneasy détente after many years of friction. But it all flared up again recently, after"—Dr Blackwood scowled—"after she told me I should stop mourning my wife. She said I'd been self-indulgent with my moping for far too long. Helen had only been gone nine months."

Olivia's heart constricted. "That's awful! Grief doesn't have some timer. Everyone's different."

"My mother also hinted that I was better off without Helen. Oh, all sorts of ugly things came out of her mouth that night." Dr Blackwood suddenly went still. The frost was back in her expression, and her unapproachable mask now seemed to be welded back on. "I appear to be rambling. Or oversharing. Either way, I'm quite sure you're not interested."

"Why do you think that?" Olivia asked. "Because I'm very interested."

"Why?" Dr Blackwood asked suspiciously. "We're not exactly friends."

"We're not *not* friends, though." Olivia smiled. "I mean, if you consider the fact that I feed you delicious snacks and you hang out with me? That's friendship, isn't it?"

"It's…transactional. We made a deal."

"Nah, it's more than that." Olivia prayed she was right, or this was about to get embarrassing. "I mean, why did you ask me for cat names?"

"I needed ideas. I have recently adopted my late neighbour's cat. Or, rather, the animal adopted me, regardless of my views on the matter." She rolled her eyes.

"Really?" So it wasn't some test. Olivia tried to imagine Dr Blackwood stroking a cat like a Bond villain and talking to the feline about her day and almost laughed. "Which name did you settle on?"

Dr Blackwood gave a huff before admitting: "Wednesday."

Olivia beamed. "Awesome. There, see? Friends seek out friends to name cats for them."

"Perhaps." Dr Blackwood clearly wasn't budging on this one. "Why did you put a smiling emoticon after that name?"

"Because I thought you'd think it's funny since…" she faded out, suddenly realising her error. Just because Olivia thought of this woman as goth-librarian Morticia didn't mean Dr Blackwood saw herself that way. "I, um, never mind."

"No, tell me."

"You remind me of Morticia Addams. I thought it'd be cute if you named a cat after another member of that family." Olivia held her breath. Would she see this as insulting?

"I remind you of Morticia Addams. She of the plunging cleavage and the decapitating of roses and the fawning husband. That Morticia?"

It was really hard to get a bead on Dr Blackwood's mood with those dark sunglasses on. "Yes. She's cool."

"She is." Dr Blackwood conceded and inclined her head. "Excellent fashion and parenting skills."

Unlike Dr Blackwood's own mother, by the sound of things. "And, yeah, there are way worse things to be than like Morticia. But I truly just meant looks-wise."

"Morticia is beautiful, though." Dr Blackwood's unreadable eyes were focused squarely on Olivia now.

Hoo boy. Well, in for a penny. "Yes—very beautiful. Like I said. You're physically similar."

Was that a small blush now edging onto Dr Blackwood's cheeks? Surely not.

Olivia opened her mouth to say something else, but the other woman had leaned forward and smashed a few buttons. Soon, Siberian Indigenous folk music was blasting from the speakers.

Olivia's horizons were getting broadened whether she liked it or not.

Three hours later, they'd had some muffins and water, discussed various topics—from book club picks Dr Blackwood recommended to the woeful state of the local Prahran public library, eternally undergoing storm damage repairs.

"Okay, new topic," Olivia said. "Why do you like bushrangers so much?"

"Ask me again after you've met my mother," Margaret deadpanned without so much as a thought.

Olivia turned that over. What relevance did a university's vice chancellor have to the lawless rabble of over a hundred years ago who lived off the land, fought, stole, and…*ohhh*…openly mocked the repressive, authoritarian power structures of the day. Margaret *liked* that they irreverently poked a stick in the eye of rigid authority. "I think I get it," she said with a knowing smile.

"I thought you might." Margaret didn't smile back but seemed pleased nonetheless. She paused and asked: "Will you tell me about Timothy?"

Olivia stiffened. *God.* She supposed she would have to talk about her first boyfriend sooner or later. But the shame of it. She slumped.

Dr Blackwood looked at her in alarm. "You don't have to. I just thought since we're dealing with him after Tina…"

"No, you're right. I just…" Bile rose up into her throat. "I hate myself for what happened with him."

"Will you tell me?" Dr Blackwood asked again, more kindly this time. "Since it's henchperson-critical information?"

She wasn't wrong. Olivia drew in a shaky breath. "Timothy and his brother, Rodney, were thick as thieves. They did everything together. Gaming, cars, playing footy, you name it. So, when Timothy started to date me at school—we were in the same classes—I was treated like a third wheel. And it was made a hundred percent clear to me that Rodney did not like me at all."

"I see," Dr Blackwood said.

"Timothy was my first boyfriend. I had no experience with relationships or how I was supposed to act or be treated. I was just muddling through. And sometimes he would make comments about my 'fat arse'."

Dr Blackwood scowled. "Your rear is not fat."

Well, it kind of was. Certainly, it was rounder than the women in every ad she ever saw.

"It's not," Dr Blackwood repeated more adamantly.

"Well, anyway, that's what he called me, 'a fat arse'."

"He sounds charming. I trust it was hard for him, being perfect in every way."

Olivia tried to laugh, but it came out flat and sad. "Sometimes Timothy's brother would prevent us from going out. Like, Rodney would tell him they had to go to some car show he'd gotten tickets to when he knew I had something special planned. Whatever Rodney wanted to do always took precedence over anything I wanted to do with my boyfriend. Rodney loved to make it clear I wasn't important, or required."

"And Timothy let him do this? Went along with it?"

"Most of the time Rodney was clever enough not to act up too much when his brother was around. But I noticed sometimes it felt a bit like Timothy didn't really like me either." She bit her lip.

Dr Blackwood's jaw clenched. "Did he hurt you?" The hands on her thighs curled into tight bundles.

"No, not like that." She had a sudden urge to smooth out those angry fists. She smiled at Margaret's protectiveness. "It was just a sense I had. Like, I was threatening the brothers' relationship. How close they were." She hesitated, hating what she was about to reveal. "The thing was, I was just too stupid to not put the pieces together sooner. I feel like such a fool in hindsight."

"What pieces?"

"Timothy and Rodney are twins. It's extremely hard to tell them apart. And one day, I was kissing Timothy on the couch and Rodney wandered in.

And then he started laughing hard. Then Timothy started laughing." She swallowed. "They'd swapped for a joke. I wasn't kissing my boyfriend."

Dr Blackwood's eyes narrowed.

"I hadn't realised. I certainly hadn't agreed to kiss that slimy bastard." Her heart started thudding faster. "I went home that night, ashamed and appalled, and angry at Timothy for treating it like a joke. And then I wondered if it wasn't the first time they'd swapped. And what if…it had been more than kissing?"

Dr Blackwood's face had turned to stone. She hissed in a breath. Her fisted hands tightened to white.

"I went back over there and confronted them. They denied everything. Timothy looked incredulous at even the suggestion. I broke up with him then and there. God, I was so filled with shame. Then I felt stupid. And that morphed into trying to tell myself it was nothing. And if it had just been one kiss, then it wasn't *too* bad. I was an emotional wreck."

Dr Blackwood looked incensed. "It's irrelevant even if nothing 'too bad' occurred. You had your right to consent stripped from you."

Olivia lifted her head in surprise. "You don't think I'm an idiot not to have noticed I wasn't kissing my boyfriend?"

The other woman's nostrils flared. "I'm sorry, I couldn't hear you over my jaw grinding. This is a worthy case for vengeance."

"I'm really glad you think so," Olivia said. "Because for years, I felt maybe I'd overreacted, breaking up with him over that. Timothy, later that night, sent me a 'calm down' text message, saying I took it all wrong. But I just felt so…creeped out. Icky. Not to mention dumb. I also felt completely betrayed. Like, why wasn't my boyfriend supporting me? But he was such an immature little shithead." She sagged. "And I was too young to know how bad a relationship that was."

"Did you ever find out the truth? How far it went?"

"I tried. I called Timothy a month later, asking a lot of questions, but he got so defensive. He denied everything again, and he really did sound like he believed it. It was easier to accept that was the truth and move on. Even so, Kelly threatened to kick both of them in the balls. But I just wanted to go into denial because it was too much to deal with. And then along came Martin with his older, wiser, man-of-the-world routine. And after dealing with Timothy's immaturity, he felt like a relief. I was dating a grown-up. I thought he'd be safe to trust."

"Out of the frying pan, into the fire?"

"Pretty much."

"And then you lost everything you owned to Annalise."

"Yes." Olivia huffed out a breath. "I'm well aware."

"Before Tina stole the one thing that meant everything to you."

Olivia turned to stare across to Tina's building, wondering where Trip was now. She hoped he wasn't being mistreated. Would Tina do that? She didn't think so, but it was such a weird thing to do in the first place. "Yeah. I can sure pick them."

"Indeed you can." There was no bite in the words. Almost…sympathy?

"Kelly says I attract red flags somehow. I used to think I had really lousy luck. But it's more than that. Why did I so easily fall for their sweet words and charm? Why couldn't I see past that? Or did I subconsciously pick people who would treat me as if I don't matter? Is it because deep down I think I don't deserve more? I never listened any time Kelly tried to warn me about their red flags. If I didn't see it myself, I didn't believe it. I always thought she was just being overprotective."

"You could probably pick up on those red flags now," Dr Blackwood suggested. "You must have learned a lot from that unholy foursome."

"You'd think so, yet I gave Tina another chance and she turned around and stole Trip. So I learned I'll probably be single for life now because it's impossible to trust myself anymore." She meant it as a joke, but it came out sounding defeated.

"That would be a waste," Dr Blackwood said softly, "if you gave up dating."

"It would?" Olivia gave her a surprised look.

"Well, of course. The world needs romantics, without whom many of the books in my store would not exist. If everyone was as bitter and cynical as me, no one would want to read a single one."

Olivia could hear the smile in her voice and studied her face. "Are you really bitter and cynical? Or is that just the image you project to keep people away?"

Dr Blackwood took off her sunglasses and peered at her. "What's the difference?"

"The difference is what's in your heart."

"My heart." Dr Blackwood gave a bark of laughter. "My heart has been fossilised for three years since Helen died. And it's no less than I deserve."

Whoa. Olivia would dearly love to pick that comment apart, but she knew the moment Dr Blackwood said it that she regretted it.

The other woman slapped her sunglasses back on, glanced at her watch, and said sharply: "You told me Tina only buys coffee in the mornings on the Saturdays she gets it?"

"Yes."

"Any exceptions?"

"No."

"It's 12.23. She's not coming out today. Our stake-out is officially a bust."

"Looks like it." Olivia regretted how the conversation had shifted from free flowing to tense and heavy. "Well, Dr Blackwood, looks like I've wasted your time. I'm sorry."

"I'll drive you back to Mary Bugg's," Dr Blackwood said curtly.

They'd only driven a few minutes when she added, "You know, you can call me Margaret, if you wish."

"I can?" *Since when?* Kelly had told her that absolutely everyone called the woman "Dr Blackwood".

"Yes." She changed lanes, then glanced across to her. Her lips quirked. "I understand it's what friends do. Or rather *not* not-friends."

And with that, Olivia grinned happily. "Yep. Absolutely. I understand that's totally correct." Okay, she was gushing. But just like that, her mood lifted.

Saturday, April 4

Sunset: *7.07pm*

Temp: *12.8C-16.6C*

Rain: *35mm—I thought it would never stop raining. All day, just a constant, driving downpour.*

Drink: *Old Vine Barossa Valley shiraz—one glass. Still not an improvement. I think it's not really a match for my taste at all.*

Reading: Non-fiction—JALIA, *Vol 69, issue 1. "Trusting Records in the Cloud". I'm torn by my natural urge to trust nothing to cyberspace. As long as there are physical back-ups, I suppose I can be grudgingly in favour.*

Fiction—The Wife and The Widow *(Christian White)—Alas, this predictable whodunnit lost me at: "Her bowels felt like slippery eels trying to escape a bucket." I pity the state of the author's bowel movements.*

General Observations: *My first stake-out ended in failure. I'm not certain what to make of it either. There was too much sharing. I almost told Olivia the truth about Helen—my inexcusable behaviour. Mercifully, I stopped myself in time.*

She's doing it again, though: that superpower of hers where she's able to draw my secrets from me. How does she do that?

My desire to murder Olivia's exes went up another notch today on learning what the Immature Twin did. She couched her story in terms that the non-boyfriend brother did not like her and had pretended to be her boyfriend to hurt her. My suspicion is both young men did not like her. A man who cares for the woman he is dating protects her from all harm. He doesn't find it funny that she's groped by another man. That's not just immaturity. There's misogyny underneath it.

I could easily detect Olivia's shame, even before she admitted to it. It's as if she thinks she's responsible for not seeing what was taking place—a situation no one would think of or look for. Rodney seems like the lowest of them all.

Jealous and venal. Punishing and cruel. And his brother...an enabler? Weak and pitiful, certainly.

How shall we destroy them? For both of them need their comeuppance, not just the ex.

Wednesday finds my mood too agitated. The feline just made the most baleful noise, sat up on my lap, and glared at me for my angry stress writing. I apologise, Wednesday. Go back to sleep. I'll try to scribble in my diary in a less agitated way.

On a surreal note, I'm apparently beautiful—at least in Olivia's eyes. That was unexpected. I admit her admiring confession caught me so flat-footed, I had no customary acidic retort. I have never thought of myself in that way. I'm aware I'm too tall for most, too severe in looks. I'm neither gentle nor delicate in how I speak or walk. I dress for my own comfort— in suits that allow me to travel at pace. Helen's rose-tinted glasses praise aside, I'm usually only ever called "striking". I'm fairly sure that's just code for "memorable". But beautiful? No. Still, Olivia and I can at least agree on one thing: We are, apparently, friends. Or not-not friends. That description makes me smile, hours later. I'm surprisingly gratified.

Meanwhile, Emma loved Anne of Green Gables *and asked about the sequels. I had to break it to her that they deserved to be catapulted into the sun. I did also point out that if any reprobate boy pulls her hair and calls her "carrots" because he likes her, she is under no obligation to forgive him, let alone marry him. She smiled at that. As well she might. I am quite amusing.*

Emma said the last boy who tried to insult her was punched repeatedly in the groin by her four-year-old brother. I think I might like that child.

Perhaps I should hire him for when Sasha next drapes himself artistically across my door in an attempt to be amorous.

CHAPTER 15

TO CATCH A THIEF

AFTER THE UNSUCCESSFUL STAKE-OUT, OLIVIA had tried twice more to catch Tina leaving her apartment at times she knew her ex sometimes would go out—to no avail. Tina really had gone to ground. Or was she away?

All Olivia's messages to her had gone unanswered, and she was beside herself with worry for Trip. Why had Tina taken him? To sell? But who'd want a worse-for-wear stuffed penguin? No pawn shop would touch Trip. They'd told her so. It was bizarre.

After the next book club meeting, as everyone was leaving, she pulled Damien aside. "Hey, did you ever have any success getting intel from the security guard at Tina's apartment building?"

"Yes and no." Damien returned to his armchair and resettled himself. "I was going to talk to you about that when I'd solved it. We have a bit of a logistical challenge. I had to bring in an expert."

The office door behind her made a sound, and Olivia turned to see Margaret Blackwood now leaning against the doorframe, listening in, arms folded. That was new. Margaret out of her office? Did this almost count as being sociable? If you squinted?

"An expert?" Olivia asked.

Damien called Bo over and then asked her: "Should we present our findings now?"

Bo was his logistical expert? Although, anyone building sets for musicals like *Les Misérables*—rotating, climbable French barricades and all—would know a few things about logistics.

"Can't hurt," Bo said amiably and plonked herself into the chair beside him.

"First, the guard, Christos, says no one can just go up to the penthouse floor without being seen and challenged by him. No deliveries go up there either—he takes them up himself. All part of the service for the penthouse."

Nodding, Olivia said, "That's true. I've seen it myself."

"Right. So there are cameras on the lifts, outside and inside, so you can't just distract the guard while someone else sneaks in. It'd show up on his monitors."

Damn.

"And he's not someone you can bribe to look the other way. He takes his job seriously. The night shift guard is even more serious. He's not for the turning."

Well, there went all the usual methods for getting to Tina's apartment door.

"Does this mean we're screwed?"

"Not exactly. It just means we can't get to her from inside. That just leaves the outside of the building."

He pulled out of his bag an A3 copy of a photo that he unfolded and spread across the coffee table. It was the rear face of Lonsdale Heartland Tower.

Olivia already did not like where this was going. She studied the back of the regal building. It was six storeys high. On the far right were a stack of small balconies, one per floor, all the way down.

On the far left of the building, zig-zagging up, was a metal fire-escape. At each change of direction on the right was a landing. There was one of these per floor. Each landing was beside a small window. Which made sense: in the event of a fire, you'd want to be able to hop out of the window and haul yourself over the railing onto the landing, then scramble down to safety.

The distance between the fire-escape on the left and the balconies on the right was huge, so that ruled out leaping across to the penthouse's balcony.

Each balcony was too far apart, top to bottom, to attempt to climb up from a floor below. Which only left coming down from the roof above. *Oh God. Abseiling?* Was that the plan?

Her stomach lurched. She was not built for dangling off ropes. She prayed Damien and Bo had something else in mind.

"This is what Bo and I have been studying all week," Damien said. "We looked at the fire-escape as an access point. Unfortunately, it starts high enough off the ground so burglars can't access it. In a fire, an extension is dropped down from the first-floor landing. To close the gap, we thought about just propping a ladder on the ground, right under the fire-escape, and getting up that way. But it won't work."

"Why not?" Olivia asked.

"Under the first floor's landing is a camera that points straight down. Christos would see the ladder suddenly appearing on his monitors. So ground floor access is out. Despite that, I have found a way to get to here..." He tapped a balcony two below the penthouse balcony, "But no higher. That's where we're stuck."

Olivia stared at the balcony halfway up the apartment tower. "How on earth could you get to there?"

Damien grinned. "All those beers I bought Christos paid off. He told me this corner apartment"—he tapped Level Three's balcony—"is for sale. The real estate company with the listing has been showing groups of people through on the regular. Christos just checks the agent's business card and lets them up. The place is totally empty, so it's no risk for him, security-wise. He doesn't go with them."

"So we need to get a business card from that real estate company?" Olivia suggested.

"Done and done." Bo reached into her wallet and plucked one out. "Sorted it on my way in to work yesterday. I rolled up there, told them I was thinking of selling my place, and then got a business card from the agent most suited."

"Most suited?"

Bo slapped it on the table. "All the agents are men except for this one. I picked the card with the woman's name."

It had in one corner a headshot of the real estate agent. Olivia examined the picture in dismay. "I don't look anything like her," she said, squinting. "I can't impersonate her. She's all angles and cheek bones. Looks a bit regal too."

"No, you can't pull it off," Bo agreed. She looked past Olivia's shoulder. "I'm thinking your henchperson could, though."

Margaret strode forward immediately and slid the card off the table to examine it. She scowled. "Blonde? Dear God. But…if the security guard didn't look too closely, and a wig was involved…I suppose I could pass as," she peered at the card, "Anita van…" She stopped.

"It's pronounced the same way it's spelt," Bo said, eyes bright with amusement.

Margaret sighed and finished, "van Dyke."

A soft titter came from near the window. Clearly homework was not being done.

"You're Dutch," Bo added. "Congratulations. And don't skimp on playing the part. I spoke to Ms van Dyke, and she's got an accent, all right."

Olivia decided right then she would give every dollar she owned to witness the mind-boggling spectacle of Margaret Blackwood role-playing a regal Dutchwoman.

Margaret blinked. "*I* haven't agreed to any of this yet. And what exactly is 'this' anyway?"

"Right. Well, it's like this," Damien said, "and bear in mind we've only got the first half of the plan locked down. But I'm suggesting that you, playing Anita van Dyke, rock up to the front desk, wave your business card at Christos, say you're here to take the clients through for a viewing but that you left the apartment key at the office; he'll loan you one. Like I say, there's nothing up there to nick, so no skin off his nose. You've just gotta make him believe you're her."

Bo nodded. "Just be slick but a bit haughty. That's what that lady was like. I don't think it'll be too much a stretch, hey?" She grinned.

Olivia gulped back a laugh. *Oh shit.*

"Rude." Margaret's flinty eyes narrowed into slits.

Damien grinned too. "She means it as a compliment."

"I do," Bo claimed with a nod. "Okay," she pushed on, even as Margaret glowered at her, "next, you and Olivia and whoever else head up to the third floor."

"But once we're in the lift, why can't we just select the button for the penthouse?" Margaret asked.

"The lift won't go up to the top without a special key. It's a security thing."

Margaret inclined her head in understanding. "Continue."

"So now," Bo said, "you're inside the corner apartment of Level Three. That means access to this window," she pointed to the one in the left of the photo, "as well as access to the fire-escape right outside it." Bo tapped the elements as she said them.

"And then what?" Olivia asked, already terrified as to where this plan was going.

"And…that's where we're stumped," Damien admitted. "Because although the fire-escape goes all the way up to the roof, there's a huge overhang on the right half of the building. So no one on the roof can drop down onto the penthouse balcony, even with climbing apparatus."

"Even if we could do that, it won't help us because I'm not doing anything involving a vertical drop," Olivia said with a shudder. "I'm already dreading just getting onto the fire-escape from a window."

A shadow shifted over them, and she glanced up to find Sasha absorbed in proceedings.

"Yes?" she asked him.

"Nothing," he said. "Go on. This is better than spy movie."

"There's not much to go on with," Damien replied. "We only got this far. Access to halfway up the back of the building. And by the way, those other windows?" He tapped the vertical line of them beside each of the landings. "Security advises apartment owners to keep them locked. So we wouldn't be able to access Tina's apartment through there."

"And, sadly," Olivia said, "I can confirm Tina keeps all her windows locked. I used to joke about the lack of breeze in her place. She doesn't lock her balcony doors, though. Why would she, given how impossible it would be for a burglar to get to it?"

"Someone fearless could get to it, though," Sasha said with a gleam in his eye, pointing from the roof overhang to the balcony tucked away underneath. "Like a movie stuntman—one could swing back and forth from the roof on a rope until he was in position to let go and land on the balcony."

"No!" Olivia said in dismay. "Absolutely not. No one is going to swing from a rope six floors off the ground and hope to nail the landing. You're not Paul Hogan in *Crocodile Dundee*."

"Who?" He peered at her.

"Never mind. You're not doing that. *No one* is doing that."

"Exactly," Bo agreed. "And that's why we're stuck on Level Three."

Silence fell as everyone peered at the photo on the coffee table.

A small voice broke in. "For grown-ups, you're really missing the obvious. No offence."

Everyone turned to see Emma perched by the window in her school uniform, gazing at the photo.

"Emma?" Olivia asked hopefully. "You have an idea?"

The ten-year-old slid from her chair. "Not really me. It's more from the mind of the climbing expert I live with."

The climbing exper... Oh. Toby. "Go on."

"You ask yourself: what would Toby do? Then how to get to the penthouse balcony is pretty obvious."

It is?

Emma came over to the table. "You do this." She traced her finger from the third-floor window of the vacant apartment to the escape ladder, then moved up the stairs and stopped on the sixth-floor landing of the fire-escape. "When Toby wants to get to another tree, assuming he can get away with it, he doesn't climb down and then up, he looks for a way straight across." She traced her finger from the landing all the way over to Tina's apartment balcony.

"That is much too far for anyone to jump," Sasha said gently. "Even me."

"You don't jump it," Emma said, "you scoot your bum across a ladder you've laid from here to here like a tree branch." She tapped the landing's railing and drew a straight line across the building face to the penthouse balcony's railing. "It's in exact alignment, see? It's so simple."

Oh. My. God. It *was* so simple.

Bo chortled. "All hail fuckin' Emma! And Toby! Oh shit! Sorry about the language." Then, realising she'd just sworn again, she said, panicked: "Shit! I mean, uh, crap. *God damnit!*"

Everyone laughed.

Well, almost everyone. Margaret's voice was icy when she said: "And who, pray tell, will be volunteered to scamper along this ladder, six floors up?" She hissed in a breath. "Because I can assure you it won't be me."

"I volunteer!" Sasha said. "Heights are no trouble to me. In fact, I could walk across it, not crawl. As a dancer, I have impeccable balance."

"And then what will you do on the other side?" Margaret asked, her tone disdainful. "Do you even know?"

"I…" He deflated. "No." Sasha glanced at Olivia. "What *is* the plan?"

"The plan is my penguin. This is a retrieval mission. But Sasha, you can't do this. If Tina's home, and I expect her to be, she'd freak out if some enormous man just walked into her apartment from the balcony. No offence, Sasha, but you do look intimidating."

He shook his head to get his perfect floppy hair away from his eyes in a move straight out of a shampoo commercial and said, "Thank you. But I still volunteer. You will need someone to carry the ladder and put it in position, yes? You need someone who does not fear heights to do this."

"Wait," Olivia said. She tapped the space between the fire-escape and Tina's balcony. "That's at least eight metres between these two points. We'd need one seriously long ladder for this. Do they even make them that long?"

Margaret cut in: "And even if they did, how would you smuggle it past your man on the front desk?"

"Actually, that's not a problem," Bo said. "Either question. At work, there's a thirty-foot telescoped aluminium ladder—that's, like, nine metres. Cost them a bundle, but it's brilliant. It folds right down to the size of a small suitcase. Has a maximum weight rating of 150kg, so it'd take you easy, Liv."

Olivia swallowed. "Right," she said uneasily. "Good."

Margaret looked at her incredulously. "You people cannot be serious."

"Don't worry," Bo said confidently. "It'll work like a charm. Remember, I'm an expert in securing things to prevent people from falling to their deaths. So I'll come along too and make sure the job's done right: set up safety ropes, supply harnesses, and the like." She glanced at Sasha. "I could use a collaborator with no fear of heights. Can't use Damien, of course."

"Why not?" Damien asked indignantly.

"Because Christos will recognise his drinking buddy." She glanced at Margaret. "I'm sure Dr B can talk us all up as 'interested buyers' to get us past Christos."

"Yes. I am in." Sasha puffed out his chest.

Olivia licked her lips nervously. "Um, great, but we'll practice first, though? If yes, then okay."

"Not okay!" Margaret looked even paler. "It's insane to risk your life like this!"

Well, at least she hadn't said "over a penguin", but still. Olivia folded her arms. "Who are you to tell me what I can or can't do? And as my henchperson, I'd expect a little support here."

"Support, yes. Enabling your suicide, no! I refuse. This whole plan is absurd! Can't you hear yourselves? Ladders invariably have a joint in the middle to give the option of being folded into an A-frame. That's a dreadful weak point. Can you imagine what will happen the moment Olivia slides onto that joint? It will bow and maybe even buckle the instant any weight's put on it. Ladders are not designed for this. It's a recipe for disaster."

Okay, good point. Olivia glanced at Bo, who nodded.

"Excellent arguments, Dr B," Bo said earnestly. "That's why we'll be testing it properly first. What if we get a couple of big crates out into that car park of yours, put the ladder between them. See if it holds when it's in position with Olivia's weight. And we'll especially stress test that middle join. Yeah?"

Margaret didn't answer and sank into the closest armchair. Fear flickered into her eyes. "No. *No.*" Her voice was rough.

Never had Olivia seen her looking so rattled. She turned to the rest of the group. "Bo and Damien, thanks for your help. It's a good plan. We'll talk later. Sasha, ditto, and I appreciate you volunteering. I'll get back to you. Emma? Awesome idea. Please can you go and hang with Kelly for ten? I need some space here."

The crowd got the hint and left them to it.

Olivia sank onto her knees beside Margaret's chair and looked at her. "You're terrified of heights, aren't you?"

Margaret didn't reply.

"That's okay," Olivia said, "I'm not fond of them either. But I'll have Bo doing my safety lines and making sure the ladder is locked in place and tied down at our end. Not to mention, we'll be doing a rehearsal. Or five."

Margaret didn't appear to have registered any of her words.

"So," Olivia rushed on, "the thing is, you'll be in charge of making sure no one enters the third-floor apartment while we're outside. Just, you know, stay inside and keep the perimeter safe for us."

"The perimeter. Safe?" Margaret finally said. "How? By just…standing there while you risk your neck? This is so foolhardy. You will be SIX STOREYS UP!"

"I have faith in Bo. She's been tying expert knots since she was in the Brownies." She smiled. "I'll be across and into Tina's apartment in no time. If she's not there, I'll search for Trip and enact a little vengeance. And if she is there, I'll confront her and demand to know where Trip is."

"What 'little vengeance'?" Margaret frowned and seemed closer to her usual bad mood. "We haven't discussed this."

"I know. It only came to me last night. Okay, picture it: A syringe filled with milk. I inject it into the upholstery of Tina's favourite chair. She has this striped one she adores. When the milk starts to go off, the smell will be awful. She'll look everywhere trying to find the source; it'll drive her nuts." She paused and added: "I might also go the raw prawn too. For extra vengeance."

"Go the raw prawn?"

"Okay, so I take half a dozen prawns—or any tiny fish, really—slip them into the hem of her curtains. They'll start to reek, especially when the sun hits them. Between that and the sour milk, Tina's apartment that she adores so much will smell like vomit. I'm not sure she'll ever find the cause."

"Clever, I suppose," Margaret murmured. She closed her eyes. "But I really don't want to have any part in doing this. Or you to have any part in doing this. It seems reckless in the extreme."

"Well, any risk is for me alone. All I'm asking is for you to be the haughty Dutch real estate agent who breezes us all past security, and then your job is done. We'll do the rest."

"You're all insane."

"The cause is just. I really want Trip back. He means everything to me."

Margaret exhaled. "And what of the legal implications? So far, we haven't crossed any legal lines in our vengeance planning. This will be trespassing at the minimum."

"It depends on whether Tina's home or not, I guess," Olivia said. "If she is, I'll stand at the balcony threshold and get her to invite me in."

"Why would she do that?"

"Because she'll be so busy panicking that she stole my penguin and trying to talk herself out of trouble that she'll forget she could just tell me to get lost."

"And if she's not home?"

"Then I play a ghost. I was never there. She'll never know. But she'll have a smell to last a lifetime."

"That's still breaking and entering."

"If we get caught. I'd be in and out so fast that even if someone sees us up there and reports it, we'd be gone before police could arrive."

Margaret said nothing for the longest time. "You plunging to your death would be most inconvenient. I've become accustomed to critiquing your little book group."

"Critiquing? You mean heckling, right?" Olivia laughed. "I also have no plans to meet my Maker yet."

Margaret didn't laugh back. "You will be careful? I need you to promise you will be. I'm not joking about this. I will not assist with this plan at all if you're unprepared."

"I promise we won't go up until we've practised our arses off. We can use your car park for that, right? Hell, you can watch us and see for yourself that the ladder holds."

Margaret sighed. "I will observe your practice session. And, if it works, only then will I agree to help. But I should warn you, I do the worst Dutch accent."

"Wait, you've tried one in the past?" Olivia asked. "When? Why?"

Margaret's cheeks reddened. "No comment." She huffed. "Can we focus? Please?"

"All right. So, to recap, you do a bad Dutch accent. You'd better get practising." Olivia placed a reassuring hand on Margaret's arm. "I have faith you'll nail it, Ms van Dyke."

Wincing, Margaret said: "I wish that agent had a…gentler…name that didn't remind me of the worst slurs I heard tossed around when I was at high school."

"I don't think Anita van Lesbian is an authentic Dutch surname some-how," Olivia teased.

Margaret rolled her eyes, but the edges of her mouth threatened an actual smile. "I can't believe I'm actually going along with this. *How* did you talk me into it?"

"I'm not sure," Olivia said truthfully, "but thank you." She squeezed Margaret's arm gratefully. "I mean it."

"Mmmph." Margaret did not look mollified. But an agreement had been struck.

Tuesday, April 7

Sunset: *6.03pm*

Temp: *11.9C-16.4C*

Rain: *1.4mm*

Drink: *Vodka with lime. Half a glass. What on earth possessed me to have one of H's old favourites? It still tastes foul, Helen dear. No, I'm not 'finally won over'.*

Reading: *None. My mind is too frantic.*

General Observations: *Daylight savings has ended, so it's darker an hour earlier. I'll have to get my heating lamp out on the balcony soon. Or maybe not quite so soon as Wednesday has proven herself an excellent heat source.*

I can't believe I'm going along with this idiotic scheme. It was one thing when the missions involved my feet firmly on the ground, but this is potentially deadly. Did a ten-year-old really come up with this plan?

Are we trusting Olivia's life to the plottings of a TEN-YEAR-OLD?

The vodka is growing on me. I just drank another.

If anything at all happens to Olivia Roberts, I will personally track down Tina Whateverhernameis and pull her tonsils out through her nostrils.

Sorry, Wednesday. Don't look so disgruntled. I'll be fine in a moment.

The fact is, I'll have palpitations regarding this risky endeavour for days. Yes, I have a terror of heights. Almost tumbling off a cliff at age six will do that to a person. Only my mother's lightning-fast reflexes saved me. But it's more than that. I have come to a disturbing understanding recently that I can't stand the thought of anything happening to that ridiculous muffin baker. I wasn't lying when I told her I've grown accustomed to critiquing her book club.

But even more than that: I've grown accustomed to her as well. She has a gentleness that soothes. Also, a smart tongue. She can be amusing in her own bumbling, blurting, unpredict-

able way. She's determined. I might have barricaded myself in my office when life became too unpalatable to bear; not Olivia. No, she decided to wreak revenge on all who wronged her. It's admirable. Oh, and she's unaccountably kind.

I once asked myself how she exists in this world. I still don't know.

It's not just me who'd notice her absence, either. The Garrity children clearly adore her.

Did I mention that this is a terrible idea? It is. But now I have to source a blonde wig and develop a Dutch accent.

CHAPTER 16

THERE'S NO I IN CREAM

OLIVIA ROLLED UP TWO DAYS later to Mary Bugg's car park and stopped dead.

Someone—Margaret, obviously—had had the two large industrial bins moved to what seemed to be exactly eight metres apart. Their lids had been closed too. It was the perfect distance for practicing a ladder-crawl mission.

"If you're going to do it," said a familiar voice behind her, low and cool, "the least I can do is ensure conditions are as identical as possible to those on Tina's apartment building."

"Thank you!" Olivia turned, meeting her eyes. "I appreciate it."

"All part of the henchperson service." She studied Olivia. "Do you really have no doubts about this idiotic scheme?"

"Plenty." Olivia nodded at the two enormous bins. She hoped she wasn't going to give new meaning to dumpster diving. "But one way or another, we'll know soon just how idiotic it is."

The ladder held. Even at the midpoint, which had been everyone's greatest fear. It had sagged a little, but Olivia had moved past it as fast as she could, so it didn't have time to buckle. She had no doubt that on a cheaper apparatus, she'd have been dropped in the dirt. At least Bo's theatre company had paid for quality.

Kelly had briefly come outside to observe one run-through, her face a grim mask, and Olivia knew she'd be hearing all about it tonight from her sister. All she said in the here and now was, "Well, I see your button is apt."

It read: *There's No I in Cream.*

"Yep," Olivia agreed. Teamwork abounded today.

After the sixth pass with no injuries or unforeseen wobbles, the practice mission was deemed a success.

Bo ran around high-fiving everyone in sight except Margaret, who'd given her such a ferocious look that Bo had wisely dropped her arm. Then the sturdy woman set about seeing how fast she could collapse her ladder, flicking clips and locks furiously.

Three minutes, twelve seconds.

Next, Bo unlocked and re-extended it, handing the towering structure over to Sasha, who practiced lowering it into place and collecting it again.

When that got boring, Sasha ran from one end of the ladder to the other, showing how easily it could be done. The man didn't even slow for the rungs. He just had some sort of innate sense of knowing exactly where to put his feet. His enormous albatross-span arms held out horizontally probably had something to do with his incredible balance.

"Get off of there, ya big show-off," Bo ordered him. "We're working!"

Five more tests of the ladder being expertly stretched, laid flat, pulled back, and shrunk down to its packed-away form and Bo called it a day.

All of this meant it was "go" time. They could do this. It would work. And Olivia wanted to throw up.

"You can still call it off, you know," Margaret murmured in her ear.

Olivia hadn't even heard her come up behind her.

"No shame in it at all. In fact, I was thinking: we can do a stake-out every Saturday morning until Tina finally shows to buy her coffee. That would be a lot more sensible and considerably less illegal."

"We can't wait any longer," Olivia said tightly. "I need Trip back. I'm not taking a chance she'll get rid of him or hurt him or who knows what she has in mind."

Margaret shook her head minutely. "I wish you wouldn't do this."

"I know." Olivia met her eye and conveyed all the gratitude she felt. "But thank you for agreeing to help us anyway."

"I barely did," Margaret pointed out.

Olivia nodded. "I know. But thanks even so. That's being an excellent henchperson. You're worth every muffin."

Margaret snorted and folded her arms. "Just get it right. I really don't want to be the one to say 'I told you so' in your eulogy."

"Well, someone'll have to," Olivia said with a grin. "May as well be you." Without thinking, she grabbed Margaret's hand and gave it a reassuring squeeze. *Another one.* Apparently, that was something Olivia did now. Her cheeks heated at the realisation of what she'd done. Margaret's hand felt so warm beneath hers. "I'm sure you'd be really good at pointing out all my shortcomings at my funeral."

"Indeed I would." The flicker of concern was back in Margaret's eyes. She quickly dropped her hand, turned on her heel, and strode back inside.

"You know," Emma Garrity said, joining her a few moments later. "You'd make a cute couple."

Olivia turned. "Excuse me? Who would?"

"You and Dr Blackwood."

"You don't have any idea what you're talking about," she told Emma firmly. "Dr Blackwood has no interest in me like that."

"You know you two forget I'm here half the time, right?" Emma said thoughtfully. "I see the way she watches you. She wouldn't watch you if she wasn't interested, right?"

"Or she's making sure I'm not recommending terrible books to my group."

"I don't mean just during book club." Emma huffed and simultaneously rolled her eyes as only a ten-year-old girl could. "She watches you constantly, you know. She *likes* you."

"Nope. Come on. You've heard some of the mockery she unleashes on my book club. Ever since that first time, it's like she can't resist heckling. She's got so many barbs, she's an echidna."

"Kelly says she's been listening in on your club since it started. For two years!"

"See what I have to put up with?"

"But that's even more proof."

"Proof she thinks I'm appalling at book choices and isn't afraid to let me know."

Emma looked at her as if she thought her a bit slow. "Olivvvvia," she said in exasperation. "Look, there's this boy at school, Jonathan. I can't stand him. He says the *worst* things all the time." Emma shuddered. "Whenever he says something annoying, which is, like, *always*, I don't tell him he's an idiot. I avoid him because I don't want to start a conversation with him. I don't want to be anywhere near his stupid face. That's what you do when you don't like someone. But this has been *two years* of Dr Blackwood listening to you. And don't forget how she loves to give you all those critiques in book club now."

Olivia snorted. The girl hadn't factored in how much Margaret loved to be contrary for the sake of it. She seemed to prefer arguing with *everyone*. It was her resting state. "Even if it were true that Dr Blackwood finds me in any way interesting in that regard—which it's not—what makes you think *I* like Dr Blackwood in that way?"

"Because you watch her too." Emma had her *duhhh* face on. "Because you're always looking at her office as if you wished you could see past that big blind. *And* you didn't deny it when I said you'd make a cute couple. You just said *she* wouldn't like *you*."

Oh Jesus. The kid was way too smart.

"Well." Olivia fidgeted and tried to focus on Bo attempting to squeeze her telescopic ladder back into its bag for the last time.

How embarrassing that even a ten-year-old had noticed she spent way too much time wondering what Margaret was doing or thinking at any given moment. And it was true, much as it pained her, that she found the woman attractive. Of course she did. Book Woman had captivated her for far too long for Olivia to forget the effect she'd had on her. Knowing her more recently as Margaret Blackwood—abrasive, intelligent, condescending, and yet undeniably interesting—didn't erase any of her charisma. Her...undeniable sex appeal.

It just meant that the one-sided attraction was still there, just below the surface where Olivia had pushed it. And that was fine. She doubted she'd be able to handle an intense and complicated woman like Margaret even if the attraction were mutual. Which it wouldn't be. Emma was imagining things on that score.

"Guess we'll never know if you're right," Olivia finally said. "Because the mind of Margaret Blackwood is entirely a mystery."

"Not ex-actly." The little girl's face turned mischievous.

Uh-oh. "What did you do?" Olivia asked, her stomach clenching in dread.

"I asked her if she likes you back," Emma said innocently.

"*What*?" Back? *Back*! She'd told Margaret that Olivia liked her *romantically*?

This was a disaster! As if the bloody woman wasn't already smug enough! She'd be impossible now! Her mockery would be tenfold. "You said that to her out of the blue?" Olivia asked, astonished.

"It wasn't out of the blue. We were discussing *Anne of Green Gables* and how to know if someone likes you. Did you know she gave me a copy?"

She had? That was thoughtful. Olivia was momentarily distracted.

Emma barrelled on: "She said pulling a girl's hair and calling them 'carrots' is a terrible way to say you like someone. And I said, 'So, is listening to them talk about the books they like for two years a good way to say it?'"

Olivia almost swallowed her tongue at the audacity. "You didn't!"

"I *so* did." Emma beamed.

"Oh God." That would have gone down like a lead balloon. Olivia was almost scared to ask. "What did she say?"

"She glared at me like I'd told just her Ned Kelly deserved being an Aussie legend." Emma giggled. "She didn't say anything else after that. Just told me to do my homework and went back to her office."

Olivia snorted. "Poor Margaret." She sighed. "You're such a meddler. Not to mention delusional."

Emma shrugged. "Yeah, yeah. Do you think you'll ever ask her out?"

"No, thanks. I'm not a masochist. I need to know a woman likes me back before I ask her out."

"You said 'like her back'." Emma looked gleeful. "I *knew* it!"

Olivia scowled. "Do your homework."

Emma laughed hard.

Olivia wiped her slick hands down her navy pants. She was wearing a white cotton blouse and a navy jacket. She'd dressed up, as befitting a client who could afford to buy an apartment at Lonsdale Heartland Tower.

Sasha looked absolutely dashing in a smart grey suit with a mustard tie and matching pocket square. He wore black boots, military grade—"for grip", he explained. Olivia really hoped Christos the security guard didn't decide to look down and wonder why an apartment buyer was wearing combat boots.

Bo was looking sharp—butch and beautiful in all-black mission gear—which could pass as "eccentric theatre director". She carried an oversized bag which contained the safety ropes, harnesses, and steel carabiner attachments. Sasha's bag contained the compact ladder. It weighed well over twenty-five kilos, but somehow, each time he moved it, he made lifting it look effortless.

Damien had turned up for moral support—staying hidden from the security guard inside—and said he'd be watching proceedings from the ground.

That just left "Anita van Dyke"—who'd yet to show. Olivia bit her nails as the assorted group hung around out front like a nervous groom's party at the church waiting for a bride.

Margaret Blackwood was never late. Had she decided to bail? Olivia's worrying grew worse as the time ticked down.

Finally, that signature Jaguar rolled up to the curb and parked. Margaret exited and…holy Jesus!

Olivia had to stop herself from gaping at that ridiculous blonde wig. It looked big and floofy and absurd against her pale skin and those black-framed glasses.

Margaret was also wearing a pastel blue pantsuit with some sort of swirly pattern. Where on earth had she found that? It seemed far too frivolous—and colourful—to have come from Margaret Blackwood's wardrobe. The fact it was too short meant it certainly wasn't hers. An apricot and blue scarf finished the outfit.

Gone was any sign of the intimidating, forbidding Morticia Addams. Enter…well, whatever this was.

"They only had a Farrah Fawcett wig left at the costume shop," Margaret hissed as she joined them. "If any of you laugh *or so much as twitch*, I will walk right now."

"No, no," Olivia said hastily. "We're all good." It was, however, *really* hard not to twitch.

"All right." Margaret nodded curtly at Bo and Sasha, ignored Damien, and looked more murderous by the minute.

Bo began to hum the theme from *Charlie's Angels*, stopping only when Margaret turned a poisonous gaze on her.

"You look as beautiful as a coral reef," Sasha opined.

What a suck-up. Wait, *had* that actually been a compliment?

"No," Margaret snapped and patted down her outfit self-consciously. "I look like an air hostie for TAA from the seventies."

"What's TAA?" Bo asked.

Sasha looked blank too.

"Oh my God," Margaret spat. "You're children."

Olivia was about to point out she was thirty-two and not a child when Margaret pinned her with a questioning look.

"*Et tu*, Olivia?" Margaret asked, tone silky.

"You do know Trans Australian Airlines hasn't been around for decades?" Olivia replied. "But, hey, I know the theme song." She sang *Up, Up and Away* until she got to the high bit about my "beautiful balloon" and Margaret's mouth fell open.

"You are *absurd*. That wasn't even close to in tune, and never mind." Margaret rubbed her temples. "I'm clearly the only one over forty here."

"You are over forty?" Sasha asked in faux shock. "This I would never have guessed!"

Margaret glared at him. "No. Stop that." She waggled a stern finger at him. "I already look ridiculous. Do not add to my foul mood with your... *antics*. Now, let's get this done."

With that, she strode up to the apartment building's main doors, not even glancing back.

Everyone scrambled to follow, except Damien, who scuttled around the back.

Margaret placed the agent's business card on the counter in front of Christos and said, "Anita van Dyke." She tapped the card, right on the tiny photo, cleverly partially obscuring it. "I am 'ere to show these people through the apartment on floor thrrree."

Olivia winced. The accent was...terrible. Margaret had not been lying. She peered into Christos's impassive face. He was a big Greek man with a manicured beard and watchful brown eyes.

With a careless wave, Margaret added: "My aparrrrtment key iss back at worrrk. I have noh time to retrieve it."

Did she just lapse into...French?

Margaret powered on. "Do *you* have the power to asseeeest me or must I return for it?" Her taunting eyebrow shot up to impressive heights.

Oh my God. The sheer cockiness. The absolute "prove to me you're good" attitude was off the charts. Olivia's body gave an inconveniently approving quiver of delight.

Christos blinked at Margaret, glanced at the business card, then at the motley crew. He hesitated. "You're all together?" He waved between Sasha and Olivia and Bo.

"I'm the interior designer," Bo said gruffly, hitching her shoulder bag a little. "I've brought samples to see what will go with what. Depending on lighting." She paused. "And, uh, the fen shi. You know."

"You mean...feng shui?" Christos asked dubiously.

Bo's cheeks reddened. "Yes, that," she powered on. "Rooms have to be aligned for positive ionic power. And energy in line with the body's chakrams."

Christos's brow furrowed. "The...*chakrams?*"

"But my specialty's really um...shades. Colours. Shaded colours in all their gradients of multiplicitous hues and so on."

Oh God.

Christos then glanced to Sasha inquisitively, as if asking who he was in the scheme of things.

"I am here to buy a home with my beautiful princess," he announced, suddenly tugging Olivia into his side so hard that she made a tiny *oof.* He turned one of those dazzling smiles on her that was his trademark. He was beaming like a lighthouse lamp.

Olivia attempted to smile back and wondered how constipated she looked.

Based on the sharply narrowing eyes Margaret threw at Sasha, *badly* was the answer.

"You two?" Christos blurted in surprise.

I told you! Hadn't she told Sasha during his henchperson interview that no one would ever buy him as her ex? She had to save this mess! "I am very rich," Olivia suddenly announced.

Margaret let out a soft sigh of disbelief.

Sasha gazed at Olivia lovingly. "Very," he said with extra enthusiasm.

After a pause, Christos merely nodded. "I see. Well." He fetched a key. "Good luck with the viewing. And the…feng shui. And, er, chakrams." His frankly sceptical gaze raked Bo.

"Right you are," Bo said cheerfully, hoisting her bag of "colour samples" so hard that the steel carabiners within clanged loudly.

Christos's eyes clouded with confusion. "What…?"

But Margaret swept them all towards the lift. "Theees way, please, people. I must not be late for my next viewing."

Within moments, they were inside the lift, the doors closed, and they'd done it. They were heading up to floor three.

CHAPTER 17

TOWER OF TERROR

THE THIRD-FLOOR APARTMENT WAS SPACIOUS and completely empty. They made their way into the master bedroom which had the window they needed.

Olivia unlocked it and peered out. Sure enough, the fire-escape landing was right beside it.

"We have to move fast," Bo said and dove into her bag. "Sasha, put this on. It's a chest harness. You'll be closest to the end of the ladder, and I need you secure while you keep our apparatus in place. Olivia, this is for you. It's a seat harness. Goes around the waist, and you put a leg through each hoop. I'll be attaching your safety rope to it at the back of your waist."

Olivia caught it and did as instructed, feeling Margaret's worried gaze on her the whole time. "What about you?" she asked Bo.

"I'll clip on directly to the landing. I don't need my own rope because I'm not moving. I'll be who's holding yours. I'll feed you your safety rope. It will loop around a strut above us that I'll be using as a fulcrum point to keep it out of your way."

Whatever the hell that meant.

"Sasha," Bo said when he'd finished with his harness, "come with me now, and we'll set up. Olivia, when you hear me whistle, you can join us. No point in crowding the landing when we don't need everyone there. It'll just get in the way of ladder deployment."

Olivia rather appreciated how in charge Bo sounded. She radiated competence. It was what Olivia needed right now in the face of her rising nerves. She'd chosen her *Whisk Taker* button pin today (hidden discreetly inside her jacket) to give her courage and cheer her up.

"Everyone, can you remember to keep your voices down during the mission," Bo instructed. "We don't want a curious neighbour to hear us halfway up their wall and call the cops."

Sasha and Olivia nodded. Margaret looked ready to snap with tension.

Bo climbed out the window, followed by Sasha. Olivia passed him his ladder bag, and then she was alone. Well, except for Margaret. Who had begun pacing.

"Did I mention this is an idiotic idea?" she began.

"Once or twice." Olivia tried a smile. It was met with anxiety. She slid a small backpack she'd brought onto her back. It contained raw prawns, a milk-filled syringe, and enough space to hold Trip.

"We are trusting everyone's safety to a woman who tried to convince the guard she was into channelling body chakrams. Xena's weapon?" Margaret objected.

"Yeah, that was a bit dodgy. Wait, you watched *Xena*?"

She sniffed. "Under sufferance. Helen enjoyed it. She had a…broad… sense of humour. I suspect she liked how schlocky it was. And the lesbian subtext."

"Good for her. What about you? Did you like anything in it?"

That stymied Margaret for a moment. "It was pretty. The scenery." Then she scowled, distraction forgotten. "I can't believe you're doing this. Or that I helped you! It's so high up there!"

"Okay, but look at how expert Bo is at this. She won't let anything happen to me."

"Mmmph." But at least Margaret didn't look quite so fretful.

A low whistle sounded.

"That's my cue." Olivia gave Margaret a long look. "I'll be fine."

"I will hold you to that," she ground out, eyes flashing. "Or I'm resigning." This time, it was Margaret's hand that flew out and seized Olivia's. "I will haunt you if you foolishly choose to die," she said, almost vibrating with anxiety.

"Isn't it the other way around?" Olivia pointed out with a smile. "Don't the dead do the haunting?"

"Don't think I won't find a way. Stay safe." She squeezed Olivia's hand so hard, it was painful.

"Okay," was all she could think to say.

And then she was out the window.

The ladder was in position, tied to the sixth-floor fire-escape's landing railing. It stretched across the void and had been laid over the railing of Tina's balcony—unsecured at that end. It gave a little rattle in the wind and moved slightly.

The wind! Olivia suddenly registered there was a strong breeze up here, something they hadn't allowed for during training. She shot Bo a worried look, but the other woman grinned.

"It's fine," Bo said. "Your weight on the ladder will stop it moving around." She snapped a carabiner clip onto the back of Olivia's harness, then tugged hard to test it. "You're all good. See?" Bo pointed up. The rope went up and up, had been passed through a fire-escape metal brace bolted just under the roof, and came down again to the ground, where a large coil of excess rope lay.

"I'll be holding that end and feeding you more rope as you inch along," Bo explained. "If, worst-case scenario, the ladder fails, I'll be able to swing you straight back to the landing. Easy. And Sasha will be here as backup too, so no worries."

Indeed, he was standing obediently by the end of the ladder which had been tied to the landing railing in an array of so many knots, it suggested Bo was taking no chances.

He, too, had been tied to a landing strut, and his coiled safety rope lay at his feet. That seemed like overkill since he wasn't going anywhere. Was he?

Bo followed her gaze. "That's my Plan B," she said. "If you freeze in the middle of the ladder crawl or can't continue for any reason, just raise one arm, and Sasha will immediately retrieve you. But that's only as a last resort. We really don't want that to happen."

"No," Olivia shuddered. "Because that'd mean I've turned to jelly."

"That, and the fact the ladder's only supposed to hold one hundred and fifty kilograms. I'm not sure how well it'd do with both of you, given your combined weight is a little more than that."

"I cannot help how many muscles I have," Sasha announced.

"You kind of can, big guy," Bo pointed out. She patted her round stomach. "Sadly, the fact I don't have skills at anything involving bending means I can't be the one to do retrieval. But, as I say, that's a worse-case scenario."

She turned to the ladder. "It's time. You're up, Liv. Remember, arm out if you need help. No shouting. And go get yourself a penguin."

Olivia inched along the ladder and stopped three feet in, the headwind making her blink furiously. Maybe Margaret had a point. This *was* ridiculous.

She'd made the mistake of looking down just once, spotting Damien watching from the ground—little more than an enthusiastically waving blob. Olivia had shuddered. *Way* too high.

Bo's tension on the rope she was holding was excellent. Meanwhile, she didn't have to look to know Sasha had a rock-solid hold on the end of the ladder, just to be sure all those knots held. Wind aside, conditions were optimal.

"One Day More" from *Les Misérables* suddenly blared out, rattling Olivia with shock. She clenched the ladder so hard, her knuckles turned white and she felt pain.

"Oh shit, sorry!" Bo called, tone low. "It's work. Everyone hold tight. No moving."

The hell. "Now?" Olivia hissed back.

"Work emergency number. I wouldn't answer it otherwise." Her voice changed to professional. "Go for Bo." Then. "The hell? What? No! Shit, I'll be right there." She hung up. "I'm so sorry, but I have to go."

"What?!" Olivia said, forgetting the "no shouting" edict. As best she could, she twisted around and saw Bo unclip herself from the fire-escape and hand Olivia's safety line to Sasha. "Take this," she told him. "Don't let go."

"Bo!" Olivia said as loudly as she dared. "Why?"

"Um…" Bo sucked in a mighty breath. "The *entire* barricade on my theatre set just collapsed. There will be no revolution tonight if I don't get there to help fix it. I'm sorry. But I have to put my job ahead of your penguin." Then, more reassuringly, she added: "It'll be all good. Just stick to the plan. Sasha's got you." And then Bo scrambled down the ladder.

Olivia watched her, frozen to the spot.

There was only the sound of the wind and an occasional honking car from Prahran's impossible traffic until Bo crawled into the window. Then came a muffled eruption of fury that sounded an awful lot like Margaret, interspersed with Bo attempting to get a word in. Occasionally, a long arm was flung out the window, pointing up. There was an unmistakable: "Get back up there right now!"

And then nothing. Apparently, Bo's fallen French barricades were more powerful than even Margaret's impressive ire.

Then the bookstore owner's pinched face was peering out the window. "Mission cancelled," Margaret called, her voice low. At least, that's sort of what it sounded like, although it was hard to hear. "Get down here at once."

Olivia shook her head and began to inch again along the ladder. It was now or never. This mission had no do-overs. How could it? Christos would never buy them returning for another viewing with Anita van Dyke forgetting her key a second time.

She tuned out whatever else Margaret was saying, trying to forget how rigid with fear the other woman's face was, and focused on making steady progress.

Her heart thudded as she neared the middle. The weakest point. Although the structure hadn't bowed during training, it also hadn't been subject to these winds before either.

She probably also shouldn't think about the fact that the person she'd trusted with her safety in this mission was not only no longer here but had been responsible for barricades that had just *collapsed*.

Oh no. No, no, no. That was not a good thought at all.

The centre point was right ahead. Should she lie down for that part? To spread her weight so it wasn't all concentrated on it? Yeah, she probably should.

Olivia lay down and then pulled herself across the join, even as the wind began to howl in her ears. The whole ladder gave an indignant rattle, and to her horror, the end point began to shift slightly on the balcony.

No! If it slides off the balcony, I'll fall...

She wasn't going to fall, she told herself. She wasn't. Just to be sure, she decided to wait a moment to let the wind die down before sitting back up and continuing.

And right about then, the wind gusted once again, even more strongly, making her face ache…and—*oh God!* She ducked as a small bird flew right at her face. Olivia lurched into upright position, waving it furiously away, and the whole ladder bounced with her sudden movement.

And…kept on bouncing.

What. The. Hell?

Then she heard Sasha's voice, strong and urgent: "I am coming. Hold on."

Holy shit! She'd waved! At the bird! She'd inadvertently given Sasha the signal for help. But if Sasha was speed-walking along the ladder—and it sure as hell felt like it—that meant no one was holding her safety rope. If the ladder dropped now, or Olivia did, she was dead.

In terror, she clung hard to it, and slowly started to turn.

Enormous Sasha, face wreathed in worry, filled her entire frame. Barely breaking stride, he was suddenly bending down and scooping her up under the armpits and propelling her forward with his considerable momentum. It was as if she weighed nothing at all. Then he'd somehow changed his grip, and suddenly she was being held by the waist and rushed to the end of the ladder and the balcony.

When they got there, in a split second, two things happened at once.

First, the balcony door slid furiously open, framed by an even more furious-looking woman.

And second, Sasha froze at the sight of her, in the act of holding Olivia aloft over the balcony like Simba from *The Lion King*. She felt ridiculous with her feet just dangling, as Sasha, behind her, went so rigid that his locking muscles felt like a physical "oh fuck".

Then time recommenced. He placed her gently on the balcony floor and hopped down behind her. And three sets of eyes reviewed each other.

Olivia blurted out to the woman: "You're not Tina."

"No," not-Tina replied, eyes narrowing to slits. "And who the fuck are you?"

CHAPTER 18

OPERATION RAW PRAWN

THE ENRAGED WOMAN IN FRONT of her did have a passing resemblance to a rabid raccoon, Olivia thought as she undid the carabiner from the harness, freeing herself from her tether. Not that it was tethered *to* anything anymore.

She glanced back to where she'd come from. Her eyes fell to the last thing she ever expected: Dr Margaret Blackwood—the woman in terror of heights—was standing where Bo had been, clutching Olivia's safety line, face as white as an ice storm.

Even from eight metres away, her fear was rolling off her in waves. And, unlike Bo, she had nothing to tie herself with to the landing. She had wrapped her arm tightly around one side of the railing but still looked about to bolt every time the wind picked up.

And the wind *was* picking up, getting stronger by the second. Margaret was putting herself in danger. *For me.*

Hold on! Olivia tried to telepathically send her the signal, but Margaret just looked even more grim. Frightened. Olivia never wanted to see that expression on her face ever again. Strong, competent women like Margaret Blackwood should never look terrified.

"I'm not sure what's so fascinating over there," the woman in front of her snapped. "Answer my question: who the fuck are you?"

"I'm Olivia," she said, turning. "And you are?"

"Absolutely calling the cops on you."

"Right." Well, that made sense. "Where's Tina?"

"In the gym. She'll be back any minute." The woman folded her arms. "I'm her cousin. Chloe."

The cousin was real? She wasn't just Tina's code word for scoring drugs? That was a relief. Or maybe she used the cousin excuse only half the time.

"I remember her mentioning an Olivia, from a few months back. Didn't you two date?" The woman was eyeing her suspiciously.

"Yes, we did," Olivia said. "Well, until she stole my mother's bracelet."

Chloe's eyes narrowed at that. She showed no surprise. "I see."

"You know she's a thief?" Olivia asked. "She stole so much of my stuff."

"No shit, Sherlock. Why do you think her parents cut off her allowance?"

"They still left her this nice place," Olivia couldn't help observing.

"This?" Chloe stared at her in disbelief. "Is that what she told you? I'll have you know my parents own this place. They've let her stay in it rent-free for years because she has them wrapped around her pinkie. When she got into trouble with her parents for the klepto shit, my parents said she could remain here but couldn't put a single toe out of line from that moment on. And I get roped into checking on her every now and then to make sure she's keeping their place up to scratch." She rolled her eyes. "Lucky me."

"Wait, so Tina will lose this place if your parents find out she's stolen one more thing?" Olivia checked. Her heart rate picked up. Could it be this easy?

"Yeah. Why?" Her gaze lifted to Sasha. "And who's he?"

Sasha beamed as if just delighted to be remembered. "I am Sasha," he said solicitously. "It is an honour to meet you, Chloe the cousin." He gave a half bow and smiled so charmingly that Chloe's eyebrows shot up.

"Well, you're not the usual burglars, I'll give you that. Not that we get any burglars up here."

"I'm not a burglar at all," Olivia said. "I'm just a woman with an access issue."

"Chloe?" came Tina's voice from somewhere inside. "Who are you talking to?"

"You'll never guess," the cousin replied, turning. "Your ex decided to see you by way of a ladder, six floors up."

Tina, looking tired and sweaty in gym gear, appeared at the balcony door. Her face went through myriad expressions, from astonishment to fear.

Of course she'd be afraid. She was probably worried Olivia had told her cousin about a certain stolen penguin…and knew what that would mean for keeping her free luxury apartment. Then Tina said urgently: "Just wait right there, I'd like a quick word with Chloe."

Tina bustled her cousin inside, and they disappeared towards the bedroom.

"Now's my chance," Olivia whispered to Sasha. "Operation Raw Prawn. You cough if you see them coming back." She didn't wait for an answer and flung herself inside.

Shooting milk into Tina's chair from the syringe took only five seconds. She then crawled over to the curtains and rummaged around for the frozen prawns in her backpack. Four of those soon-to-be smelly little suckers were into the hems before Sasha loudly coughed.

Olivia scrambled back to the balcony doorway but was still on her hands and knees as Chloe and Tina returned, seeming to be having a hissed argument.

Chloe stopped. "What are you doing down there?"

"I needed a rest," Olivia huffed. "I'm not really built for ladder-crawling *Mission Impossible* stuff."

"Huh." Chloe glanced at Sasha.

"Indeed she is not," he intoned.

Grr. He didn't have to agree so quickly. Sasha shot her a winning smile nonetheless.

Chloe turned back to Tina and seemed to resume their conversation. "If you're sure. I don't mind being a witness or whatever."

"No," Tina said and smiled reassuringly. "This is between me and Livvy." With that, she waved Chloe away and dragged Olivia by the elbow into the lounge room.

"Okay, what the fuck?" Tina demanded the moment they were alone. "Chloe almost called the police on you."

"I want Trip back."

"It's long gone."

At least she didn't deny stealing him.

"I'm well aware, and I want him back."

"It. Is. Gone." Tina folded her arms. There was no trace of deception on her face.

"Then you don't mind if I search your place."

"No!" Panic filled her face.

"Why? Because Chloe will ask what I'm looking for and I'll tell her it's my penguin that you just STOLE!" She lifted her voice.

Tina slapped a hand over her mouth. "Shut up!"

Olivia nipped at her hand.

Tina removed it with a muttered "ow".

"I know what'll happen if she learns you're stealing again," Olivia said hotly. "Tell me where Trip is."

Tina's hand fell to Olivia's arm and stroked it.

Olivia stared at her disdainfully, recognising the gesture for what it was now. An attempt to manipulate her.

"Look, here's the thing," Tina began with a bright, forced smile. "A little while back, I was telling Horrie about your penguin."

"Horrie? Your loser drug dealer?"

"Ssh!" Tina snapped her head around worriedly. With no Chloe about, she continued: "My...associate. Did you know the man has this whole wall of collectible animals? He's got all sorts of trophies and shit hanging in his office. No penguins, though. So when I sort of came up a little short to buy merchandise recently, I had an idea."

Dread filled Olivia.

"I asked if I got him a penguin, that'd square us. Horrie said, 'Penguin first'...and so here we are." She gave Olivia a dazzling smile. "I figured you'd understand. I mean, you're so sweet, right, hon?" She smiled harder until her TV-commercial-cute dimples showed. "I love that about you."

"Cut the crap," Olivia blurted in disbelief. She wondered if every vein in her forehead was about to pop. "You seriously think you can butter me up and I'll be fine that you stole my penguin? After everything else you've nicked from me too?"

"Well, I admit, I had hoped you wouldn't be too mad, but it was a bit of an emergency. I'm still so short since..."

"Since your parents cut you off for stealing." Olivia brushed that manipulative, stroking hand away and said: "Here's the deal: I won't tell Chloe about Trip, but you're going to get my penguin back from Horrie today. And if you screw me over again even once, in the smallest way, I'll track down Chloe and fill her in that you're still a thief."

Tina actually looked shocked. "Livvy? Why are you talking to me like this?"

It *was* unlike her, Olivia supposed. All she'd ever done in the past was be unfailingly respectful and kind to a woman who had stolen from her repeatedly. She'd even given Tina a second chance and had it thrown back in her face. She'd had enough.

But for Tina, so used to her cute, elfin looks winning over one and all, bluntness probably felt like rudeness if you were unaccustomed to hearing it.

"I've finally worked out how I deserve to be treated," Olivia said and ran a hand tiredly through her hair. "And it's a long way from what you've been doing."

Tina's expression lit with surprise. "I...see."

"Bottom line: get Trip back and I go away. Your family won't hear about your latest theft from me."

Tina pursed her lips. "Except Horrie and I have had a bit of a falling out since our penguin deal. He said I'm dead to him and that if I darken his doorstep again, I'll be dead in every sense." She scowled. "He's full of shit, but I won't risk it on the off-chance he really means it."

"Then give me his address."

"That won't help. Horrie's got guards on his doors. He only sees people he knows or with an invitation."

"Let me worry about that. Address. Now."

Tina's jaw looked set hard in that stubborn way it did when she was about to dig in. But then there came a crash from the kitchen of something being dropped. A reminder Chloe was still there.

"All right." Tina looked pissed off. "Wait here." She disappeared and returned with a scribbled address. "You can't tell him where you got his info, though. Promise me."

"I won't," Olivia agreed and took the paper. She checked that the address looked real. It did. Olivia knew the building. Shady as hell. She had seen goons hanging around it too. Were they Horrie's security? She stuffed the paper into her bag and regarded Tina with a dispassionate eye. "I was a fool, wasn't I?" she asked without bitterness.

"You're going to have to narrow it down," Tina said with a small smirk. "Which time?"

Olivia straightened. "I can't believe I ever thought you liked me for me."

Tina studied her a moment. "This is new. What's gotten into you?" she asked curiously.

Hadn't Annalise asked her the same thing? Said she was different? What *had* changed? Losing Trip? Acknowledging her anger at how her exes had treated her? Margaret Blackwood's uncompromising influence? Learning her own worth? All of the above, most likely.

"Everyone has a limit," Olivia finally said. "You pushed me past mine. I'm never putting up with shit like that from anyone ever again." As soon as she said the words, she knew they were true. As she met Tina's eye, she wondered if she'd even get an apology.

"I see." Tina said nothing else. Of course an apology would be too much to hope for.

"That about sums it up, I guess," Olivia said. "If you'd said sorry now, I might have even believed you since you'd have nothing to gain from it."

"Why would I?" Tina asked, tilting her head. "I have nothing to apologise for. We both got something we needed."

Olivia stared at her, a sick feeling rising up. What had Tina needed? Stuff to pawn, obviously. But was there really nothing else to it? She searched Tina's face but saw no deception. Steady blue eyes held hers.

"Christ. I thought you knew," Tina said, sounding faintly surprised. "You turned a blind eye to what I was up to so often that I figured you knew the score, deep down."

Oh. Olivia inhaled sharply. Was that how she'd come across to Tina? So desperate to be touched, to feel wanted, that she'd knowingly put up with having her worldly goods stolen?

Tina blinked. "Huh. Guess not."

Olivia glared at her. "Well, if that was the deal, you weren't too good at keeping up your end, were you?" Tina's lack of reciprocation in the bedroom still burned. Was it worse now, knowing Tina thought it was her duty? *Her* side of the bargain? "Did you even *want* to be in my bed at all?"

Tina shrugged. "Sometimes."

Humiliation burned through Olivia.

"Can you stop looking at me like that?" Tina's eyes squinted in annoyance. "Come on, Livvy. The world is full of people who mutually use each other."

Olivia could barely speak through her embarrassment. "For it to be mutual, Tina, *both* people should know what the deal is."

"And like I said, I thought you did. I thought it was obvious what I was up to."

No. It wasn't. Not to me.

Tina studied her expression for a moment and then sighed. "Well, it's done now," she said, her face back to granite. "We're done too. You can see yourself out." With that, she grabbed Olivia by the elbow, propelled her to the balcony door, and shoved her outside. The lock clunked into place on the door, and she disappeared.

And that was that. Tina was out of her life for good. But the pain of that parting blow about how little Tina had cared was brutal. She'd never felt so unworthy and unlovable. But then Olivia looked over to the fire-escape, and Tina's indifference was nothing compared to the sudden warmth in her chest at what she saw: there stood Dr Margaret Blackwood, white as the whitest sheet, clenching Olivia's safety line. She was in danger of being blown off the building herself, but she was waiting. For Olivia.

Sasha wordlessly hooked Olivia back to her safety line. It was as though he sensed her self-worth had been put through a wringer and she was struggling with her emotions. Or he just couldn't think of what to say. It was obvious from the lack of bulge in her backpack that she'd failed to retrieve Trip.

Her gaze drifted to Margaret, who watched Olivia like a hawk—albeit a trembling hawk.

Sasha held the end of the ladder as Olivia slid onto it and began to make her way slowly back to the landing. It was colder now, and her backside felt numb as she moved steadily along. The ladder didn't rattle or move this time because Sasha leaned firmly on the end of it, watching her progress.

Don't look down; just look at Margaret.

The other woman was like a beacon. Not a beacon of hope, more like one of doggedness. It was the sense that if Margaret could be up here, enduring her worst fear for Olivia, then Olivia could damned well get to the other side. Besides, she didn't doubt Margaret would find a way to haunt her if Olivia did die. She was contrary enough.

She'd reached the end. Olivia slid off the ladder onto the fire-escape landing, then caught the astonishing sight of Sasha, with those enormous long arms held out wide for balance, speed-walking towards her with the sureness of a mountain goat. His safety rope was still firmly attached, but knowing him, he'd probably be just as sure-footed and confident without it. *Amazing.* But his form and balance weren't what mesmerised her right now.

Her heart, mind, and body were all focused on Margaret, who had rushed up here despite her fears. Now she stood, unmoving, her frame almost locked up, still clutching Olivia's slack safety rope with white knuckles, eyes darting wildly about. Her blonde wig was gone, clearly ripped off by the wind.

Olivia placed her hands gently on Margaret's rigid biceps and rubbed soothingly. "Margaret? You can let go of the rope now."

Margaret blinked, as if not fully registering Olivia was there until now. "You made it," she croaked. "You're here."

"I'm here," Olivia confirmed, then unclipped herself from the carabiner, dropping it and its attached rope line to the landing with a clatter. She met Margaret's dark gaze again. "I know how hard this was for you. Thank you for climbing up here to save me."

"Someone had to," Margaret said, grinding out her words. "Since that disloyal stagehand bailed on you." Her eyes held a murderous gleam. "I tried to encourage her to stay, but she refused." She looked genuinely enraged.

"Bo had a work emergency," Olivia said gently. "I don't blame her for leaving."

"I don't care. And I *do* blame her. I might ban her from my store for life for her reckless actions." The wind picked up, and as Margaret swayed, fear again flitted across her face. Her eyes tightened. "I might ban Sasha too for forgetting his primary duty was to hang on to your safety line." She shot the rapidly incoming figure on the ladder a glare.

"You won't ban them," Olivia smiled. "And thank you."

"Don't thank me yet," Margaret said curtly. "I'm entirely unsure how I'm going to get down from up here." Her ferocious grip on the railing tightened. She craned her neck around Olivia as if trying to see her backpack. "You don't have your penguin?"

"No." Olivia bit her lip. "He's been sold. Tina gave me the buyer's address—Horrie, her drug dealer. But Operation Raw Prawn was a success, at least. Vengeance was enacted."

"Well, that's something, I suppose." Margaret sniffed. "And at least Tina was forthcoming."

"I…kinda had to threaten her."

Margaret's eyebrows shot up. "You…*threatened* her? *You?*"

"Yeah." Olivia gave her a tiny grin. "I think your influence might be rubbing off on me."

Looking pleased, Margaret said, "Glad to hear it." The wind gusted, and she trembled again. It wasn't surprising, given what she was wearing.

"Where did you get that suit from?" Olivia asked, appalled. "That's more polyester than I've ever seen you wear. It's not even in your size. It does nothing to protect you from the wind."

"Well, I didn't expect to be clinging to a building face today when I got dressed, did I? Or clambering up a rickety escape ladder in heels, for that matter." Margaret blew out a breath. "This was Helen's. I found it at the back of the wardrobe when I was looking for something that screamed *real estate agent*. I didn't even know I still had it. If I'd known, I'd have put a flamethrower to good use on it before now."

Olivia laughed. "I believe you would."

Margaret opened her mouth, but before she could reply, a clatter sounded.

Sasha had reached the landing. He leaped easily off the ladder and raised his arms like Rocky Balboa, turning to Damien on the ground. In return, Damien waved furiously up at them while holding a familiar blonde wig in one hand—impersonating a cheerleader waving a pompom. Well, at least Margaret would get her deposit back.

"You make that look so easy," Olivia told him. "Thanks for rushing to my aid, but I have to tell you, I was only waving away a bird."

"But you went flat on the ladder all of a sudden, then your arm came out." He peered at her. "You were not calling for help?"

"No." She gave him a sheepish look. "Sorry."

"Then *I* didn't need to be up here either?" Margaret asked, looking askance.

Oops. "There was a bird," Olivia repeated in vain. "Right up in my face. I couldn't *not* wave it away."

Sasha snorted. "Well, it is no matter. I appreciated the challenge. It is good rehearsal for me if I want to do my own movie stunts. Now I will take down the ladder." He flicked a glance to Margaret and then back to Olivia. "Maybe you should assist Dr Blackwood, yes?"

Oh yes. For all her threats, the bookstore owner was looking paler and wobblier by the second.

"Come on," Olivia said, sliding an arm gently around Margaret's back and unclenching the woman's white knuckles from the railing with her other hand. "Let's get you down from here."

Four minutes later and Olivia had finally managed to coax Margaret back into the third-floor apartment. Her angular body had trembled against Olivia's the whole time. The final moments, easing her over the railing and into the window, were the worst. Her eyes had widened with fear.

The moment they were safely inside, Margaret sagged against a wall. Then she turned on her. "*Never* do that again," she hissed. "Never!"

"I promise I won't crawl across another ladder six floors high," Olivia said. "But you should talk! When I saw you up there, no safety line, just clinging to the fire-escape and being buffeted by the wind, you gave me the fright of my life!"

"*You* had a fright?! I had to watch that Russian idiot take off like a rocket when you waved. He was supposed to be holding your safety rope! What was he thinking?" She stalked right up inside Olivia's space and glowered, fear bright in her eyes. "I had to run up that fire-escape to grab your rope because the imbecile had forgotten *why* he was meant to be holding it." Her eyes drew tighter, and she suddenly grabbed a fistful of Olivia's shirt and gave her a shake. "You could have *died*."

"I didn't." Olivia whispered hoarsely. "And you could have been blown off the fire-escape!"

"I didn't." Margaret swallowed.

"My hero," Olivia murmured appreciatively. "Racing to my aid, so high up. So impressive."

"I"—Margaret seemed stymied by that—"suppose."

She was so close, Olivia could feel the warmth of her breath. Short little puffs of air. God, up this close, she was beautiful, especially now with her blood up. She seemed more alive than Olivia had ever seen her. "You are so very impressive, Dr Blackwood," she whispered. "Thank you."

And then Margaret Blackwood tugged her even closer. And kissed her.

CHAPTER 19

FLIRTING WITH DISASTER

OLIVIA HAD NEVER BEEN MORE stunned in her life. Margaret was kissing her. *Margaret.* The woman who seemed to make an art form out of mocking Olivia. Margaret's hand was buried in Olivia's hair, her other one cupping the back of her neck, a thumb stroking the underside of her jaw.

Olivia kissed her fervidly, holding nothing back. She slipped her arms around Margaret, pulling her close. Those small breasts and warm belly were pressed against her, and Olivia found even the thought of that impossibly arousing. As was the sensation of their tongues tangling, which made her whimper.

How had she ever doubted she'd wanted this woman?

Margaret's hand was stroking her cheek. Where else might that elegant hand explore? She moaned at the thought as Margaret's other hand slid to her ass and fondled it appreciatively.

Oh God. Olivia wasn't sure she'd survive this. Her underwear was already drenched.

A bang sounded, making them leap apart.

Sasha had thrown the packed-up ladder through the window—all twenty-five-plus kilos of it—and now one long leg was climbing in after it.

Margaret and Olivia stared at him, mouths slightly open. Olivia's breathing sounded harsh and ragged to her own ears. Margaret's hungry, wild eyes darted about.

Ropes were looped all around Sasha's body—the safety lines—and he looked like a mountain climber in a fancy suit as he came to full height.

No one spoke. Sasha cast them a long look as the weird, charged vibe settled between them, but then he set to work, deftly stripping himself of all the ropes.

Olivia wondered what would have happened if he hadn't arrived when he had. Would Margaret have slid her roaming hands somewhere intimate?

Would Olivia have started unbuttoning Margaret's blouse? Slipped her hand inside her bra? What sort of bra did Margaret have? Would it be pale? Sheer enough to see her hardening nipples?

Whimpering inwardly, Olivia watched in wonder as a visible heat rose up Margaret's throat and into her cheeks. Had she read her mind? Or were Olivia's fantasies showing on her face?

Margaret inhaled sharply and looked away.

Or maybe she had just remembered she shouldn't have done that. Or hadn't meant to. As Tina had implied, Olivia wasn't terribly alluring. Her confidence wilted.

Sasha was the only one moving. "Did you know," he said conversationally without looking up, "adrenalin makes us do things we might not otherwise?" He began shifting the ropes into one big pile. "Speaking as someone who had much adrenalin in his former career. This is simply fact." He was now pushing the ropes into the bag Bo had left behind. "In case you wanted to pretend it did not happen."

It being…the kiss??? Alarm shot through her.

"I always look inside a window first before I throw something through it," he said by way of explanation, his voice even as ever.

Ah shit. He'd seen.

"At least now I know why Dr Blackwood is so opposed to my advances," he continued with a small grin as he zipped up the now rope-filled bag. He finally looked up.

"It couldn't just be that you're repellent to me?" Margaret suggested, eyebrow lifting. Her voice sounded unusually raspy. "That not every woman wants you?"

"No," he said, his smile widening. "I'm very sure it is not that." Sasha rose and handed the bag of ropes to Olivia to carry, then returned to the window.

After closing and locking it, he faced them again. "I chose Dr Blackwood to pursue to make Kelly jealous. I was not serious in my attentions."

"No shit," Olivia murmured, adjusting the bag on her shoulder.

"You knew?" He gasped.

"Everyone knew," Margaret said dryly.

"Even Kelly?" he asked, sounding miffed now.

"Especially Kelly," Olivia said.

"Oh." He sagged. "Well, it is of no matter." Sasha offered Olivia a hopeful look. "Will you tell your beautiful sister how I saved your life today? Maybe she will give me a second chance?"

"Only if you swear to stop ogling other women when you're dating her," Olivia said, deciding his daring deeds merited a good word in Kelly's ear.

"I swear!" He raised his hand as if taking a solemn vow. "Only Kelly. I have learned a powerful lesson."

"Wait, daring deeds!" Margaret sputtered, suddenly coming to life. "You *dropped* Olivia's safety line! You didn't save her life; you put it in danger!"

Sasha shook his head and turned to fully face her. "No. Did you not notice that the rope you were holding so tightly was secured at your end? Did you not see me bend down and tie to the landing strut the end of her safety line?"

Silence fell.

Margaret turned pale. "I was too busy trying to get out that damned window when you shouted to her that you were coming for her! But…" She stopped. "Then I…didn't really need to have gone up there?" she hissed. "At all?"

"You did not," Sasha said simply, grabbing the ladder bag and inclining his head at her. "But you will now have the bright side, yes? Would you and your Olivia have kissed if you had not been so brave? Hmm? I think not."

Your Olivia? Olivia was too scared to check out Margaret's reaction to that.

Sasha winked and headed for the door. "I will meet you at the lift. Do not be too long."

Margaret and Olivia shared a brief, embarrassed glance as Sasha left.

"Well," Margaret said awkwardly and then gazed intently at the floor skirtings. "I suppose he has a point. Adrenalin is a powerful thing. We mustn't read too much into it."

So she had only kissed Olivia because of adrenalin? Between that admission and Tina's, her ego crumpled into a sad little heap. Did no one ever kiss her because they desperately wanted her? "I…guess so."

Sharply, Margaret looked at her. "You did kiss me because of the adrenalin?"

Hadn't she just said the same? And hadn't *Margaret* initiated that kiss? Olivia glared at her. "Apparently." It was unconvincing. She scratched her neck and looked away. "Tina pretty much said that I wasn't that alluring either. I get it." Her cheeks flamed, and she felt utterly humiliated. "Like you say, adrenalin must be pretty powerful."

Margaret stared at her, eyes warring with emotions. "I didn't say you were…" she paused and looked awkward as hell, "un-alluring."

Olivia's head snapped up. "It wasn't nothing to me, that kiss," she said, screwing her courage to the sticking place—to misappropriate Shakespeare. Because she couldn't pretend it hadn't been amazing. Olivia wasn't going to play games. She was useless at them.

Margaret sighed. "I think this is a discussion for another time and place."

Ah. Olivia felt foolish all over again. She was being fobbed off. At least Margaret was being kind about it. Olivia looked away, blinking hard. Maybe she should try a vow of celibacy next because…

A gentle hand tucked under her chin, lifting her eyes to meet Margaret's. "I didn't say anything but that we should discuss this later. Don't read anything else into it."

"Except you're not going to say yes to anything else, are you?" Olivia pulled away. Her face burned where Margaret's touch had been. "You agreed so fast to Sasha's adrenalin excuse. Next, you'll pretend our kiss never happened. But it *happened*, Margaret. And I felt something. Because I'm an idiot and because I'm always doing this."

"Always doing what?" Margaret asked, sounding puzzled. "Kissing people in moments of high stress?"

"Having my head turned by the wrong people who then hurt me. I'm an idiot."

"Olivia," Margaret said softly. "You are, unquestioningly, an idiot. Your absurd missions speak volumes on that topic." She said that as if she'd uttered the most heartfelt compliment. "Scholars could write peer-reviewed papers on both our idiocy for participating in these vengeance schemes. But

I always mean what I say. In this case, I do mean we will discuss this later." And then, as if unbidden, her fingertips trailed from Olivia's temple down her cheek, then ran along her jaw. She gave a little huff of something between disbelief and fondness and turned and led the way out of the apartment.

As they walked together to the lift where Sasha waited, Margaret suddenly asked Olivia: "What on earth would a drug dealer want with your penguin?"

"Horrie collects taxidermied animals, apparently. Has a wall full of them. The problem is Tina says he won't see anyone without an invitation. I don't think she's lying. I know that building, and I've seen goons lurking outside. We can't just sneak in."

"Then we don't sneak in," Margaret said, sounding like her old self, before she'd been terrified into a new reality. Before she'd kissed Olivia senseless because *adrenalin*. "In fact, I've an idea."

"Already?" Olivia asked, impressed

Margaret supplied a cautious smile. "Yes, already." Her chin lifted imperiously. "You didn't hire an unimaginative henchperson. And I know how to get us an invitation."

It was intoxicating seeing her smile at Olivia like that. A thrill shot all the way down to her toes. Their gazes locked and held, and Olivia had a hard time remembering to breathe.

"You two will please get a room," Sasha noted as the lift doors opened and he stepped inside. "*My eyeballs…*"

Olivia followed him in and sharply elbowed him in the ribs. "Behave, or I'll forget to put in that good word with Kelly."

He straightened instantly and, with over-the-top earnestness, said: "Olivia and Dr Blackwood, I apologize with most sincereness. You make a beautiful couple."

A beautiful couple? Olivia wasn't sure whether to laugh or cry. Embarrassment crept up her cheeks again, and she sneaked a peek at Margaret, who watched Olivia, expression as inscrutable as ever, before abruptly looking away.

Friday, April 10

Sunset: *5:59pm*

Temp: *12.7C-22C*

Rain: *0.2mm*

Drink: *Silver Lining Adelaide Hills Sauvignon Blanc 2020—the whole damned bottle. Enjoyable acidity is a nice counterbalance to my cartwheeling brain, on account of the fact I KISSED OLIVIA.*

Reading: *As if one could focus on reading at a time like this.*

General Observations: *What have I done? I'll narrow that down. What was I thinking, kissing Olivia. Not to mention enjoying it thoroughly.*

I also clawed my way up a fire-escape despite being in no way over my childhood terror of heights.

I badly cosplayed a Dutch real estate agent. Really, Helen, why did you have that outfit? It's as appalling now as it was the day you bought it. I trust you laughed seeing me in it? I almost ripped it off twice before leaving home, which was what made me so late. But I wore it because Olivia needed me to look the part.

And then I climbed a six-storey building because Olivia needed me.

And then I KISSED Olivia.

The preceding not-me-at-all antics I've decided to chalk up to protective panic. I need Olivia to be safe, and I feel protective of her.

But the kiss?

I couldn't believe how alive I felt and how alive she looked with those bright eyes and her sweet face lit up in excitement. I'd never seen her look so enticing.

It's impossible not to admire the woman's uniqueness and determination and her amusing personality, pickled as it is in a mix of cleverness and optimism.

When she gazes at me, it's as if I'm the most important person in her world. She sees me as something complete, more than I see in myself.

Opening myself to sexual or romantic indulgences is not something I've had any interest in since Helen died. I have also been quite sure that if I ever kissed another woman, crushing guilt would be the inevitable result. Instead, I received such a bolt of arousal, it set me back on my heels.

So apparently now I'm attracted to Olivia? How has that crept up on me? Or perhaps the kiss was just a fleeting lapse? A primal reaction to the powerful way she was looking at me?

Either way, nothing can come of it. I don't like feeling unprepared or out of control, least of all by...arousal. It seems so embarrassing. Needy. I'm forty-three, hardly a teenager lost in the haze of hormones. And yet my body's reaction was instant and unmistakeable. It craved more. More is the last thing I can offer her.

I'd be terrible at dating again. What if I'm constantly comparing her to Helen? That's not fair to Olivia. I do feel guilty about today—because I'm worried I gave Olivia false hope.

I wish we could avoid this conversation I promised her. I'll only disappoint. But I just couldn't stand seeing her embarrassment and sadness at the thought that I felt the same way about her as that appalling Tina creature.

I was horrified Olivia might conclude I kissed her because my blood was up. As if I might have kissed Sasha or Bo if she hadn't been there. As much as I might wish to explain our kiss away, the act itself was definitely about Olivia and no one else.

I loathed Tina in that moment for making Olivia doubt her own worth.

I worry for her. She's not like me. I'm bone cold—or so everyone tells me. I'm bitterness, toughness, and hide. She's warmth. An open heart, trembling as it beats, hoping that others won't hurt her yet again. Olivia brings out my territorial instincts like no one else, the determination to keep the monsters from her. I can't explain it.

Not everyone deserves access to me. It's a short list, and I prefer it that way. Odd how it's been growing of late. Olivia has also done that to me. Drawing me out of my safe little shell.

She is a curious, baffling woman. Her courage is astonishing. For instance, she could have pretended to feel nothing after the kiss; swept it aside as I did, to save face. Instead, she admitted it. She held out her emotions to me—pointed right at them as if they were a small, helpless bird—and asked to know mine in return.

That is bravery I cannot even imagine.

CHAPTER 20

MUFFIN TO SEE HERE

"Are you really sure you want to do this?" Olivia asked Margaret nervously. They stood on the footpath across the street from Horrie's grungy building. Olivia was wearing jeans, a warm corduroy jacket, and her *Muffin to See Here* button, which seemed apt on multiple levels. Margaret had already eyed it and firmly said nothing, glancing away again.

Because they absolutely weren't talking about kisses, pending conversations about said kisses, or anything else remotely personal. Olivia wondered when Margaret would raise the topic but had decided to leave it to her to get to. She was, however, existing on very little sleep due to a combination of Kelly's diatribe about Tina's callous comments yesterday and Olivia's memories of how Margaret tasted—how she felt pressed against her. And how…

"Yes."

Olivia sucked in a breath and focused. "Hmm?"

"I said yes." Margaret glanced at the mean-eyed brutes loitering out front of Horrie's building. "If I play this right, we'll have your penguin back in ten minutes." She adjusted her extra-long military-green duffle bag. "And if not, if that cockroach refuses to help, I will simply threaten him."

"What with?" Olivia asked in astonishment.

"I'll explain how I know the *Herald-Sun's* deputy editor and that he probably won't want the harsh light of the media shone on him. Or some variation on that."

"You can't blackmail a drug dealer!"

"No?" Margaret eyed her. "Have you *met* me?" One haughty eyebrow arched higher than Olivia had ever seen.

Arousal flooded Olivia instantly. "Stop that," she protested in frustration.

"Stop what?"

"Your awesome badassery is distracting. Cut me some slack."

"Oh?" Margaret turned, eyeing her curiously. "So you like me being a bad ass?"

"You must already know that," Olivia complained. How couldn't she know? Olivia had practically told the woman yesterday she was putty in Margaret's hands. "Stop milking my weaknesses."

"I'm your weakness now?" Margaret inhaled in what looked to be surprised delight.

"I didn't say that. It's just..." Olivia wondered how she'd gotten stuck in this conversational cul-de-sac. "It's just that you're a powerful force, Margaret, okay? With all that charisma, take pity on us mere mortals."

Margaret puffed up a little at that and offered Olivia a small smile. "Well," she said, "I'll try to bear that in mind."

Olivia rolled her eyes. "Can we just focus on getting Trip back?"

"Of course. Penguin first. Your weaknesses later." Her smile widened to almost playful for just a moment before falling away. "Sorry," she said and looked annoyed with herself. "I forgot for a moment." Then she shook her head.

"Sorry for what?"

"Never mind. Come on."

Olivia was rooted to the spot. Since when did Margaret apologise for anything? And why did she look so regretful?

"Well?" Margaret paused. "Or do you intend for me to do this alone?"

"No!" Olivia scampered up behind her. "Let's do this."

Margaret had been accurate about being able to wrangle an invitation to meet Horrie. Once she'd shown the security goons the contents of her duffle bag, they'd escorted her straight to their boss.

Horrie was a small, balding man in his fifties with thick spectacles. He looked exactly like an accountant—well, if accountants wore Rolexes and supplied a small chunk of inner-city Melbourne with ecstasy and ice. Olivia might have found it hard to believe he was a drug dealer at all if she hadn't seen through an ajar door behind him four young men packing pills into plastic baggies.

Behind Horrie's desk in his main office was a wall of stuffed animals. Heads of a lion, giraffe, gorilla, and jaguar sat beside an eagle, a quokka—wait, weren't they endangered?—and…Trip!!! Olivia bit back a squeak of recognition.

Immediately, Margaret gave her arm a warning squeeze.

Horrie came around his wide wooden desk to stand in front of them, a sceptical expression on his face. "Show me."

Margaret opened her bag and reverently removed her watch peacock. She placed it on Horrie's desk with great care, as if it were invaluable, and unfurled its feathers. Then, laying on her most cultivated, polished academic tones, she said: "Before you sits the watch peacock once owned by Ned Kelly's grandfather. It would alert the bushrangers whenever police were near. I have brought the appropriate documentation."

She removed a photocopy of the letter Helen had been bequeathed that outlined Quincy's alleged heritage. "You will note," Margaret intoned, "that this fine specimen was kept by a historian who believed in its authenticity as a rare artefact before passing it on to me."

"And you are?" he asked. "Expertise-wise, I mean. I don't give a rat's what your name is."

"The founder and former director of the world-leading Australian bush-rangers collection at RMIT."

Horrie reviewed the letter then put it down. "And you believe this peacock is what the letter says?"

Straightening, Margaret said honestly: "It is not worth my professional reputation to manage goods that are not authentic."

Nice evasion. But Horrie hadn't seemed to notice the dodge, and a smile was creeping over his face as he looked at the letter again. He started rotating a garish gold ring on his finger as he gazed at the peacock.

Margaret cocked her head. "In sum: that's about as authentic as it gets."

"So Ned Kelly's family really owned this?" Horrie asked, sounding close to awed.

One of his security guards craned his head for a better look while another edged closer.

Well, leave it to criminals to appreciate another criminal. For once, Margaret would be delighted Australians revered Ned Kelly so much. Anything directly linked to him would be the Holy Grail to someone like Horrie.

"How much?" he asked, lowering himself to eye level of the bird, inspecting every detail. "It's in good nick, I see."

"One penguin." Margaret pointed to the wall over his shoulder. "That one."

Horrie glanced up in surprise. "You want to swap a historical artefact for some dingy old bird?"

Olivia stiffened, but Margaret gave her a quick warning glance and Olivia's protest died unspoken.

"Yes." Margaret said evenly. "Quite the bargain for you. Consider it your lucky day."

"Why would you make such a trade if it doesn't benefit you?"

"Does it matter? Why do you care?"

That gave him pause. "Fine. What if I don't want to part with the penguin?" Horrie glanced at Trip and back, a mercenary gleam in his eye. "Or, better yet, what if I just take your bird?" The threat might have been politely offered, but his goons stiffened, clearly readying themselves for a confrontation.

"Then I'm assuming you don't mind being named and shamed in Victoria's biggest newspaper as the thief of an Australian historical artefact that should belong in a museum." She lowered her voice to conspiratorial. "You know, it's a bit cheeky I kept it out of a museum, but I did so for sentimental reasons. You would have no chance getting your hands on it if I'd donated it as I probably should have."

Horrie eyed her speculatively. "Mmm."

Lifting her chin, Margaret continued: "So that's the deal. A piece of history for a *dingy old bird*. And if you take it by force, which of course you could, I will raise a ruckus on a national scale. Every media outlet in the country will immediately know where the Ned Kelly family's watch peacock resides. It'll be seized by police and probably wind up in a museum before too long, benefiting neither of us."

"All right, all right," he said, eyes still sharp. "Can I keep the letter?"

"You may. So, do we have a deal? May my associate take the penguin?"

He nodded. "Go ahead."

Olivia didn't need to be told twice. She gingerly collected Trip from his stand and slipped him into her backpack, whispering, "I got you. It's okay," as she did.

Margaret had moved closer to Quincy. "I'll miss my peacock. Do you mind if I get a photo of him before I go? Something to remember him by? In fact, a photo of him with his new owner as a memento, perhaps?"

Horrie shrugged. "Don't see why not." Gently, he picked the bird up, holding it proudly. Margaret reached for her phone. "Can't blame you wanting a keepsake of it."

Lifting her phone to take the photo, Margaret paused. "The light's not right here. Just move that way three steps?" She pointed to his left.

He did so.

Margaret fiddled with her phone, then also moved herself a little to the right. Then she smiled. "That's perfect." She clicked the phone camera and nodded. "Enjoy your peacock. I hope it brings you the same luck it brought the Kelly clan."

Wait, hadn't the Kelly clan been arrested when the peacock had gone missing to avoid a storm? Olivia met Margaret's dancing eyes and knew that, *yep*, that was exactly the kind of luck she meant.

"Thank you," Horrie beamed.

They left him fussing over the bird, surrounded by impressed security guards chattering excitedly.

Back in Margaret's car, Olivia freed Trip from his confines and began cooing her delight at him. Then she paused and looked at her amused henchperson. "*Please* tell me you didn't swap a rare artefact that meant everything to Helen just to get me Trip? Tell me you have another plan for Quincy?"

"That's not his name," Margaret said placidly. "And do you really think I'd let Helen's peacock stay in the hands of that reprobate? Hardly." She removed her phone from her pocket and scrolled through it, bringing up the photo she'd taken of the drug dealer.

"What do you see?"

"Horrie holding Quincy."

"What else do you see?" Margaret zoomed in on the background and pointed.

Olivia laughed. "Oh shit." In the gap between the door and the frame was a glimpse of two men bent over, packaging drugs.

"Exactly." Margaret looked pleased with herself. "Horrie's obviously so used to it, he forgot they were there. Or maybe he thought the door was shut. Either way, this looks like the sort of evidence that would spark a police raid. I just need to report my peacock missing first so it's returned to me afterwards."

"Um, sorry to break it to you," Olivia said, "but Victoria Police don't give two shits about tracking down someone's stolen stuffed animal for them. It might be a long wait before they care."

"Oh, they'll care. This picture will give the drug squad cause to raid. To protect my identity, I'll get them to say they received an anonymous tip-off. Further, my subtle threats of media involvement will give them impetus to move fast, and the bird itself being an important historical figure of national interest will put a rocket up their backsides."

"You didn't say *alleged*." Olivia studied her face. "Not even once."

"Hmm?"

"You usually say alleged when you're talking about Quincy. Do you think the peacock is the real deal now? That it really is Ned Kelly's grandfather's watch peacock?"

"I'm taking the Schrödinger's Peacock approach to it. The bird is both an authentic artefact and *not* an authentic artefact for the purposes of getting it back. After I've retrieved it, I'll return to thinking of it as…potentially authentic. Personally, I'm leaning heavily towards it not being so. I know Helen would have hated me to disprove its heritage, so I'll never get it tested. At least this way the bird has its mystery."

"Understood." Olivia nodded. "It's sweet how careful you are to protect Helen even now."

"Well," Margaret looked a little startled by the observation, "it's what she would have wanted. Now, we should get going. Surely Trip must be missing his van."

"Oh yes," Olivia said and trembled with excitement. "He will be."

Margaret started her car. "By the way, I've decided I'm having you over to dinner."

"What? Wait, you are?"

"I believe we have an overdue talk."

That they did.

"Whatever day it is, it'll have to be only a light meal. And early," Olivia said, her cartwheeling mind racing to all the possibilities of that talk. Would Margaret be open to a relationship? Or was it going to be a gentle let-down and Olivia trying to pretend she didn't care? "I fall asleep by nine-thirty. It's a baker's thing."

"I assumed as much. Do you have any allergies? Preferences? I won't prepare anything you dislike. And, yes, I can cook something light. So, is tonight acceptable?"

Margaret was going to cook for her? Olivia stared.

"What?" Margaret asked, eyeing her in confusion.

"No one's ever cooked for me before. Well, except Kelly. But that's more a reheating deal."

"No one? Ever? Surely your romantic partners?" Her eyes widened the tiniest bit.

Olivia shook her head. "Nope. I think everyone I've ever gone out with never really liked me enough to bother impressing me." *Oh God.* Had she just said that aloud? Olivia wanted to bury her face in her hands. "Hell. Can we just pretend I never said that?"

Margaret studied her for a long moment, her jaw working hard. Her eyes seemed to suggest she would be happy to plan a murder or four with Olivia. Her nostrils flared, and her lips briefly thinned. But, in a tone as even as could be, as if she'd decided she absolutely wasn't going to draw more attention to Olivia's embarrassing admission, all Margaret said was, "So, tonight—any allergies? Preferences?"

And that was the moment Olivia knew she was gone on Dr Margaret Blackwood.

CHAPTER 21

IT'S NOT A DATE

ALTHOUGH THIS WASN'T A DINNER date—it was a conversation about *maybe* dating—Olivia was a mess. She'd tried on three outfits and still couldn't work out which one said: *interested, and I hope you are too, but I'm cool if not.*

Although, truly, she wasn't cool if not. She was anything but that.

Kelly knocked on her bedroom door and, at Olivia's answering "yeah?", stuck her head in. She paused at the pile of discarded outfits on the bed and then glanced at Olivia. "Date night?"

"No! Not a date. Nope."

"Liv, you're wearing your date-night gear. Black jeans and a white shirt crisper than a lettuce. Lez bait, right? Plus, it's a Saturday. And also…" She pointed at the clothing reject pile.

"Still not a date."

"And the *Bake it Happen* button?" Kelly noted. "Not very subtle."

Oh. Oops. Freudian, much? She hadn't even remembered putting that on. Olivia quickly unpinned it. "What'd you want?" she asked evenly.

"Is your phone off?"

Olivia frowned, turning around, hunting for it. She found it half under the bed. Sure enough, the screen was black. "How'd you know?"

"I got this text from my boss," Kelly said mysteriously. "Wanna hear it?"

Olivia gave a shrug that she hoped conveyed complete disinterest in the textings of one Margaret Blackwood.

Kelly, Bureaux Collective informs me there's a delay in deliveries next week. Please promote a different coffee to the specials board on Monday morning. Also: review for errors the new printed menu I've left under the back counter, on the left.

P.S. What is your sister's beverage of choice?

Kelly's eyebrows lifted dramatically as she repeated: "What is your sister's beverage of choice?"

Olivia's cheeks reddened. "What'd you tell her?"

"Beer."

Damn it. How unsophisticated did she sound now? She'd dearly love to have edited that response to *sometimes beer, but loves a good Yarra Valley red.* Or something cultured like that. Margaret Blackwood was a cultured woman, after all.

"It's interesting you find nothing odd about the question." Kelly pointed at her outfit. "You are *so* going on a date. And it's with Dr Blackwood?" She looked astonished.

"It's not a date," Olivia protested. "But, yes, I'm going over to her place. It's more…a strategy meeting?" She hated how her voice rose in question. "She is my henchperson, after all."

"Well, I'm *her* employee, and she never asks for my drink preferences or invites me over for strategy discussions. Are you two dating? For reals?"

"No." Olivia's cheeks turned hot. "No!" she repeated in the face of Kelly's frank scepticism.

"But…you want to?" Kelly guessed.

She sank onto her bed. "Yes," Olivia admitted. "We're going to talk about that tonight."

Kelly gave her a long look. "I mean, that's…unexpected. She's so imposing and intimidating and all; I'm amazed you're up for it."

"Gee, thanks."

"You're braver than I am." Kelly shuddered. "If I was into chicks, I mean."

"Why brave?" Olivia's tone sharpened. "Margaret is beautiful and smart and kick-ass. Did you know she bolted up a six-storey fire-escape in heels even though she's terrified of heights? She did it to save me! Why wouldn't I want to date someone like that?"

"Whoa!" Kelly lifted her hands in a surrender gesture. "I didn't know she'd done that. I thought Sasha was the one doing your safety line."

"He helped too." She couldn't be bothered explaining that mess now. "On that note, can you do me a favour? Give Sasha one more chance?"

"Why?" Kelly eyed her. "You know what he did."

"I do. And he says he learned his lesson, and he'll never look at another woman again when he's with you."

Kelly snorted. "Uh-huh. And why are you taking up his cause all of a sudden?"

"Because, like Margaret, he did try to save me. He thought I'd given the signal I was in trouble and came flying along the ladder to rescue me. He was incredible."

"Really?" Kelly gave an approving *hmm*.

"He also admitted he wasn't interested in Margaret and had just been trying to make you jealous."

"As we suspected." Kelly didn't look too put out, though. "That's so stupid. But all right. He can have one date. Only because he saved my baby sister."

Olivia grinned. "Thank you."

"And don't think I didn't notice the little conversational pivot. You and my boss?" Kelly wagged her finger. "But we can talk about it later when you're not melting down over what to wear."

"I'm no—"

"You so are. God, imagine what a mess you'd be if she actually kissed you!" She laughed.

The memory washed through her so fast, Olivia's cheeks felt as if they'd turned scarlet.

"Oh, fuck." Kelly's eyes went wide. "When?"

"None of your business. Now, can you leave me to get ready for my not-date?"

"Oh. My. God!" Kelly's eyes were even wider. "She's *into* you!"

"Not necessarily. Hence the reason for tonight's meeting."

"She is," Kelly said adamantly. "Otherwise, she'd have just said, 'This was a huge mistake; forget it happened'."

That was annoyingly true. Hope filled Olivia. "We'll see."

But she felt lighter than she had for hours.

Margaret Blackwood was dressed in an outfit Olivia would not soon forget. She looked like a wraith, and Olivia had never wanted to dance with the devil more.

Tailored black pants, black-matte snub-nosed boots, a black silken blouse, three buttons undone, and a sleek silver necklace which drew the eye to a pale, kissable throat.

"Wow," Olivia said, forgetting how *hellos* worked. She passed a bottle of a (cultured) Yarra Valley red into Margaret's hands and smiled. "You. Wow. *Amazing.*"

Looking faintly startled by the praise, Margaret inhaled and then took the bottle. "Thank you. You like wine?"

"Yes. Or whatever's good."

"I see."

Olivia waited for her to confess to milking Kelly on the topic, but Margaret instead said: "Come on through. It's too nice a night not to be out on the balcony. You can meet Wednesday, the cat you named, while I finish up."

The cat? Olivia bounced in excitement. She loved cats. Her and Kelly's landlord had forbidden pets so they'd never been able to have one. "I'd like that."

They walked through Margaret's tastefully designed, austere apartment—all modern, clean lines and elegant art. Not exactly lived-in and comfy but beautiful in a cool, aloof way, like a poised European model in a museum. Not unlike Margaret herself.

"I'll just be in the kitchen." Margaret pointed to an alcove to one side. "I'll join you very shortly." She slid open the balcony door and closed it behind Olivia.

A snoozing black cat looked up from a chair and narrowed her eyes in recognition that this was not her mistress.

"Hey, girl," Olivia said, slipping into the wooden seat beside her. "It's good to meet you."

The cat stared at her, unblinking.

Olivia dared stretching out a hand, which the animal sniffed with little interest. Then Wednesday's teeth bared, and Olivia withdrew her fingers barely a millisecond before getting chomped.

"Black cat says no," Olivia murmured. "Prefer an ear scratch, then?"

Slowly, so Wednesday could see where she was going, Olivia shifted her hand to behind one ear. That seemed to do the trick. Wednesday allowed this familiarity and, after a moment, closed her eyes and began to purr. Two minutes later, she relocated herself to Olivia's lap.

"Welcome. Here for the warmth?" She took in the animal's shiny coat and contented face and glanced at a squishy cat pillow in one corner of the balcony. "You seem to have a pretty cruisy life. Good for you."

For all Margaret's feigned indifference over the cat, it was obvious that she cared about her new pet.

"So," Olivia said, deciding some introductory talk was in order, "you're probably wondering who I am. My name's Olivia Roberts. Aged thirty-two. Muffin baker. And I'd like to date your mum." She then proceeded to fill the animal in about an average day in her life while Wednesday gave a little huff and went to sleep.

That's how Margaret found them five minutes later.

"I'm glad you explained to my cat exactly what goes into a three-cheese zucchini muffin," Margaret said dryly, holding a platter while sliding the door closed behind her with her foot. "Who knew it had to be Humboldt Fog cheese from California? I'm sure Wednesday would have died not knowing."

Olivia grinned. "Right? That's important information to have. It adds to the zest."

"Is that so? Well, I hope you like tapas. They're light but filling." The platter containing all sorts of delicious-smelling Spanish treats was slid onto the small table between the two chairs.

"That looks amazing." Olivia gazed at the assortment of tiny tasting dishes. "Wait, did you make all these yourself?"

"Yes." Margaret lowered herself into the other chair and crossed her legs. "You said nobody had ever cooked for you, an oversight I felt needed correcting."

Olivia suddenly was overcome by the thoughtfulness. "Thank you," she croaked out, but that didn't feel sufficient as she forked a sampling, "so much."

But Margaret merely shrugged. "Think nothing of it. Now, what would you like to drink? I have six different types of beer."

"Six?" Olivia said in surprise. "Seriously?"

Margaret had said that casually, as though she hadn't run out and bought them after texting with Kelly. Because that sounded like six more beer varieties than Margaret would normally drink.

"Or there's wine. Yours, of course, or a red from the Barossa? I have others, too. It just depends on what you prefer."

Wait, was Margaret rambling? *Margaret*? A faint blush appeared on her milky, white throat, and she looked a little cross with herself.

"Whatever you're having sounds great to me," Olivia said. "And this looks heavenly too." She indicated the food, the source of delectable aromas. Even the sleepy cat had sat up and was looking interested in the closest dish.

"All right," Margaret said, rising to her feet. "One moment. And don't let Wednesday sample the tapas. I don't think jalapeño poppers, empanadas, or wine-glazed chorizo are intended for feline stomachs."

"No." Olivia laughed. She stroked Wednesday until the furball got the hint that food wouldn't be forthcoming, huffed, and closed her eyes again.

Margaret returned with a wine bottle and two glasses. "I hope you'll like it."

"I'm sure I will."

They sat for a while in companionable silence, helping themselves to the tapas and wine. It was as delicious as it looked. Margaret was quite an artisan with food, but she waved that compliment away when Olivia offered it.

"It's not difficult. I followed the recipe scrupulously. If you can read, you can cook."

"But this is so good."

"Thank the recipe book, then." But still, Margaret smiled. "Thank you, though. I'm pleased you're enjoying it."

After that, conversation flowed easily from topic to topic, ranging from how to remove demonic cat hair from pantsuits to digging into French philosopher Michel Foucault—"He gives my mother an anxious tic," Margaret said with a glint in her eye. "I love to bring him up with her."

Half an hour later, Margaret leaned back and said: "I had an interesting talk with Samantha Garrity yesterday when she came in to collect Emma for the walk home." She paused. "Home is barely the right word, is it, when it's a car."

"It's not ideal. But Sam told me it was still better than this shelter they'd stayed at briefly. She said it had terrible energy that felt like decay and despair. Sam decided their car was the better option for her family's mental health."

"I see. Well, things will be much improved soon. Ms Garrity told me that they've made it to the top of the waiting list. She's due to move in to public housing in three weeks."

"That's awesome. I worried about them living in that old car. It doesn't even run."

"Yes, that is a bit of an issue, because their new apartment is some distance away. She's not sure how they'll relocate there. Tow truck, perhaps?"

Olivia sighed. "I'd loan her my Torana indefinitely if she'd say yes. I could sell it, but I can't be bothered with the hassle. And Sam could really use it. If only she'd take it."

"She wouldn't." Margaret said firmly. "She's a proud woman. I think she struggles enough just with accepting your groceries. She only does that because of her children."

"How do you know about that?"

"My storeroom window looks out over the back car park. I witnessed Rhinoceros Art Day."

"Ah." Olivia smiled. "And a classic day it was."

"I also know Samantha will be paying you back every cent you spent on her down the track."

"I don't expect her to, but why so certain?"

"Because today she repaid me for letting Emma stay at the store after school each day. I assured her no debt was owed, but she disagreed. She handed me a folder with a detailed promotional plan for Mary Bugg's that she'd spent hours working on."

"A…promotional plan?"

"Indeed. In it, she proposes that my bookstore runs a Bushranger of the Month display. I'd put it on a noticeboard in the window with a photo, biographical notes, the bushranger's nickname, and so on. Then I'd discount any book in the store about that particular bushranger. She included mocked-up layouts, all the research, and a USB drive with her design that I can get blown up into posters for the store window. And she did all of it by borrowing a colleague's laptop in their lunch break, and her manager allowing her to use the office printer just once."

Olivia stared at her. "I didn't know she could do any of that."

"Nor I. In fact, I asked how she knew how to do all this, and she said from a previous job."

"What job?"

"She used to be the assistant librarian at Prahran Public Library until the storm wiped it out. Ms Garrity did all their educational programs and store displays. She casually dropped that bombshell on me and said that she hoped her work might be useful. She even apologised if she was presumptuous but said that she couldn't think of how else to pay me back for making Emma happy and keeping her safe."

Olivia was astonished. "Sam's such a dark horse. All I knew was she'd become unemployed, then her husband died, then she had to pay all his debts—he apparently loved to buy on credit using their joint account. The bank took her house when she got behind on payments and she couldn't afford the rents in Melbourne. Everything's so overpriced."

"She has had a terrible run of luck," Margaret said.

"Are you going to use her idea? Is it sound?"

"Absolutely." Margaret's voice warmed up to her pet topic. "The overall design for the poster is good, and the written detail on the bushrangers is meticulous. I appreciate her efforts at research, although I disagree with some of the biographical information she included. But I can't expect a layperson to know more than me on a subject I've examined for decades. Even so, her proposal showed a great deal of promise."

"Wow." Olivia shook her head. "All this time, I had no idea. She was a librarian, just like you!"

The warmth dimmed in Margaret's face. "Not just like me."

"Sorry—I know you headed a department at a major academic library and Sam only worked for a small public one. I'm not diminishing your achievements."

"I know you're not. That's not what I meant, but never mind."

"No, tell me?"

Margaret hesitated for a moment. "I meant that few people would have chosen the path I took to have the success I did. In that regard, Sam is fortunate she's not me. She can still look herself in the mirror. Anyway, would you like a top-up?" She indicated Olivia's wineglass.

Olivia held her glass out, watching Margaret's jaw work as she refilled the glass.

Still look herself in the mirror? Was she feeling guilty about something? Had she done something wrong? It was hard to picture the perfectionist woman failing at anything, including her own standards. But whatever had happened obviously still troubled her. That clenching and unclenching jaw seemed to indicate she was debating whether to tell Olivia the rest of the story.

Instead, the moment passed back into silence and Margaret didn't return to the topic.

The sun sank lower in the sky, and Olivia took in the gorgeous streaks of light, framed neatly by the balcony. "Oh, it's perfect! The sunset!"

"Yes. I watch it every night. I find it a relaxing way to end the day, along with a glass of wine, Wednesday, and my diary."

"You keep a diary?"

"An old habit from my academia days when I wanted to keep track of professional materials I was reading and so on."

"Do you miss those days?"

"Not especially." Her lips pressed together tightly before parting, as if she'd forced herself to relax. Then she lifted her chin, and it seemed as if she'd come to a decision. "But, I suppose, it's because I wasn't focused on the right things."

Olivia snagged a bite of chorizo. "Didn't you create the world's foremost library collection on Australian bushrangers? That hardly sounds like a bad thing to focus on."

Margaret's head snapped up. "You've been busy, I see. You read Helen's obituary. That was the exact wording in it."

Olivia inhaled. *Damn.*

"How neatly that article encapsulated who I was in two short, sharp sentences."

Nervously, Olivia admitted: "Yes. I saw Helen's obit."

Margaret's expression turned flinty. "So, during your research into my past, did you also enjoy the story about my long-running feud with another RMIT library department head? Oh, that makes for particularly salacious reading. Our little war caused quite a buzz around campus. It made it onto a few online academia gossip sites."

Olivia couldn't imagine anyone foolish enough to lock horns with Margaret Blackwood. "I only saw Helen's obit. I didn't see anything about you fighting anyone."

Margaret folded her arms, then drew them closer around her ribs. "That was who I was back then. I was at my professional peak. Oh, I was an impressive sight. I had respect, power, international accolades. I had a ruthless, laser focus on three things: running the world's peerless bushranger collection; beating the weasel who wanted a slice of my funding; and winning, above all. That was what my world shrank to. To the exclusion of all else."

To the exclusion of all else.

I wasn't focused on the right things.

"You weren't focused on Helen," Olivia guessed quietly.

"No. She begged me to take a break. She could see I was getting too worked up. She even suggested I quit entirely and we follow our dream. We had this not entirely serious fantasy where we'd retire and run a sweet, little crime-and-mystery bookstore together with a focus on bushrangers." Margaret's eyes tightened.

"You did do that."

"So I did." Margaret's jaw worked.

Olivia hesitated and softly asked: "What happened?"

Margaret bolted to her feet and went to the balcony. She leaned on the railing. For a few moments, she said nothing. "I was too blind to see what was happening beneath my nose. Helen had become unwell. She'd kept her illness from me to keep further stress off my plate." Margaret gave a derisive snort. "I was too busy crushing my rival to even notice."

"It's clear you loved her."

Margaret turned and pinned her with a quelling look: "Love isn't enough, Olivia. Being present is. Not just physically. Emotionally." Sorrow flooded her face, along with anger and guilt. "When I finally realised the truth, I was too late. I didn't have time to make things right or do much more than hold Helen's hand in the hospital before she was...gone."

"I'm so sorry."

Margaret's pain radiated off her. She didn't speak for long minutes. Finally, she walked back to her chair and sank into it. "I'm not sure why I'm telling you any of this. It's difficult to talk about. I haven't really discussed my wife with anyone since she died."

What a heavy burden to face alone. Olivia had already noted the tension between Margaret and her mother. But what about the rest of her family? "Not even your friends?" she asked delicately.

Margaret sighed. "I let all my friendships lapse. Most were Helen's friends first anyway. It became too difficult to engage with them. All I wanted was time alone to grieve in peace. And all they wanted to do was feed me casseroles and tell me how special Helen was. I *know*!" She shot Olivia an aggrieved look. "Of course, I know. I married her! And them eulogising her every time we met just made me feel worse because it was a constant reminder that I'd allowed someone so special to slip away without her knowing how much she meant to me."

"She knew, Margaret," Olivia said with conviction. "She had to."

"Well, either way, it's done now. I remind myself it's been three years. More than three, actually. And I've tried to make amends and do what Helen would have wanted. I'm just not sure I've succeeded."

"By creating the bookstore you two dreamed about. You don't see that as a success?"

Blowing out a frustrated breath, Margaret said: "Technically, yes. I ticked off Fulfilling the Dream from the list. But the result wasn't exactly what I expected."

"Let me guess: all those pesky customers wanting their Ned Kelly merch," Olivia teased gently.

"Yes. *Them*." Margaret's eyes narrowed in faux outrage before she became serious again. "I kept waiting for the contentment to appear. It never did."

"So...you don't really like running your bookstore?"

"Truthfully?" She gave a rueful snort. "I've been bored out of my skull."

"Shit."

"Exactly." Margaret shook her head. "But until recently, I haven't been feeling interested in doing much else. Anything that required actual energy seemed a bridge too far. Is it any wonder I've been listening to your book club for two years? It's been about the only thing interesting in my week."

Had Margaret been depressed? Or maybe just trapped in some grief-fuelled rut? It would certainly explain some things, like why she'd never seemed to leave her office. "So when you applied to become my henchperson, you really did mean it when you said you were bored?"

"Among other reasons, but yes. And your chaotic book club is many things, but boring isn't one of them." Margaret smiled. "I assumed anything you masterminded would be the same. And I wasn't wrong."

Olivia was entranced by how much softer her face became when she smiled. "I'm not sure if I just got insulted or not," she joked.

"Definitely not." Margaret's eyes gleamed now. "If you'd been insulted, you'd know."

"I suppose that's true," Olivia said with a short laugh. "You're never a mystery when it comes to mockery. Just everything else."

"Oh?" Margaret regarded her with interest. "How am I a mystery?"

"I think this leads into the reason for tonight." Olivia inhaled. "I'm unsure as to your intentions towards me, to use some old-fashioned language."

"Straight to it, I see," Margaret said quietly. "I suppose that's very you."

"I guess it is," Olivia agreed. "I'll even go first, if that'll help?"

"All right." Margaret leaned back in her chair and regarded her with hooded eyes. "You have the floor."

Where to start? Olivia gathered her thoughts. "You may have noticed that I've dated a lot of people who have been bad for me."

"I did, in fact, notice that," Margaret said, "on account of being your vengeance-seeking henchperson."

"Yeah." Olivia rolled her eyes. "That was kinda obvious, huh?"

"It was."

"In the past, I've picked people who, it turned out, barely liked me. I was a means to an end. I put up with their crap because I'm an idiot."

Margaret's expression was inscrutable.

"Sorry, wasn't that your cue to agree that I am, *unquestioningly an idiot?*" Olivia asked, cocking an eyebrow.

"You are," Margaret agreed, her lips twitching, "but I thought it rude right at this juncture to point it out."

"Uh-huh." Olivia turned to gaze at the last red streaks of the setting sun. "I just want to date someone who wants me too. Is into me as much as I am into them. Who actually likes me as a person. And I want to date someone who, when I kiss them, makes me feel like my world just exploded." She glanced at Margaret. "I have to say you especially qualify on that last point. You're an incredible kisser."

"Oh?" Margaret's cheeks seemed suddenly pink. She fidgeted. "Well."

"Yes. My problem is it's always been hard to work out who's good for me and who isn't. I seem to have a missing red-flag detector. Kelly says that if I want to know someone's true character, I should look at what people do, not what they say. So, on that score," Olivia waved at the tapas dishes. "You cooked for me."

"That seems a low bar."

"Not to me." Olivia smiled. "You also asked my sister what I like to drink."

"Only because you didn't answer my text."

"You bought *six* varieties of beer when she told you it was beer," Olivia guessed.

"Ah." Margaret said sheepishly. No denial.

"And you ran up that fire-escape to save me even though you were petrified."

"*Petrified* seems like a strong word."

"Margaret, I had to peel your fingers off the railing!"

"Fine. But I didn't *actually* save you, though," she pointed out. "If you recall, Sasha had already secured the rope."

"You didn't know that," Olivia said incredulously. "I'm not sure why you're downplaying your awesomeness."

"I'm…unaccustomed to being thought of as 'awesome'," Margaret suggested dryly. "I'm much more primed for a stream of veiled insults by inferior colleagues. But go on."

"You're intelligent and witty and brave and really attractive, for one thing."

"Just one thing?" Margaret's eyes twinkled.

"Well, it's a *big* one thing." Olivia grinned and then turned serious. "But the other, much bigger, thing is that you seem to actually care about me. Tina had just told me how little I meant to her, and then I looked over and saw you there, clinging to my safety rope, looking so petrified."

Margaret lifted a protesting finger.

"Or…a *tiny* bit scared. And it was everything. You cared. That's a good feeling—one I've never had with anyone outside family. It's irresistible. I want more. More of feeling wanted. More of you. More of your smart-arse comments and beautiful, rare smiles you sometimes share with me. I'd be honoured to date you…if you'd be interested."

Margaret hesitated.

Dread filled Olivia. Her cheeks blazed with heat. Had she really read this so wrong?

Olivia scratched her arm nervously and rushed on. "And I understand if you're not interested. I know I'm not a catch. I'm, as you point out quite often, an idiot. I'm also just a uni dropout who works stupid hours that most people get sick of. But I'm loyal, Margaret." She met her gaze earnestly. "And I give the people I care about my whole heart. I'll have your back, and I'll be honest with you. And we share the same passion for books, so we have that in common."

Margaret still hadn't spoken.

"And I know I'm just *me*, not someone polished or cultured or beautiful. But I'm smart enough to know I can't walk away tonight without giving this my best shot. You're amazing. And I care about you too." She looked down again. "That's it. That's…my pitch, I guess."

Margaret drew in a tight breath. "You really don't make it easy, do you?"

"What do you mean?"

"I had a whole speech prepared about how I don't think it's a good idea for us to date. I haven't gone out with anyone since Helen died. It's unfair the pressure that would put on you. How can anyone match up to someone I loved for fifteen years? I thought it might be better to just spare us both the grief and say no."

Olivia sagged.

"Yet your speech…I'm not unaffected." Margaret gave her an intense look that was in no way reassuring.

"I sense a *but* coming."

"*But*…I have to consider this with my head not my heart. Intellect not emotion."

"Why?" Olivia asked. "Why not your heart?"

"Because my heart has been bitter and broken and useless for three years. I'm furious at myself for what I lost and how. When I listen to my head, it says one thing over and over: I don't want to hurt you, Olivia. I can't risk it. I'm not good for you. Conclusion: there should be no 'us'. And I need you to know that it's not you; it's me."

"When people say that, they always mean it really is you."

"In this case, Olivia, I can assure you it is me. I would not be good for a soul as gentle and kind as you."

Olivia blinked.

"Yes. I'm aware that sounds strange coming from me." Margaret swallowed. "I'm rarely *nice*. I push people away. I prefer to be left alone. Unfortunately, you didn't seem to get that memo. But don't you see? You're too breakable to be with someone so broken."

"How do you know I'd break?" Olivia protested. "You can't just decide that for me. Ask me. Let *me* decide if I'll take the risk."

"It's for the best."

So much finality. "Whose best?" Olivia persisted. "Not mine. I know what I want. And if we crash and burn, well, at least we'd know. But what if we were spectacular?"

Margaret was already shaking her head.

Olivia rushed on anyway. "And I think you'd benefit from connecting with another person again. You've been in your own headspace too long. It's not healthy."

"Olivia…"

"No. Look, I came here tonight worried you might say no because I'm not someone you'd want to date. Or you might say no because you aren't over Helen. I get that. Totally valid reasons. But I never thought you'd say no because you're tempted but you've decided *I'll* be broken if you even try dating me. You've twisted it all around and decided saying no is for my benefit. That's bullshit, Margaret."

Anger flashed into Margaret's eyes. "It's not bullshit."

"Be honest. Tell me you're not ready to date yet. Or tell me it's me. But don't tell me you can't because you'll break me."

"But what if I do? Especially after those last four awful exes. What if I'm number five?"

"Then I'll need a new henchperson because that'll be a massive conflict of interest!" Olivia threw up her hands.

"I truly don't wish to hurt you," Margaret said quietly.

"Then don't! Just…don't. You make it sound like you have no control over what happens when you date someone. You're not a passive observer, Margaret."

"It's not that simple! I don't want to try!" Margaret's eyes flew wide at her own words.

And there it was: the truth. Squirming awkwardly in front of them. It was never about protecting Olivia. Margaret didn't want to try.

"Thank you," Olivia said quietly as sadness filled her. "I understand now."

"What, exactly, do you think you understand?" Margaret asked, anger again flickering on her stormy face.

"Everything." Olivia's voice was flat.

"*What* do you understand?" Margaret demanded. "What do you *think* you see?"

Olivia licked her lips. "I see that you hid yourself away in your office at Mary Bugg's after Helen died. It was your safe space. Now, three years on, your need to hide is not about Helen anymore. You don't want to leave a place of comfort because to do so requires you to be stronger than you feel."

Shock flitted across Margaret's face. Then…irritation.

"It's a sign of just how bored you've been that you decided to become my henchperson," Olivia continued. "You've been so comfortable hibernating, so this was a spur of the moment decision, I'm guessing? Did you hear all the other deadbeats applying and thought how you'd be so much better? Did your competitive instincts kick in? Either way, I think it was probably wildly out of character, you braving the world for the first time in years."

"You think I lack courage?" Margaret's eyes narrowed. "Even after trying to save your life?"

"You misunderstand me. I think you are very courageous…about protecting others, if you think they're worth your notice. But personal courage? Taking a risk with your heart? No. A doctor once told me the scariest thing for a chronic pain sufferer is the thought of more pain. It's the fear it'll be more than they can cope with. I don't blame you if you feel terrified of more pain, Margaret. I'm just sad about it."

Margaret folded her arms and glowered. "You make me sound like some pity case! Pathetic and weak."

"I don't pity you, Margaret. But I think I really do understand you now."

Margaret's face was ashen. Her voice shook as she said roughly: "You don't know me."

Olivia fell silent. A prickling sensation shot up her neck at Margaret's darkening expression. Had Olivia gone too far?

Then Margaret's whole face shifted to closed off and cold. Without inflection, she said, politely: "I can see this isn't working." The hands she'd brought to her knees curled into fists, then went flat. "We're incompatible, that much is clear. What do we even have in common? You bake muffins and blurt out idiotic things and drive an eyesore." She smiled as if it had been an attempted joke, but her empty eyes didn't agree.

"Don't do this," Olivia said softly, feeling sick, knowing where this was going. "Please don't."

"It wouldn't have worked out, Olivia. We were never even meant to be friends, when you think about it."

Olivia shivered. How clinically Margaret could write the obituary of their friendship as if it were something of little consequence.

"I know what you're doing," Olivia said, her voice shaking. "Can't we just talk this through? This doesn't have to end like...like...one of your eviscerations of your rivals at uni."

"I'm not doing anything but stating a fact." Margaret's face was a granite mask.

"No, not a fact. Our friendship isn't nothing. Even if we're not going to date, our friendship is valuable. It's worth keeping."

"Valuable? Hardly. Seriously, we're not really even friends." Margaret's hand briefly curled back into a fist before it pressed flat on her knee.

Olivia's eyes narrowed. "What would you call us, then?"

"We are...associates. And once the business involving your final ex, Timothy, is concluded, we'll be back to what we were before: bookstore owner and baked-goods provider. Why make this into something it's not? Don't force it, Olivia."

Something it's not. Did she actually believe that? And *force it?* As if Olivia had been the only one making an effort to interact? What crap. Here they were, surrounded by the remnants of a painstakingly created meal that proved the exact opposite of Margaret's words. Olivia desperately searched her face for any hint of softness. "Come on, you *really* don't think we're friends?"

Margaret peered at her. "We've barely interacted until quite recently. We're like a cat and a dog. Contentious. We don't agree on much at all. This thing…" she waved a finger between herself and Olivia "has been merely an…alliance of necessity. But soon it'll be done. Then we'll return to our earlier parameters, which is for the best. And to be clear: I certainly do not want you in my life for anything further."

"Our…" Olivia's breath caught. *Earlier parameters.* That felt like an execution of a friendship.

I certainly don't want you in my life.

I don't want you.

Olivia's whole heart trembled.

"It's not like we gained anything from a closer association either," Margaret added in a tone devoid of emotion. She was barely even looking at Olivia now. "On the contrary, I almost lost my life over it." Her eyes went even icier.

"So you weren't lying before, were you?" Olivia said, tone dead. "When you told me, 'If you'd been insulted, you'd know'." Blood pounded through her heart and roared in her ears. Her stomach turned queasily. "But you can stop now. You've made your point. You don't want there to be an us. And you don't want me at all, in any capacity."

Margaret froze. She opened her mouth, then closed it again. But there was absolutely no denial. She looked away, lips tightening. Her eyes were chips of ice.

Silence.

And just like, that Olivia's heart shattered. Margaret didn't even want her a little bit. She would have said something if she did. This was definitely the end. There could be nothing more. How do you come back from *I don't want you?*

"*Fuck.*" The word was almost gasped out as Olivia drew her arms around herself. Pain sliced through her body, and she fought not to cry at the icy rejection. "Well, you'll be relieved to know I'm releasing you from your obligations as my henchperson. I'll deal with Timothy myself."

Margaret showed no visible reaction. "I'm a woman of my word," she said, tone clipped. "I can—"

"No. You won't. It's done," Olivia cut in. "I sure as hell won't force myself into someone's space when they don't want me there." Her eyes pricked, and she blinked the tears away viciously.

Margaret's jaw worked.

"So, fine." Olivia's anger flared. "We're no longer friends. I say 'no longer' because we *were*, Margaret. And we were great together! Screw you for not even acknowledging that. But I'll bow out of your life entirely now."

Something indefinable flashed in Margaret's face, and she asked, as if seeking to clarify, "You'll no longer come to Mary Bugg's? Do you intend to no longer supply the store with muffins?"

"I'll still do daily muffin drop-offs to Kelly and attend book club, assuming you don't fire me or ban my club. But you won't have to look at me again. You can stay in your little office as always and even resume offering cutting criticisms of me and my idiocy from within, if you want."

Margaret inhaled sharply. "Offer cutting crit... Is that how you viewed those interactions? Attacks on you?"

"What else am I to think?" Olivia asked tiredly. "That *is* your area of expertise." She slumped as the anger ebbed out of her. Why was she even bothering? It took two for any kind of relationship to work, and Margaret had made it clear she'd withdrawn her interest. "You're probably right about us. We wouldn't have worked out. How could we when you don't want me in your life? You don't want me at all."

Emotions suddenly returned to Margaret's face, and then it was like she folded into herself. She hunched over; now more vulture than wraith—albeit a disturbed and miserable one.

Olivia steeled herself against that achingly vulnerable expression and rose, dislodging from her lap Wednesday, who mewled in protest.

"Thank you for a delicious dinner," Olivia said honestly. "And thank you for being the first person in my life to cook for me who didn't have to. I will never forget that. As for the rest? Message understood. I'll leave you alone. Goodbye, Dr Blackwood."

Margaret did not move a muscle as Olivia took her leave.

Olivia didn't make it home. Halfway there, she had to pull over at an abandoned bus stop. Through watery eyes, she stared at the weeds around the graffiti-ridden shelter.

Then she let the tears fall. Margaret didn't want her. She'd literally said that. And it stung. That wasn't just a rejection of Olivia's hopeful advances. It had been a cutting repudiation. Her emotions had been slammed into concrete.

The tears slowed. She wiped her exhausted eyes and glanced at Trip in the passenger seat. "Well, that was not how I'd hoped tonight would go."

He eyed her sympathetically.

Olivia had known, of course, that Margaret had the capacity to shred people. She'd told her as much. "Academics can peel the skin off a rival in two bloodless sentences, then offer the poor corpse a coffee," she'd said so casually.

Margaret apparently had some truly expert skills at verbally gutting someone. Olivia had seen hints of these hidden skills: the dry mockery coming from Margaret's office over the past month of book clubs. Cutting little jabs that spoke of her capacity to do much worse if she ever took the gloves off.

I just didn't think she'd ever turn her shredding skills onto me. At least, not in a way so deliberate. The intention being to draw blood. To…hurt.

But why had Margaret done it? Taken off the gloves and been so ruthless? Was it simply her personality? The scorpion and the frog parable? The scorpion would always sting the frog—even as the frog rescued the scorpion trying to cross the river—because it was in its nature.

Or was it something else?

Thoughts twisted and curled in Olivia's tired brain, and a few glaring truths started smacking her in the face.

She sniffled, wiped her eyes, and tried to push her emotions further out of her thinking space. Then she picked up her phone.

"Liv?" Kelly answered in surprise. "Why are you calling? Aren't you on a date with my boss?" Her sister's tone was light and teasing.

"Before I went out with Timothy," Olivia began, her voice devoid of inflection, "how many red flags did you see?"

"What?" All humour drained from Kelly's voice. "What's this about? Are you okay? God, did something happen?" Concern flooded down the phone.

"Please answer," Olivia said. "How many?"

"Um, I suppose about three? He never seemed that into you before he asked you out. He was weak around his brother. He cared about his car and doing what Rodney wanted more than anything else. It didn't feel like a good match."

Olivia inhaled. *Three*. Before she'd even gone out with him.

"And Martin? How many red flags there? Before I'd gone out with him. Not in hindsight."

"Hell, um, a fair few. He was so creepy in the way he glommed on to young women. He did it with me too, telling me things 'for my own good', imparting his life lessons, his wisdom. I wanted to slap him and say he wasn't fifty. He always made me a bit uncomfortable. He also stood way too close to women, as if trying to impose himself in their space."

Great. He'd screamed red flags. "What about Annalise?"

"You remember that I knew her before you did, right? She used to hit the bar I worked at. There were enough red flags for me to notice her in a crowd of people. She always gravitated towards the most powerful person in the room. She stopped talking to friends she was with—in mid sentence—if someone more important walked in. She treated all the bar staff like crap. That's a *big* red flag. And I noticed she often disappeared when it was her turn to shout a round of drinks."

Cheapskate even then. "And Tina?"

"So, so many. She was as fake as a Balinese gold watch. Come on. She's so insincere. I was shocked you bought her bullshit—and even worse, went back for seconds."

Olivia's stomach tightened. "And Margaret? How many red flags does she have?"

Silence fell.

Olivia observed a cockroach scuttle up the side of the bus shelter.

"What did she do?" More concern filled the phone line.

"Answer the question. Please?"

"None. She's a fair boss and treats her staff with respect. Stephanie, the book sales assistant, loves her. Dr Blackwood's generous with giving her time off so she can attend classes. She doesn't lie to us or play power games. I don't get any creepy or deceptive vibes from her. I'd have said something if I did. Didn't I warn you about the others?"

"Yes." She had. And Olivia had ignored her every time.

"If you're trying to work Margaret out—or, hell, anyone—remember what I always say: look at what people do, not what they say."

Olivia sagged as a reminder hit her. "I don't want you to go out with Sasha for me," she said suddenly. "I'm the worst sister for asking that of you. He hurt you. I don't want you hurt again. I didn't mean to put you in an awkward position."

"I wasn't going to go out with him again *for you*," Kelly admitted quietly. "That was just an excuse. I'm… I wanted to give him one more chance before you asked, but my pride got in the way. Sometimes people deserve another shot if they screw up something that's fixable *and* they take ownership and mean it. Sasha says he's sorry he hurt me and that he won't do it again. I believe him. Time will tell if I'm right. But he's worth a second chance."

Olivia breathed out hard. All right.

"Are you okay, Liv?"

"Yeah. Well, I hope I will be. Sorry to freak you out. I just had a…difficult night. Thanks. I'll talk later when I get home." She hung up.

So it wasn't in Margaret's nature; she wasn't stinging Olivia because she was a scorpion. Margaret was stinging her for other reasons. And, now that Olivia's brain's fog had cleared a little, those reasons were startlingly obvious.

Olivia had gone too far. No one liked a mirror being held up to them, but it was ten times worse when you're already fragile and in denial about some of your choices. Olivia had inadvertently humiliated Margaret, calling her out on hiding out in her office for three years. She'd made the proud woman feel pathetic.

Margaret had reflexively kicked back hard in anger and embarrassment. There had been fear in her eyes too. Olivia had probably been close to the truth when she'd suggested Margaret was terrified of being hurt more.

Whatever was driving her, Margaret's next move had been predictable. Her expert evisceration skills had made the source of her anguish disappear: she'd said exactly what she needed to in order to make Olivia leave.

Winner of the round by technical knockout: Margaret Blackwood.

The question was, what did Olivia want to do about it? Did Margaret deserve a second chance?

On the one hand, Olivia had given Tina another chance, and that vicious little schemer had never deserved it. Didn't Margaret deserve the same chance?

On the other hand, Margaret had deliberately drawn blood tonight. Because she was hurting. Because Olivia had hurt her. Still, she'd done it *on purpose.*

Look at what people do.

Olivia tried to mentally step back and look at the bigger picture. Apart from tonight's panic-fuelled, icy shutdown, Margaret had consistently shown herself to be on Olivia's side. She'd shown who she was, over and over. Wasn't that someone worth giving the benefit of the doubt?

Turning, she gave Trip a long look. She'd be lost without him. Margaret knew that. She'd found a way to bring Olivia's penguin back at huge personal risk. Margaret might have lost Quincy forever. She'd had no idea how this would play out, but she'd done it anyway.

That said something about who she was. Her character. What she really thought of Olivia.

It was settled. If anyone deserved a second chance, it was Margaret. But first, Olivia would have to take the sting out of the scorpion's tail. Although it was more than one stinger. She had a quiver full of them. Margaret was an especially angry, lethal creature right now. Closer to porcupine than scorpion.

Even if Olivia managed to navigate all those barbs, there was something else to address. She'd learned a thing or two about boundaries in the past few months. But in her bones, this felt like exactly the right thing to do. It felt too important not to try.

Margaret Blackwood was too important.

But first she needed to make a detour.

Saturday, April 11

Olivia crossed every line I had tonight.

How much her words scratched and bit and stung. Did she have to do that? Reveal she knows my every failing and vulnerability? Shake them out like a blanket for all to see? How I view my office as my escape? Some days I can barely leave it. It's too hard.

It's safe in there. She says I'm hibernating. Like I'm some dopey, useless bear, unwilling to poke its head outside. Olivia ripped away my dignity. And so I shut her down. Shut everything down. Made it end.

Well. It's done now. I'm perfectly fine without Olivia Roberts in my life. I probably won't even notice her absence.

God, my heart just spasmed even writing that. Correction, then: I'm quite sure I will adapt without her around so frequently.

Anyway, now she knows the whole truth: I am broken.

Wth? Who on earth is making that racket this late?

CHAPTER 22

SECOND CHANCES

OLIVIA BANGED AS BEST SHE could on Margaret's door with her hands full. It took almost a minute for the door to open a little, and more seconds for Margaret to open it wide, surprise evident on her face.

"Hi," Olivia said, crab walking in with a heavy bag that pulled her arms straight. "Do you mind if I drop this here?"

Margaret stared, then nodded before closing the door behind Olivia as if on autopilot. "Why are you dropping a twenty-kilogram sack of cat food on my floor?"

"It's for Wednesday," Olivia said, unkinking her back and shaking out her arms.

"I didn't think it was for me." Margaret's words were dry, her shoulders tense. Everything about her screamed wariness.

"Well, I wanted to bring you a peace offering, but the little shop I stopped at had only an eclectic bunch of stuff. And I know pets are expensive, so…" She pointed to the bag and straightened. "And I got *this* for you." Olivia reached into her back pocket and brought out a small steel file, the kind used for filing through metal.

"A file?" Margaret took it and could not have looked more confused.

"Yep. It's symbolic. I'll explain in a second. But first: what's the comfiest chair you own?"

Frowning, Margaret pointed to an armchair in the lounge.

"Great." Olivia waved her towards the chair and said with firmness: "Sit. Please?"

Margaret obeyed without comment, sinking into the leather, before glancing between Olivia and the metal file she held in her own hands. When she spoke, she sounded tense enough to crack. "I didn't expect to see you again."

"I know," Olivia said evenly. "Hang on one more sec." She scanned the room until she spotted Wednesday snoozing on a cat pillow on the balcony and went to fetch her.

On returning, she gently placed the sleepy animal in Margaret's lap. Then Olivia sank onto the floor next to Margaret's knees—in the least intimidating position she could manage—and looked up. "Okay?"

Margaret had morphed from confusion to utter bewilderment. "What's going on?"

"I want you to feel comfortable. Warm. Safe."

"While holding a metal file and with my cat purring in my lap?"

"Yes." Olivia grinned. "Exactly." She drew in a deep breath. "I was heading home when I realised what happened tonight."

"Oh?" Margaret's expression became watchful and dark.

"I've learned a lot about relationships, Margaret, by being in so many bad ones. I know how I don't want to be treated. I know what I did wrong in them too, when I should have said something and didn't. I'm planning on never repeating my mistakes."

Margaret shook her head. "I truly have no idea where you're going with this."

"I made a terrible mess of things tonight, Margaret. I handled your pain poorly. You pushed me away to protect yourself. And you knew exactly which button of mine to press to ensure I didn't stick around to argue." Olivia drew in a breath, pain stabbing her at the reminder. "You said that you didn't want me."

Looking down, Margaret focused on the hands she now clenched on her knees.

"I'm not going to lie," Olivia continued. "After my dating history, that's my tender spot—as you know. It worked. I bolted."

Margaret did not reply or even look up.

"Which brings us to the here and now. I know what you did and why, and I know how to fix it, at least a little bit. Right now, you're like a cornered porcupine—and I'm not fool enough to mess with those spikes. I have to flatten your biggest prickles. The lashing out. So, prickle number one: us having a romantic relationship."

Margaret stiffened.

"It's off the table," Olivia said instantly. "I'll never bring it up again. You can, if you want, but I won't. Okay?"

Margaret relaxed marginally.

"Prickle number two: your office. I'll never again mention what it means to you or why you stay in it for prolonged periods. I never meant it to come out like mockery or an accusation. It's good you have somewhere that gives you comfort. I'm sorry I made that awkward for you. I truly never meant to hurt you."

Nostrils flaring, Margaret looked away. A blush spidered up her neck, and Olivia realised she was feeling self-conscious all over again about the topic.

"I lived in my van for three months," Olivia blurted out. "I was effectively homeless. Why? Because I was too embarrassed to tell anyone that Annalise had changed the locks on our apartment while I was at work one day, and that she kept all my stuff. Annalise already had all my savings, so I was broke. Even after she moved in with my boss later, she kept my things. I was too humiliated to go to the police because I'd have to admit that I'd been thoroughly conned. They'd think I was such a loser. It's the worst feeling, fearing being made fun of when you're at your lowest."

Margaret's shoulders seemed to lose a little more of their tension. She removed her hands from her knees and buried them in Wednesday's fur.

"Prickle number three: our friendship." Olivia turned the word over in her head. "What is a friendship? Sharing thoughts and common interests? Hanging out together? Choosing to be in one's company when you could be anywhere else? Margaret, by that definition we've been friends for close to two years. I was just too obstinate to notice."

Margaret gave her a startled look, meeting her eye for the first time since she'd sat down.

"Every week at book club, I'd twist around behind me to check if your office door was ajar. And every week without fail, *for two years*, I felt you watching. Listening. I wondered for the longest time what you were thinking. And then you started joining in. Your little murmured commentary from the office. I took every word you said to heart."

"I know," Margaret said quietly. "I know you did."

"We were friends even then in a sense, don't you think?" Olivia asked.

Margaret's brow puckered.

"Well, we were certainly friends in recent weeks. Not acquaintances. Never that." Olivia dared her to disagree.

Guilt slipped across Margaret's face, but she looked as if she might be stubborn enough to argue.

"Margaret, no one who's scared of heights climbs a six-storey-high fire-escape for *an acquaintance*. My free muffins aren't that good a lure. And no one trades away their beloved peacock to help *an acquaintance*."

"I'm going to get it back," Margaret protested, chin lifting in defiance.

"I know you will." Olivia smiled gently at her. "I'm also sure you're reluctant to be friends with me right now because you're afraid I'll hurt you again."

Uncertainty flitted into Margaret's expression.

"Here's my idea: a trial friendship separation. We try *not* being friends for a little while. If you don't like it, just tell me the trial is cancelled and we're back to being friends." Olivia pointed at the metal file. "Here's where my awesome prop comes in. Remember the legend about Mary Ann Bugg supposedly rescuing Captain Thunderbolt from jail on Cockatoo Island, swimming there with a metal file between her teeth?"

"That's just a myth," Margaret said with scorn, eyes brightening at the familiar and safer topic. "Several historians have convincingly argued it didn't happen."

"Yes. But, for argument's sake, can you consider the metal file as a symbol of what might have been Mary Ann Bugg's courage? In the same way Quincy may or may not be a famous watch peacock? When you look at it, think about what Mary Ann Bugg would do when faced with a challenge. In this case, the challenge is whether to toss aside a friendship or look at what might be gained from it."

"What could possibly be gained from it?" Margaret's eyes were hooded.

"Me. In your life. As an ally. Making you laugh. Being someone to share stories about your day with, or who allows you to blather on about your book verdicts as though they're peer-reviewed fact when we both know they're just an opinion, same as mine."

Margaret looked outraged at that, but her lips betrayed her, twitching upwards. "Actually, my opinions *are* peer-reviewed facts."

"Only on bushrangers. Everything else? Mysteries and thrillers? Come on, you know as much as I do." Olivia rested one hand lightly on Margaret's knee. "The bottom line is, I think we're good together as friends, so I'm willing to step back and wait for you to see it too, and give you that trial separation."

"What if I don't see it too?" Margaret asked quietly.

"If I'm wrong, I'm wrong. But I'm not wrong." Olivia smiled, but it faded and she hesitated. "Now then, because I'm a forgiving sort, and I know you were panicking, I am prepared to forget all the shitty things you said tonight as long as you do one thing."

"What?" Margaret asked after a moment.

Olivia looked down, and embarrassment stained her cheeks. "Don't ever tell me again you don't want me. As a friend or as a person. Not like that; find another way if you have to step away. But those words cut deep for me. If you can't agree to my terms, or if you agree but do it anyway, I'm walking immediately. It's a boundary I need you to respect."

Margaret inhaled and looked shamefaced. "Olivia, I fail to see how anyone could not want you."

"I'm not talking about anyone. I'm talking about you." She held Margaret's gaze unwaveringly.

Straightening, Margaret said: "I will not say or imply that again." Real regret tinged her voice when she added in a soft voice, "I'm sorry that…I… hurt you."

At least she hadn't said that it hadn't been her intention. It had been, and they both knew it. She'd wanted Olivia to leave so desperately that she'd knowingly pressed on Olivia's bruise.

"For argument's sake, how does this trial friendship separation work?" Margaret asked tentatively. "Will you stop visiting my store? Will you stop speaking to me?"

"No. I'll simply interact with you politely, exactly as I would with some-one who is not my friend. I won't offer anything more to a conversation than

I would to a stranger. You can then assess what our friendship is worth to you. But either way, Margaret, I want it on the record that we *were* friends."

Margaret drew in a long breath and then inclined her head. "Yes. I suppose we were. And I agree to your terms."

At least the defensiveness was all but gone now.

"Okay, great." Olivia smiled and rose to leave. "With all that out of the way, I'll leave you to it, Dr Blackwood."

Margaret winced at the formal use of her name. Edging Wednesday from her lap, she stood too, her eye falling to the twenty-kilo bag of dried pet food. "Why did you buy so much cat food?" she asked, looking genuinely puzzled.

"Because buying just a metal file at Harry's Supermarket looks weird and kinda criminal-ly. I don't want Harry to think I'm a weird criminal. And he was out of the smaller bags."

Margaret hesitated and seemed about to say something else but instead just nodded.

Olivia waited, but when nothing else was forthcoming, she saw herself out.

And that was how Olivia and Margaret very politely ended their friendship.

Kelly met Olivia at the door the moment she arrived home, eyeing her pensively. "After that call, tell me if I have to quit my job or kill my boss."

"Neither. But it's not going to work out. Romantically speaking." Olivia forced a smile. "Margaret doesn't want that."

"Are you sure?"

"Yeah. She said as much. We're too different to even be friends, according to her."

"Oh, Liv." And then Kelly's arms were around her, and she was suddenly pressed into her sister's shoulder.

"Honestly, it's okay," Olivia said, voice muffled. "We eventually sort of reached an understanding."

"An understanding?"

Olivia stuck her head up to meet Kelly's sympathetic eyes. "She pushed me away—hard. I decided to go back. I told her she didn't have to say cold things to get the distance from me she needs. And now, we're having a trial friendship separation to see how she likes it. Either way, we're not friends anymore. Margaret tried to argue that we never were."

"That's not true, you know," Kelly countered, anger lighting her eyes. "She came alive when you were around."

Olivia drew in a deep breath. "I'd like to believe that. And maybe she'll believe it too one day. We'll see. But if I've learned anything from the past month vengeancing, it's that I'm done with being anyone's doormat. I'm never doing that again, letting myself be treated like I don't matter. I set some boundaries, which she agreed to. And I fired her as my henchperson."

"But don't you still have Timothy to do?"

"Yes. But that won't take long."

"It won't? Have you already worked out what you're doing to him?"

"I've known for ages. You remember what a rev-head he was? Hell, he found me my first car."

"Your Torana came from Timothy? How did that happen?"

"He knew a guy and got me a nice deal for it. One of the few things Timothy was good for." Olivia rolled her eyes. "Anyway, he always said he and his brother were going to start their own mechanic business when they left school. He even told me what he'd call it: Mitchell Brothers Mechanics. And sure enough, I found his company's website. One of the online photos shows he still has his favourite car, this old Holden he was restoring when we were dating. Based on the pic, which I cross-checked with Google Street View, I know exactly where to find it too."

"And then what?"

"Okay, so Mitchell Brothers Mechanics is pretty near Port Melbourne Beach. I can ask the fishermen on the pier for fish guts. Then I'll spread it over Timothy's beloved car."

"That's it?" Kelly peered at her. "Can't he just…wash it?"

"Fish guts will attract seagulls. They'll be all over it, pecking and shitting on his pride and joy. Very…Hitchcockian." She grinned. "The kicker is, he'll be working inside his garage and won't notice for hours. It'll be *so* ripe and disgusting by the time he does."

"Hmm." Kelly digested that. "And then what happens? Or is that it? He just drives his sticky, smelly, possibly seagull-covered car to the car wash? Or gets out the hose himself? And that's the end of it? Done in five minutes? After all your years of agonising about what he and Rodney did?"

Olivia deflated. "I don't know. I hadn't really thought that far ahead. Margaret was better at the dastardly stuff. She's the one with the creative imagination." Sagging, she added: "I guess my plan is kind of pathetic. Which is sort of the theme for the day I've had. I'm pretty lame all around."

Kelly hugged her again. "You're actually impressive. Dr Blackwood is as intimidating as hell, and it was brave you asked her out in the first place. Firing her as your henchperson also took guts. I'm proud of you for getting better at standing up for yourself. And if it helps, I can give my boss the cold shoulder every day in solidarity."

"No, don't. You need your job. Besides, this is between her and me. We worked it out in a weird kinda way. After I gave her a peace offering: cat food and a metal file."

Kelly stepped back. "Huh?"

"Long story." She shrugged. "Anyway, it's over. For now."

"Can I ask you something?" Kelly suddenly asked. "Why are you going after Timothy but not Rodney? He's the one who tricked you into kissing him."

"They both tricked me. But Timothy was the one I cared about and who betrayed me. Timothy's the one who was supposed to protect me and instead let his juvenile brother put his creepy mouth on me. I may think Rodney's a jerk, but my boyfriend's the one who broke my heart. It hurt twice as much because he was my first relationship."

"Ah. Okay."

"But maybe I'll post on social media a pic of the car getting Hitchcocked with Mitchell Brothers Mechanics signage in the background just to piss them both off."

Kelly smiled. "Good plan." She clicked her fingers. "Hey, it's not even nine-thirty yet. Want to hang out, stream B-grade shit, and eat ice cream? That zombie show maybe?"

"I'm not in the mood. But thanks."

Kelly fell silent for a moment. "You really care for her, don't you?"

"What?"

"Like, really, *really*."

Olivia scowled. "No idea what you mean."

"You *never* turn down ice cream and zombies."

"It's past my bedtime. I'm going to my room."

"Okay. But the other offer stands: I can be frosty as fuck to Dr B on Monday." Kelly gave a dramatic glower to prove it. Of course, she just looked adorable. She just couldn't pull off a mean look to save her life.

"Thanks for the offer, but it's fine. Or, it will be. Besides, maybe Margaret...Dr Blackwood...will barely even notice us no longer being friends." Olivia had her doubts, though. She really hoped she was right.

CHAPTER 23

PREVIOUS PARAMETERS INITIATED

It was weird being back in Mary Bugg's for book club after all that had transpired. Olivia felt oddly discombobulated as she took her old armchair and settled in.

Unlike every other Tuesday, though, she didn't look behind her to see if the office door was ajar. She no longer assumed Margaret Blackwood would be there and no longer assumed the bookstore boss would be interested in anything Olivia had to say.

Damien was in fine form, filling everyone in on a night out at the pub with the security guard from Tina's apartment building. Olivia forced herself to focus as he told his story with gusto.

"So you got out by the skin of your teeth," he was saying.

She blinked. What had she missed? "Sorry, I vagued out. What happened?"

He grinned from ear to ear. "Two minutes after you, Sasha, and Dr Blackwood bugged out of the building, the real Anita van Dyke arrived with clients for a showing."

"Oh shit!"

"Right?" Damien slapped his thigh, laughing. "Christos was SO flamin' confused. He got the poor woman to show every form of ID she had. Then he took them up to the third-floor apartment personally and went over every inch of it to try and see what we'd been up to. Couldn't find a thing. He was also going on about how the fake agent he'd let upstairs had been a blonde and he could have sworn that she'd left a brunette. He half convinced himself he'd remembered wrong."

Olivia laughed. "I'd wondered why he looked so confused when Dr Blackwood dumped the key on his desk."

"Poor Christos. Anyway, the real Anita van Dyke was enraged someone was impersonating her, but she couldn't work out who. Said the only woman she'd recently given her card to was 'not impersonation material' cos she was a 'short, stocky lesbian who embraced denim-on-denim as a style palette'." He glanced at Bo. "Sorry, direct quote."

Bo nodded sagely. "I own it. But denim is vastly underrated as a fashion statement." She turned to Olivia. "Can I say again I'm really sorry I had to bail in mid operation? It was life or death at the theatre, or I'd never have shot off like that. Those French barricades when they come apart are lethal."

"Did you resolve it?" Olivia asked. "Did the revolution go ahead?"

"The show went on, yep. The revolution didn't succeed, though because it never does. That's the plot."

"Of course." Bo had her there. "Glad it worked out fine."

"Not fine, since Bo left her post in mid mission." Margaret's voice, soft and goading, was clear to Olivia, and low enough that she was probably the only one who could hear it.

She didn't acknowledge it. They weren't friends. That's what Margaret wanted, right? "So," Olivia said. "On to the book."

"Wait," Damien said, "I haven't gotten to the good part yet."

"It gets better?"

"Tina is getting her thieving arse kicked out of her apartment!"

"What?" Olivia gaped.

"Two days ago, according to Christos, this woman came flying out of the lift with Tina right behind, pleading with her. She was screaming at Tina for cooking something so rancid it had gotten into the furniture and saying she'd tell her parents to take back the apartment. And Tina's all 'but I didn't do anything!'"

"That has to be Tina's cousin," Olivia said. "Her parents own the place."

"Ah." Damien nodded. "Okay, so then Tina started crying. And the cousin goes, 'You can cut the crap with your weaponised tears, they don't work on me. Start packing; you're going back to your parents' place', and she stormed off. Tina moped back on up to her apartment."

"Operation Raw Prawn for the win!" Olivia punched the air.

"Excellent." Breanna said approvingly. "And I can't *stand* weaponised tears. It's so repulsive and evil. Always a white woman too."

"I dunno," Tess said, brow puckering. "My sister weaponises her tears pretty hard, and her bum's just as brown as mine."

"Well, if you want to get technical, that example is probably not weaponised tears," Breanna said thoughtfully. "See, it's about the power dynamic. Is your sister using her tears to bring some entitled status into play and force an undeserved win? If she doesn't have an entitled status in the first place, then I'd argue her tears aren't weaponised, merely manipulative."

And off they went down a rabbit hole of racial, social, and gendered politics.

Olivia wanted to bang her head on the table. Especially when Damien burst out laughing, which pissed off Breanna enough to tell him his amusement was enabling the patriarchy. Which only made him laugh harder. He never minded Breanna too much.

Margaret said something inaudible behind Olivia. For once, Olivia didn't strain to try and make out what she'd said over the rabble.

That was the moment she realised she'd done this all along. Been acutely aware of the elusive bookstore owner's presence. Listened hard for what was going on behind her in case she came out of her office or spoke. It seemed she'd been invested in Margaret Blackwood for a lot longer than she'd realised.

"The book," Olivia said tiredly, breaking into the conversation. "Did everyone read it?"

"Well, about that," Bo began. "I meant to but…"

And life was back to normal.

When the hour was up, Olivia announced their next book would be Ruth McIver's *I Shot the Devil*, then stood and strode from the book club, not bothering to look back.

Tuesday, April 14

Sunset: *5:53pm*

Temp: *12.1C-23.4C*

Rain: *0.6mm*

Drink: *Turkey Flat Rosé 2020. One glass. Opened too soon. I should have cellared it for at least a year. It was like bathing in rose petals...and not in a good way.*

Reading: Non-fiction—*I've finally finished all of the JALIA Vol 69, issue 1 and have a rather intense urge to never read any further library journals. It's as though that part of my life is now over.*

How...curious.

Fiction—*I've made a start on* I Shot the Devil *by Ruth McIver, next week's read for book club. It's about a journalist with clearly zero common sense or self-preservation instincts. (How clever to meet alone with a suspected killer in the middle of nowhere.) Plus satanism. Janice would love this one purely to point out all the reporter's professional malfunctions. Think I'll give it to her next.*

General Observations: *Today was not acceptable.*

I attempted to re-engage with Olivia via book club as per usual. She didn't so much as turn in my direction. I cannot explain how much this felt like a punch to the gut. It shouldn't matter of course, as we are _not_ friends.

Yes, it is my own choice that we're in this position. I can't very well object now.

Meanwhile, I'm...concerned as to how Olivia will handle Timothy on her own. She had planned for us to defile his car next Monday with a coating of fish guts. Perhaps I should attend—discreetly, of course—just to ensure she is fine.

I did make an undertaking as her henchperson, and I would like to ensure all goes to plan. I am a woman of integrity in such matters, even if circumstances have changed. Olivia shouldn't have to suffer because I forced her hand in suggesting we sever our arrangement.

CHAPTER 24

TERRIBLE TIMOTHY

Timothy Vengeance Day dawned grey and windy. The bruised clouds threatened a tempest, but Olivia's weather app said it wouldn't eventuate until later. She hoped it was right. She'd taken a few deep breaths, told herself she could do this alone despite it feeling so weird without Margaret, and then slapped on her go-getter *Here I Crumb* button pin.

Kelly snorted at it over breakfast, shaking her head, which Olivia chose to take as a thumbs up.

It was midmorning when Olivia arrived at Kerferd Road Pier and said hello to the handful of rugged-up anglers, clutching her little white bucket. After begging for any fish guts they might have, several shrugged and obliged.

With the stinky pink cargo in possession, Olivia headed off to Mitchell Brothers Mechanics.

The Holden HK Monaro of Timothy's dreams was parked around the back. It wasn't hard to spot, in that its bright rust-red paint gleamed from having been waxed to within an inch of its life.

Olivia crept closer. She could picture the cow-skin car seat cover and dangling fuzzy dice from all those dates with Timothy as a teenager. Peering inside, she confirmed the same decor, although the dice was now a dangling, scented cardboard pine tree.

One thing she hadn't expected was the baby seat in the back. Was Timothy a dad now?

The wind whipped her hair into her eyes, and the bucket's wire handle bit into her hand as she tried to work out whether his paternal status changed anything.

No. It changed nothing. Timothy had gotten off scot-free and hadn't felt the faintest hint of remorse. He'd denied all her feelings and acted as if she were unhinged for being upset over a small "joke".

With a quick glance around, she noted no movement from within the open rear garage doors, which were huge. A car was up on a hoist, and a radio station played loudly. Masculine voices called out to each other, but no one was visible.

Now or never.

Olivia hurled the bucket with all her might, propelling its contents over the car's roof with a gross *blurrrp.*

A sickening slick of blood, guts, and entrails splashed over the roof and windshield, then skidded right off the car—the wax finish aiding its impressive whoosh.

Just then, the wind gusted back towards her, and a wash of slurry blew into her face and hair.

"Argh!" she cried out, dropping the bucket in disgust.

The masculine voices stopped abruptly.

Olivia was flicking fish guts from her eyes and out of her nose, mouth, and collar when a man's voice said: "Shit! My car!" And then: "Uh...Livvy??"

Bedraggled, she turned, blinking away disgusting goop. Timothy, in grease-stained overalls, was jogging towards her.

He looked older than thirty-three, his hair greying at his temples and receding at the front.

Timothy skidded to a halt and stared at his car in dismay. Then at her. And back at his car. His mouth opened and shut.

Olivia glanced around, resentfully wondering where the promised seagulls were, because this mission had already gone tits up. Not only had Timothy found the mess prematurely, but there were no birds mobbing his car and making him cry.

He didn't look remotely like crying. He didn't even look angry. He just studied her with a resigned look.

"Timothy," she said with a sigh. Because it seemed the thing to say when someone said your name.

"Great," he muttered, staring at the car. "Do you mind if I hose it off now, or do you need it to sit a while longer and really get gross?"

"I was waiting for seagulls."

He glanced around the heavens. "Don't see any. Too windy, probably. Maybe should've waited till tomorrow?" Timothy considered that for a moment. "But it's kinda a sound plan, I guess."

"Thank you," she said tightly.

"Come inside," he suggested. "I've got a towel. You can wipe yourself off."

"No thanks," she said primly. "I don't need anything from you."

"Beg to differ," he said, eyeballing the car. "Kinda looks like you needed something."

"I...suppose." And in case it wasn't abundantly clear, she added: "Revenge."

Timothy scratched his jaw absently. "I see." He waved at a line of up-turned crates outside the garage doors. "Wanna sit and talk a bit? Get it off your chest?"

Olivia scowled at him. "Do you even know why I did that?"

Silence fell long and heavy. He sighed. "I reckon I do. And I...probably deserved it."

Capitulation was the exact last thing she expected. Olivia stared in confusion.

"Come on," he said. "We'll talk. I think maybe there's some stuff you don't know."

"Where's Rodney?" she asked, peering around suspiciously. He could always be relied on to ruin any conversation with his sly comments.

"Not around. He's what we should talk about."

Olivia nodded then and followed him to the crates.

"Wait here," he said. "I'll be right back."

Worry prickled up her spine, and she wondered if he was about to wreak some nasty payback on her. She looked all around, then up, half expecting a car engine to land on her head. But the area was clear. Except for an idling Jaguar down a small laneway.

Olivia squinted at it, shading her eyes. If she didn't know better, she'd say that was Margaret's car. But that was ludicrous. The woman had made it perfectly clear a week ago that she wanted nothing further to do with Olivia.

"Here."

She turned back to find Timothy holding out a bottled water and a towel.

"Use it or don't, I don't care. But I figure you won't want to stink up the Torana on the way home with fish guts, hey?" He paused. "You still have the Torana, right?"

"Yes." She decided not to inform him a different shitty ex had had custody of it until quite recently.

"I'd love to check her out again, if you don't mind. That car was a beaut."

"Timothy," she snapped. "We're not here to reminisce! I'm here to commit vengeance for what you did to me when we dated."

"Yeah. Sorry." He looked shamefaced.

"Do you remember?"

His cheeks darkened, and for a moment, he looked like the teenager she knew years ago. A big galoot. So young. Could be sweet. Until he wasn't.

"Your brother forced that kiss on me. He took away my consent," Olivia said. "And you let him. You were in on it. I never liked Rodney, especially after that. But it was *your* betrayal that hurt."

He dropped his head. "I know."

"You do?"

"Yeah." Timothy sighed. "I was a bit of a dick, okay? That was really fucked up, and I didn't see it for what it was at the time. I didn't understand a lot of shit."

"And now you do?" Olivia asked sceptically. "What changed?" She twisted open the lid on the bottle, poured some water onto the towel and then wiped the crud off her face. She turned the towel over and did the same for her hair and collar.

Timothy waited for her to finish and then said: "I changed. And Rod changed. And, well, it was hard not to get a clue when he went to jail," he said softly.

Olivia froze. "What?"

"Yeah. He's still there." Timothy squinted up at the sky for a moment as the wind picked up. Then he pointed at his car when a seagull landed on the bonnet and began pecking at it. "Hey, you got one."

She gazed at the bird in astonishment and then turned back to him. "Can you go back to the part about your twin being in jail?"

"You were the first, Livvy," he said solemnly. "But you weren't the last."

"I wasn't the…" *Oh.* Her eyes widened.

"He had me convinced what happened with you was nothing. A kiss. You were being hysterical and not taking a joke." He lifted his hand to prevent her protest. "I don't believe that now. I did then. He wasn't just my brother to me, he was my hero. I looked up to him. He was the brave one of the two of us, the fun one, the confident one. The leader. He called himself Hot Rod, and I thought, *yeah, he's cool.*"

Cool? Olivia side-eyed him.

"I know he's not. Now." Timothy kicked the dirt beneath his boot and inhaled. "See, my brother wasn't done. He got a sick pleasure in what he did to you. He really enjoyed it and wanted to do it again with my future girlfriends, but he knew I'd never agree to more 'jokes' after how you reacted. He figured the solution was to just not get caught next time. To tell no one. I just kept weirdly losing girlfriends. Out of the blue, they'd start ghosting me or calling me shitty names, like I'd been mean to them. I couldn't work out what was going on. I was too stupid to realise."

"Oh, hell."

"Right? And from my point of view, it was just that one swap thing with you. One kiss. But for him? He'd escalated. He was jealous. He hated my girlfriends and loved driving them away as cruelly as possible. The court psychologist said he resented anyone getting between me and him but that he also hated women in general. Some of the nicknames he called them when he was pretending to be me were really fuckin' low."

Olivia stared. "What?"

"He had names for them that he'd use and then pretend he was joking when they got upset."

"Timothy? By any chance did you ever call me a 'fat arse'?"

He gaped at her. "Never! Fuck no. I loved your arse!" Then he blushed.

She sighed. "Rodney did more than just kiss me, then. He bullied me too."

"I'm so sorry, Livvy." He looked genuinely remorseful.

It answered that question though: why you'd date someone if you thought they were unappealing. Timothy wasn't the one who'd thought she was ugly.

"How did you find out what he was doing?" Olivia asked.

"One day, I came home from work early and caught him on top of my girlfriend. He was tearing her clothes off. I'd hate to have been five minutes later. I heard Penny say, 'Timothy! Stop being so rough'. And I lost my ever-loving shit on him. And then Penny clocked my arrival, worked out what was what, and she lost *her* shit too. Next thing, everyone's at the cop shop. Police went back to all my exes and found Rod had been a busy little creep."

"I never heard from the police."

"I know. I didn't give them your name because I knew exactly what he'd done with you: One kiss. I wasn't sure about the others, though. I gave the cops names of all my other exes, just in case he'd done worse. Fuck, Rod was mad as hell. He thought I should have protected him. How could I after what he'd done? He was sick."

"Timothy, how many of your girlfriends did he exploit?"

"All of them. They were all groped and kissed. Only two he tried to go further with, and both women caught him in time because he acted so creepy and not like me at all. Those two pressed charges. That's why he went to jail. It's not why he's still in jail, though. He went bunta. He intimidated the witnesses, insulted the judge for being a woman, threatened his lawyers—who resigned and sued—attacked the media outside court, and generally made an absolute dick of himself." He sagged. "When he was jailed, the *Herald Sun*'s headline was *Good Roddance!* Mum cried for a week. You really didn't see any of this on the news? I thought everyone knew."

"I don't watch the news. With the hours I keep, I don't like being filled with depressing content just before bed."

"Really?" He looked interested. "What do you do?" His gaze darted curiously to her *Here I Crumb* button and back.

"I'm a baker. I run a muffin van around Prahran's cafes mainly. It's…fun. I like it."

"That's so cool." He sounded like he really meant it. Timothy grinned. "I thought you were going to do literature, so this is outta left field. But it's great you're doing something that makes you happy." He glanced past her, then pointed at his car. "Hey, look, you got another one."

Sure enough, another seagull had landed. He seemed far too excited on her behalf.

"Aren't you worried about the mess it's making of your car?" Olivia asked, a little peeved her vengeance efforts were backfiring, yet again. "I know you love your old Holden."

"Oh yeah. I'm a bit dark about it, not gonna lie. But I figure you must be feeling way worse to plan this whole thing out, then come down here and do it. If I'd known you were still hurting, I'd have looked you up years ago and said sorry. And I am, Livvy. Really fuckin' sorry. I acted like an immature dick, going along with Rod, and I should have listened when you told me how it felt. I deserved to have my arse dumped. I was the worst boyfriend."

He sounded so sincere that Olivia couldn't even feel glad that three more seagulls had turned up. But the whole topic of Rod's skeezy actions made her suddenly bilious. She scrambled for a new topic. "What are you up to now? How are things?"

"Can't complain." Timothy shrugged. "I got my shit together, bought out my brother's half of the shop. Oh, and one day, a young woman came in with a clapped-out Hillman Hunter. Jesus, that car was a sight!" He laughed. "Held together by rust and a prayer. But I fixed it right up. Even so, Amanda kept coming back. Finally, I got a clue she wasn't really after *that* many oil changes. Married her. We have a kid now. Wanna see?" He reached into his pocket, pulled out his phone, and scrolled through it.

Timothy proudly showed her a picture of an adorable, curly-haired three-ish girl with the cheekiest grin. "Takes after her mum, obviously, with looks like that, hey?" Timothy gazed fondly at the picture, then looked up. "How about you? Anyone in your life? Kids?"

Olivia hesitated.

"Sorry," he said hastily. "Shit, it's not my place to ask. I didn't mean to put you on the spot if you don't want to talk about it."

"There's no one I want to talk about," Olivia said frostily. Then she sighed. "By the way, you can hose off your car now."

"Really?" he asked with so much hopefulness. "I mean, if you want it to sit overnight and get *really* manky, I'd understand. I'd be gutted, but I'd figure, fair enough."

"No, not necessary. I've decided I accept your apology. But for your sake, I'm glad Rodney's out of your life. You're a much better man without him."

"No argument from me. Our parents disowned him, you know. He's got nothing now but his bitter bullshit and a prison haircut, and I'm not sorry."

Olivia stood and put the towel and water bottle down. "I think I'm glad your life's worked out for you."

He smiled then, wide and relieved. "I'm stoked to hear that. And I'm glad you came today. Squared the ledger and all. Y'know?"

"I do." She held out a hand to him. "Thanks for not making this harder."

He shook it. "If there's anything I can do for you, just say the word."

Olivia was about to say there was nothing, but then a thought hit. "I don't suppose you're feeling charitable?"

"Huh? How so?"

"I have a friend who's homeless. She and her two kids sleep in their car. It's an old station wagon, and it's dead. Do you think you'd be able to donate a bit of time and resources on helping her out?"

"Be happy to. I can go to her too. Got a mobile mechanic van now," he said proudly.

Olivia smiled. "That's great. I'll check with my friend that she's fine with it, but if so, expect to hear from Samantha Garrity."

He nodded. "Shall do. Well, I better go find a hose and ruin the party those birds are having. I gotta say, it's good seeing you again, Livvy."

"Timothy?"

"Yeah?"

"It's *Olivia*." It felt good to insist on her name. A boundary. About time she started enforcing them.

"Right-o." He shrugged, as if not in the least bothered by the correction. "See you around, Olivia."

Was it really that easy to get people to call her by her name? She should have done this years ago. With that, Olivia left him to it—"it" being eight seagulls and counting.

As she walked away, she looked around for the stalking black Jaguar, but it was gone. Probably not Margaret, then.

Olivia was almost back at her van when she remembered she'd planned to take a photo of the car being bird-bombed to humiliate the business. But now she had no interest in revenge. At all. The burning urge had left her. She stopped and realised something else: she was done with her list, her exes, and her vengeance. It was over. She'd finished.

She smiled at the sense of completion. Her vengeance planning days were officially over. It was a good feeling.

Monday, April 20

Sunset: *5:45pm*

Temp: *12C-20.8C*

Rain: *3.4mm*

Drink: *Vodka neat. The smell of fish gut has put me off wine tonight. The vodka wasn't much of an improvement.*

Reading: *I've cracked* The Dry *by Jane Harper. Small towns, big secrets...well, now there's a theme I've never read before. I'm leery of multi-multi-award-winning books because I feel as though my tastes are at odds with the world's literary judges. I can appreciate slow-paced reads, and I'm still side-eyeing the ending. In sum: my jury remains out.*

General Observations: *Well. That was spectacular. If by spectacular, one also means a grotesque, wretched, fish-gut-propelled tsunami of absurd proportions.*

I did not, in fact, have "Olivia splatters fish entrails all over herself" on my expected outcomes bingo card today.

Clearly Timothy is not too much of a boor as I witnessed him supply a towel and water. The least he could do, of course.

Nor did he run around pointing, shouting, and crying over his vehicle as Olivia had anticipated.

I would love to talk to her about it. Determine what took place. I left after a handshake where they apparently reached some sort of agreement.

I can't, however, let the matter rest entirely. I have now texted Olivia four different recipes for removing fish smells from fabrics, cars, hair, and general clothing. Vinegar is key. But variations include toothpaste, lemon, boiled cinnamon sticks, and so forth.

It's been three hours. Olivia has not replied to any of my helpful suggestions. This gives a somewhat...hollow feeling.

Four hours.

Six hours. I'm turning in.

CHAPTER 25

FROSTY ISN'T JUST AN ICING

IT HAD BEEN THREE WEEKS since Olivia lost her friendship with Margaret. That was how it felt to her. A loss. A friend whose opinion and presence she'd sought out so frequently in recent weeks that she hadn't realised how often she'd been doing it. She really hoped Margaret was noticing the loss too, given that was the point of the exercise. Perhaps she had, given the array of texts about fish smells. Okay, that had been embarrassing. She'd been the driver of the Jaguar after all. Trust Margaret to have witnessed Olivia in that humiliating condition.

But missing the other woman right now was okay because it felt temporary. Because if Margaret hadn't wanted a friendship with Olivia at all, she'd never have agreed to a trial separation. She'd have just told her to go away and stay gone. She hadn't. She'd wanted to try. And that meant the world.

All Olivia could do while she waited for Margaret to see sense—that they were too good together to throw away the friendship—was to keep her vow to maintain boundaries.

That meant not indulging in replying to Margaret's commentary during book club, tempting as it was. Not responding to mocking texts—because for sure, Margaret was making fun of her with those fish-smell cures.

Not acknowledging her if they passed each other. Which wasn't often, but still. That one was hard. Margaret was still captivating to look at. Olivia had also spent a great deal of effort trying to forget what she tasted like and the small sounds she'd made when she'd kissed Olivia.

On the topic of boundaries, Olivia had now started telling everyone to stop calling her Livvy—Liv was okay for those closest to her, but nothing else. And that included telling her favourite customer, Andy, in the park not ten seconds ago, to quit it with all the terrible nicknames.

He paused, mid purchase, and looked up at her in surprise. "Like… forever?" he asked while clutching his Parma Sutra.

"Yep. Can you also take 'Love Muff' out of rotation too?"

"Awww!" he whined. "That's your best nickname."

"Only to you." She tilted her head. "Do you *really* want to piss off your favourite muffin supplier?"

He considered that for a moment, then sighed. "Okay. Fair enough."

"Thanks, Andy."

The engineering student waved good-naturedly and made his way to sit on the low wall where he always had lunch, hunched over his phone.

Olivia had almost sold out of everything today, but her three-cheese zucchini muffin was a harder sell. She glanced around for more customers.

To her surprise, Book Woman was back at her old bench. Margaret hadn't been there since their friendship ceasefire.

With a new, critical eye, she regarded the other woman. Still as angular and interesting as ever.

Kisses like a demon, her brain whispered.

Shut up!

Still hellishly attractive. But as Margaret flicked through the pages of her book, Olivia saw something else now. Or rather, remembered something else.

Margaret was introverted. Aloof. She wanted to be left alone. Her office was her sanctuary. And yet she'd often come here to the park to read, long before she'd come out of her shell and taken on the bold role of henchperson. Why?

As Olivia studied her, wondering at that choice, Margaret glanced up and their gazes locked. It was too far away to make out her expression, but Olivia shivered anyway from the intensity.

No. Bad Olivia. She would not tumble into those brooding eyes and fall off the wagon. She would not wander over to chat with Margaret, nor offer the woman her last muffin. That sounded way too friendly.

Instead, she scooped the remaining muffin onto a paper plate, shivering at the way Margaret's eyes never seemed to leave her.

Margaret put down her book, seemingly in anticipation.

Olivia instead pivoted and headed over to Andy, offering him the last muffin.

"Oh my God, thank you, OLIVIA!" He beamed happily as if she'd given him the universe.

She chuckled at his enthusiastic correct use of her name. Olivia returned to pack up her van, making sure not to look at the tempting siren on the bench. Ten minutes later, she glanced over at her.

Margaret was gone.

The next day was book club. The office door did not crack open. There was no commentary. Olivia wasn't sure what to make of it. Had Margaret finally learned to control her impulse to comment?

She tried to pick apart how she felt about that. The meeting had been somewhat bereft, as though absent an essential element.

"Yo, Liv," Bo said as everyone finished up and started to leave. "Why so glum?"

"Nothing."

"You missing your shadow?" Bo prodded. She glanced at the office door and back. "Dr B's not in there."

"She's not?" Well, that explained her non-contribution.

"Nah. Hot lunch date." Bo gave a low whistle. "Not back even yet."

"What?" Olivia started. "Who with?" she demanded.

"Not sure, but the woman checked out my fine ass when I had my tool belt on, so there's no doubt in my mind that she's 'family'. Conclusion…her and Dr B? Hot date."

"Don't listen to her," Kelly said gently, arriving to pick up the cappuccino cup Olivia had left on the coffee table. "I recognised the woman she left with."

"And?" Olivia asked impatiently. "Who is she?"

"I don't remember her name, but she has a column in the paper. She's the deputy editor of the *Herald Sun*. Pretty sure that's the same woman who left the comment under Martin's Instagram post. Didn't you say she and Dr Blackwood were friends?"

"Oh." Bo pouted. "But they were wearing *date* clothes!"

They were? Olivia's eyes narrowed. Then her brain did some quick arithmetic. "What were you even doing here so many hours before book club? And why were you wearing a tool belt?"

"Dr B hired me to put up the new Bushranger of the Month noticeboards around the place. They'll be fitted with posters later. And I'm also going to build her the new office."

"What new office?"

"She's sectioning off some of the store to make space for an assistant manager."

"What?" Margaret had never made any comment on changing the way her store was running. "Is that why she took her friend to lunch? Is she going to be working here?"

"Nah, nah." Bo then grinned and turned to the smallest, unofficial member of the book club. "I'll let Ems fill you in."

Emma, at her usual seat by the window, had spun around and was grinning widely. "Mum's going to be the new Mary Bugg's assistant manager! Dr Blackwood created the position just for her! She'll have a full-time job again. And it's doing what she loves! Books!" She wiggled in her seat in enthusiasm.

"That's wonderful!" Olivia was truly thrilled for Sam. And, admittedly, a little put out that no one else had thought to share the news with her. Like…Margaret, for instance. Even via text. Which she seemed to have no problem using when she wanted to mock Olivia for her smelly fish ordeal.

Margaret, who was apparently busy having a hot lunch date with a friend. What was the woman's name? @RealJMMorrison… *Janice.*

So, reclusive Margaret had no problem seeking out friendship—or more—with Janice.

On the one hand, Olivia was pleased Margaret was finally getting out socially. On the other hand, Olivia couldn't deny it stung.

Irked, Olivia snatched up her phone and googled the hell out of Janice M. Morrison. To her dismay, she found an attractive older woman with a cheeky lopsided smirk, flashing green eyes, cropped salt and pepper hair, and a leather jacket. She exuded a distinct lesbian player vibe that was hard to ignore.

Margaret was lunching with *her*? Jealousy slithered through her. Just wonderful.

Olivia waited for Margaret's return from lunch and vowed to show none of her inner turmoil. She reminded herself repeatedly that she was not her friend and didn't (officially) care what Margaret did on her lunch break. Or, more importantly, who.

Upon Margaret's arrival, Olivia allowed her a full two minutes to settle into her office before knocking.

"Who is it?" came the terse voice. It usually was when anyone dared bother her.

"Olivia." And then, because she couldn't help herself, she added: "Olivia Roberts. Your muffin supplier."

A small snort sounded and then: "Come in."

Olivia got straight to the point. She dropped a set of car keys on her desk. "Here. I heard you're employing Samantha Garrity as an assistant manager. I'm really glad. She's going to be great. I thought it might a good idea if you offered her a company car in the package. This way she won't feel guilty taking my Torana. Timothy patched up her station wagon temporarily but says it needs a new engine and is close to dying for good. Won't last long. So this way, she'll always have transport. And you'll get a reliable employee."

She stopped and wondered if this was a conversation a stranger might have, under the terms of their friendship separation. To cover all her bases, she added, "Dr Blackwood."

"Timothy fixed Ms Garrity's car?" Margaret prodded. "Timothy your ex, who you can't stand? *That* Timothy?" She was clearly nudging Olivia for information on revenge day.

"That's not a story I'd feel comfortable sharing with someone who isn't a friend. Sorry." Olivia pointed to the car keys. "So, about the Torana?"

"A generous offer, Ms Roberts," Margaret said. "Will you assume the costs of insurance and registration, or was that something you thought Mary Bugg's should take on board?"

Oh. She hadn't thought of that. Olivia bit her lip. "I'm not sure. Is it too much of a financial burden?"

"No, no. I was just seeking clarification. If I go ahead, I'll pay those costs. Thank you for this offer."

Olivia nodded and hesitated. *How was lunch,* she wanted to ask. *Are you and Janice friends again? Lunch buddies? You know, we could have been lunch buddies. If you wanted.*

"Was that all?" Margaret asked evenly.

"Uh, yeah. That's it. Unless…"

"Unless?" Margaret gave her an intense look now. "You have more left-over muffins to hand out to strangers?" Okay she sounded positively frosty now.

"What?" Olivia frowned. "Andy isn't a stranger. He's my best customer. He's definitely worthy of getting my last muffin." Was Margaret annoyed about that? That Andy had scored the muffin Margaret assumed she would receive?

"I thought Mary Bugg's was your best customer," Margaret shot back, her expression tight. She compressed her lips, looked down, and shuffled some papers.

This was about her store now? Who was she kidding? Olivia cleared her throat. "The Torana's out the back in your car park right now." Actually, it had been moved there the day Martin had dumped it outside Mary Bugg's, and they both knew it. Olivia hadn't decided what to do with it until now. She made a mental note to hire Timothy to give it the once-over before Margaret handed it over to Sam.

Margaret nodded. "Understood."

That sounded altogether too final, so Olivia backed out of the office. Well. That had gone as blandly as she'd feared.

God, she missed Margaret. The real one. Her friend.

Tuesday, April 21

Sunset: *5:44pm*

Temp: *8.5C-19.6C*

Rain: *0mm*

Drink: *Water. I had too much overpriced wine at lunch.*

Reading: *I missed book club and am unsure what their selection is. I'll make inquiries with Emma. That girl doesn't miss a trick.*

General Observations: *Janice thinks I'm being ridiculous. Janice usually thinks that, but this time she said it with her whole chest.*

I only asked her to lunch to seek clarification on a matter that's plaguing me. The Olivia Situation. Why it bothered me not to be offered a stale, leftover muffin. Why I wanted to pluck the eyes out of the concave-chested man-child who accepted it with the enthusiasm of a game show prize winner.

I brooded over this for far too long. Finally, I called Janice.

We enjoyed a perfectly adequate pasta and salad at Ricardo's Trattoria. I caught up on her diabolical dating exploits. Still can't keep a girlfriend to save her life. Well, too busy keeping many girlfriends to keep just one, it seems.

And then she wheedled until she found out why I'd called her. We both know I've turned down multiple lunch invitations with her over the past three years, and now, here I am, initiating one.

So, it all came out. The book club. My inability to not participate. The vengeance schemes. Janice laughed so loud about those, she reached for her asthma inhaler.

When I got to my clinging to the side of a building, she said: "But you're in terror of heights, woman! What would possess you?"

Good question. Olivia possessed me.

She didn't buy my "good henchperson fulfills her duties" line and peered at me with her green, searching eyes. "Are you kidding me?" she began. "You really don't know?" Then she came up with an absurd theory that doesn't bear repeating. And a long, irrelevant speech about how Helen would have wanted me to find love again. That I shouldn't feel guilty.

I pointed out I don't feel guilty. At least not about Olivia. One random, spur-of-the-moment kiss doth not a romance make. It's irrelevant! Attraction certainly does not equal love. In fact, I'm in a trial friendship separation with the very same woman Janice has decided I'm falling for.

I stared at her as if she were a slow infant and explained I simply want to murder the engineering student who was gifted my muffin.

Janice became rather circumspect after that. "Your muffin?" she murmured. "Yours?"

Yes, mine! I've always been territorial. I explained that to her too.

"Territorial," Janice had repeated. "Over...a muffin?"

Was she being deliberately obtuse?

Janice was absolutely no help. Also, she thinks being given a twenty-kilogram bag of cat food is a sign of lesbian devotion.

Delusional woman. I suggested she gift it to one of her paramours and see how that goes down. She vowed to do exactly that.

Did I mention delusional?

CHAPTER 26

I CHEWS YOU

IN THE END, IT TOOK exactly six weeks for Margaret to crack. Olivia had started to think she'd misread everything and that Margaret truly wasn't interested in her friendship. That it had been of no consequence losing it.

Until…

Until.

Olivia wrapped up another week's book club. This one had yet again suffered from the absence of Margaret, who Kelly had told her had gone out at lunchtime. Was Margaret off with Janice again? Olivia hated her petty curl of jealousy at the stray thought. It was beneath her. Margaret could lunch with whomever she liked.

This week's book club did have the addition of Sasha, who had taken to lounging artfully in one of the armchairs, clearly hoping to catch Kelly's attention, while offering a commentary on how Australia's "murder books" were positively cheerful compared to Russian ones.

By the end of book club, she'd concluded two things: she would never read any Sasha-recommended Russian mysteries. And Sasha had indeed caught Kelly's eye.

Her sister had come over no less than three times during book club for no good reason. That was interesting. The pair had planned a date for after Kelly's shift ended—officially fulfilling Olivia's request they give it one more try.

Unofficially, Kelly's gaze was not subtle. And Sasha's biceps were rippling magnificently under his muscle shirt—exactly as he'd planned, no doubt.

Well, then. Good for them.

And that was the moment Dr Blackwood arrived, striding through her bookstore like an arch villain, all black on black with calf-high ebony boots while clutching a peacock under one arm. Its long tail feathers trailed behind her like a bride's veil.

Oh. My. God. What a vision. Margaret and her glorious peacock. The dramatic image of the pair made Olivia forget to breathe.

"Quincy!" Olivia exclaimed, bolting to her feet. "You got him back!"

Dr Blackwood stopped dead, staring hard at Olivia, then at the rest of the curious eyes, then back at Olivia, who held her breath.

Finally, Dr Blackwood seemed to sort of sag. Or, well, capitulate. "Fine," she muttered as if the word physically pained her. "We can talk in my office."

Olivia blinked and didn't move.

"Some time before my peacock loses its lustre, hmm?"

Olivia snapped out of it and followed Margaret into her office. She closed the door behind her, and when she turned, Margaret was situating the peacock back in its old spot on a shelf.

"Well." Margaret exhaled with a rueful gust of air. "It seems you win," she said, sliding into her chair and eyeing Olivia with wariness. "Consider the white flag run up the pole."

"What did I win?" Olivia dropped into the visitor's chair.

"The trial separation is over."

How utterly Margaret to simply decide their friendship was restored and announce it as a done deal.

Olivia split into a grin. "It is?"

Margaret gave a weary sigh. "Yes. Previous parameters should be initiated. How did you know I'd choose this? Friendship with you once more?"

"I didn't. But I hoped."

"Mmm." Margaret looked dissatisfied.

"So what changed? Why now?"

"I found myself, the whole way back from the police station with my peacock, trying to tell myself it was *fine* I wouldn't be able to tell you all about it. And this I discovered to be greatly disagreeable. As disagreeable as you not informing me of what took place with that last ex of yours. And you giving away your last muffin to that pimply man-child when clearly you should have offered it to me."

Olivia burst out laughing. "Look at you having all that bottled up. Out it comes…"

"Well. Apparently, even I can't withstand the powers of Olivia Roberts forever. It seems I *chews* you," Margaret said, eyes rolling as she quoted Olivia's button pin.

"I'm so glad," Olivia said, and happiness radiated from every pore. "I think you've made an excellent choice, if I do say so myself."

Margaret cocked her head. "Modest in victory, I see."

Olivia laughed. "I've missed you. I hated book club without you."

"I was right there," Margaret pointed out. "You were the one who ceased to engage with me."

"Yes, and we both know why." Before Margaret could fire up into argument mode, Olivia changed subjects. "Okay, are you going to tell me how you got your peacock back?"

With a satisfied smile, Margaret filled Olivia in on the peacock's retrieval, which began weeks ago with showing the police photos of drugs being packed by Horrie's men. She'd told them she'd "innocently" gone to buy back Trip for a friend but that Horrie had in turn stolen the peacock that she'd only brought along to get her in the door.

Olivia laughed at the angelic way Margaret had said the word "innocently". "What happened next?"

"A drug squad raid occurred. Horrie is in custody awaiting a court hearing. Quincy was initially collected as evidence, but they've taken photos and released him back to me today." Margaret smiled. "Meanwhile, Horrie's lawyer was telling some incredible tale about how I *voluntarily* surrendered a historically valuable peacock in exchange for one unremarkable penguin, a story absolutely no one believes. And that's where we're at."

"Trip isn't unremarkable," Olivia said moodily.

"Oh, I know. Kelly filled me in last week."

Olivia asked. "What do you mean?"

"Trip's name? His origins?"

Olivia paused in confusion. "His name comes from his many trips with my nan. His origins are that she bequeathed him to me as a lucky charm."

Margaret stared at her. "You really don't know?"

"Know what?"

"Well, this is awkward." Margaret hissed in a breath. "Kelly informed me that the first time she packed up your grandmother's things to take over to her place, she had Trip in the front seat of her car. She went over a speed bump, and something fell out of him."

Olivia gaped. "What fell out?"

Hesitating, Margaret said, "A stash of marijuana. According to Kelly, the reason Trip was her lucky charm was because all the times your grandmother was stopped by police, they'd search her van looking for the weed they could smell. They never found it because it was in a little pouch sewn inside your penguin."

"Oh my God!" Olivia's eyes went wide. "No!"

"So Trip is called Trip because… well, your grandmother would have many a drug-induced trip thanks to him."

Olivia put her head in her hands. She couldn't believe it. Except that this was exactly something she could envision Nana Betty doing. Damn. "Why didn't Kelly ever tell me?"

"I'm guessing it's because she thought you had an idealised vision of your grandmother and didn't want to ruin it? Was I wrong to tell you? It only came up because we were discussing Horrie and his animal collection. It's not as though Kelly was informing all comers as to the truth about your penguin."

"That's… Oh, I'm going to kill her!"

"You are?" Margaret eyed her. "Why?"

"I should have been told! Years ago!"

"I agree. I'm sorry if you think less of Trip now, knowing he was a drug mule—er weed penguin—all this time." There was the faintest hint of amusement in her voice.

"Oh, you are loving this, aren't you!" Olivia sputtered, trying to maintain her indignation. It was a lot harder in the face of the normally aloof Margaret leaking her mirth.

"A little bit." Margaret smiled. "Your family is rather delightful. It makes mine look even more boring than they already are. Take my mother, for example."

"Yes?"

"No, I mean it. Take her. Please."

Olivia laughed. "Is she really that bad?"

"No, she's worse. She invited me to some big Monash Uni fundraising event on Saturday and told me I was required to attend. Not 'please come'. Or 'it'd be great if…'. No. *You will be there.* She knows I hate those things. She's trying to reignite my interest in returning to academia, the only pursuit in life she thinks is noble."

"What a narrow view," Olivia said, appalled.

"As if that's not bad enough, she always tries to pair me off with some dull academic she's hand-picked. She thinks she's being subtle, but it only takes until I'm at the bar for my first drink before someone is suddenly chatting me up. And I'm sure half of the women she chooses for me aren't even into women, just trying to get into her good graces by doing as instructed and making small talk with me."

"Whoa." Olivia couldn't even imagine her own mother taking half as much interest in her life, let alone this much overkill. "That's out there."

"Yes." Margaret sighed. "My mother is going to be even more impossible than usual because she's just found out about my new project. She does not approve in the least. She's declared I'm shaming her if I proceed."

"What project?"

"Remember when you dared me to write a certain book? You even pointed out I had all the right credentials." Her eyes were sparkling now.

Olivia was entranced. "Book?"

"Yes. *Why Bushranger Mary Ann Bugg Is Better Than Buckethead.* Subtitle: *Ned Kelly's An Overrated Son of A Bitch.*"

"Oh my God!" Olivia's eyes widened. "You're actually doing it?"

"I am." Margaret actually grinned. "My mother is so appalled by the lowbrow title, I think she might disown me. That doesn't exactly dissuade me. But even if I'd had a mind to write my book before, I had no one who could take over Mary Bugg's. But then I discovered Ms Garrity's former career and realised she would make an ideal assistant manager. And that leaves me free to…" She waved airily.

"Besmirch a national icon!" Olivia laughed.

"Exactly. I told Janice about my book idea, and she laughed hard at my title before telling me she'd make sure it was a bestseller. I believe her." An amused expression spread over her face. "This is going to put the cat among the pigeons. Thanks go to you for putting the thought in my head to write it."

"Yeah, please don't thank me in your author interviews," Olivia said hastily. "I don't need obsessed Ned Kelly tragics gunning for me and one-starring Love Muffins for being unpatriotic or something."

"Noted. Well, enough about me. What's going on with you? What happened with Timothy?"

"Oh, I think you caught most of it on your stake-out, if your mocking texts were anything to go by." Olivia snorted.

"Mocking texts?" Margaret froze and looked at her in astonishment. "Don't you mean my sublimely helpful texts? I spent some time ensuring you had the best information to remove those fish smells from your person."

"I thought you were taking the piss."

"I was doing no such thing!" Margaret protested. "I was trying to assist. Why do you think I was there in the first place?"

"To snoop?" Olivia shrugged.

Margaret glared, but there was no fire behind it. "No, I was making sure you were safe. Which I couldn't do officially since you terminated my services."

"Well, it's done now. I'm fish-free, and things are settled with Timothy." She quickly ran through the whole story.

"Rodney is in prison?" Margaret regarded her in surprise. "Good place for him. And what idiot threatens a judge?"

"Rodney?"

"True. What else is afoot?"

Olivia rehashed the gossip on Tina's eviction, which Margaret had overheard but they'd never discussed given their friendship separation.

The delight in Margaret's eye was something she'd never seen before. Olivia decided she'd do rather a lot to keep that look there as long as she could. "Hey, Margaret?"

"Olivia?" One teasing eyebrow quirked up.

"Any chance you have a spare ticket to that fancy uni thing you have to go to on Saturday?"

Margaret blinked. "I get a plus one. Why?"

"I'm thinking it's time I met your mother." Olivia smiled her most mischievous smile.

"Oh?" Margaret peered at her. "Are you insane? Why would anyone voluntarily enter my mother's lair?"

"I think you should have some backup," Olivia said. "An ally in your corner. In case she gets on your case. Or worse, some woman she's picked out for you decides to get handsy."

"Ah. My hero," Margaret drawled. "Flinging yourself at ambitious lackeys to save my honour? And stepping into the dragon's maw, no less!"

"That's me. A regular Saint George." Olivia grinned. "What are friends for, anyway? See, I told you having me as your friend would come in handy."

"So you did." Margaret chuckled. "Well, this should be something to see."

CHAPTER 27

FINAL BOSS FIGHT

Olivia dressed with care for her meet-the-parent extravaganza that Saturday. She'd consulted Kelly, who could be counted on to tuck in her collar's label and look scandalised when she explained she wasn't wearing a bra.

The most eye-catching component of Olivia's look was the daringly open white blouse that showed off a lot of cleavage.

She'd paired that blouse with a beautifully cut-in black jacket that cinched at her waist. It was Kelly's *get-laid, never fail* jacket. So: *eww*, but also, hot. Black skinny-leg pants met stark white Converse sneakers that matched the snow-blinding brilliance of the blouse and—according to Kelly—"screamed so effing gay".

Olivia contemplated wearing her final boss fight button pin—*Go Ahead, Bake My Day*.

"Nope," Kelly said, snatching it out of her hand. "Not tonight. Not cool."

Which was a pity because that button was totally *on message* if you were planning on scoping out and possibly metaphorically kicking a certain ass-hole vice chancellor in the ankles in support of her daughter.

Kelly then teased Olivia's chestnut hair up with all manner of gel and spray until it had a "careless, just fallen out of bed, don't-give-a-shit pixie look". Olivia decided Kelly should never work as an ad writer.

From behind, Olivia thought she could pass as stylish, like a high-class-restaurant maître d'—until you spotted those ironic sneakers.

From the front, she projected, according to Kelly, "cute lesbian rocker looking to start a fight she can't possibly win." Olivia wasn't sure if that was a compliment or not.

Right, then. Dressed for success? Check. Time to hit the road.

Olivia had never been to Clayton campus when she'd studied at Monash Uni; all her literary studies classes had been at Caulfield campus. She'd been doing a neck swivel, taking in all the new locations, from the moment she'd parked her Love Muffins van out front of The Chancellery.

The building face looked as if a wall of metal origami had been welded to it—curving, folded triangles and diamonds made up a geometric pattern. Behind the façade sat darkly tinted glass. Architect porn, for sure.

"Hello?" came an officious woman's voice the moment she stepped out of her van. "Yes, you there. You're late! And you should be around the back with the rest of catering."

Olivia turned and inhaled sharply, recognising her challenger. She'd not expected to meet Margaret's mother quite so soon.

Imposing was the word for Professor Neubold. Not to mention intimidating. Olivia had seen her photo in the university's promotional literature and occasionally in newspaper interviews back when Olivia had been a student. But meeting her was a whole other experience.

For one, she wasn't tall like her daughter at all. She was about Olivia's height—five-foot six. But she made up for it with an imperious attitude. She wore tortoiseshell glasses that framed her pale, oval face while her pencil-straight, shoulder-length light-brown hair was streaked with grey. Professor Neubold wore a sleek midi dress with a cowl neckline that was sleeveless—showing off gym-toned arms—and swept down to her slender ankles. The garment's steel-blue shade matched the colour of those dissecting eyes now pinning Olivia.

"Excuse me?" Olivia asked politely.

"You are not where you should be," Professor Neubold barked, pointing off to the side. "Around the back. Go! If you park here, our guests will assume we're offering catering tonight by way of *food truck*. Move that…

vehicle…" she said, tone laden with distaste, "to where the rest of the cater-ing team is at once!" She then snapped her fingers as if addressing a dog.

"Um, no," Olivia said firmly. As she straightened, the deep vee in her four-buttons-undone blouse drew the vice chancellor's narrowing eyes. "I'm not with catering. I'm a guest."

Professor Neubold's sharp gaze slid to the van, paused on its name, and then slithered back to Olivia's face. "*You* are a guest? I dread to think who added a muffin purveyor as their plus-one."

Olivia took that to mean "I'm embarrassed I screwed up so will now insult you to hide it".

"Perhaps the History Department?" Professor Neubold suggested sweet-ly. "They do have some…colourful characters there."

"Not History, no. And there's nothing wrong with making muffins for a living," Olivia said evenly. "Are you in charge of the catering staff, then?" She couldn't resist. "Since you have firm opinions on where they should be?"

Professor Neubold's expression flashed with irritation. "Insolent," she muttered under her breath. Then, louder and crisply she added: "I'm Monash University's vice chancellor!"

Olivia shrugged and didn't answer, which seemed to irritate the other woman to no end. Well, she wasn't going to hang around and be insulted further, so Olivia headed toward the Chancellery. She opened the door only to have Margaret's mother push past her indignantly.

Chuckling softly to herself, Olivia followed her inside and immediately stopped. She looked up. *Oh. Wow.*

How beautiful The Atrium was. The timber floors were a pale, polished honey colour. In the middle lay a giant puddle of dusty pink and white sandstone pavers. Directly above those, matching the puddle shape exactly, was an enormous hole cut out of the ceiling. Looking up through this void, you could see the railings to the next half a dozen floors, all the way up to the ceiling, upon which was printed a beautiful native hakea tree's leaves and flowers.

All around this room was glass, giving views to the outside of funky moulded pillars seemingly shaped by an eccentric collector of antique chair legs.

A makeshift open bar was on one side of the room near a slick string quartet playing in the corner. On violin was a pretty blonde woman attracting much attention from the assembled suited men—academics most likely. But Olivia's eye was drawn to a dark-haired cellist who seemed as much skilled in the art of cello-ing as she was at exuding disdain. She was like a broodier, more intense version of Margaret, which was probably why Olivia appreciated her.

And…speak of the devil. Margaret was gliding towards her in a stunning, chic black suit. Of course it was black.

"You made it," Margaret said softly. "Thank you for coming." Then she startled Olivia completely by kissing her cheek.

Oh! Whoa. Okay, social protocol. Nothing to see here. She forced herself not to rub the still-tingling spot where those lips had pressed to Olivia's skin.

Stupid body with its stupid out-of-control hormones.

"You look dapper," Olivia said lightly, as though her heart wasn't galloping. She patted Margaret's black lapel. "Are you the Model T of fashion?"

"Black *is* timeless," Margaret said, but she seemed pleased with the compliment. "By the way, be warned: I think I saw my mother lurking around here somewhere." Margaret scanned the room.

"About that? We've already met." Olivia gave her a sheepish look.

"Oh?" Margaret's eyebrows shot up. "Do tell."

"Okay, so first she confused me with the catering staff."

Margaret's eyes did a slow wander down Olivia's cleavage. Her nostrils flared. "How on earth could she make that mistake given…" she waved at Olivia's chest.

"Well, she did."

"You look beautiful," Margaret added as if suddenly worried Olivia would think she was being judged. "I probably should have led with that. I'm a woeful date!" she teased.

"The worst," Olivia agreed, smiling back, trying not to let the unexpected compliment go to her head. "So when I set her straight that I was a guest, she tried to work out who'd made me their plus one before deciding it had to be the History Department because they have so many *colourful characters.*"

Margaret tittered. "She never did forgive Helen for flipping her the bird on their first meeting."

"I'll bet. You know, your mother's got quite an 'I run the universe' aura. She's very intimidating." Olivia eyed her. "I mean *very.*"

"Yes." Margaret sighed. "I know. So was that the extent of your interaction?"

"I did ask if she was in charge of catering since she had so many opinions on where I should be. I know it was evil of me, but I couldn't help it."

Margaret's eyes lit up. "You didn't!"

"I definitely did. I got called insolent for that one." Olivia laughed. "Your mother's absolutely adding me to her blacklist as we speak. I'm toast before we've even formally met."

"Well, that's impressively fast. Now then, speaking of the History Department, I should do a quick catch-up with the professors. They were Helen's closest friends, and I've been a bit recalcitrant in staying in contact."

"That's fine. I can dance to the string quartet with a beer in each hand and really set your mum's teeth on edge."

"Try not to get thrown out before I get back, hmm? I'm looking forward to introducing you properly."

"I'll do my best." She grinned.

Before Margaret could leave, though, she glanced up and murmured: "Oh dear. No time like the present. Showtime."

"I'm sorry," came a cool voice that did not sound sorry at all, "could you remind me of who you are?"

Ah yes. The vice chancellor was back.

Professor Neubold flicked a dismissive glance at her daughter. "Margaret," she said as an afterthought. "One moment. I have this…situation…to attend to."

Margaret opened her mouth, but her mother immediately put up a finger to silence her.

"Your name," Professor Neubold said curtly, cold eyes fixed on Olivia. "Please."

"Olivia Roberts."

"Olivia…Roberts," Professor Neubold repeated slowly. "How do I know that name?" She frowned and peered thoughtfully up into the void—an actual void, as it happened.

Olivia had no clue how she could possibly know her, so she said, "My muffins are popular around Prahran's cafes."

Professor Neubold scoffed. "No. I don't think it's because of your *muffins*. Who are you with? On whose invitation are you claiming to be here?"

Olivia smiled then and looped an arm around Margaret's waist. "I believe you already know my date rather well."

Margaret smirked. Quite possibly the smirkiest smirk of all time.

"You are Margaret's *girlfriend*?" A frankly sceptical look raked Olivia's body.

Girlfriend? That was quite a leap. Maybe not, though, as Margaret almost certainly wouldn't bring anyone along to these events normally. Olivia waited for Margaret to object to the term, but instead she simply froze as if out of her depth.

"That's…unexpected." Professor Neubold's lips pursed. The condescension oozed off her like sludge. Her eyes sharpened.

Margaret stiffened under her assessing gaze.

Olivia squeezed her waist reassuringly, trying to tell her, *Relax, I've got this.*

"I don't know why that's unexpected," Olivia said casually, deciding she didn't like how ludicrous the vice chancellor seemed to find the thought of Olivia dating her daughter. Needling her over the wrong assumption suddenly seemed like a powerful life goal. "Margaret seems to like me a whole lot. Well, me and my cooking."

"Ah yes, the *cooking*." Professor Neubold gave a small, tight smile. "That reminds me of when she was a girl. She was *obsessed*. Wanted to be a chef so desperately. Until I pointed out the obvious: unspecial people cook. After all, if you can read, you can cook. Anyone can follow a recipe. It's hardly that taxing to do some community TAFE course and wind up utilising basic kitchen skills for the rest of your life. I didn't want my daughter to lack ambition. I told her anyone can play with their food. People like us choose academia."

And that explained both Margaret's love of cooking and her dismissal of her own skills at it.

Olivia felt terrible for that little girl with dreams of creating wonderful dishes, only to have them belittled as nothing. She sneaked a glimpse of Margaret. She was now rigid, face blank, as if walling herself off from an impending wave of vitriol. Olivia squeezed her waist again. *It's okay*, she tried to convey to her. *They're just empty words.*

She didn't care that Professor Neubold had just blatantly insulted her too. The woman was just a garden variety snobby bully who happened to share bloodlines with someone Olivia cared about. It was also disturbing that she was completely indifferent to how much she'd hurt her daughter just so she could taunt Olivia.

Well, Olivia wasn't putting up with that. She met Professor Neubold's eye and said casually: "I know, to an amateur, food preparation can seem simple and be dismissed as nothing special. That's because they don't know what they're talking about. It's a common error, though."

"Don't you just bake muffins?" Professor Neubold asked sweetly. "It's not exactly high art. Hardly science or literature."

"Having studied both cooking and literature, I can assure you only one requires me to be on top of my game at all times: practically and creatively."

"Having studied both…" Professor Neubold regarded her for a long, long beat. And then an unsettling dawning recognition crossed her face. Her expression twisted into mockery. "I know who you are."

What?

"Some years ago, my then department head for Literary Studies came to see me about a student. Someone called *Olivia Roberts*. I remember the story because it was so absurd. The head told me this sorry tale of a remarkable second-year student who was such an asset to the university but might have to drop out because she'd just been conned out of all her money. The head asked if there was some way, some scholarship we could put her on, to help her stay in college."

Olivia's jaw tensed. *No! Of all the times for someone to remember her!*

"I asked the department head how this alleged literary wunderkind had lost all her money. And do you know what she said?"

Margaret tensed beside Olivia, and her head had dropped as if she were ashamed. But it was hardly her fault her mother was an asshole.

Olivia stared straight back at the vice chancellor and braced herself.

"She said," Professor Neubold continued with relish, "that the student gave it all away to her scheming girlfriend who'd conned her out of it on a host of broken promises." She snorted. "Gave it all away? To a romantic interest? I told her that I hoped this Olivia Roberts got what she deserved for her stupidity." She leaned in a little. "Given your current career's in *muffins*, I'd say you did."

Margaret's tension tightened to that of an ironing board.

"You know, I don't have to explain my choices to you," Olivia said crossly. "But I don't see how mocking me for something I did when I was young—trusting someone I loved—is helping you in any way now. What do you hope to achieve by rehashing my old mistakes?"

"I'm simply pointing out the failings of my daughter's latest paramour in case she is blind to them...for whatever reason." She glanced at Olivia's cleavage, to unsubtly point out exactly what might be blinding Margaret. "I'd hate for her to choose the wrong partner..."

The *again* was unspoken but clear.

Margaret was now trembling faintly beneath Olivia's fingers. She soothingly stroked her waist, wishing she could tell her it was fine. Because it would be fine. This annoying woman might have power over Margaret, but Olivia was bulletproof.

"Although..." Professor Neubold ran her eyes up and down Olivia derisively. "Are you two even really dating? Or is this falling for the working-class fluff"—she waved at Olivia's cleavage and glanced at Margaret—"just a ruse to make me pull my hair out? I know you'd love to manage that one day."

Olivia was kind of impressed she'd sussed out they weren't dating. But *working-class fluff?* Elitist much?

Margaret sighed softly, but it was just loud enough that her mother caught it.

"Oh dear. Did I guess correctly?" Her eyes were sharp. "Well, my ineffective daughter, what's another failure in a long line of them? From throwing away a fairly decent career in academia to selling potboilers, tawdry thrillers, and tales of illiterate bushrangers."

Olivia had a burning urge to point out Mary Ann Bugg wasn't illiterate. But then she caught a glimpse of Margaret's face. While still an aloof mask, she betrayed small clues if you knew her well enough. The tightening around her eyes revealed that barb hurt. The slightest pull of her lips showed she wished she had a comeback and didn't. Or had one but felt too beaten down to say it. She seemed exhausted, as all the fight had drained out of her.

Powerful beautiful, magnificent Margaret brought to heel. It was an outrage!

Olivia snapped straight. "How many people are there in this world, Vice Chancellor?" Olivia said suddenly. "Roughly?"

The other woman blinked in surprise. "Eight billion or so."

"Eight billion," Olivia repeated. "Imagine being the best in the world at something, better than eight BILLION other people. That'd be amazing, wouldn't it?"

"Is this where you tell me you're the world's best muffin maker?" the other woman said snidely.

"Nah. Only best in Melbourne, according to the *Good Food Guide*." She smiled. "But your daughter, who you just belittled as a failure, is the world-leading expert on Australian bushrangers. She knows more on the subject, has published more papers, received more accolades than any other person on earth. Margaret Blackwood is a name that scholars *worldwide* turn to when they need a reputable source on this topic. No one is better. *Not one single academic anywhere.* And you act as though she's just slithered out of jail on parole. She's not a failure or a disappointment. She's *remarkable*. She's also one of the most interesting, intelligent, and bravest people I know."

"Brave!" Professor Neubold sputtered. "She's been a hermit inside her little bookshop for three years!"

Olivia didn't dare look at Margaret. It occurred to her suddenly that Margaret hadn't said a single word since her mother had turned up. Not one word. What must it be like being raised by such a woman as to learn silence was the only way to win? Or at least to avoid more abuse?

"I'm sorry—does *this* look like her bookshop to you?" Olivia waved at the room. "Margaret's right here. Outside her store. Enduring your insults. Because, for some reason, she wishes to have your respect. And she *is* brave. That's why I hired her to be my henchperson."

Professor Neubold's mouth seemed to unhinge like a snake about to swallow a buffalo. "Excuse me? You...what?"

"I needed some matters of vengeance taken care of. I do that when people really piss me off." She glared at the woman in warning. "Your daughter was a brilliant choice. Do you know only two months ago she was clinging to the side of a six-storey building in the course of her duties. It was magnificent. And brave as hell."

For the first time, Professor Neubold seemed robbed of speech. "But... she's terrified of heights," she whispered.

"Yes. She did it anyway. It seems you don't know your daughter at all. So, let's review," Olivia said, tone brisk: "Your so-called failure of a daughter is the best in the world at something. Your coward of a daughter is brave.

And your hermit of a daughter has driven all the way out here to socialise, because you asked, even knowing you'd try to humiliate her." Olivia cocked her head. "It's hard to know what's more dubious at this point: your maternal skills or the way you think your opinion on her matters at all. Spoiler alert? Too close to call."

"Do you have *any* idea whom you are addressing?" Professor Neubold said, arching one incensed eyebrow. Her voice was irritated. "The amount of power I hold?"

"Being vice chancellor, I guess you'd be used to that. Having all that power." She glanced around. "But it's an illusion, isn't it? In fact, I'd argue my job is more valuable than yours. It's certainly more noticeable."

Professor Neubold scowled. "What? How could you possibly come to that conclusion? I have sixteen thousand staff. Eighty-six thousand students. A budget in the hundreds of millions. An endowment in the billions. International-leading research. But do tell me how a little muffin maker is more worthy!"

Olivia cocked her head. "Look at Foucault's argument on Bentham's panopticon. He points out that a prison needs only the central watch tower. It doesn't even need the guards. So just the awareness that people might be under surveillance is enough to make them obey the rules. Why do we stop at stop signs in the middle of the night on empty roads? We are self-governing. The knowledge of the power is making us act a certain way, not some nebulous person in charge with a fancy title."

Yep, so sue her: Olivia had paid attention to Margaret's gleeful recounting at dinner of the one philosopher who gave her mother heartburn. And Olivia was bound and determined to give the vice chancellor cause to reach for the antacid tonight.

"If you were hit by a bus tomorrow, nothing much would change at Monash," Olivia pressed on. "Your multi-million-dollar institution would work just as seamlessly whether you were there or not. But if I were hit by a bus tomorrow, there'd be dozens of coffee shops and cafes across Melbourne without my muffins, a tonne of people would go to work hungry and grumpy, and my absence would be felt a hell of a lot faster than yours. I'm not saying I'm more important than anyone else. I'm just saying you're less important than you think you are."

Margaret gave the softest snort of laughter beside her.

And there it was, in the clench of Professor Neubold's jaw, that anxious little tic Margaret had told her about. Just by reminding the vice chancellor how the worth of her lofty career was just an illusion.

Professor Neubold finally let her mask drop. Her expression was pure loathing. Instantly, Margaret placed her glass of wine, still half full, on a nearby table. Then she grasped Olivia's wrist to pull her back and stepped in front as if to protect her from whatever was about to happen.

She was protecting Olivia from her own bully? Margaret might not be saying anything at all, but her bravery was clear. Her back was rigid, and the fingers clenched around Olivia's wrist were slick with perspiration.

However, with a cluck of dismissal, as if both women were too beneath her to bother with further, the vice chancellor spun on her heel and stalked off.

Olivia immediately turned to face Margaret. "Are you okay?" she asked, searching those brown eyes that seemed unnaturally lit up.

"I am now," Margaret said, her voice barely a croak. "She's gone to fetch Security, you know. She'll kick you out in a minute."

"Ah." Olivia swallowed. "She did seem to leave too easily."

"Come with me," Margaret said urgently.

"I…okay."

She was being pulled towards the back of The Atrium, and then into a small room. Inside were cables, light bulbs, plastic cups, and tissue boxes.

"Okay, what…?" Olivia began as Margaret closed the door and spun around to face her.

"What were you *thinking*!" she said with an incredulous look. "That was idiotic! Taking on my mother directly like that? With witnesses? People were listening to us, you know. Her employees and lackeys were all getting an earful. It was insanity! Now she'll do everything in her power to ruin you."

"She can try, but I'm not in academia. What can she do?" Olivia shrugged, but she was fascinated by how bright Margaret's eyes were. "Anyway, I don't care. It was worth it."

"You beautiful, brave, insane idiot," Margaret murmured. "You were magnificent." And then her lips landed on Olivia's.

Desire flooded her. Olivia pushed back against her with abandon, kissing her thoroughly and revelling in the sensations. Finally, she pulled away and said, voice rough: "This doesn't feel like a friendship kiss. Not that I'm complaining."

"Oh?" Margaret murmured teasingly against her mouth. "I thought kissing was something we *did* do under our previous parameters."

"Ah, I misunderstood." Olivia grinned as elation filled her. "So, just to be clear, uh, what did I do to earn this, exactly?"

"You stood up to my mother. Usually, she never faces off with anyone directly. Any adversary she's ever had backs down. Not you, though. You just...went for it." Margaret kissed her again, slipping her tongue in Olivia's mouth, exploring her.

As if that wasn't arousing enough, Margaret's hand was suddenly between her breasts. Olivia broke away to look down. Her nipples knotted tightly in appreciation, and the skin beneath Margaret's roaming fingers tingled with awareness.

"Is this all right?" Margaret asked, her voice low and deep.

"Y-yes." Olivia swallowed. "Very."

Margaret's fingers slid across the bare skin of Olivia's cleavage, disappearing under her shirt, and then...God, she was cupping her naked breast. Seeking out her nipple. Rubbing it. Pinching it.

A delicious shiver ran through Olivia. "Oh, *fuck*." She briefly closed her eyes at the erotic sensation.

"I've wanted to do that from the moment I saw you tonight." The material moved as Margaret's fingers worked beneath it. "You've been driving me crazy. I was almost able to put your tempting wiles out of my mind, but then you had to go and ruin my resolve by defending me to my mother and, well. Here we are." She leaned in for another kiss, this one luscious and languorous.

Olivia twitched between her legs. She whimpered. "You're going to have to stop doing that really soon or I'm going to have an embarrassing situation." She bit her lip regretfully. "Besides, I don't want our first time to be in a supply room."

Margaret's laugh against her mouth was throaty. "How about this: once you're thrown out, which should be pretty soon, given the look on my mother's face, come back to my place. I'll leave too. I just have to catch up with Helen's History Department friends first, but after that, will you join me?"

"I'd love to."

"All right, then." Margaret pulled away. She sighed at herself. "No. I need one more for the road." She leaned in and kissed Olivia once more, softly and wistfully. Margaret found Olivia's breast again, this time massaging it over the top of her blouse. "That outfit really is sinful."

Olivia sat outside the Chancellery on a long wooden bench and contemplated her next move. Should she just…go? Straight to Margaret's apartment? Or wait here for Margaret, and they'd each leave in their respective vehicles at the same time? Was that too…eager?

The door opened behind her, and Olivia turned hopefully. Only it wasn't Margaret.

"I just thought I'd see you off," Professor Neubold said briskly.

Wanted to have the last word, more likely.

Olivia made to rise.

"Oh, no, don't get up on my account. You just stay down there. Now then, I've been ruminating about your pulling up Foucault out of nowhere." Her lips thinned. "Somewhat of a shock, I admit." She folded her arms. "But now I also recall Margaret's lack of surprise. That tells me she was well aware you might do that. She coached you."

Damn. She was good. *Coached* wasn't exactly right, but the woman was in the ballpark. "What, a common baker can't have read Foucault?"

"Even a graduated literary student wouldn't have read him, my dear," Professor Neubold said. "No one's *that* curious about sadomasochistic French philosophers, even if academia's old guard worships him. And speaking of *common*—yes, you are. Finally, something we agree on." Her smile was full-bodied this time.

Olivia's heart sank. They couldn't even have their one win against this woman. She was far too shrewd.

"My goodness, I've rendered you speechless," Professor Neubold mocked. "Although I'm starting to wonder if it's because you've run out of speech *literally*? Have you used up all the talking points you've been fed?"

Olivia said nothing. What could she say? That Margaret *hadn't* fed her all the Foucault arguments that annoyed her mother? She absolutely had.

"Well, I only have one thing left to say to you. A single sentence to change everything." Professor Neubold looked positively gleeful now as she finished: "You'll *never* be able to replace Helen in her heart."

Olivia gulped back a gasp. That burned.

"How interesting. I was actually betting you were just some strumpet my daughter had found to play the role of girlfriend. But it seems you really do care for her. Well, well. I suppose that just makes it all the more sad, doesn't it?" And with that, Professor Neubold offered a smile that was pure crocodile.

She pivoted on her heel and headed back inside.

Two minutes later, Margaret exited and strode over to Olivia. "Sorry to be delayed," she said quickly. "I couldn't get away faster. I kept being stopped by people who wanted to tell me how missed I was, which is absurd because I don't ever think of *them*." Her eyes twinkled.

Ah, joking. Probably.

"And all I wanted was to get to you," Margaret finished.

"And here I am. You'll be happy to know Security didn't rough me up, although I'm sure your mother suggested they try."

Margaret laughed. "I did cross paths with her again before I found the history professors."

"Was she civil, at least?" The woman's cruel parting words still stung.

"Oh, she's always civil. She can reduce those she disdains to a bloodied smear all while adopting the veneer of politeness. On that note, she demanded to know what I see in you." Margaret snorted. "I told her the list was too long to name, but that your loyalty was impressive. Then I added, 'And that's why we're eloping to Perth'." She snorted.

"Wait, we're fake fiancées now?" Olivia couldn't help but laugh. "Dare I ask why? And why Perth? Isn't Bali the go-to spot for elopers?"

"My mother knows I'd never hit some massive tourist hotspot. It lacked credibility. And, on the former, I guess the devil in me came out. Perhaps you've inspired me? So she thinks we're going to Perth so that we can hit Rottnest Island and you can take silly selfies with the world's cutest marsupial, the quokka. It sounded like the sort of excruciating, inane detail newlyweds-to-be would have planned."

"You've thought it all through." Olivia chuckled. "Did you succeed in melting her brain?"

"I really think I did." She looked so satisfied. "I finally got a win on the board against that impossible woman."

"Yeah, about that," Olivia said regretfully. "She's worked out you told me about her sore points on Foucault. She actually ran outside to taunt me for it and said there's no way I could have known about him otherwise. And she got in one last spectacular dig about…other stuff." Her shoulders slumped.

"Damn." Margaret murmured. "What did you say back?"

"Nothing. I was out of smart-arse replies."

"I'm so sorry. She's a heat-seeking missile when it comes to finding people's tender spots. Whatever she said, can you remember that? She uses partial truths to get under people's skin. Maybe I should have warned you better."

"I don't think there's any amount of warning you could have given. She is a force of nature. I don't know how bad it must have been growing up with her, but I'm sorry you did. I'm an idiot not to have realised she must have been brutal to make someone as strong as you so tightly wound." Olivia huffed. "But that's me. Idiot."

"Yes, you are an idiot." Margaret said the word so affectionately. "I keep saying that, don't I?" She stroked Olivia's cheek with her thumb. "But don't you understand by now? You're *my* idiot."

Olivia swooned.

CHAPTER 28

WANTING

THE MOMENT OLIVIA REACHED MARGARET'S apartment, its owner flung open the door and dragged her inside. Okay, not exactly like that, but the fire in her eyes told a whole-ass movie about what she wanted to do.

They kissed briefly against the door. And then Margaret cocked her head and murmured, "This way."

It dawned belatedly on Olivia that this was *actually* happening. Should they slow down? Talk about it? Discuss what they wanted out of a relationship? Whether this was just a one-night deal or much more?

But it seemed absurd to Olivia, after all their dancing around each other, after getting to know Margaret on a fundamental level, that it was anything but exactly what it felt like: real and whole, a relationship of two people who connected so well it felt wrong not seeking more from it.

She followed Margaret down a short hall and stepped inside the room at the end. Margaret closed the door firmly behind them, explaining, "Wednesday's asleep on the couch right now, but I don't wish any interruptions later."

Olivia leaned back against the door and beheld Margaret's bedroom. It was a spacious room painted in off-white with a queen-sized bed that had a chaotic collection of pillows. In one corner sat an armchair with an assortment of black clothes draped over it, along with a discarded bra.

Margaret followed her gaze and then hastily scooched the clothes together neater, hiding the bra. "I hadn't anticipated a visitor," she admitted, looking sheepish. "I'm not normally so…" She sighed. "Actually, I am. Sometimes. When I get distracted."

"It's fine." Olivia slid her arms around her from behind, resting her chin on Margaret's shoulder. "I actually might have freaked out if your bedroom was straight out of a magazine spread. Imperfection is surprisingly reassuring."

"That's a relief."

Olivia enjoyed the warmth of Margaret's body leaning back against her. She slid her hands up Margaret's waist to her breasts and rubbed them over her black shirt. "Fair's fair," she said softly. "You had your way with my boobs earlier."

"Just the one," Margaret observed. The breath caught in her throat. "But I cannot argue with your logic." She turned to face her. "I know you've had a lot of people in your life who didn't want you enough or didn't care about you the way you deserved, and I need you to know that stops with me."

"It does?" Olivia whispered.

Slowly, Margaret stroked her cheek with the back of her knuckles. "It does. Anything you want, ask me. If I can give it, I will try. And to be very clear," she said intently, her gaze locked on Olivia's, "I *do* want you." Then she kissed her.

This kiss was different than the others. It was fierce and excited, probing and delicious. Olivia felt as though she had to hang on for dear life as she clutched Margaret's shirt. Then she wondered why she was clutching it when she could be ripping it from her body.

Olivia's fingers scrambled across the buttons, nimbly sliding them out of their little holes until she reached the bottom. She flattened her hand onto the soft, naked skin she found beneath and sighed into Margaret's mouth.

She pushed Margaret away for a moment so she could slide the shirt off her shoulders. *Beautiful.*

Margaret was so pale—evidence of a life spent indoors—and so exquisite. Her bra was black—of course it was—and her body soft and long and lean.

Olivia reached behind Margaret, unhooking her bra, then removed that too, feeling her lover's smouldering gaze on her the whole time. Small, soft breasts came into view topped with dark-pink nipples, erect and tempting.

She lowered her lips to the closest nipple, sliding her tongue across it, as her fingers gently kneaded the other breast. A soft exhalation issued from Margaret, a sort of strangled sound of half-arousal, half-frustration, and Olivia's stomach clenched at the knowledge she'd affected her.

After long, delicious moments of worshipping Margaret's tight nipples, Olivia stepped back to admire them again. Gorgeous.

Margaret's nostrils flared, her eyes darkened with arousal. She removed her black glasses and tossed them onto the nearby chair. "Undress, Olivia," she said with a hint of imperiousness. "I need to see you."

"I will if you will," Olivia croaked out. "Take off your pants. Please?" She had to admit, she was dying to see what type of underwear Margaret wore. Olivia had spent a little too much time in bed lately wondering about it.

Margaret's lips curled into a knowing smile. Slowly, teasingly she obliged, undoing her top pant button, then her zip. She pulled the black material easily to the floor and stepped out of her pants.

Margaret Blackwood wore *boy shorts.*

Olivia's whole body melted down. *Fuck. Just holy fuck.* So the austere, cool, elegant Margaret wore lesbian catnip panties?

"I take it you approve?" Margaret drawled.

Olivia's face warmed. "So much," she said in awe.

"Mmm." Margaret put her fingers on the waistband of the black boy shorts to draw them down her long legs.

"Wait!" Olivia swallowed. "Let me?"

"If you undress first, I'll allow it."

Okay, Imperious Margaret was Olivia's favourite thing right now.

Nodding, Olivia quickly shucked her Converse sneakers, then shed every last stitch of clothing with Margaret's gaze burning her skin the entire time. When she was stark naked, Olivia looked up.

Margaret's eyes swept her body, and a blush began working its way up Margaret's chest, neck, and to her cheeks. "You do not disappoint," she said approvingly. "I'll be devouring every inch of you shortly."

Oh God. Olivia had never expected Margaret would be so forthcoming during intimacy. So direct about what she wanted. It was such a turn-on.

Olivia took a step closer until she was right inside Margaret's space and slid her fingertips under the waistband of those boy shorts. "My turn." And then she tugged.

Margaret was *so* wet. Her arousal was blatant on her slick curls.

"Oh, Margaret," Olivia whispered reverently, removing the garment entirely.

Glancing down at herself, Margaret sighed, and her cheeks burned. "Well, what did you expect, what with you wearing that scandalous outfit tonight? I had to tell myself, no, we were just friends. But all I wanted"—she swallowed—"was my mouth on you."

"Where?" Olivia whispered. "Where did you want your mouth?"

"On your breasts. Your lips… And lower. I wanted to taste all of you." She inhaled and offered a rueful smile. "And now you have me at a disadvantage, because I don't think I can stay standing much longer."

"On the bed," Olivia said immediately, tugging Margaret towards her. She lay down first, on her back, so she could enjoy the incredible view of Margaret crawling towards her…naked. That sight would be in her fantasies forever more.

"Now you're mine," Margaret announced, laying herself precisely, full-length, over Olivia's body.

Skin on naked skin for the first time, Olivia's brain liquefied. She would never get enough of this. Never.

Margaret's weight rested on her forearms, and her whole body seemed to cover and surround Olivia. She felt cocooned by her. Their breasts were touching. Their thighs were tangled tightly, and Margaret kept languidly rubbing her pelvis against Olivia's, sending erotic flares through her.

"I wanted to have you exactly like this," Margaret murmured. "To *slowly* press myself into you. To feel your body perfectly fitted beneath mine." She rocked again. "To feel all of you."

It was impossible to miss Margaret's wetness. Olivia gasped out: "Well, now you have me."

"I do." Margaret's dark eyes burned deep into Olivia. "I *do*." Then she kissed her again. She was thorough, taking her time to map Olivia's mouth, an approving *mmm* sounding in the back of her throat as their bodies continued to rock together.

The kissing was addictive. So meticulous, so very *Margaret*. She seemed in no rush to hurry anything along, merely to enjoy every second with Olivia now that she had her.

Olivia, on the other hand, was dying of frustration. She arched up, seeking more pressure to tip her over the edge.

Margaret shifted off her and suddenly her mouth was disappearing down Olivia's trembling body. She created wet trails down Olivia's breasts, her stomach, and then… Oh God. And *then*. That contrary, clever mouth was tasting Olivia at her source. Margaret drew her in, worshipped her with her tongue, and slid all around her clit and entrance with teasing swipes.

And that was all it took. Olivia came—so suddenly that it shocked her. A delicious heat ricocheted through her body, leaving her twitching and incoherent, sticky and delirious.

Even then, Margaret didn't slow. She gathered up Olivia's quivers with a most enthusiastic groan. Finally, she lifted her head the tiniest amount and whispered against Olivia's swollen folds, "So beautiful." Her tongue flashed out and licked her playfully. "Come one more time, darling."

Olivia would have protested that she'd never come twice in a row before. Instead, her body trembled harder and arched into Margaret.

"Like that. Oh yes." This time Margaret's tongue raked firmly over her folds. "That's a good girl."

And…*oh fuck all over again*. How had she made "good girl" sound arousing? From Margaret—commanding, imposing Margaret—it felt so fucking naughty. Like a stern governess talking dirty. Her nipples went rock hard, and Olivia's clit gave another final, exhausted, happy twitch as she spasmed again.

With endorphins washing through her, Olivia weakly pushed Margaret's head away. "No more," she whimpered. "You win."

"I most certainly did," Margaret said, slowly sitting up. Her chin was glistening, and her eyes were sharp and bright. *God. Pure sex*. Margaret gave Olivia a long, knowing look. "You are delightful to watch as you come."

"Oh God," Olivia muttered, slapping a hand over her eyes. Was she going to talk about it? Olivia's orgasm face?

"It's like you can't believe so much pleasure exists, so you look half stunned."

Apparently, she was. "In my defence, you did supply a lot of pleasure," Olivia protested and removed her hand.

Margaret gave a pleased smile. "That was the aim." She rolled onto her back, and those petite, enticing breasts wobbled.

Olivia was entranced and licked her lips. "I want you so much, I don't know where to start."

"What a dilemma," Margaret noted, as if contemplating the problem with some gravity. "Perhaps, if I gave you a helpful suggestion?" And then... then. *Oh Lord!* She parted her legs slowly in invitation.

A searing bolt of desire shot through Olivia. Because Margaret Blackwood did *not* just expose herself for Olivia's inspection. That was so hot.

"You can begin anytime," Margaret intoned, eyes bright. "Don't mind me."

With a laugh, Olivia took the unsubtle hint and shifted between Margaret's spread legs.

Olivia melted into Margaret, tasting every tremble and shudder, discovering which places made her moan. Teasing just to the left of her clit drove Margaret crazy. She jerked and gasped, her neck snapping back, her hands clutching and grasping at the sheet.

A rush of arousal pooled on Olivia's tongue as Margaret went rigid and let out a tight almost shriek. She then dropped back to the bed, her fingers clamping on Olivia's head, pressing her hard between her pale thighs.

"I want..." she cried. "I want, I want..."

Olivia took that as encouragement and flickered her tongue over her again and again.

Another groan. More trembling. Then Margaret arched and wailed.

Silence fell for a few minutes as Margaret panted, and stared straight up at the ceiling. "I want *you*," she finally said, her voice raw. "Do you hear me?" She stared straight down at Olivia, meeting her eye, as if to say, *Let there be no mistake.* "*I want you.*"

Olivia smiled softly, warmed beyond belief. "I want you too."

"Good." Margaret's eyes closed. "Stay here tonight. I want to wake up with my idiotic muffin baker beside me."

"Yours, huh? And *again* with the idiot?" Although the affectionate way she said it was impossible to miss.

"Haven't you been paying attention? Honestly." Margaret huffed. "I told you earlier and I meant it. Olivia, you are *my* idiot. Don't you forget it."

Olivia slid up behind Margaret to spoon her. On its own accord, her hand curled over Margaret's hip and cupped her centre. It twitched. "We both know I'm not an idiot," Olivia said, her breath hot against her ear. "If I were, you wouldn't want me at all."

"And yet," Margaret murmured sleepily. "You took on my dragon for me. If you don't like being called an idiot, I'll call you a dragon slayer. It's the same thing."

"I like that. Except I didn't actually slay your mother. She beat me."

"Olivia, my beautiful dragon slayer..." Margaret was definitely falling asleep now, her words half mumbled. "The fact you are neither cowed by her nor minus a job because of her means you most definitely won. She was powerless to destroy you, and she was itching to."

"She tried. After Security kicked me out, she came outside to tell me I'd never replace Helen in your heart."

"Of course you won't." Margaret said with an indignant huff. Her eyes snapped open, and she turned to peer at Olivia. "Helen's not some goldfish that I won't notice if it's been replaced. She was my wife. I loved her. I'll always miss her. But in the same vein, Helen can't fill the Olivia-sized hole in my heart either. That's a place that's reserved for you." She thumbed stray hairs away from Olivia's temple and offered an affectionate quirk of her lips. "Please tell me you're not torturing yourself over anything my mother said? It's an appalling waste of emotional resources, as I know only too well."

"Uh...you hold me in your *heart*?" Olivia repeated, trying not to squeak. "Me?"

"Obviously. Didn't I just say that?" Margaret rolled her eyes. "I might have been a little slow to join the dots on what you meant to me, but it occurred to me there's a long list of things I wouldn't have done of late unless they were for *you*. I know I decided it would be best to be friends, but then you went and ruined my nice, safe, platonic intentions by wearing that shirt and putting the vice chancellor of Monash University in her place."

Olivia grinned. "Oops?"

"Exactly." Margaret sounded faux aggrieved. "Now stop talking about my mother and hold me. I hate being cold."

That sounded like an awfully good suggestion, so Olivia did exactly as requested. "I love you too," she mumbled, snuggling nice and tight. "Just for the record."

A soft, contented sigh filled the room. "Yes," Margaret said idly, but there was just so much warmth in her voice. Then: "Good."

Olivia woke the next day with a naked body draped along her side that made her eyes snap open.

"About time," came a low voice. "I wondered if you were going to sleep the whole day away. Which struck me as odd for a baker used to getting up before dawn."

"Hey, you wore me out, okay?" Olivia protested while her brain still processed just who lay beside her. It hadn't been a dream. "And it's Sunday. I've trained my body not to wake up early when I'm not working."

"Impressive." Margaret's eyes were so bright, they bored right into Olivia.

God. She was not going to be able to withstand anything this woman ever asked of her. She was in trouble. "Did you tell me you loved me last night, or did I imagine it?" Olivia blurted out.

"I did not," Margaret said blithely. "You inferred it. Correctly. I'm glad you did. I'm so rusty on the emotional side of things, it would have taken me months to actually say it if you hadn't. Now, then, what do you want to do today?"

"Besides you?" Olivia asked, a blush rising up her cheeks. "I just want to do you a lot from now on, if that's okay."

"I see." Margaret appeared to consider that. "Well. I'm not opposed."

"No?" She grinned.

"No." Margaret smiled back. "I give you permission to do whatever you wish with me. I suggest you be creative." Her gaze turned smouldering.

Three hours later, Olivia woke to the smell of breakfast—well, brunch— and singing.

Margaret Blackwood could sing! She listened to the tune, and pieced together some operatic number. It made for an unexpected change from the music she played in her car, that's for sure.

Olivia listened a little longer until she recognised *Flower Duet* by Delibes, a number she only knew thanks to excessive watching of the hot lesbian sex scene in *The Hunger*. Her mind suddenly froze at the thought that that's where Margaret might know the song from too. Her mouth went dry at the intoxicating thought of Margaret…enjoying…that film alone the way Olivia had. She swallowed. There was an image.

She slid out of bed, found a long, black T-shirt draped over Margaret's chair, and padded, otherwise naked, through the apartment to find the source of the singing.

Margaret froze, spatula holding aloft a pancake, the tune dying in her throat. Her gaze turned hungry as she absorbed what little Olivia had on.

"Hey," she said with a teasing smile.

Margaret was wearing yoga pants—black—and a slim-fitting pale green T-shirt. No bra. Her nipples were suddenly punching through the sheer material.

"Hell-o." Margaret licked her lips, then dropped the pancake back in the pan, removing it from the heat. "Excuse me one moment."

She came around the counter to Olivia's side, pulled her into her arms, and kissed the hell out of her. "Now, put some actual clothes on or I'll set fire to the kitchen. I've put a towel next to the shower—through there." She pointed.

"Okay." Olivia chuckled and headed for the bathroom. So worth it to see how quickly Margaret's eyes had filled with desire. Worth it to know what Olivia needed to know: she *was* wanted.

Of course she was twitchy about that. It was hard to trust again after her exes. Hard to feel desirable. It was amazing how Margaret could wash that away with one heated gaze.

In the shower, she began to sing herself. The shower head was enormous. So much water! She chose a song appropriate to her deluge. Two minutes later, the door flew open.

"Do not," Margaret said tightly, "sing the *Titanic* theme. Ever!" And then the door closed again.

Huh. Interesting.

Then the door opened again, and Margaret re-appeared. "Fine, you can if you must. I just…overreacted."

The door closed again.

Olivia waited—hair wet, eyes blinking—for a third appearance, but nothing happened. She finished her shower at her leisure.

Before long, she was ushered to a table laden with food. Pancakes, egg, bacon.

"That's quite a breakfast spread."

Margaret shrugged. "I spent a lot of time in hotels overseas as a kid; my mother would drag us along to wherever her conferences were. I spent a greater part of my childhood assuming the full hotel buffet breakfast was how everyone ate. I'm used to doing it now when I have someone staying over."

"Which isn't often, I'm guessing?" Olivia asked.

"No." Margaret smiled. "I trust you understand your importance now?"

"I'm starting to."

"I just want to say this once," Margaret's tone became serious, "and then we never have to go near it again. The night I said those awful things… that we weren't friends and that I didn't want you in my life, I was rattled terribly. I was not my best self." Margaret looked down. "I was sorry the moment I said those words. It's no excuse, but I felt…"—she shook her head—"stripped bare. Hurt."

"I know," Olivia said gently.

"It had also been a long time since I felt more for someone. That was unsettling to discover. I never thought I'd be there again, *needing*…It shook me to my core and I rejected it. Now, I find I want nothing but you."

"I feel the same." Olivia inhaled. "I've wanted you even when you were being a pain in my neck during book club. That should have been my first clue. I thought about you far too much. And when I discovered the book woman in the park who I loved to watch was the same woman listening in on my book club for two years, you became all encompassing."

Margaret regarded her a long moment and gave a small, reluctant sigh. "I sat there at that park for you, you know. It's funny because until you came along, I rarely used to eat outside of my office. One day, I overheard you talking to your sister about where you sold your leftover muffins and I went there without analysing why. It seemed I wanted to see you more than once a week. But every time, I told myself it was just a nice park and a lovely view and I needed to get out a bit more. I am truly excellent at denial." She offered a tiny half smile. "I suppose it really was a lovely view." Her smile broadened.

"Flatterer," Olivia teased, but Margaret's confession was heartening. She bit into the eggs. "Sinfully good," she announced, waving her fork. "If I ever need a muffin-making assistant, are you in?"

Margaret considered that. "To be discussed after I've defamed Ned Kelly."

Olivia laughed. "Okay, topic change. What's your beef with the *My Heart Will Go On*, anyway? I think it's kind of dreamy."

"It's an abomination. And my mother would put *Titanic* on as a babysitting movie when my brother and I were teenagers and she wished to go out to dinner with a colleague or her latest husband. She chose it because it was the longest movie she owned."

"Oh no! Why didn't you just turn it off?"

"My brother insisted we obey my mother. So I'd put headphones on and do my studies. However, the little cretin would always turn the volume up full whenever *that* song came on to annoy me." She rolled her eyes. "Brothers do things like that."

Olivia grinned. "I'm rather enjoying getting to know you on a domestic level."

"I'm sure it's fascinating," Margaret said with a doubtful look.

"It is." Olivia nodded.

Wednesday rubbed up against her legs under the table and looked up at her hopefully. Olivia broke off a piece of bacon and lifted it…

"Do *not* feed my cat. Bacon's terrible for her."

"Sprung." Olivia popped it into her own mouth instead. "You don't miss anything, do you?"

"I missed falling for you. Janice had to point it out to me. Well, she tried. I didn't grasp her meaning initially. Or, rather, I did, but I called her delusional. I can be exceptionally oblivious when it suits me. My oldest friend is going to be impossible now."

"You got there in the end." Olivia reached for her orange juice. "I'm still a little astounded you applied for the henchperson job."

"That makes two of us."

"And what surprises me even more is just how bad we were at it. We'd have these great plans, and nothing ever went according to them."

"But all our plans *did* work," Margaret pointed out. "Eventually. Just not the way we expected. Martin didn't get stranded for an hour or rethink his life choices, true. He did get humiliated on Instagram and lose his beloved car." She ticked that off her finger.

"I suppose."

"Annalise didn't get shamed to her whole office with that cake. But she did pay you the money she owed. And I hear her fiancé broke up with her, so she's lost him now too."

Olivia's eyes went wide. "What? How do you know?"

"It was in the *Weird About Town* column three days ago. It was a blind item, asking which prominent bakery-chain owner was breaking up with which prominent lawyer, and did it have anything to do with something salacious written on a cake. And they included that photo of your cake." Margaret smiled. "So it did get a mention after all. I trust Annalise's colleagues have put two and two together now."

"Wow."

"Tina didn't give you back Trip," Margaret went on. "We did very nearly get caught out by Security too. But you did stink up her apartment so badly that she got kicked out. And we did—eventually—get Trip back."

"Only because you sacrificed your peacock. Without that, we'd never have succeeded."

"Irrelevant." Margaret gave a dismissive wave. "And then there's Timothy. Who didn't apparently need revenge at all because he was genuinely sorry. And his evil brother is in prison. So our schemes didn't work in the least, but the end result was achieved. We won right across the board."

"Not exactly across the board." Olivia sighed. "What about the last mission: the final boss fight?"

Margaret frowned.

"Your mother? I took her down a peg for all of five minutes before she came after me to crush me. She was pretty vicious too."

"So she thinks she won," Margaret mused.

"She does, yeah."

"But she's wrong. *We* won." Margaret's eyes bored into hers. "I'd never be with you here, now, like this, without that showdown." She reached for

Olivia's hand. "I'd never have seen your loyalty and your courage in the face of her power and fury, and I'd never had made a snap decision."

"What decision was that?"

Margaret's gaze became intense. "I thought: screw just being friends. I want all of you."

"And you have me."

"Yes. And further to your earlier point?" Margaret cocked a haughty eyebrow. "Just to be clear?"

Olivia blinked in confusion.

"I love you too."

Sunday, May 31

General Observations: *I'm in love with Olivia. And I told her. She feels the same way.*

My heart is three sizes too big for my chest. Somehow it neglected to explode. There's a relief. I find myself clutching my chest just to check. No, the pounding is normal. It's my emotional state that's not.

I worried how I would feel...moving on. I miss Helen still. It helps knowing she would adore Olivia. It helps knowing she wouldn't want me wallowing in grief. It helps knowing she'll always be with me.

In the end, what helps most is that I've learned the biggest lesson from my years with Helen: It's important to be entirely present and to focus on what matters most. And that's simple. I love Olivia.

CHAPTER 29

ALL YOU KNEAD IS LOVE

Ten days later

Olivia scrambled into Mary Bugg's embarrassingly late and brought the book club to order. "I'm so sorry," she said. "But I have a surprise this week: a new member."

The door behind her creaked open, and she didn't have to look behind to know her girlfriend had appeared. It had occurred to her lately that she could always sense Margaret whenever she was around. Her vibe felt so distinctive.

"Dr Margaret Blackwood has agreed to join us instead of offering her comments to me from her office, which, as you know, she's been doing of late. I'm hoping you'll welcome her in person."

Margaret slid into the vacant chair at Olivia's left. Dead silence greeted them.

What the hell? Had Olivia misjudged her book club? She'd thought for sure Margaret would get a warm welcome, especially since the Tina special op, where everyone had met her during their rehearsal ladder work.

Margaret stiffened.

"Ah, hell," said Damien, reaching for his wallet.

Emma grinned happily.

Breanna scowled and was also fumbling for her purse.

Rifling through a notepad that appeared out of her backpack, Bo announced, "The bet is concluded as of 3.23pm on June 10." Then she reached into her pocket and passed a fiver to Emma. "Bloody hell. Fleeced by a kid."

Tess coughed, and Bo slid her ten bucks.

"Two kids," Bo amended. "Cos I've got leftovers older than you, Tessie."

"Um, excuse me?" Olivia interrupted. "Is someone going to explain?"

"Oh, right," Bo said. "Emma here claimed you two were a couple ages ago. Tess agreed with her. The rest of us begged to differ on the grounds that Dr B would never, ah…"

"Take the stick out of her uptight arse," Damien finished, chuckling. "No offence."

"I'm pretty sure there were *several* forms of offence in that one sentence," Margaret said acerbically. "And what makes you think we are now a couple?"

"Simple," Bo told her. "We all agreed the only way you'd ever join us was if Liv dragged you into book club. And she wouldn't try that on unless you two were…" She tapped her two index fingers together suggestively, "y'know."

Olivia's face turned into a furnace. "Oh God."

"Am I wrong?" Bo turned to her. "Besides, look at your button pin."

Everyone stared at it: All You Knead is Love.

Crap. Freud strikes again.

"Are you two official now or what?" Bo pressed on.

"I don't suppose 'none of your business' would be effective?" Margaret asked dryly.

"If you weren't, you'd just say it, so yep. It's on." Bo grinned.

"How did you know, Emma?" Breanna asked turning to the girl.

"Everyone forgets I'm sitting right here whenever they talk or make goo-goo eyes at each other. And Olivia is, like, *totally* besotted. It's obvious."

And Olivia's blush returned in force. *Kill me now.*

"Besotted? Is that so?" Margaret drawled, lips twitching. "Well, well."

"I wouldn't be too smug there, Dr B," Bo noted, putting her wallet away. "You only think you have a poker face."

"True," Emma said. "You talk about Olivia to me all the time."

"Because she's a mutual acquaintance!" Margaret protested.

Bo snorted. "Oh, *that's* why. Come on, you two have been eye-fucking for months and months." She coughed and glanced at Emma. "Ooops. Shit. Um, sorry."

"If you believe we've been doing that," Olivia asked silkily, "why did you lose the bet?"

"Oh, I thought for sure you were going for the long haul on an unrequited love. Happy to be proven wrong, though, hey." Bo became serious. "Uh, by the way, nobody tell the assistant manager *anything* about this, okay?" She shot them all a shifty look. "I think Sam Garrity might put a hit on us if she found out her kid was betting on Dr B's love life."

Emma giggled. "Yeah, please don't tell Mum. She'd say you're corrupting me."

"This just gets worse and worse," Margaret muttered. She glanced to Olivia. "Tell me why I agreed to join this rabble?"

Damien laughed loudly. "You're too funny, Doc. You *already* joined us. Years ago! First time you opened that door to listen in. We were just bein' polite and pretending we didn't notice you doin' that. So when you started throwing out comments during book club and Olivia was getting all worked up, I guess even then you were flirting with each other."

"We were *not* flirting!" Olivia protested. "She was being awful! To all of you! And she was defaming some very good books!"

Margaret coughed faintly. "Well, maybe there was a *little* flirting."

"Oh my God!" Olivia spun around to look at her in astonishment. "Was that your idea of flirting? Insulting people and their book preferences?"

Margaret scratched her neck. "Not...consciously." She pursed her lips. "Hindsight is 20-20 and so forth. Looking back makes for some rather startling conclusions. But either way, that's not a conversation for public consumption."

"Unlike your other ones." Damien grinned. "We didn't mind, you know. And it was good Liv was getting so worked up over someone who seemed just as into her too."

"Hey, I'm right here!" Olivia protested.

"And, yeah, gotta say, we've all been worried for you," Damien told her. "Those bad exes were dragging you down into a pit of shit."

"They really were," Breanna chimed in.

"But just lately, when you and Dr B were up in each other's dials," Damien went on, "it's like you forgot to be miserable. So that was a good thing, right?"

Olivia blushed to her roots.

"And now here we are. It'll be good to have another opinion at book club," he finished.

"Well," Margaret said staunchly and flicked lint off her black pants, "my opinion is you're a bunch of bleeding-heart pseudo intellectuals with all the taste of a Barry Manilow concert. However, you are loyal friends to Olivia, and that counts for a lot. So I'm prepared to listen to all your outlandish *theories* on our selected book each week and not laugh outright. Any and all subsequent eviscerations will be…mild. This time."

"Big of you," Bo said, eyes crinkling.

"I thought so." Margaret shot her a million-dollar smile. "Who's first?" Her brown eyes had lit up like it was Christmas as she scanned the group.

"Me!" Tess's hand shot up. "I'd like to be mildly eviscerated. It's good character building for my acting process. Like…grounding, you know? I want to get good at accepting withering criticisms."

Margaret beamed.

One month later

Olivia woke in her own bed as Margaret attempted, badly, to leave it without waking her.

"Sorry," Margaret whispered. "I need a glass of water. Go back to sleep."

"Time is it?" she muttered.

"Six. On a Sunday, before you panic about not being up and baking." She pulled on Olivia's blue terry-towelling robe and belted it at the waist. It was way too short on her naked body, sliding perilously close to indecent.

"Okay." Olivia rolled over. "Is good."

Her bed felt sadly empty the moment Margaret left it. Even temporarily. It was funny how she'd never felt like this with her other partners. Whenever they'd left, she'd always exhaled and mentally started her list of chores. Whenever Margaret left her side, her brain went to wondering when they'd next be together again.

Barely two minutes later, Margaret reappeared with an odd look on her face. She was not holding a glass of water.

"Margaret? What's wrong?" Olivia sat up.

"Right," she said firmly. "That clinches it. You're moving in with me."

"I am?" She blinked.

"Yes." Margaret strode back to bed and pulled the borrowed robe off. "Immediately."

"Okay?" She studied Margaret's wide eyes and said with alarm: "What happened?"

"Sasha was sitting in the kitchen in next to nothing. I didn't know they made men's underwear that small. If that wasn't bad enough, your sister wandered in wearing an even more revealing robe than I just borrowed. We all sort of looked at each other in surprise." Margaret inhaled. "I said, 'We will *never* speak of this again'. Then I left. I have no intention of seeing my barista wearing so little ever again, and I'm quite certain she never wishes to see her employer in a similar state of dishabille."

"Ah." Olivia tried to hide her smile. "So now I'm moving in with you? After only a month? That's so lesbian."

"I don't care." Margaret slid closer to Olivia and wrapped her arms around her. "So, will you?" She paused. "I'll get my kitchen updated with a second oven like the one you have here. So you can make your muffins at all hours. Plus there's the fact I live in the heart of Prahran instead of half an hour away, which makes my place much closer to your clientele."

"That's the least romantic move-in-with-me proposal I've ever heard." Olivia wasn't sure whether to be amused or faintly insulted. Still, she knew how much Margaret valued her own space. Asking Olivia to share it with her was huge. She either really hated being seen with bed hair by her employee, or…there was a lot more to it.

Margaret sniffed. "Well, I mean, obviously, it'd be nice for us to wake up together every day, don't you agree?"

"You understand I get up at around four or four thirty every working day? This isn't fun for partners of bakers."

"I'm well aware." Margaret sighed. "I've actually given it some thought before this. I'm sorry if it came across as reactive as opposed to…romantic."

"Now we're talking." Olivia wiggled closer. "Ask me again. Romantically this time."

"Olivia Roberts," Margaret said promptly, "make me the happiest semi-retired academic and move in with me?"

"Weird flex including your professional qualifications," Olivia said with a grin.

"Just being accurate. Well?" She slid closer still. "Yes?"

"Yes." Olivia kissed her. "I'll be your live-in muffin maker."

"Why does that sound so salacious?" Margaret murmured. "Never mind. I'm sure I'll find out."

Olivia laughed.

CHAPTER 30

SWEET POTATOES FALL FOR SPUD MUFFINS

One year later

"I NEED YOU TO TELL me everything that goes into making muffins."

Olivia looked up from her latest book club read in the lounge of Margaret's apartment. Correction, *their* apartment. She felt a sense of ownership over it now.

Margaret had swept in holding a large notepad and pen, looking earnest and enthused.

"Why?"

"I have an idea. But to enact it, I need to learn your special skills."

"What idea?" Olivia put down her book. "And it better be good if I'm coughing up my secret recipes. Especially on my day off when I don't even want to think about baking."

Margaret huffed. "Of course it's good. *I* came up with it." She smiled then and sat beside her. "I want to invent my own range of muffins just for my bookstore. The Bushranger Collection."

"The…Bushranger Collection?"

"I'll feature the three Marys. There will be a Mary Ann Bugg muffin— 'The Thunderbolt'. 'The Black Mary'—that was Mary Cockerill's bushranger name. And 'The Winterberry'. That's for the infamous Mrs Winter, who many believe was convict Mary Herd."

Olivia had never seen Margaret so excited. Was it because she was back to her childhood dream of cooking? Or was it because it was all about bushrangers, her adult passion?

After a moment, Margaret hissed in a breath. "And, of course, I'll include 'The Ned Kelly'." She gritted her teeth. "Even I can admit it would be an oversight to do a bushranger muffin selection and not include Australia's most overrated, beloved icon."

Olivia tilted her head. "So how does this work? You'll come up with your own recipes going off my base mix?"

"Yes. I've already contacted one of Helen's history professor friends, a Wurundjeri woman who has a long line of Aboriginal bushtucker experts in her family. I'll hire her as my expert, and together we'll identify the ingredients native to the areas that specific bushrangers roamed, in order to be authentic. It will be *very* scientific."

Her lips thinned as if even the suggestion of anything less was heresy. "Every other half-baked cook who features a Ned Kelly-themed anything just shoves potato in the dish and calls it a day. Because: Man food? His Irish parents? I don't know why they've decided Kelly equals potatoes. *My* recipes will be flavour-packed, nuanced, and accurate. And there will be no potato in sight."

"And…then what?"

"Then, once perfected, you'll bake my recipes for Mary Bugg's customers. It'll be good to have it perfected for when my book comes out in six months."

"I see." Olivia's eyebrow hiked up. Well, it wouldn't be a Margaret request if it didn't have assumptions in it that Olivia would just go along with her grand plans. Hadn't that been how Olivia had wound up living with her?

Greatest outcome ever, by the way. Margaret was adorable to live with… once you understood her patterns—her early morning and once-a-month grumpiness and preferred ways of doing things. She was firm in her habits, yet absolutely committed to doing her best to make space for Olivia.

Additionally, her efforts at being present emotionally for Olivia and fighting her own rigidity and stubbornness made Olivia's heart ache, given she knew the reason for it.

In return, Olivia tried to be as accommodating as possible to ease Margaret's anxiety at having someone cramping her style and space. She'd even agreed not to go ahead with threats to make a *Sweet Potatoes Fall for Spud Muffins* button pin and wear it every time she was in Margaret's office. Still, Olivia wouldn't make her latest request easy on her.

"What if I say no, I don't want to expand my repertoire?" Olivia asked mischievously.

Profound astonishment filled Margaret's face. "You wouldn't want to have a unique, historically accurate, groundbreaking quartet of Australian muffins on your menu?"

Well, when she put it like that... "It sounds like a lot of work."

It didn't really. She could swap out some of her less popular lines with these.

"I'll find you an assistant, then. I'll pay her wages, don't worry." She waved her hand. "Is that all your objections sorted?"

"All except the big one. You understand I'm a trained professional, and you implying it's easy for an amateur to just come up with a whole new line of my muffins is pretty insulting?" Olivia shot her a peeved look. She was used to others minimising her skills but not Margaret.

"I'm actually a good home cook when I put my mind to it," Margaret began and then petered out. She sighed. "Fine, yes, good point. That was presumptuous. I don't even understand how you make muffins as sublime as you do."

"So it's *not* just following a recipe then?" Olivia's lips twitched. "Despite you saying that's all it is every time you cook."

Margaret rolled her eyes. "Yes. I acknowledge it's a lot more than that. Flair and taste and nuance go into it too. Okay, how about this: I work out the regionally correct ingredients as well as the flavour mix for each bush-ranger muffin and then I give you that blend to develop further and turn into actual muffins?"

Olivia pondered that. Flavours were tricky to perfect and balance. It usually took her weeks of trial and error to come up with a new muffin, and she'd been at this game for years. Margaret would have her work cut out for her. However, her lover did have a knack for spices and seasoning. If anyone could pull this off, it'd be her.

"Don't worry," Margaret said at her silence, "between the two of us we'll invent muffins so beyond compare that even my own mother would love them."

"Maybe set the bar a little lower, hon," Olivia teased. "Your mother is impossible to please."

Margaret's eyes flashed. "Okay, one, I never settle for less than the best. Which is why two, I chose you. And three, if you love me, you'll never call me that risible nickname ever again. So, do we have a workable plan?"

What nickname? *Hon?* Olivia threw up her hands in surrender. "Fine, yes, go ahead, darling. You have my full support."

Margaret considered that. "Darling is acceptable." Her eyes grew bright. "It'll be wonderful, I should add. So very good." She was glowing now. "Wait and see."

As if Olivia could say no to that face. And hell, she believed her.

Sixty-two days later

Olivia awoke to the smell of something savoury and hot breath near her ear.

"Wake up," Margaret demanded impatiently. "The morning's wasting."

"You know, I think I preferred you as a bored bookseller," Olivia protested, peeling open her eyes. "All this enthusiasm is a lot to take in first thing."

"Stop complaining about your girlfriend being finally fulfilled and taste this." Margaret was fairly quivering with anticipation.

That was when Olivia saw it. A muffin on a small plate Margaret was handing to her with the gravitas of an Olympic medal. It looked a lot like the Mary Ann Bugg 'Thunderbolt' muffin Olivia had been working on last week.

"Yesterday morning I realised what was missing: I doubled the pepperberry. Taste it now."

Olivia felt like complaining it was too early to be in the least hungry, but Margaret's excitement was infectious. She took a small bite, and oh. *Oh!*

Margaret had been busy. The flavours leaped off her tongue and did a little tap dance in her mouth. "That's so zesty!"

"It's the finger lime combining with the extra pepperberry. If you wait a second, the wattleseed will kick in. And then the smoothness of the creamy feta cheese will even it out."

No doubt about it. Margaret had a real gift for flavours. Her muffins themselves weren't quite at Olivia's high standards of fluffiness and crunch, but the taste? Now *that* she'd nailed. Between them, this would be a truly exceptional range. Olivia felt a rush of excitement.

Margaret watched her closely as she ate. "I fed these to Janice yesterday and she was so impressed, she wants to get the Food Editor at the *Herald Sun* to do a story about our authentic bushranger muffins." She pulled a face. "However, she threatened to make the Ned Kelly muffin the centrepiece."

"Janice is hilarious." Olivia had another bite. She really was. They'd had her over to dinner enough times now that Olivia counted her as a friend and an amusing stirrer.

"No, she's not hilarious; she just thinks she is." Margaret smirked. "My publisher says the book's almost edited, so the two events should tie in perfectly: muffins launch and book launch."

Olivia swallowed and had to admit that it was one seriously tasty muffin. "Well, I may be biased, but I think we've got a hit on our hands."

Margaret didn't say anything to that; she just seemed to radiate satisfaction. Then she picked up the plate and straightened. And that's when Olivia noticed what she was wearing.

One black cotton shirt, unbuttoned almost all the way down, and absolutely no underwear. *At all.* Which was evident by how the garment only barely made it to the tops of her thighs. It was utterly scandalous.

"Did you forget something when you got dressed today?" Olivia asked, her mouth going dry.

"On the contrary, I forgot nothing." Margaret's eyes sparkled. "I thought we might celebrate this successful muffin achievement with some attention to another muffin entirely." She said it so archly that it took Olivia a full ten seconds to grasp her meaning.

Olivia stared at her. "You didn't just make a muffin sex joke. *You?*"

Margaret merely smiled. "I'll put this plate back and then we can go forward with my latest excellent plan."

Olivia decided then and there that, aside from hiring a henchperson, helping Margaret dabble in the muffin business had been far and away the Best. Decision. Ever.

Sunday August 22

Sunset: *5.49pm*

Temp: *11.3-22.2C*

Rain: *0mm*

Drink: *Mug of hot chocolate. Prepared by Olivia who thinks too much wine in the evening is bad for me. I chose not to point out how much caffeine is in hot chocolate.*

Reading: *Final, final, FINAL readthrough of my own book was finished this afternoon. I'm...satisfied. It's back to the editor. She seems to think I have an axe to grind about beloved Australian legend Ned Kelly. Nooooo...what gave it away? I've already pointed out every cutting criticism I make in my book is <u>exhaustively researched</u> and backed up with multiple credible sources. I could almost read a sigh in her editing note where she wrote, "I know".*

I'd say 'Sorry I defamed your national icon' but I'm not. Ned Kelly is not even one tenth as cunning or clever or talented as Mary Ann Bugg and it's time the world knew it. All he had going for him was that he was white, male, charismatic, and put a good spin on his hard-luck tale. His myth was built on his perceived invincibility, eye-catching armour, and derring-do, more than his achievements. He inspired people, yes, but that doesn't make him better. He was simply incredibly lucky. Until he wasn't.

My publisher says media interest is very strong in my book but I've been informed that I'm not allowed to "crow or sneer" in interviews when asked anything about Ned Kelly.

Please. Just watch me.

General Observations: *The Mary Ann Bugg muffin has been perfected at last. That means we've finished the complete set.*

I am entirely satisfied with the outcome.

But my brief diversion into creating muffin flavours is of secondary importance to something else: It's the first anniversary of Olivia moving in with me. She hasn't realised it. Nonetheless I trust she found my present this morning both delightful and hands on. I'm not talking about the muffin tasting, either. Erm...the edible muffin tasting. Why does everything about muffins always sound so salacious?

Back to the point: I never thought I'd ever allow another person to share my space again after Helen. Especially not someone with a disruptive job like a baker. I admit it's hard not to be a little grumpy each day when my bedmate wakes me, despite trying so hard to stay quiet. I've always been a light sleeper, so it makes me irritable.

However, when I awake the second time, the apartment is filled with delicious smells, and it feels so right. Warm. Inviting. The way it should be.

About six thirty, I get a visit from Olivia, whereupon I'm pecked on the cheek, occasionally nuzzled on the neck in farewell, and I feel warm all over again. A different warmth: belonging.

I'm aware I've been set in my ways for a long time. I try my best to overcome my various rigid personality quirks to accommodate her presence. I don't comment on the absurdly long showers or the off-tune populist music she warbles.

In turn, she likes to make sure the pile of clothes on my chair doesn't build up too high before finding the washing machine. But I get so distracted by my projects. And then I remember I should be in the present. I should never again take someone I love for granted. So I gather up Olivia in my arms and express with a kiss and words my absolute, profound conviction that I'm glad she chose her henchperson to love.

She always laughs at the reminder of my old role. I love reminding her. Because it is absurd, isn't it? How we met.

I tell her how it feels to love her. That I get friendship, a silly book club, and her. "Quite the trifecta." I'd arch my eyebrow high to hide how vulnerable I always feel on this baring topic.

And she'd always smile, squeeze me, and say, "And I get an incredible woman who blows my socks off".

How remarkable that she thinks I'm incredible. For so long I felt anything but. A grumpy, reclusive, guilty, wound-licking hermit, at best.

And now, here we are. Life is nothing as it was. I barely spend much time in my old office. I shift from project to project, excited for a new discovery or avenue of research. All because Olivia stumbled into my life, inflicting on my sedate existence a group with the worst book opinions ever.

Look at what's happened since.

My mother and I are speaking civilly now, ever since I did something she pleaded for regarding my book that she believed I could have easily refused. She took my agreeing to her request as a sign of respect. (I'll never tell her what really happened.)

Now the impossible woman has fully retracted her talons and laid off her usual criticisms. I'm cautiously optimistic the cease-fire will hold. She's even being polite regarding Olivia. Will wonders never cease?

What's next for me and for my lovely muffin-maker? It's actually appealing that I don't know. But I'm quite sure it will be exhilarating.

EPILOGUE

Samantha Garrity, Assistant Manager of Mary Bugg's, strode through the store with a grim look on her face. When she reached the Women in Crime book club, she said with authority: "I need to borrow Olivia for a work matter. Are you all done?"

She always had a grim look on her face for this group ever since she'd been alerted to a certain bet involving her daughter that had taken place eighteen months ago.

Olivia had often wondered who the stool pigeon was who'd told her about it.

"I'm done, yep," Olivia said. "Everyone cool with next week's pick?"

"Yep," came a chorus of replies. Plus one acerbic, "If we must delve into potboilers, I suppose it will do…" from Margaret. And one, "Uh, I may not get to it…but I'll try".

Bo's sheepish voice was followed by laughs. Some things never changed.

Breanna walked out with Damien and sternly launched into a debate with him. "I really can't see why you'd ever think…"

Sam eyed the two arguing good-naturedly. "I don't know who they think they're kidding," she said under her breath as she and Olivia veered off in the other direction. "They've been dating for longer than you and Dr Blackwood, haven't they?"

"At least," Olivia agreed with a grin. "But when I asked Breanna about it, she said she'd never date a foot soldier of the patriarchy."

"So no denial, then, that she wouldn't date Damien." Sam chuckled. "Just who she *wouldn't* date."

"Exactly."

"It's a very incestuous book club you're running there. Have you noticed?"

"Not just within book club." Olivia smiled as she followed Sam into her neat little office. "Sasha and Kelly are now making noises about possibly getting engaged. There may be something in the water around here. How about you? Anyone caught your eye?"

"Please. I'm too busy."

Sam wasn't lying. The woman had proved an exceptional assistant manager over the past eighteen months. She'd streamlined all the bookstore's processes, removing so much work from Margaret's desk that she'd found time for all manner of diversions, from inventing bushranger muffin flavours to writing icon-deriding biographies.

While Sam rummaged through her desk drawer, Olivia slid into the visitor's chair and asked: "Hey, I always wondered. Who told you about the bet? The one on whether Margaret and I were dating?"

"Emma." Sam smiled as she removed a large yellow envelope. "She's terrible at keeping secrets. I exercised all sorts of self-control in not telling off the book club for involving my daughter in illicit bets, don't you think?" She arched a playful eyebrow.

"Your restraint was very impressive," Olivia agreed with a snicker. "Margaret especially thought so."

"So she should. Okay, here." Sam pushed the envelope over and sat back, beaming.

With a questioning look, Olivia emptied it and found a cheque and a car key. "What's this?"

"The cheque repays all the help you gave me when I was homeless. Plus, a little extra for interest and wear and tear on your Torana."

"*My* Torana? But…"

"Please. Who chooses a collectible Torana as a company car? Anyway, I knew it was yours before I even took the job. Emma told me all about the day your ex, Martin, turned up and flung the keys at you. She described the car in vivid detail. I did need it very badly back then, but as soon as I didn't,

I planned to give it back. I've finally sold the old station wagon and bought a much more reliable car. But I'm grateful to you and Dr Blackwood for making sure I could stay on the road when I needed to most."

Olivia examined the cheque. It was a generous amount. She instantly worried it was too much. "You don't have to pay me back a thing. I was happy to help."

"Yes, I do. For *me*, Olivia. I have been looking forward to this day for a long time. I have my pride. And I'm grateful for all that you've done, but please, let me have my clean slate by paying you back."

"Okay." Olivia tucked the cheque and keys back in the envelope and shoved them in her jacket pocket. "So, what are the latest plans afoot at Mary Bugg's?"

"So much," Sam said, her eyes lighting up. "I'm getting the shipment of Dr Blackwood's book next week. The preorders have been phenomenal thanks to the story in the *Herald Sun*. It's almost certainly going to be a bestseller, especially with that other story on the upcoming Bushranger Collection of muffins. People are going to be queuing up to get into Mary Bugg's very soon. However…" She hesitated.

"What is it?"

"I have an idea, but you have to tell me how I'm going to break the news to your girlfriend."

Olivia leaned in. "I'm all ears."

"We feature Dr Blackwood's new book in a big display in the window as well as inside the store. But we also put up a Ned Kelly biography display next to her in-store books. Side by side. Capture the Ned Kelly fans, especially those who'd get all worked up about Dr Blackwood's book and might come in to argue about it. If they *really* want to show their displeasure, we can suggest they buy the Ned Kelly book. You know, vote with their wallets. And either way, they're still buying one of our books."

"That's so clever!"

Sam smiled shyly. "You really think so?"

"Yes!"

"Well, there's more: I'd also like to offer readers a deal: Buy Dr Blackwood's Mary Bugg book, and you can also buy the Ned Kelly one for a discount. Double the sales. We'll shift a lot of copies regardless. We could maybe throw in a Bushrangers Collection muffin of choice too. What do you think?"

"I detest it," came a low voice from behind them. Margaret stuck her head in the office. "And you should absolutely do it. Never listen to an author on a promotional decision. They're full of themselves. Samantha, I trust you. I mean that."

Sam looked inordinately pleased. "Well, if it helps, Dr Blackwood, I'll make your book display twice as big."

"I should think so," Margaret said, her lips quirking. "Keep this up and I'll promote you to manager."

It was a long-running joke. Sam was already practically in charge now. Margaret had all but retired as a bookstore boss, and, apart from her various minor diversions, hadn't decided what to do with herself yet. Her publisher was pushing her to write more bushranger books, though.

In the meantime, she'd volunteered to edit Tess's Aboriginal outback sci-fi novel, a story she'd declared was "not wholly without merit". Which Olivia had deciphered as "pretty good" in Margaret speak.

Having a spirited, unmoored former bookstore manager seeking distractions had also meant Olivia found herself flung into bed quite often as Margaret explained without words how much she wanted her. So Olivia definitely didn't mind Margaret was between vocations right now.

"On that note," Sam said. "Prahran Public Library's up and running again. The storm repairs are finally done. They offered me the manager's job."

Olivia went still.

Margaret's face paled even more than normal. "Oh." She pursed her lips. "I'd hoped you'd stay with us," she said quietly. "Do you need more money? I can work something out." She frowned. "Maybe cut some costs elsewhere. Please stay."

"I already turned them down," Sam said. "You both looked out for me when I needed it most. I'm not about to leave now. I'm loyal."

Margaret exhaled. "Do *not* terrify me like that again. Just for that, I'll promote you to manager anyway."

"You will?"

"Yes. With a pay rise. It makes sense: I need you firmly in place for when I go on holiday in a month's time."

Olivia peered at her. "Holiday?" Why was this the first she was hearing of it? "What holiday?"

"Will you excuse us, please?" Margaret said to Sam. "I need to outline my latest schemes to my partner in crime." She slid her arm around Olivia's waist to propel her out the door.

Schemes? Oh boy. Now what?

"Go right ahead. We're finished," Sam said with a smile. "I'll be here finalising the book launch arrangements."

Margaret whisked Olivia out of the office and glanced back. "Just make sure that Ned Kelly display is *distinctly* inferior to the Mary Bugg one. Uglier, even."

"Can't do that," Sam called after her, voice laced with amusement. "You just told me to ignore authors on promotional matters."

"Hoisted by my own petard," Margaret muttered dramatically. "Ah well." Her eyes crinkled as she led Olivia to her own office.

Once they were alone, Olivia studied the room. It felt warmer somehow, and she wondered if it was just knowing Margaret intimately that made her feel that way. She glanced at the wall Quincy sat in front of and smiled at the newest addition to it.

A metal file framed in a little white box was affixed to the wall. A teasing Post-It note in Margaret's handwriting was stuck to it: *Mary Ann Bugg's mythical metal file. Sourced by Olivia Roberts.*

She loved Margaret's sense of humour, especially now she got to experience it rather often. Olivia, in turn, had stuck a Post-It note on the base of Margaret's peacock with the words:

Quincy*, the mythical watch peacock, owned by Ned Kelly's grandfather, James Quinn.

* His actual name.

It made her laugh that Margaret hadn't removed it yet or corrected it.

Margaret cleared her throat. "My mother has offered you a chance to cater the next big Monash Uni fundraiser. She'd like those Bushrangers Collection muffins on display. It's for an Australian history event, so it'd be on theme."

Olivia stared at her in surprise. "Your mother wants to help me? What's the catch?"

"I'm aware there might have been some tension between you both in the past," Margaret said angelically. "But she assures me she wants to be an ally to us both moving forward."

"No, seriously, what's the catch?" Olivia asked. "Come on, she hates me."

Margaret laughed. "Okay, fine. My mother got wind of my book title and was utterly scandalised. She asked me what it would take for me to name it anything but that. Apparently, she thinks it's crass, lowbrow, and will reflect terribly on *her* for me to call it *Why Bushranger Mary Ann Bugg Is Better Than Buckethead.* Subtitle: *Ned Kelly's An Overrated Son of A Bitch.*"

"Well, I mean, it's expressing a certain point of view," Olivia said diplomatically.

"I am aware it's provocative to the point of rude. That was the point. To make people react to it and think about why they assume the Ned Kelly myth is fact. My mother despises the title so much she offered a bribe of allowing you to cater several key university History Department events in future if I change it."

"Ahhh." Now it all became clear. "But don't you love that title?"

"The thing is, my publisher absolutely won't allow my original title due to the obscenity, so it's being changed anyway. I've told my mother I've now altered the title. Her feathers are no longer ruffled. You get a very lucrative university event contract if you want it. And I get to enjoy that she thinks I changed it for her when I did no such thing."

"What's the new title?"

"*Mary Ann Bugg vs Ned Kelly: The Forgotten Bushranger and The Overrated Icon.*" Margaret shrugged. "I don't hate it. Janice, though, was overcome with grief. She loved the scandalous other one."

"Of course she did. She runs a newspaper! She lives for controversy!"

"Exactly. So—do you want to cater my mother's big event? The pros are they overpay a great deal and there's a lot of kudos in being chosen. Also, you'll finally get to meet my History Department friends. They're dying to meet you, by the way. They're like gossipy, eccentric little meerkats dying to pick over a fresh carcass."

"Interesting they're *your* friends again," Olivia said thoughtfully. "Only a few months ago they were Helen's friends."

"Yes, well. When I was researching bushtucker ingredients with Merindah, they somehow pulled me back into their absurd little web. I found I missed them. And they've stopped mentioning Helen every two minutes too, which makes things easier."

"I'm so glad." This was an excellent development. Margaret had spent too long trapped by grief. Expanding her social life was wonderful.

"But back to the event. The cons are just one: my mother. She'll doubt-lessly initiate passive-aggressive conversation and be smug about it."

"Oh, I'm quite used to smug women." Olivia nudged her under the desk with her foot. "Tell her yes from me."

Margaret smiled and rose, coming to sit on the edge of the desk right in front of Olivia. "I will."

Did she seem…nervous? But Margaret said nothing further.

Olivia gave her a questioning look. "So, after your book launch, I thought you were considering writing bushranger biographies of the other Marys. But now apparently you're having a holiday of some sort?" She lifted an eyebrow.

"Not just me. I was hoping *we* might get away for a week? Especially now that you have a baking assistant who can fill in. We can travel to Perth. Visit Rottnest Island. Take a selfie with a quokka or two."

"Take a…" Olivia stared at her. "Oh, you want to make your mother think we did it. That we eloped."

"You're half right." Margaret held her breath and waited.

"Margaret, are you…*proposing* to me?" Olivia asked incredulously.

"That depends," she said, voice quiet and serious. "Will you say yes?"

Olivia's heart began thudding so hard she wondered if Margaret could hear it.

"You want to marry me?" she asked, not quite believing this. "Me, the muffin maker who runs a bad crime-book club and sometimes hires henchpeople?"

"If you'll have me." Margaret smiled. "I'm a semiretired academic lay-about with one book to my name. I'm not that much of a catch."

"This is the weirdest proposal ever," Olivia pointed out. "Like how you asked me to move in so you wouldn't see my sister and her boyfriend in next to nothing."

"I disagree; this is a far superior proposal." Margaret cocked an eyebrow. "I'm not involving your sister in it, for one thing. So—will you marry me?"

"You are an impossible woman." Olivia laughed. "And I love you very much. So, yes!" She kissed her soundly.

"Good." Margaret looked delighted. "Does this mean we can indeed post some selfies so my mother's head explodes? Asking as an excellent henchperson."

Olivia chuckled. "Oh, honey, we'll tag her with quokka photos; splatter them all over her feed until the embarrassment of knowing us kills her."

"You say the sweetest things." Margaret's eyes glowed warmly. "Thank you." Her lips quirked. "I'm the luckiest henchperson alive."

"That position has expired," Olivia said solemnly. "But I do have a new posting open for select applicants."

"Oh?" Margaret leaned in. "I'm listening."

"Wanted: One Future Wife."

Margaret blinked and then a slow smile curled her lips. "Sounds like it has potential. What are the duties?"

"Occasionally assisting in bushranger-themed muffin creations."

"I can do that. I have extensive experience in it already, as it turns out."

"What an amazing coincidence."

"Right?" Margaret snorted.

"Plus, the successful applicant also would be required for occasional wining and dining, book discussions, and sexual favours."

"A little unorthodox, but it doesn't sound too arduous." Margaret's eyes were bright. "What is the preferred skillset? I need to know if I'm qualified."

"I'm seeking an excellent kisser and cuddler, naturally. Snuggling on cold nights. Fondling would be viewed favourably too. Not to mention…" She whispered in Margaret's ear several naughty deeds she knew got Margaret's engine purring.

Her lover hissed in a breath and her cheeks went pink. "Oh my. This is a *full*-service position."

"Oh yes. The fullest."

"I imagine competition would be fierce."

"Not at all because I'm really only interested in one applicant." Olivia slid her thumb over Margaret's pursed lips. "And, to save you asking, the payment will be in reciprocal deeds. So, that's everything. If you're interested, apply in person to: Olivia Roberts."

"Oh, I'm *very* interested, Ms Roberts," Margaret purred.

"Then the job is yours." Olivia leaned up enticingly. "Now and for as long as you'll have me."

"A job for life? How appealing." Margaret's eyes crinkled, affection filling them. "I accept—starting immediately." She lowered her lips to Olivia's, kissing her with great attention to detail, and sealing the deal.

OTHER BOOKS FROM YLVA PUBLISHING

www.ylva-publishing.com

CHANGING THE SCRIPT
Lee Winter

ISBN: 978-3-96324-296-0

Length: 317 pages (104,000 words)

LA-based indie filmmaker Alex Levitin finds herself in New Zealand to save the "worst movie ever". Things might go easier if she didn't almost run over the standoffish local cop, Sam Keegan, and if the film wasn't being sabotaged. As Alex and Sam reluctantly join forces to find the set saboteur, attraction flares.

A funny, small-town lesbian romance about clashing cultures and daring to dream.

LOOKING FOR TROUBLE
Jess Lea

ISBN: 978-3-96324-522-0

Length: 312 pages (109,000 words)

Nancy hates her housemates from hell, useless job, and always dating women who aren't that into her. She'd love to be a political writer and meet Ms. Right.

Instead, she meets George, a butch, cranky bus driver who's dodging a vengeful ex.

When the warring pair gets caught up in a crazy Melbourne election, they must trust each other and act fast to stay alive.

A quirky lesbian romantic mystery.

SCISSOR LINK

(The Scissor Link series – Book 1)
Georgette Kaplan

ISBN: 978-3-95533-678-3
Length: 197 pages (72,000 words)

Wendy is in love with Janet Lace. Janet is beautiful, she's intelligent, and she is also Wendy's boss.

Still, a little fantasy never hurt anyone. Or so Wendy thought until Janet got a look at the e-mail she sent. The one about exactly what Wendy would like to do to Janet.

But when Wendy gets called into the boss's office, it might just be her fantasy coming true. If it doesn't get her fired first.

LOST FOR WORDS

Andrea Bramhall

ISBN: 978-3-96324-062-1
Length: 300 pages (104,000 words)

Massage therapist Sasha's meddlesome mother and best friend conspire to shake up her mundane existence by entering her into a scriptwriting contest. She's not entirely sure how she feels about the life-upending chaos that ensues, which includes meeting an attractive, perfectionist film producer. A bittersweet lesbian romantic comedy about the fun of never knowing what life will bring.

ABOUT LEE WINTER

Lee Winter is an award-winning veteran newspaper journalist who has lived in almost every Australian state, covering courts, crime, news, features, and humour writing. Now a full-time author and part-time editor, Lee is also a 2015 and 2016 Lambda Literary Award finalist and has won several Golden Crown Literary Awards. She lives in Western Australia with her long-time girlfriend, where she spends much time ruminating on her garden, US politics, and shiny, new gadgets.

CONNECT WITH LEE
Website: www.leewinterauthor.com

Vengeance Planning for Amateurs
© 2024 by Lee Winter

ISBN: 978-3-96324-865-8

Available in e-book and paperback formats.

Published by Ylva Publishing, legal entity of Ylva Verlag, e.Kfr.

Ylva Verlag, e.Kfr.
Owner: Astrid Ohletz
Am Kirschgarten 2
65830 Kriftel
Germany

www.ylva-publishing.com

First edition: 2024

Credits
Edited by Genni Gunn and Michelle Aguilar
Cover Design and Print Layout by Streetlight Graphics

Printed in Great Britain
by Amazon

44145923R00189